SLICKER

ALSO BY LUCY JACKSON

Posh

SLICKER

LUCY JACKSON

ST. MARTIN'S PRESS ⚞ NEW YORK

This is a work of fiction. All of the characters, organizations, and events portrayed in this novel are either products of the author's imagination or are used fictitiously.

SLICKER. Copyright © 2010 by Lazybones Ink, LLC. All rights reserved. Printed in the United States of America. For information, address St. Martin's Press, 175 Fifth Avenue, New York, N.Y. 10010.

www.stmartins.com

Book design by Gretchen Achilles

Library of Congress Cataloging-in-Publication Data

Jackson, Lucy.
    Slicker / Lucy Jackson. — 1st ed.
        p. cm.
    ISBN 978-0-312-56500-8
    1. Self-realization in women—Fiction.   2. Women college students—
Fiction.   3. Chick lit.   I. Title.
    PS3610.A3535S57 2010
    813'.6—dc22

2009047036

First Edition: August 2010

10 9 8 7 6 5 4 3 2 1

CHAPTER 1

DESIRÉE CHRISTIAN-COHEN, born and bred on Manhattan's Upper East Side, will, in the near future, be forced to admit the disappointing truth—that she is far from the worldly, whip-smart person everyone seems to thinks she is. This epiphany will come to her at the tail end of the summer, just before she returns from Honey Creek, Kansas, a place seemingly so dusty and provincial, its inhabitants had never had even a peek at a New Yorker of any stripe at all before *she* came to town.

Though she's home in New York now for her summer break, in the fall she expects to return to New Haven, where, in her just-completed sophomore year at Yale, she somehow managed to take all the wrong courses and lose her virginity to the wrong boy, who murmured during sex that he really did like her "veeery, veeery much." A declaration that fell far short of what she'd been prepared to hear. What she'd been listening for was a sentence or so that included the word "love," announced breathlessly in the heat of the moment or shyly whispered immediately thereafter as the two of them lay, still smoldering, their limbs still entangled, on her cheap and uncomfortable secondhand bed.

Well, at twenty, you can't have everything, can you?

Frankly, Desirée doesn't see why not. She understands, though, that love, or at least newly discovered love, is always a miracle. It takes you by surprise, fills the emptiness in you with something sweet and airy, and leaves you buoyant. Of course, if the object of your affection isn't feeling quite as buoyant, there's nothing much you can do about it. Except perhaps hope that sometime soon he'll wise up and see what *you* see—that clearly the two of you are made for one another. Or if hope is in short supply, you can always take an overdose of Xanax. Or throw yourself in front of the Eighty-sixth Street crosstown bus, which Desirée happens to be boarding this particular Thursday night, finally heading to the Upper West Side to visit her father, someone she'd refused

1

any contact with these past six months, distressing both of her parents with her stubbornness. Neither her mother nor her father know that, to Desirée's sorrow, Nick Davenport likes her veeery much but has failed to love her.

Hurtling through the Central Park transverse now, its air-conditioning working only intermittently, the bus seems a cramped holding pen for a load of stony, world-weary passengers. Desirée finds a window seat next to a young mother with a collapsed umbrella stroller tucked awkwardly under her arm and a toddler in her lap. A large diamond-and-sapphire engagement ring adorns her left hand. Desirée is gazing out the window as the little boy says winsomely, "Do you love me, Mommy?"

Desirée and the woman both smile. "Of course I do, baby," the woman says.

"Mommy, do you love me?"

"Yes, Maxie, you know I do."

Maxie fools with his mother's ring; he raises it to his mouth and licks the sapphire at the center and the diamonds that surround it. "Do you love me, Mommy?" he asks.

"Sure do."

"Do you *really* love me, Mommy?"

"Jesus Christ, just STOP IT ALREADY!" the woman says, and rolls her eyes for Desirée's benefit. "Do you believe this?" she says.

The truth is, Desirée doesn't know *what* to believe anymore. She could have sworn, right up until the very moment they'd broken the news to her, that her parents' marriage was rock-solid. They, who rarely raised their voices to one another, who slept side by side in the same king-sized bed night after night for twenty-three years, who shared their dinner hour, moviegoing, annual concert subscriptions to Lincoln Center. Often enough, she'd seen her father sneak up behind her mother and fling his arms around her waist; she'd seen them settled in the love seat watching television, her father's fingers playing idly with her mother's hair. So what had she missed? What had her mother missed? And what's so remarkable about her father's boyfriend, Jordan, that he somehow managed to throw a wrench into the works, bringing their whole family to a sudden, shocking halt?

Desirée hasn't a clue. She, who has always regarded herself as someone sensitive to nuance, ever able to recognize the flicker of doubt that crosses someone else's face, that instant of hesitation before this friend says yes or that friend says no, the momentary, icy silence that a careless word of her own may have caused. She's not the oblivious sort; she *sees* things, things other people routinely miss. If her father had been so unhappy with her mother, wouldn't Desirée have noticed? Not that, ultimately, it would have made a scintilla of difference. Because when it comes to falling in or out of love, who's going to listen to the impartial voice of reason? Probably no one and certainly not Desirée herself. If anyone were to point out to her that she and Nick have virtually nothing in common and are temperamentally unsuited to one another, she would, like Maxie's mother, roll her eyes, knowing that she'd fallen for Nick precisely because he is nothing like her at all. The youngest of three boys, he'd grown up in suburban Wisconsin, in a family where church on Sunday was mandatory, along with a baked ham that, like some sort of crudely conceived and executed homemade cake, was ornamented with canned pineapple rings. A talented student and tennis player (gifts that secured him a place at Yale), Nick has an outlook that is serenely, unrelentingly sunny. It never occurs to him that things might not go his way, because, in fact, they always have. He understood long ago that medicine was his calling, that he would become one of those family practitioners who actually makes house calls and distributes small bouquets of colorful lollipops to weepy kids with ear infections. Cynic-in-training though she is, Desirée continues to find him irresistible. If only she could, like an alchemist, transform his affection for her into the pure gold of love.

"Dream on," she says aloud, and makes her way off the bus.

THE DOORMAN IN JORDAN'S BUILDING high up on Riverside Drive is busy on his cell phone when Desirée arrives, and she waits impatiently as he says, "I refuse to see anything with subtitles, Sienna. Why should I have to read when I go to the movies?"

"Excuse me?" Desirée says. "Apartment eleven A?"

"The thing that really gets me is the way she refers to movies as 'films,'" the doorman says after he hangs up. "It's so—"

3

"Pretentious?"

"There you go!" the doorman says. "And you have a nice night now."

Desirée's father, Patrick, lanky and handsome, opens the door to the apartment he shares with Jordan on the eleventh floor, casting his arms around her the moment she steps into the foyer. *"Enfin! Finalement!"* he says.

She allows his embrace but keeps her arms rigidly at her sides. She and her father haven't seen one another since her Christmas break from school, only days before he officially came out to her mother and announced that there was a man named Jordan he couldn't live without. For half a year, Desirée would not pick up the phone when her father called her, or answer even a single one of his e-mails. She simply couldn't. Today, her stubbornness eroded by both of her parents' strenuous urging, she has, at last, given in and permitted herself to visit.

"I'm thrilled you're here, Desi," her father says. "You can't imagine how happy this makes me."

"Super," Desirée says, perhaps sounding cooler than she means to. And as much as she loves him, she wants the chilliness she still feels toward the very notion of him and his "partner" (this new word in their vocabulary) to come across loud and clear. She notes that except for his jaw, now frosted with a graying beard, her father resembles his old self—a middle-aged husband and father, a professor of chemical engineering at Columbia whose life had followed one of those utterly straightforward, ordinary paths, one that had raised not a single eyebrow. Desirée has only an instant to contemplate the tidal wave that has so recently hit their cozy little family of three, before a balding man wearing his hair gathered into a tiny, ludicrous ponytail appears without warning. There are gloomy, blackish half moons under his dark eyes; Desirée would prefer to think otherwise, but she just doesn't like the looks of him.

"Jordan Sinclair, this is my Desirée," her father says delightedly.

"Hey," Desirée says. She takes the hand Jordan offers her, gives him another appraising look. He is slightly younger than her father, somewhere in his early forties, she guesses, and like her father, is a professor at Columbia, where he teaches French lit, and is an authority on Flaubert, about whom he's written a couple of books. Oddly, he's wearing a jean jacket, though it is midsummer and none too cool here in the apartment. There is a single gold hoop about the circumference of a dime pierced through the cartilage at the tip of his right ear. He is smiling at her warmly, expectantly.

So here it is staring her in the face, the pure and bitter truth. And the truth, spelled out in its simplest terms, cannot be mistaken for anything other than what it is.

Her father isn't coming home to her mother anytime soon, of that Desirée is certain. She thinks of Emma Bovary's arsenic-induced suicide, and allows herself to imagine an equally wretched death for Jordan. And then is immediately ashamed of herself.

Jordan is cradling her moist hand between both of his. Is he ever going to let go? He's so, so pleased to meet her after such a very long wait, he says.

Desirée thanks him. Her heart is thumping quickly, her breathing rapid and shallow; it's as if she's suffering a small anxiety attack. She reminds herself, as her mother often has, that she is descended from a long line of strong women who successfully weathered pogroms in czarist Russia, the Great Depression of the thirties, and early widowhood.

At last Jordan drops her hand. "Your father and I are hoping to see a lot more of you this summer," he says.

Don't count on it.

"Please please PLEASE don't be a stranger," her father adds.

If only she were a young child, young enough not to comprehend the sea change their family has endured. If only she could say to her father, as she would like to, *Whatever turns you on.* Chacun à son goût. *I'm down with it, dawg!*

She has a handful of gay friends at school, both male and female. But this is her father, and he and his boyfriend have rent her poor mother's heart and sent her into a fucking tailspin.

She will not tell her father that she and her mother refer to Jordan as "Loverboy," that they can't even bring themselves to call him by his real name. For all she knows, all she suspects, Loverboy is a perfectly decent guy, someone she might, under vastly different circumstances, be more than happy to meet. But when her father says that of course she'll be staying for dinner, won't she, and wants to know which she prefers, Thai or Cambodian, Desirée says, "Maybe some other time, okay?"

Like the twelfth of never.

Sorry, but as open-minded as she is about nearly everything, on this particular subject of her father and Loverboy, that mind of hers remains firmly, insistently, shut.

Later, at home, she has dinner (two slices of pizza, one white, the other embellished with prosciutto) with her mother. Both of them stand at the kitchen counter in the comfortable but unexceptional apartment she grew up in on the Upper East Side, a three-bedroom, two-and-a-half-bath apartment with a small terrace—where, in high school, Desirée and her friends sometimes smoked pot when her parents weren't home. Her mother sips at her Diet Coke straight from the can and asks what her father's new digs look like; Desirée answers, truthfully and apologetically, that she forgot to pay attention to the couches and window treatments and lighting fixtures and the rest of it. All she remembers is how hard her father and Loverboy had tried to make her feel comfortable, and how she would not give an inch.

CHAPTER 2

TWENTY-EIGHT YEARS AGO, Desirée's mother, Nina Cohen, was voted "Best Looking" in her high school's senior poll. She and another girl received exactly the same number of votes and amiably shared the title. (A dubious honor, though, Nina thought; after all, she'd done nothing to earn it. "Most Likely to Succeed," on the other hand, would have been something to be proud of.) The other girl, Anna Spargo, became, in the decade after high school, a big-time coke dealer, and acquired a collection of homes for herself in Waikiki, Rio, and Paris, along with a pied-à-terre on Fifth Avenue. But eventually she was brought down by a pair of DEA agents in Manhattan and served nearly ten years in federal prison. There were articles about her trial and conviction in the *New York Times,* and Nina had read them in disbelief. She remembered the yearbook photographer snapping pictures of her and Anna posed against the curved wall outside the high school auditorium, and that afterward, she and Anna shared a cigarette in the bleachers surrounding the football field. This had been in 1979, in a town on Long Island's North Shore. Unlike Anna Spargo, Nina's life after high school went undocumented by the *New York Times.* She enrolled at Wellesley, met an MIT student named Patrick Christian at a mixer while she was still a freshman, and, unfortunately, as it turned out, fell happily in love. She found Patrick both exceptionally smart and uncommonly sweet, an unusual combination, in her experience, and she loved his baby-fine red hair, nearly invisible eyebrows, and the freckles that adorned his long limbs. Twice during college, for several months each time around, Patrick broke up with her, for reasons so vague, Nina can no longer remember them. Both times she believed he would come back, and both times she was right.

News of their wedding plans delighted neither the Christians nor the Cohens. Patrick's mother immediately tried to convince

Nina that any children they might have should be baptized. An unbaptized child would, at its death, go straight to hell, she explained. Nina, someone for whom the concepts of both hell and heaven were absolutely untenable, smiled politely and kept her mouth shut. It was Patrick who told his mother to mind her own goddamn business. "Over my dead body will a grandchild of mine be baptized," Nina's father said when he heard of Patrick's mother's request. He threatened to be a no-show at the wedding—an extravagant affair, the payment for which necessitated a home equity loan from his bank. The ceremony was conducted by a priest and a rabbi, and though the two sets of parents were cordial enough to one another that evening, they kept out of each other's way in the years that followed, barely speaking to one another again, even when Desirée was born and they all had something to celebrate.

There was, as it turned out, no baptism, no baby-naming ceremony in a synagogue; there was only a Christmas tree and a sterling silver menorah that, year after year, was lit, as prescribed, eight nights in a row.

Patrick's parents eventually retired to Palm Beach, where Nina and Patrick always visited them for a week every winter. (Now, of course, Nina doubts whether she'll ever see them again.) Several years ago, Nina's own mother died—shockingly—of an aneurysm; shortly afterward, Marvin, her father, exhibited the hand tremors that proved to be the first sign of Parkinson's. Confined to a wheelchair and unable to live on his own, he's taken over the extra bedroom Nina and Patrick had long used as a den. Better to have her father here under her roof than in a "senior residence" or nursing home, Nina is convinced, though the cost to her mental health has been steep.

Here is the news that greets her and her daughter now at the breakfast table: somehow managing to slip out of his diaper in the middle of the night, Marvin has soaked the bed again. This information comes to them from Porsha, the woman who helps look after Marvin, from the moment he awakens in the morning to the time he drifts off to sleep for the night. In between, she takes him for walks in his wheelchair; changes his diapers; listens attentively to the virtually incomprehensible strings of words he occasionally murmurs; spoon-feeds him the applesauce and rice pudding that, along with three cans a day of chocolate-flavor Nutrament, are the staples of his diet—all with a perpetual cheeriness that springs from who knows where. It is obvious to Nina that Porsha is a saint, the very best of all the women who'd been hired and then fired by her—some so fast Nina hardly had time to get their names straight—since Patrick moved out and her father gave up his own apartment and moved in. But Marvin, despite the attention lavished upon him, is never going to get better, only worse. This, too, is evident, though sometimes Nina pretends she simply doesn't understand the nature of his disease: it's as if she's convinced herself her father will someday outgrow his need for diapers and graduate to the toilet, progress from a diet of mush and canned liquid to ordinary solid food, and rise up out of his wheelchair like one of those phonies planted at a revival meeting by some fabulously wealthy, silver-tongued minister with a fleet of ultraluxury cars. The strain of pretending that an incurably sick old man is going to get well and that she herself is going to help him along the way has, not surprisingly, rendered her depressed and high-strung all at once, and nearly impossible to please. If only she could blame every bit of her misery on Patrick, which—you can bet on it—she would dearly love to, unfair though it might be.

"All right, coming through!" Porsha calls brightly, returning with Marvin in his wheelchair and parking him in the kitchen doorway so she can keep an eye on him as she fixes his breakfast. Though Porsha is slender, her bosom is a large shelf you could, no doubt, balance a collection of miniature teacups and saucers on; her bras, she's confided to Nina, have to be made to order for a princely sum. She moves gracefully in and out of tight spots, like the space she is negotiating now between the dishwasher and the glass table. "Oh, and I forgot to mention he's got some diaper rash this morning," she says. She stirs a bowl of rice pudding, adds a sprinkle of cinnamon, and ties an apron patterned with pots of showy geraniums around Marvin's neck.

"Can we please not talk about this at the breakfast table?" Desirée requests, sipping at her mango-orange juice.

"A little bit of baby corn starch on his bottom will fix that rash right up in a day or two," Porsha says. She tries to get Marvin to open his mouth, but he isn't cooperating. "Come on, darlin'," she urges, "you got to keep your strength up. If you don't eat, bad things are going to happen."

Marvin sits tight-lipped, his hands folded in his lap. Nina can read his mind: *What bad things? What could possibly be worse than this?* Most of the time he stares vacantly, but he seems to appreciate watching the news on television, and Nina, who is teaching a literature and writing class to undergraduates at NYU this summer, reads to him every day from her required reading list; she and Marvin are currently on *The Portrait of a Lady.* His speech has deteriorated sharply in recent months, but every so often she can distinguish a phrase here or there. Yesterday he'd said, with what sounded like excitement, *Cream cheese and lox,* though when Nina spread a small sample over a piece of the softest white bread for him, he refused it. A retired trusts and estates attorney who'd been married for over fifty years, he's lived long and well; what he's left with now, in Nina's estimation, is a humiliating finale. Perhaps he fantasizes about a chance meeting with Dr. Kevorkian in Central Park and a secret exchange of phone numbers with him now that the good doctor is out of the slammer; perhaps he takes a distinct pleasure in the affectionate sound of Porsha's voice, a cool breeze blowing across his face, the taste of his favorite sorbet as it sits melting in his mouth.

Surrounded by women who are dying to know what he is thinking, Marvin remains a mystery they just can't crack.

"Open your mouth, darlin'," Porsha says patiently. "What I got here tastes real good."

Marvin shakes his head.

"Not hungry? Well, you got to eat anyway. You got all that medication to take and you can't do it on an empty stomach."

Compared to Porsha, Nina isn't much good at this. "Would you prefer a feeding tube instead?" she's horrified to hear herself say. "Think you'll be happy with a plastic straw stuck in a little incision in your belly? I can call the gastroenterologist anytime if that's what you want." She approaches Marvin, squats on the floor, rests her hands on the padded arms of his wheelchair. "I used to be a nice person," she says. "You remember that, don't you? Ask anyone, ask Desirée here." Swiveling around to face her daughter, Nina says, "Wasn't I a nice person?"

"Yeah, absolutely."

"Am I nice now?"

Desirée pours herself a half bowl of cereal from an open box of Honey Smacks (called Sugar Smacks in Nina's day), and crunches thoughtfully. "Well, at the moment I'd have to say you're pretty stressed out."

"So if I weren't under so much stress, I'd be a lot nicer, wouldn't I? I'd be the person you know and love."

"I still love you," Desirée reports.

"Thank you," says Nina, "but what I really need is for your grandfather to know I'm sorry for sounding so, well, unsympathetic." She turns back to Marvin. "Do you understand the strain I'm under these days?"

"He understands plenty," Porsha says. "Sometimes he just doesn't want to listen. He tunes you out, disappears inside himself there and doesn't come back till he's good and ready."

"That's my theory, too," Nina says. "I wonder what he thinks of *The Portrait of a Lady*? He seems interested, but who knows?"

Marvin grunts.

"If only he could be a little more specific." Nina sees that there are tears in her father's eyes. His voice is faint, not much more powerful than a whisper. *I don't know who I am anymore*, he is saying. The words are slurred as a drunk's, but she understands them. This confession is the most he's offered up in a long while, and Nina's eyes fill at the sound of it.

"Oh my," says Porsha.

"He doesn't know who he is anymore," Nina says. Her voice is suddenly edged with excitement, and Desirée is glaring at her. "Well, of course it's a terrible thing to hear, but on the other hand, it's a wonderful breakthrough."

Desirée moves to Marvin's good side, the one without the hearing aid, and sinks down onto her knees. "It must have cost you a lot to tell us," she says. "It was a secret, wasn't it?"

11

Marvin nods slightly; a single tear falls onto the collar of his yellow-and-white plaid shirt and then disappears.

"We'll keep it to ourselves," Desirée promises him. She tells Nina that she and Marvin need to go out for a walk. "We need to clear our heads," she explains.

"Who in this family doesn't?" Nina says.

CHAPTER 3

DESIRÉE PUSHES MARVIN in his wheelchair along Madison Avenue, which has lost much of its population to the Hamptons this Friday afternoon. It is a spectacular summer day, warm but not humid, with just enough of a breeze to keep you from feeling sluggish. Occasionally a bus rumbles by, but there are few cars and even fewer pedestrians. Someone dressed as a pea pod and holding a sign that says, GIVE PEAS A CHANCE—GO VEGETAR-IAN parades back and forth listlessly. Desirée smiles at him or her, but is ignored. She tries not to think of how her father had wrecked his marriage, tries not to feel stupid for having missed whatever neon signs might have been there, but finds herself thinking of little else. While she'd been sitting at her desk in her shared apartment off campus in New Haven, sweating over a paper about suicide for her abnormal psych class and the uses of imagery in *King Lear* for her Shakespeare course, her father had been screwing Jordan, an image best left uncontemplated. She wonders if her father had ever considered confiding in her; the fact that he'd kept her and her mother in the dark for so long was another disappointment. Would he have earned any sympathy from Desirée if he'd brought her up to speed and confessed what he'd been up to a year ago when he first met Jordan? In all likelihood, then as now, it's her mother she would have given everything to—sympathy, comfort, her condolences. Disillusionment falls over her now like a freezing rain. If her father is no longer someone to be trusted, then clearly she's lost her footing in this world. She just doesn't know which end is up anymore. Proof of this, she realizes, is that she's forgotten her single most indispensable possession—her BlackBerry, damn it.

She and Marvin continue heading west, toward the park. They enter at Eighty-sixth Street, where she buys him a cup of frozen yogurt from a vendor wearing a plastic crucifix around his neck on a lanyard.

"What's wrong with him?" he asks Desirée, jerking his thumb in Marvin's direction. "He doesn't look too good. He's got MS or somethin'?"

"Something like that."

"Does someone pay you to feed him?" the man says as Desirée spoons a bit of yogurt into Marvin's mouth. He looks at Marvin with frank curiosity, watches his head swinging wildly from side to side, the yogurt dripping past his chin and onto his collarbone.

Startled, Desirée says, "He's my grandfather."

"Well, good luck to you."

"Who?" Marvin asks her. She is wiping off the yogurt with a paper napkin dampened with a splash of bottled water. "Good luck?" His head is stationary now and he appears alert. "Good luck," he repeats.

"That reminds me." She's found a bench in the shade, and arranges the wheelchair next to her. Slipping her backpack off the handle of the chair, she extracts a sharpened sky-blue pencil and a manuscript of horoscopes that will fill a monthly magazine of them—one of her freelance editing jobs for the summer. "Listen to this," she says: "*Watch out who you chat with on the Internet they could be just the kind of psycho your mother always warned you about. And don't forget your vitamins today you're feeling low mentally and physically. If you get locked out of your car don't blame others.*"

"Huh," Marvin says.

"That was yours, Scorpio," she says. "Want to hear mine? *You're wondering what will save the romance, anxiety will keep you up till dawn. Bitter disappointment may be headed your way but a new pair of shoes may be just the thing to lift your sagging spirits. Above all accentuate the positive even if you feel like doing the opposite.*" She smiles at Marvin. "Not quite *The Portrait of a Lady*, is it?" she apologizes.

"Hah!"

She puts down her pencil. "It's a dirty job but someone's gotta do it," she says. Marvin's eyelids flutter. "Tired?" she asks him.

"Nah."

"I'm guessing you have plenty you want to talk about, if only you could. You used to be one of those big talkers, a distinct presence in a roomful of people."

"Yah?"

"Aren't you angry?" Desirée says. "You've got to be furious—
I'd be furious—to have lost so much, I mean . . ."

Marvin's eyes widen, almost comically, but this isn't an expression of surprise; it's just the Parkinson's.

"Well, we're all angry about something. Like me. I'm still so
freaked out over my father, I just . . ." Desirée falls silent, distracted by the sight of someone approaching, a nice-looking
woman, middle-aged, wearing khaki shorts and a fake-fur jacket
unbuttoned, and carrying an open umbrella high overhead; imprinted on it are the words SHIT, IT'S RAINING! Clearly the
woman is out of her fucking mind, and yet except for the umbrella
and the fur jacket, she looks quite sane, really, with her neatly
groomed hair, Burberry sunglasses, and a string of pearls around
her neck.

"Top of the morning to you, m'lord," she says grandly, and
strolls past them.

In the sun, Marvin dozes, and Desirée goes back to her blue
pencil, adding commas and semicolons like crazy.

When she returns home, there's a thrilling message for her
on her phone—Nick is flying in from Wisconsin tonight, the first
time he's visited her in New York since Thanksgiving! His tickets
are insanely expensive and he can only stay the weekend, but he
just *has* to see her.

Desirée listens to the message again and again, listens to that
Midwest twang of Nick's that always stirs her, even when he is saying something as heartbreaking and dumb as "I like you veeery,
veeery much."

CHAPTER 4

THOUGH DESIRÉE TRIES TO KEEP IT A SECRET whenever possible, like so many of her private-school friends who grew up in the city, she doesn't yet have her driver's license. She's failed the road test twice—the first time, because she nervously jerked the car to a sickening stop at a red light, the second time, because she knocked over a large garbage pail while trying to parallel park—and so her mother has been recruited to drive her to LaGuardia to pick up Nick.

In the airport parking lot, she considers asking Nina to wait in the car while she goes alone to meet Nick, but she knows how selfish this would sound—as if she were simply using her mother as a chauffeur—and thinks better of it. She and Nina are sitting around in the arrivals area now, her mother reading *The New Yorker* and Desirée chewing on the tip of her thumb. She gets up to check the arrivals board, and learns that Nick's plane is, as promised, exactly on time, due in any minute. Something tightens in her stomach; it has been two interminably long months since they've seen each other in New Haven, and she is afraid something may have been lost in all that time: her hold on his affections, perhaps, or, less likely, his on hers.

He is one of the first people off the plane; he has his carry-on bag slung over his shoulder and is deep in conversation with a leggy black woman who dwarfs him. Desirée waves, tentatively, as if there's a possibility she is mistakenly greeting a stranger. But he waves back and dumps his newfound friend an instant later. As their arms loop around each other, she gazes beyond Nick's shoulder and observes her mother staring wistfully, like someone in her seat in a movie theater touched by the sight of lovers on the big screen and remembering that, back home, there is no one awaiting her except her Pekingese. Selfishly, guiltily, Desirée lingers in that hug, shutting her eyes to make her mother disappear. When she opens them, Nina's face is buried in her *New*

Yorker. And Desirée, whose abiding love for her father hasn't diminished, makes a mental note to wring his neck, just a little, the next time she sees him.

ACCORDING TO NINA, these are the sleeping arrangements, as they were the last time around: Nick on the convertible couch in the living room, and Desirée where she belongs, alone in her own bed. It means nothing to her, Nina says, that Desirée is twenty years old, undeniably an adult.

"Just what I need, some horny college boy here for a sleepover," she complains.

"It's not as if we haven't spent the night together," Desirée reports brazenly, breaking the news to her mother. "Numerous times, in fact."

Her mother claps her hands over her ears. "I didn't hear that," she says. "But if I did, I'm just going to pretend I didn't."

They are in the Dog House, a neighborhood bar near their apartment, waiting for Nick to return from the men's room. There's sawdust on the unfinished wood floor, a jukebox playing U2, and a big-screen TV showing a Yankees game in progress. The air is heavily scented with the odor of fried food and alcohol, an uninviting combination that makes Desirée want to hold her breath. It is her mother who wanted a drink, and Nick who wanted a bacon cheeseburger, and so this is where they are, in a crowd of mostly twenty-somethings, loud and joyous on a summer Friday night. With her *mother,* for Christ's sake.

Nick drops back into his seat, and the table rocks uncertainly in the sawdust. Desirée takes full advantage of the opportunity to slip her foot from her flip-flop and slide it up and down the inside of his leg. He's holding her hand now, one of the simple pleasures she's missed. He lifts their linked hands to his lips and kisses her knuckles lightly, one by one.

Smiling at the two of them, Nina says, "Excellent vodka martini!" This is her third, and soon she will be completely smashed. "Very dry, very nice. And furthermore, I feel like a million bucks."

"You're going to have a hangover tomorrow," Desirée warns. "I think maybe we should get you home."

"Me? I'm fine," Nina says dismissively. "In fact, I'm so fine, I'm going to tell you, verbatim, what your father said to me the night our marriage crashed and burned. First of all—"

"Mom, don't," Desirée interrupts. "We're all going to feel bad about this in two minutes, trust me."

"As I was saying," her mother continues, ignoring her, "first of all, his eyes were closed. 'Open your eyes when you talk to me,' I told him. But he couldn't bear to look at me, which is as it should be, I guess. And as soon as he mentioned Loverboy's name, my hands and feet went numb. If there'd been a fire, I would have died right there in my seat at the kitchen table, because there was simply no way I could have picked myself up and gotten out of there. Saving myself wouldn't have been a possibility. Neither was getting my husband back—I could tell from the sound of his voice—soft, but absolutely firm. He was determined to end it, to give his life over to Loverboy. And then, just like that, the feeling came back to my hands and feet. There was a tingling; I rubbed my hands together and reached across the table to your father. I didn't know if I was going to slap him or take his face in my hands and kiss him. What happened was that I slapped the table. 'Open your damn eyes and look at me and tell me that you no longer love me,' I said. And that, boys and girls, is exactly what he did."

This is the saddest thing Desirée has heard, or at least it seems so at the moment, and she has to look away from her mother.

Nick is studying his watch. "It's late," he says mildly, politely keeping his impatience in check. "It's after midnight."

"Time to go," Desirée tells her mother. She signals to Nick and they each grab an arm and lift Nina out of her seat.

"I am bee-sotted," Nina admits. "Truth to tell, I can't distinguish my you-know-what from my elbow." As Nick turns back to the table to take care of the tip, Nina falls from Desirée's grasp and slides on her side into the sawdust.

Gently brushing the fine particles of wood from her mother's shirt and jeans, Desirée then picks it from Nina's hair as best she can. Together, she and Nick escort her to the door; outside, under the light of the streetlamp, she can see the sawdust delineating the rim of her mother's ear, and wipes it delicately with her fingertip, as if she herself were a mother tending to a child who'd tumbled in the sandbox. Where is her father, who'd removed splinters from Nina's thumb with a sterilized needle and painted it with rubbing alcohol, who worriedly slipped a thermometer in her mouth when she had the flu, fixed eggs on weekend mornings just the way Nina liked them, sunny-side up, yolks runny, whites fried crisp around the edges. What will her mother do the next time a splinter pierces her flesh? When she's sick in bed with a fever of 102, achy joints and a blinding headache, who will stand over her and lay his hand tenderly upon her burning forehead? Her mother is a grown woman and will take care of herself, but Desirée wants more for her. She can see the shadowy silhouette of a man leaning over Nina in bed, hear his voice asking sympathetically if she needs more Tylenol, more ginger ale, more anything. Somewhere, Desirée believes, there is a man just waiting to fall in love with her mother; the trick is to make sure Nina keeps her eyes and ears open, alert to the possibility that he may appear without warning anytime, anywhere.

WITH HER ARM LINKED IN DESIRÉE'S, her mother makes it home in one piece. In the elevator, though, she sinks into a corner, her face in her hands. "Life is short and so am I," she laments.

"Up you go," Desirée says, she and Nick giving her mother a hand as the elevator reaches their floor. Bypassing Marvin's room, where he and Porsha are asleep, she steers her mother straight into what was formerly her parents' bedroom, and watches Nina collapse facedown on the bed.

"Good night, sweet prince and/or princess," her mother says. "Now go away and let me sleep this off."

Nick is lazing on the love seat in the living room, his feet on the coffee table, his glasses in his lap. He squints in Desirée's direction, wrinkling his nose. "You look all blurry and beautiful, Desi."

She settles in beside him and licks his lips languidly, top and bottom.

"Is everyone asleep?" he whispers.

"Oh yes."

"All doors closed?"

"Oh yes."

"Let's go take a shower."

She tells him he is crazy, but finds herself leading the way, on silent tiptoes, to the bathroom off the hall. They leave their clothes in sloppy piles on the floor and slink behind the clear pane of the shower door, where they are soon locked in a soapy embrace, hands greedy for the feel of each other's slippery flesh.

With damp towels bunched under Desirée's head for pillows, and a single dry towel spread over a bathmat lightly seeded with lint, they have urgent sex on the bathroom floor. Perfectly formed pearls of moisture cling to Nick's chest hair; his face, as Desirée gazes up at him, looks unfriendly, set in fierce concentration. She closes her eyes, curls her toes against the bottom of the wicker hamper bulging with soiled laundry.

The back of her head grazes the base of the toilet.

"Oh God, honey," Nick says.

"What?" Desirée says. She grasps the tips of his ears and tugs at them. *"What?"*

"I like you veeery, veeery much," he says, all Midwestern charm.

"Very," she corrects him, the first time she's done so. "That's very nice to hear," she lies, and then her head cracks hard against the toilet, bringing tears to her eyes.

"I truly, truly love being here with you," Nick coos.

Here? On the floor of the bathroom, with her relatives and Porsha asleep down the hall? "That's nice," she says. Her voice sounds frail and trembly, the voice of someone who has lost all hope.

"What's the matter, honey, didn't you come?"

"I hit my head on the toilet," she weeps.

He lifts her up and into his arms and rocks her sweetly.

"Please don't," she says.

"What?"

"Go back to Wisconsin," she tells him. "Go find the love of your life and please just leave me alone."

"What do you mean?"

She rubs the back of her head; she can swear she feels a lump already rising.

"I don't understand," Nick says. "Why would I want to go looking for the love of my life when I have *you*?" Reminded by Desirée that he doesn't love her, he is briefly silent, then says, "Well . . . maybe I sorta do and just don't realize it. Or maybe I will . . . one of these days."

"You'd know by now, trust me," Desirée says.

"But you love *me,* is that it?" He runs his fingers through her wet hair and gets stuck in a tangle.

"That's it," she says, thoroughly heartsick. "In a nutshell."

"Then can't we stay together and see how things go? I think I just need more time."

It's gratifying to see the pleading in his eyes, to recognize it in his voice, but he's had all the time in the world to discover what Desirée had discovered without any effort at all. And she knows that love is something you fall into, like a deep gash in the earth that, without warning, swallows you whole. It's a simple thing, really, requiring little explanation. Confide in anyone—a stranger seated next to you on the subway—that you're in love, and he will understand in an instant precisely what you mean.

Unhooking Nick's fingers from her hair, Desirée murmurs, "Go home."

"You're actually breaking up with me?" he says in astonishment.

"We should get some clothes on," she says. It is like a tropical rain forest in the room; she can hardly breathe. Beneath her damp skin, her heart continues to beat dumbly on.

She opens the door a crack to let in some air. Nick shuts it with his foot.

"This is insane," he says. "You're breaking up with someone you love, you idiot." He lets out what sounds, to Desirée, like a strangled cry of frustration and grief, and she allows him to grab hold of her then, and to kiss her. And in that small steamed-up room, Nick quietly announces that he loves her.

"Veeery much," he insists. "Veeery, *veeery* much."

But Desirée is nobody's fool, much as she would like to be, if only for a single, rapturous moment. "We both know that isn't true," she says flatly.

"All right, look," Nick says, "I may not love you, exactly, but

I guarantee you I feel more for you than I've ever felt for anyone. So why can't that be enough, for the time being, anyway?"

SHE CALLS THE AIRLINE HERSELF, arranging, for an additional seventy-five dollars, for Nick to be homeward bound by noon. She pitches him a pillow and a blanket as he settles onto the convertible sofa, which they haven't the energy to bother opening.

Her bedroom air conditioner breathes evenly in the dark; beyond the window, trucks and cars and the occasional motorcycle travel past on the way to somewhere else. Desirée longs to be a passenger, to leave behind this room, this too-familiar apartment, this ordinary high-rise building, this city. Dozing in her bed, she dreams of exotic places she's never had even a glimpse of, of windswept deserts, mountains that might have been the Rockies or the Swiss Alps or the Himalayas. She awakens exhausted from her travels, disappointed to see that, in fact, she's gone absolutely nowhere.

WHILE HER MOTHER IS HAVING her hair colored at Hair, Thair, and Everywhair, and Porsha and Marvin are off to a program for special-needs seniors at the Ninety-second Street Y, Desirée and Nick station themselves outside in search of a cab that will take him to the airport. But when one draws up in front of the building to discharge its passengers, Nick ignores it and remains on the curb with Desirée, his hand massaging her shoulder.

"Yes?" the driver calls out. "No?"

"Go," Desirée tells Nick, though really she means "stay."

"Basically, I have to say I'm convinced you're deranged," Nick says. In the cab, he immediately powers the grimy window down and sticks his head out. "Please don't be nutty," he begs. "All you need to do is give me a little more time." He motions her closer. "A kiss?" he says. She bends awkwardly and uncomfortably from the curb; their lips meet for an instant and then she is pulling away.

Nick's cab is stuck at a red light halfway down the street. She can see the back of his head, though from this distance he might be anyone at all, even someone who genuinely loves her. There is still time to run after him, to thump her fists theatrically against the passenger side of the taxi, to blurt out in a breathless voice that she's made the most wrongheaded of mistakes, that what she wants more than anything is to give it another shot. There is still time for all of this but then the light blinks to green and she is left with the doorman, who nods at her and says grimly, "Beautiful day out there, right?"

Upstairs, she locks herself in the hallway bathroom, turns on the faucets full force, and thinks of the frenzied way she and Nick had clung to one another there on the floor. She savors, perversely, the slow trail of stupid tears down her face and into her ears and under her neck. She gives herself over to self-pity, sobbing until her nose leaks and sad little hiccupping sounds rise over the noise of running water.

CHAPTER 5

ALMOST WITHOUT THINKING, and with only the haziest notion of getting high, Desirée lights up a joint in her bedroom and enjoys it near the open window, every so often fanning the smoke toward the outside world with an indifferent wave of her hand. Her mother—who is at the other end of the apartment with her grandfather—will certainly know what she's been up to; her hair already reeks, and even when the smoke has vanished, there will be a lingering odor no matter what she does to disguise it.

Her legs folded beneath her, she sits on her bed with her blue pencil, a little stoned, but clearheaded enough to do the sort of work that comes so easily to her. After a while, though, she tires of all that optimistic bullshit the astrologer dishes out to those loyal readers of what Desirée considers a truly ridiculous magazine. (Money, however, is honey—as she herself wrote in a poem when she was six or seven—and she'll have to take it where she can get it.) She begins to delete whole lines here and there and replace them with horoscopes of her own invention.

Flirting with a guy at the mall will be like flirting with disaster. Do the three little letters STD mean anything to you?

Venus in Virgo makes you want to punch out that sullen cashier at the supermarket or drugstore. Go for it, baby!

Your boss keeps pinching you on the butt and promising you a raise. Promises, promises. Forget the raise and haul his ass into court.

She keeps this up for pages and pages, laughing her head off over what she believes to be her clever handiwork. She is taking such pleasure in her own company that she doesn't notice her mother's knock. The door swings open and then there she is, wanting to know if someone's been smoking weed.

"Excuse me?" Desirée says.

"Who gave you permission to smoke pot in this house?"

"What do you mean?" Desirée briefly contemplates confiding in her mother and revealing that she and Nick are, as of today, history. But she can see that Nina is frazzled—as is usual on the weekends, when Porsha is off—and that it's best to defer, for the moment, at least, the opportunity to tap into her sympathy.

"Okay, look, you'll just help me with Grandpa's diaper," her mother proposes, "and we'll forget about the joint it's so abundantly clear you've smoked in here."

At her mother's side as Nina gives herself over to the sorry task of maneuvering a diaper off and onto a helpless old man, Desirée trains her eyes on her own pedicured feet but holds up her end of the conversation, chattering self-consciously about nothing much. She smells ammonia and baby powder and stares at her grandfather's pale, hairless shins against the plum-colored towel her mother has arranged over the bedspread. Marvin's head is turned away, toward the TV set, sparing all three of them eye contact. On the screen, an anchor from CNN muses aloud about Britney Spears, concluding, "Someone's spectacularly lying."

Someone's in need of a grammar lesson, Desirée tells her mother, and both of them smile.

"Think Grandpa loathes this as much as I do?" Nina says, pitching the wet diaper into a plastic trash bag.

"And then some."

"You know, after changing a wet diaper of *yours* all those years ago, I'd kiss your delicious little velvety feet and tickle your sweet, satiny tummy, and everything was right with the world. Even when it wasn't. But this? This is the stuff that makes your head pound and your heart sink."

Slowly Marvin swivels his head toward them. He lifts one hand and places it deliberately over his heart.

"You, too?"

"Oh yas," he tells them; hearing this, Desirée can't help but lean over and bestow a kiss on that rubbery-veined hand crossing his heart.

She and her mother struggle to hoist Marvin's pants up around his waist. They fasten his rainbow-striped suspenders—a gift from

Desirée meant to provide a sunny touch but which end up looking pathetically clownish. Raising him to a sitting position, they ease him off the bed and into the wheelchair. He is dead weight and it's hard work, even though he's reduced to mostly bone. His gold watchband droops from his spindly wrist, in danger of falling off.

"By the way, your hair's kind of a mess," Desirée tells him.

"Mine?" says her mother, her hands flying to her head.

"Not you," says Desirée. Sunk into his wheelchair, his head droopy, Marvin looks as if he is asleep. But his eyes are open, and when Desirée asks for permission to brush his surprisingly abundant silver hair, he nods. She brushes gently but diligently, and when she is finished, she holds a large mirror trimmed in tortoiseshell up to his face. "Lookin' good, don't you think?" she asks as he examines his reflection. Anticipating an attempt at a smile, she's startled when his response is to knock the mirror from her hand onto the parquet floor, where it cracks but does not shatter. "I can see my career as a hairdresser is going nowhere fast," she observes.

"What's gotten into you?" her mother chides Marvin. "Can't you be a decent human being and say thank you to Desi? Can't you at least *try* to say those two little words?"

"Jesus, stop!" Desirée says. "He doesn't need to thank me, all right?"

Marvin's head is hung so low, his chin grazes the buttons of his shirt. It's the classic posture of shame and regret, but who knows what's really on his mind? That he's expected to engage in the impossibly difficult struggle to form the words "thank you" in the clear strong voice he no longer possesses—well, Desirée would bet that he can't be anything other than astonished by that expectation. And she is outraged on his behalf. "What's *your* problem?" she asks her mother now.

"*My* problem? My problem is that I want out. Out of this apartment that's begun to feel and smell like a nursing home. Out of the life that's been mistakenly assigned to me, okay?"

And of course, Desirée knows, there's that agonizing matter of her father and Loverboy, a subject that her mother, at this moment, can't even summon up the strength to raise. "Ever consider joining the Witness Protection Program?" Desirée says, hoping to evoke a smile. "New name, new Social Security number, maybe even new fingerprints."

"Sounds lovely." Her mother glances at Marvin, still and silent in his wheelchair, a lifelike statue of a man. "Too bad," she murmurs, and what Desirée hears is her mother's weary surrender to all that is hers, and her envy of all that is not.

A powerful wave of sympathy passes over her and she can imagine opening her arms to her mother. And then she actually moves toward her and her mother is toppling into her embrace. What Desirée wants to tell her is something she knows she must keep to herself: that after a couple of months in this city she loves but which seems to have little to offer her now but an aggrieved mother and a father who is the source of much of that grief, Desirée herself is aching to fly the coop. Aching.

Unlike her mother, whose hands are bound painfully tight by an uneasy fusion of love and guilt, and responsibilities she simply can't evade, Desirée is free to hit the road. To take her chances on the next flight out tomorrow that happens to be going her way, in any direction at all.

SHE WILL WAIT until after dinner, until she has cleared the table, and the plates and silverware are neatly in their racks in the dishwasher, and the sound of her mother's voice patiently reading Henry James puts Marvin to sleep in his bed. While Nina devotes herself to an hour-long Internet search on the newest treatment for Parkinson's (and halfheartedly checks out some dating Web sites), Desirée will retreat into the bedroom that has been hers since childhood, where shelves overloaded with Nancy Drews that belonged to her mother will wait forever to be dusted and an ancient corsage of pink roses from her father on her tenth birthday sits looking bereft, dark as parched earth and more brittle than Marvin's fragile old bones. Barefoot, she will climb on top of her bed and take down the Rand McNally map of the United States that had been thumbtacked to her wall long ago. Four feet wide, larger than the bathmat that lay underneath her while she and Nick took pleasure in each other one last time, the map, the country it depicts, will seem vast and unknowable spread across her bedroom carpet.

Wanting to create a little atmosphere—a mixture of the spiritual and the spooky—she will light a quartet of scented candles in frosted-glass jars, one labeled WIND, the others, HEAVEN, EARTH, and DREAM, all Christmas presents from Nick, in fact, that she's never known what to do with and will soon toss out with the trash. She will arrange a single candle at each corner of the map and kill the overhead light. Knees bent, fingers pressed into the carpet, she will rock nervously on her toes. Her mouth will grow dry and the hollows under her arms will dampen. She will offer herself a quick, silent pep talk, and then, eyes squeezed shut, she will go for it, drawing her arm forward over the map and lowering the tip of her index finger decisively. It will touch down somewhere in Kansas, one of those dull-looking rectangles she might easily confuse with either of the Dakotas. In the perfumed candlelight, she will read the fine print and plainly see just where it is she will be headed the next morning.

Honey Creek, Kansas. To Desirée Christian-Cohen, a place as distant and unfamiliar as the landscape of the moon.

CHAPTER 6

AFTER A RESTLESS NIGHT'S SLEEP spoiled by unsettling dreams she will only half remember, Desirée awakens to Modest Mouse playing on her clock radio and the neckline of her T-shirt moist with sweat. Except for the soothing murmur of the living room air conditioner set on low, the apartment, at 5:30 A.M., is absolutely still. Her canvas duffel bag that zips across the middle is already packed for a couple of weeks of travel; there is nothing left to do now but wash up and leave a note for her mother on the kitchen table. She writes "GONE FISHING—call you later!" on a fluorescent-green Post-it, and attaches it sheepishly to the Lucite salt-and-pepper shaker on the table next to the matching napkin holder, where it can't be missed. Armed with three hundred and fifty-six dollars in cash and a MasterCard in her own name, she tiptoes out, closing the door behind her as delicately as a thief who's just robbed a sleeping household.

It's easier than she imagined finding a cab so early in the morning, but the driver of the first one to pull up beside her doesn't want to ferry her all the way out to the airport. "It's almost the end of my shift," he explains. "I need to go home to the Bronx and get some sleep, okay, miss?"

"Yeah, but it's the law," Desirée reminds him. "You *have* to take me."

The driver's response is swift and succinct. "It's a fucking *stupid* law," he says, and tears off.

But soon enough, a cabby who is perfectly happy to drive her to LaGuardia shows up, and Desirée plunks herself down gratefully in the backseat. She can already picture her mother standing over the smudged glass of the kitchen table, that facetious Post-it in hand, wondering where the hell her only child has disappeared to. The single clue she'll have that Desirée has gone AWOL is the lavender toothbrush missing from the ceramic holder above the sink in Desirée's own bathroom. And if her mother doesn't take note of the absent toothbrush, perhaps she will regard the Post-it as a joke of sorts, imagining that Desirée has merely taken off for the day. Desirée has, as it happens, decided that it is her father she will call from the airport—she is reasonably certain he will take the news in stride, reasonably certain he can be counted on to explain the facts of the case to her mother calmly and reassuringly.

The ride to the airport clocks in at a brisk fifteen minutes, but she isn't feeling fully prepared to leave the cab yet. Arriving at the American Airlines departures terminal, she freezes in the backseat, unable to make a move toward the door.

"Twenty even, plus four-fifty for the toll over the bridge," the driver announces, and Desirée's hand moves toward her wallet, but her fingers are numb. She considers grabbing the small gray wallet between her palms and pitching it to the cabby through the opening in the Plexiglas partition. *Go ahead and take whatever I owe you. Plus tip.* But somehow she manages to fork over the money and to extract herself from the backseat.

A pair of glass doors parts smartly for her; inside the terminal, she stands in line for a round-trip ticket to Kansas City with an open-ended return. She'll have to change planes in Chicago, the clerk informs her.

"Don't look so worried," he says. "You'll be just fine."

"I will?" Desirée has traveled to Mexico, to the Caribbean, Western Europe, and, most recently, to Prague, Budapest, and Vienna—always with friends or family, never on her own. Why is it that all of a sudden she has doubts about her ability to change planes in Chicago?

She calls her father on her BlackBerry, yanking him rudely from his sleep.

"Desirée?" he says, and then she hears, in the background, an unfamiliar voice—it must be Jordan's—saying, "What time is it?"

"What's going on? Everything okay?" her father asks.

"Guess so."

"So why are you calling me in what feels like the middle of the night?"

Jordan's voice adds, "It's the middle of the night?"

Desirée begins to talk, and then, sensing her father's impatience, cuts to the chase. "So what I'm telling you," she finishes, "is that I'm in desperate need of a radical change of scenery, okay?"

"You put your finger down blindly in the middle of a map, it lands in northeast Kansas, and *that's* where you have to go?"

"You don't have to make it sound so . . . absurd and ridiculous," Desirée says, offended. "Personally, I think it's kind of exciting."

"Absurd and ridiculous?" her father says. "It's way beyond that, kiddo. What if you break your ankle, or your appendix is about to burst at three in the morning? You think there's a hospital in this godforsaken Honey Creek?"

"Oh, I'm sure there is," Desirée says, though of course she is sure of no such thing. She asks him to call her mother and deliver the message that she's perfectly safe. "Just a small favor I'm asking of you. Not a big deal, all right?"

Her father sighs. "Hold on a minute . . . What?" he says, and then adds, "Jordan wishes you a safe trip."

This is as much as she cares to hear about Jordan, and she ends the conversation right there, promising to call when she arrives in Kansas.

With hours to kill before her flight leaves at noon, she roams the airport, examining magazines at a series of newsstands, fingering souvenir key chains and shot glasses and T-shirts, all of which are imprinted with the logo I ♥ NEW YORK. When she hears her stomach murmuring plaintively, it crosses her mind that she hasn't had any breakfast, and she buys herself a Diet Coke and an anemic-looking caraway bagel freckled with no more than a half-dozen seeds. It's soft as a roll and insipid, but she eats it anyway, sitting alone at a white, wrought-iron, ketchup-encrusted table. If someone would hand her a sponge, she'd scour the table herself. She isn't squeamish; after all, hadn't she stood by her mother's side, just yesterday, as she changed Marvin's adult-sized diaper? And here she is now, about to put over twelve hundred miles between her and her family, having sneaked away without even contemplating a gentle, soundless good-bye kiss that she could have planted on the dear, familiar, sleep-drunk faces of her mother and grandfather. Well, we all make mistakes, she tells herself: the disastrous and unforgivable ones, and the other kind, the ones we can live with without too much pain. She can live with this one, though it haunts her now nevertheless, a nagging thought that she's left something undone and will pay for it later. In spades. But she's no Cassandra; she will not allow herself to believe for even a moment that her plane will go down in flames over Kansas City or that her mother and grandfather will be struck by lightning in her absence. That's the sort of thinking that gets you nowhere, that keeps you housebound in front of your DVD player with an oversized bowl of something addictive and fattening at your side.

"Honey Creek," Desirée whispers, savoring the sound of it more and more, hearing in it the sweet promise of an idyll.

WEDGED IN "PEASANT CLASS" between an elderly woman sporting two pairs of eyeglasses suspended from plastic ropes around her neck, and a middle-aged guy with what seems to be an advanced case of the sniffles, Desirée opens a paperback anthology and immediately loses herself in an old favorite, one of those Laurie Colwin stories of such great wit and charm that it wins her over every time she reads it.

The man next to her sneezes twice, then peeks over his shoulder and into Desirée's book. The sound of his congested breathing is hard to ignore.

"Laurie Colwin, huh?" he says in a gravelly voice, and clears his throat. "You've got to love those smart, cranky women of hers."

Desirée's kind of guy after all, never mind his red-tipped nose and the wadded-up tissues in both hands. His hair is a puff of gray frizz and the beard he is growing out is in its earliest, grungiest stages.

"Got to," Desirée agrees, and decides to introduce herself, first name only.

"Daniel," he says, turning his head away, and sneezing again. "Thrilled to be seated next to me and my allergy to some mysterious something or other? Though, on the bright side, the antihistamine I took should be kicking in any minute now."

Desirée smiles. "So what's in Chicago? Or is it Kansas City?"

"Kansas City. One medical convention and at least two good steak dinners."

"Let me guess . . . neuroradiologist? Neonatologist? Orthopedic surgeon?"

They're taking off from the runway now, rising in the polluted air over Queens, resolutely leaving New York behind. Desirée chews vigorously on half a piece of sweet, dense Bubble Yum and shuts her eyes. "Oncologist," she hears Daniel say. And also that he specializes in breast cancer surgery. Her ears pop, and she chews harder, telling him that her mother had had a biopsy a few years ago. "It turned out, thankfully, to be nothing, but we were all a little panicky for a while."

"Of course," Daniel says kindly. "Who *wouldn't* feel that panic?"

Patrick had taken the day off from work, of course, and Desirée had ditched school, even though her parents insisted it wasn't necessary. For a couple of hours, she and her father sat in comfortable chairs in a well-appointed waiting room, crossing and uncrossing their legs, pretending to read dingy back issues of *New York* magazine and *People*, pretending they knew for certain that there wasn't a chance in the world the walnut-sized, all-too-palpable tumor Nina had discovered herself was anything more than a nuisance, a benign clump of unruly cells that posed not even the slightest threat to their family. Afterward, when the surgeon approached them in the waiting room, saying, "Only good news," Desirée's face had flushed with relief and gratitude, and she'd sprung to her feet and impulsively hugged the doctor, a stranger with his hair in a blue paper shower cap, his mouth turned up hesitantly in a bemused smile. It pains her now to think of herself and her parents as they'd been then—their little family intact, love flowing so freely, so abundantly, among the three of them.

"Question: have any of your patients ever hugged or kissed you?" she asks Daniel. "Out of gratitude, I mean."

"Well, let's see, there've been theater tickets, an exceptionally nice wristwatch, tickets to the Philharmonic . . . and that's about all I can remember at the moment."

"Just wondering."

"I've saved lots of patients, but not nearly as many as I'd like,"

Daniel muses. "And sometimes the ones you lose are painfully hard to forget."

"Like ex-lovers," Desirée says wistfully.

"They usually don't haunt my dreams," says Daniel, "but even so . . ."

A little boy in plastic sunglasses, a chocolate cigarette tucked behind his ear, suddenly appears in the aisle. "I'm going to the bathroom," he announces loudly. "And after that, when we get off the airplane, I'm running away from home."

"Do you have a good reason?" Desirée asks, leaning across Daniel to talk to the boy.

"Because." The child takes the chocolate cigarette and pokes it into the side of his mouth. "Puff puff puff," he says pensively.

"Do your parents know where you are, tough guy?" Daniel says.

"Well, I know where *they* are. My mommy's home and my daddy's sleeping."

"You'd better get back into your seat before he wakes up and starts to worry about you," Desirée advises.

Holding the cigarette between two fingers, the little boy pulls it away from his mouth and exhales loudly. "He's a bad, bad daddy. Guess why."

"I don't *want* to guess," Desirée says. "I want to take you back to your seat, okay?"

"He's a bad daddy because he won't let me have soda when I'm thirsty."

"Does your father know you smoke?" Daniel says.

The little boy's smile reveals an endearing assortment of missing teeth. "I'm allowed. I'm in first grade next year and I can do anything except talk to strangers and cross the street without holding hands."

"*We're* strangers," Desirée points out.

The child seems surprised to hear this. "You don't *look* like strangers."

A man with a harassed expression on his face is making his way determinedly down the aisle, waving wildly in their direction. "This is what happens when I close my eyes for two minutes?" he says as he reaches his son. He clamps his hands onto the boy's tiny shoulders. "Don't do this to me, Zachary, I almost had a stroke."

"Are these people strangers?" Zachary asks him.

"What do you think, they're your aunt and uncle? Of course they're strangers." The father's hands are still on Zachary's shoulders. "About-face," he says. "Move it. And take off those sunglasses, what are you, a movie star?"

Desirée watches their slow retreat back to their seats, Zachary languidly twirling his sunglasses as he walks.

"You know, every now and then I regret that my ex and I never had kids," Daniel says. "But this, I'm sure you're not surprised to hear, isn't one of those times."

"Actually, I'm the living embodiment of Zachary's dream," Desirée hears herself confessing, and turns back to Daniel. "I'm a runaway myself."

"Really? You look a little old to be running away from home," Daniel says, amused.

"My eighteenth birthday came and went a couple of years ago, so I suppose technically I'm not a runaway. Not in the legal sense. And in addition to the note I left on the kitchen table for my mother, I made a phone call from the airport. So I'm not the worst thing that ever happened to a parent, right?"

"I'd say not by a long shot," Daniel agrees, but Desirée senses that something has cooled between them, that perhaps they have both revealed a little too much too soon, or at least that neither has a desire to continue this particular thread of conversation. And so she returns to her book, where she finishes up the short story of an unfaithful wife and her married lover, both of them so appealing, you just have to forgive them.

When she and Daniel pick up their connecting flight in Chicago, they find themselves side by side again, even though there are plenty of empty seats all around them.

"Look," says Daniel as they click their seat belts in place, "it's none of my business *what* you're doing in Kansas City, but will you tell me anyway?"

"Kansas City, you may or may not be interested to hear, isn't my final destination," Desirée says, and demonstrates to Daniel just how, back on the Upper East Side, her fingertip had swooped down for a landing in the middle of the map.

"Excellent!" he says, surprising her with his enthusiasm.

"Yeah, well, what is it they say about desperate times calling for desperate measures?" She has a window seat this time, and watches as they gradually rise miles above Chicago and head for that rectangle to the east of Colorado and to the west of Missouri. She has no idea what she is in for, and that, she reminds herself in midair, is the simple beauty of it. Even if her stay in Honey Creek turns out to be the snooze of a lifetime, it's a risk she's willing to take. She's plunging headlong into the middle of nowhere, but even the middle of nowhere at all is somewhere, isn't it?

In the airport in Kansas City, as she and Daniel part company, he asks for her parents' phone number. "When I'm back in New York," he says, "maybe I'll give them a buzz and tell them not to worry about you."

"They're not together anymore, and you don't need to call, but thanks for the offer," Desirée says, touched by his kindness.

"Who's the bigger worrier, your mother or your father? Your mother, right? Just give me her number."

He writes it on his palm, in navy blue ballpoint, a habit of Desirée's that drives her mother crazy. She shrugs, knowing that the next time he washes his hands, his good intentions will vanish down the drain.

CHAPTER 7

THE CLASS NINA IS TEACHING this summer meets three times a week, from noon to two; well aware of her students' hunger—not for literature and writing, but for lunch—she allows them, perhaps too indulgently, to bring food into the classroom if they wish. Today there is someone using chopsticks on a bento box of tempura, a slice of broiled salmon, and what looks like pickled vegetables; a student scarfing a sausage-and-pepper hero; and another sipping onion soup from a large bowl made of bread. Seated around the seminar table are fourteen students; of these, only one has heard of Primo Levi and *Survival in Auschwitz*, the next book on their reading list. One out of fourteen. Why should this surprise Nina? She read, just the other day, that nearly two-thirds of Americans cannot name a single Supreme Court justice or the three branches of the federal government. This, too, shouldn't surprise her. That her daughter had chosen to bolt on a warm summer morning and make her way—according to a text message she received from Patrick—to some jerkwater town in Kansas, well, this, to Nina, is *truly* astonishing. Not to mention preposterous, utterly contrary to reason and common sense. As if Nina herself doesn't have enough on that platter-sized plate of hers. She's left several voice mails on Desirée's cell and has yet to hear back from her. She will always regard her daughter as a lovely, smart young woman—someone Nina has never been less than proud of—but this habit Desirée has of not answering her phone is both infuriating and worrisome, and so, at this moment, this particular loving mother would like to grab her daughter by the shoulders and shake her. Or at the very least, let her know the weight of the distress she's caused.

A cell phone is calling out now, its ring tone the opening bars of the Who's "Who Are You."

"Oh Christ," a student named Kingsley says, and sets down her chopsticks to shut off the phone. She's Nina's favorite, a willowy girl with a silver tongue stud, who's written, in her most recent essay, openly and eloquently about her part-time job as an exotic dancer. "Exotic dancer," as Nina has come to understand it, is someone who earns big bucks performing lap dances wearing only a G-string. And it is this lap-dancing, G-string-sporting student, Kingsley, who is the sole member of the class familiar with Primo Levi's work—someone who actually paid a visit to Auschwitz during a high school trip to Eastern Europe.

"All of you printed out your copies of Kingsley's essay and have them here in front of you?" Nina asks. "Good, let's begin."

Kingsley's hand is already in the air. "I just want to say that I'm one hundred percent comfortable discussing my job, so please, you guys, don't be afraid to ask me questions."

The student-author of three unsuccessful drafts of her own successful battle with bulimia says earnestly, "I really want to tell you, Kingsley, that you use a lot of great adjectives and those action ones, adverbs, whatever, and I think that's really, really great, but the thing I don't really understand is whether you're actually a hooker or not." Joelle's pale face pinkens as she speaks. "I mean, you said in your essay that your friend from home called you a, um, 'worthless whore,' right, but then I just got confused by how mad that made you."

Scraping her chair back against the linoleum floor, the student with the bread bowl raises her legs and rests her bare, callused, offensively dirty feet upright on the seminar table. "How can you possibly think she's a whore, Joelle? She says right here on page two that the customers aren't allowed to touch even a hair on her head. If they so much as try, they get thrown out on their butts, right?"

The class is silent. "Please take your feet off the table, Victoria," Nina says. *For crying out loud,* she'd like to add. *And lose the word "butt" from your vocabulary, if you don't mind. Why? Because it cheapens what we do here, that's why.* Of course she has to keep this to herself; sounding priggish in front of her students is something that is to be avoided at all costs.

"I'm so, so sorry, Kingsley," Joelle begins, "but, like, you're dancing naked and getting paid a huge amount of money for it, and to me, that kinda sounds like prostitution . . . sorta."

"You need to try and understand the distinction between dancing and sex, okay?" Kingsley says, and there's a schoolmarmish quality to her voice now. "It shouldn't be that hard, Joelle."

"Okay," Joelle says meekly.

Davis, a student who has insisted—no matter what the assignment—on writing about his mother's numerous stints in rehab attempting to kick her coke habit, says, "First thing I wanted to mention is that I especially liked that paragraph on page four where you describe the bruises you sustained on so many parts of your body when you were learning to pole-dance. You really made that scene come alive for us. But the one question I have for you is whether all this money you earn is taxable income. Or is it, like, off the books?"

"Off the books," Kingsley says, sipping daintily from a can of Diet Pepsi Lime.

"So that seven thousand dollars for a single night's work is actually take-home pay?"

"In cash." Kingsley smiles. *And why* not *smile?* Nina thinks.

"Un-fucking-believable!" Davis says, then immediately turns toward Nina. "Sorry, Professor."

But she's no professor, having left her dissertation on Willa Cather to languish years ago. Nina finds it humiliating in the extreme to even contemplate her lazy-ass defection from the academy. And she can't even point to exactly what it was that made her lose interest and focus—motherhood, a series of emotionally and physically debilitating miscarriages, or, perhaps, a lack of requisite passion for the arduous work of research and discovery. Instead, she's handed the courses no one else wants to teach—variations of Freshman Comp in schools throughout the five boroughs of the city. And is grateful for them. She thinks of herself as a failure of sorts, but her students think otherwise and have almost always approved of her, more than a few of them, over the years, having referred to her as "maternal" in the course evaluations they're required to fill out at the end of every semester. And Nina's feeling very maternal right now toward Kingsley, wondering how the girl can possibly undress for strangers, night after night subjecting herself to the admiring leers of middle-aged men whose fantasies she strokes and inspires. According to

Kingsley's essay, her parents know nothing of the manner in which she's working her way through college. Nina would be happy to set them straight, to implore them to take out loans for Kingsley's tuition, but for Nina to contact them would be a dangerous and, in fact, illegal breach of ethics she simply can't afford. Begging Kingsley to explore other options for employment is also out of the question—Kingsley is not, fortunately, her daughter, and her bumping and grinding is none of Nina's business. Yet somehow it feels as if it is, as if Nina has every right to take Kingsley aside and say, *Don't do this, please, don't degrade yourself this way.* She wonders what her students would think if they knew that, on her best night, Kingsley's take-home pay exceeds Nina's salary for teaching all eight weeks of this course.

"Is it really true that it costs fifteen hundred dollars to spend an hour with you in the Champagne Room?" Davis is asking now.

"But remember that I only get half of that money, plus tip, and the rest goes to the club," Kingsley explains.

"Half of fifteen hundred is . . . eight-fifty," Davis calculates. "That's still pretty amazing."

"Or maybe seven-fifty," someone calls out helpfully.

"Whatever, it's still great. So listen, I personally think your piece could benefit from a little more description about what goes on in the Champagne Room. Like that one guy who makes you say what you refer to as 'disgusting things'—if we knew more about what those disgusting things actually were, it would really add something. I mean, 'disgusting things' is just too vague a term. Professor Cohen is always telling us that speficifity of detail is really important."

"Specificity?" Kingsley is smiling again.

"My point is that 'disgusting things' could be anything, but the reader needs to know exactly *which* disgusting things you're talking about."

"Use your imagination," Nina suggests.

"Me?" Davis says. "I'm the reader. Why should the reader have to use their imagination?"

"Why should the reader have to use *his* imagination," Nina corrects him, but why bother, really, since Davis will repeat this mistake again and again throughout the summer, paying little attention to her corrections either verbal or written. Just like almost everyone else in the class. And every other class she's ever taught. She will never understand her students' willful heedlessness, their insistence on their own wrongheaded way of doing things. There are, plainly, a good many things she doesn't understand in this world, the most painful of which is surely Patrick's inexplicable passion for Loverboy. Though it's been six months since his defection to the apartment on Riverside Drive, Nina is still in mourning, and awakens every day in nearly the same state of incredulousness and mortification. You'd think that after half a year, she might have advanced to some sort of begrudging acceptance, but she hasn't. Their lives have been intertwined for twenty-seven years— more than half her life—so how, precisely, is she supposed to extract herself from the intricate tangle of memories that, in *her* mind anyway, still connect her to Patrick? She tries not to be maudlin, tries to resist the easy pull of sentimentality, but how can she cast out from her hoard of memories the image of Patrick lifting an infant Desirée so gingerly from the plastic dish tub in the kitchen sink where they'd first bathed her? Or the afternoon she and Patrick had discovered, for the very first time, Desirée kicking with delight in her crib at the sight of the plastic *Sesame Street* characters dangling from a mobile overhead? Retreating even farther into the past, she recalls one of the many times she and Patrick made love in his dorm room at MIT, Neil Young's "Lotta Love" blasting on the stereo in the room next door as Patrick covered her breasts with kisses just before he slipped himself inside her.

"Professor Cohen?" Davis is saying. "Why *should* the reader have to use his imagination? I don't get it."

"Because," Kingsley says, "the writer doesn't have an obligation to tell the reader everything. Just like in real life, okay? I mean, we don't *need* to know everything, do we? It's too much, too hurtful, to know every last thing about the people we care about. We wouldn't be able to stand it, would we?"

"No, we wouldn't," Nina agrees. *In certain cases, we might even want to entertain the possibility of shooting ourselves.* And thank God, she thinks, for the twenty milligrams of Lexapro she takes every day for what her shrink has diagnosed as generalized anxiety. So here's another thing she finds herself astonished by: that *she* has been reduced to seeing a therapist and swallowing down an SSRI each morning. She, who has very little confidence in the benefits of psychotherapy, has actually allowed herself to confide in Dr. Quinn Pepperkorn, MD, a thirty-something with a shaved head and a vague smile who rarely opens his mouth to say two words during their fortnightly sessions together. For Nina, it is, in a way, like talking to the wall, or talking to her father, but this treatment is covered by her health insurance and it keeps that Lexapro prescription filled, month after month. And, too, every now and then Dr. Pepperkorn does say something that compels Nina to confront her darkest, most miserable thoughts about this man who is still, technically, her husband. As when, on one of her earliest visits, he asked, "In retrospect, when you think about those times Patrick broke it off with you in college, is it possible he might have been pursuing a homosexual relationship or two?" *Well, now that you mention it, it does seem likely, doesn't it?* But how could she have known all those years ago? All she'd known then, and knows now, is that Patrick is the only man she's loved. *Loves.* But oh how she would love to hate him! Because she's forty-five years old and can't afford to waste any more time continuing to harbor those secret—and, let's face it, pathetic—hopes that he'll eventually show up at her door, hers for the asking. In her classroom, she shuts her eyes for a moment. *To lowest pitch of abject fortune thou art fallen.*

Why is the class gaping at her, a dozen pair of eyes curiously turned her way?

"I sorta don't get what you mean by 'abject fortune,'" Davis says.

"That would be John Milton, from his poem 'Samson Agonistes.'"

"Uh, who's John Milton?"

Nina slams the flat of her hand against her heart. The question makes her want to weep. "John *Milton?*" she says, looking out at all those vacant-eyed students who can't possibly be as breathtakingly ignorant as they apparently are. "Someone?" she says. "Anyone?"

Kingsley's hand is up, then down again. *"Paradise Lost,"* she says.

"He was a great seventeenth-century poet," she addresses the class sternly. "Okay?"

A class full of Kingsleys—of well-read, literature-loving strippers who command fifteen hundred dollars an hour for the pleasure of their company in the Champagne Room—would, to Nina, right now, be heaven. Paradise.

CHAPTER 8

IT IS NINETY MILES TO HONEY CREEK from the bus station, about a two-hour trip, Desirée learns, when she exits the cab from the Kansas City airport and buys herself a bus ticket. There is no one else in line. Just before she steps aboard, she indulges in a brief fantasy—that Dr. Daniel has ditched his medical convention so that he can accompany her to Honey Creek instead. And that he will help her get settled and take her out to a leisurely dinner and reassure her that she is about to embark on the sort of adventure that will be just the shot in the arm she so desperately needs.

Now she is handing her ticket to the bus driver, who is busy with a cellophane bag of pork rind (not to be condescending—but eeew!) and a two-liter bottle of Mountain Dew but manages a smile for her nonetheless. The bus is air-conditioned and the seats are well upholstered; what more can she ask for? There are less than a dozen passengers already on board. One of them, seated close by, is feasting on a particularly pungent hot dog with onions; Desirée urgently needs to change her seat. She struggles to read for a while, and then her head jerks forward a couple of times and she dozes off. By the time she awakens, there is only a handful of her fellow passengers left, and the panorama beyond her window is unlike anything she's seen except in movies: miles of cornfields under an enormous and awe-inspiring blue sky ornamented with the kind of dramatic-looking clouds from which you might fully expect to hear the voice of God broadcasting. So for that reason only, she isn't particularly surprised to see an immense billboard proclaiming,

I AM THE WAY
THE TRUTH
THE LIGHT

And if that isn't enough, there's a sign that promises, LAND OF MAKE BELIEVE, EXIT 12.

But where are the farmers who will presumably be harvesting this boundless corn at the end of the summer? There isn't a soul in sight as the bus moves headlong across the highway that so neatly bisects the shiny green fields. It passes a sign stapled to a telephone pole that reminds you, in case you've forgotten, that JESUS IS LORD, and then in the middle of a cornfield, another jumbo-sized billboard that thunders, in red lettering against a black background,

SIN IS A CANCER TO ALL PEOPLE!

There's something a little sinister about the sign, something that causes Desirée's skin to prickle unpleasantly. She can personally do without anger, gluttony, sloth, and the rest, though how bad can a little lust be every now and then? Which reminds her of Nick, some five hundred or so miles away, back home in Wisconsin now, perhaps at this very instant composing a lengthy, passionate e-mail imploring her, one last time, to reconsider. *Please don't be an idiot,* she can hear him begging yet again. Well, if she wants to be an idiot, that's *her* privilege, isn't it?

At a gas station in a moribund town called Greenville, the bus discharges several passengers; Desirée is the last to remain on board. Half an hour later they arrive in Honey Creek, the last stop, where a weather-beaten sign on stilts, about the size of a movie marquee, rises above a plot of brownish, half-dead grass across from the Bambi Motel.

WELCOME TO HONEY CREEK

BANK	FIRE DEPT
BEAUTY SHOPPE	GRAIN ELEVATOR
CAFE	LISA LOU'S BBQ
COMMUNITY HOSPITAL	MORTUARY
CHURCH	POST OFFICE
(7 PROTESTANT, 1 CATHOLIC)	

Doesn't look too promising; it looks, in fact, deeply, unutterably depressing. Can this really be a town without a library, a bookstore, a Starbucks? Where can you shop if there's no Bloomingdale's, Barneys, or Urban Outfitters? And what's up with all those churches and not a single synagogue or mosque?

What the fuck is she doing so far from home in a town that doesn't even have a library? And why isn't there anyone here to meet her?

Desirée collects her canvas duffel and leaves behind the air-conditioning and her comfy seat with the reclining headrest, and steps out into the early evening heat. The bus pulls away, the harsh noise of its departure an oddly melancholy sound, and for a few moments it feels, to Desirée, as if she's been mistakenly dumped here through no fault of her own and with no hope of rescue.

Inexplicably, the place has been swept clean of living, breathing human beings—bank tellers, postal workers, morticians. It's now a bit after six-thirty (Central Standard Time! she reminds herself); can they all be home eating dinner? From where Desirée stands at the side of the road, she can see that she is at the very edge of the business district, one long street lined with stores, a single traffic light suspended in midair far down the road. Flat-bed trucks and three or four cars are parked diagonally along the street, as if they've been left there in a hurry. She may as well go into the motel, she decides, force of habit compelling her to look both ways before she crosses the street, though there isn't a moving vehicle anywhere in view. She is already thinking nostalgically of the Upper East Side, where jaywalking can, if you're not fast enough on your feet, endanger your very life.

The Bambi, a sprawling one-story building with a littered lawn and a drained, in-ground swimming pool, looks as if it has seen far better days, perhaps twenty years ago. A paint job would be a big improvement, and the series of saggy screen doors lined up one after the other need to be replaced. In the office, there is no one to greet her and she can hear a TV turned up too loud. And then she hears what sounds like bona fide laughter from someone made of flesh and blood.

She hits the bell at the desk, but there is no response. Tentatively, she smacks it twice more, alerting whoever is back there laughing it up that she's growing somewhat anxious.

"Sorry!" a voice calls breathlessly, and a skinny girl perhaps Desirée's age, and nearly six feet tall, comes running out, blond hair flying. *"Celebrity Rehab,"* she explains. "They should call it *Celebrity Fuckups,* right? And I know I shouldn't be laughing at them, but sorry, I just can't help it. So you're like the first guest we've had here in days, not counting Steve Finley, whose wife threw him out at midnight a couple of days ago, and told him she never wanted to see him again except at his funeral, where she'd be sure to sit in the front row with a big smile on her face. Which is completely understandable, since it turns out he's got two girl-friends, one in town and one over in Greenville, and the one in Greenville is pregnant with twins, and they're both Steve's! Un-believable, right?"

Too much information, Desirée thinks.

The girl is dressed—weirdly—in denim shortalls and red, high-top sneakers, and is blandly pretty, with a smooth, pink face and dark blue eyes; at her throat is a Florentine gold necklace that spells out SARAH LEE in block letters. A plastic name badge pinned beneath her collarbone says S.L. MAXWELL. "You know what, don't pay any attention to me, I'm premenstrual," she tells Desirée, who wants to scream: *Oversharing!*

Sarah Lee Maxwell lights up a cigarette, expertly blowing out the match with the first stream of exhaled smoke. "Plus, I've got problems with my dad, like I don't have better things to do than spend an hour making his damn dinner every night without a word of thanks from him."

Desirée snaps her MasterCard smartly against the counter. "I'd like a room," she says. "With a view. The nicest one you've got."

"Well, they're all perfectly nice and clean," Sarah Lee assures her. Her silent examination of the credit card seems excessive, and Desirée begins to worry. "So what kind of name is this?" Sarah Lee says finally. "I mean, Christian is Christian, obviously, but what's Co-hen?" she says, splitting the word into two distinct syllables. "And what's Desi-ree?"

"Desi-ray. It's French. And it's *cone*—like ice cream cone?"

"Okay, whatever, Desi-ray. Here we've got the Babbitts and the Johnsons and the Campbells, you know, just ordinary, regular names."

"Where I come from, Cohen's just one of those ordinary names," Desirée says warily.

"Uh-huh, so where's that?" Hearing the response, Sarah Lee says, "Awesome! We've never once had a visitor from New York. Mostly we get people from Kansas City, Topeka, or Omaha, just people coming to visit their relatives and such. So how long you staying?" she asks, handing over Desirée's key and credit card.

"Not sure—a few days, a few weeks . . ." she says. Why does this simple question make her so uneasy?

"Got yourself some friends to see?"

"I think I'm what you'd call a tourist," Desirée confesses.

Sarah Lee finds this hilarious. She laughs uncontrollably, and says, when she recovers, "What a hoot! I can't think of one single solitary thing for you to see here. We got nothing like the Statue of Liberty or the United Nations or ground zero. As a matter of fact, we got nothing. Period. Let me tell you a little secret," she says, lowering her voice. "Honey Creek isn't on anyone's top ten list of great places, believe me. That's why next year I want to try and transfer from White Cloud Community College to some-place in Florida, which is where my mother lives with her boy-friend, Buzz Emerson. They left here five years ago, right in the middle of my freshman year at Consolidated High. Because Buzz got my mom to fall in love with him and then convinces her the only place they can be happy together is Florida. So they go down to Orlando and find themselves jobs at Disney World. My mom works in some gift shop in Fantasyland selling mouse ears and such, and Buzz is the manager of the snack bar near Pirates of the Caribbean. They're forty years old but really they're two big babies, don't you think? I've been down there every Christmas to visit, and my mom throws her arms around me and says, 'Sarah Lee, I love you more than anything in this world and it just about breaks my heart that we can't be together.' And I'm thinking, if you love me so much, how come you ran off with Buzz Emerson when I was in ninth grade and let the judge award custody to Dad? Honestly, my mom and I were so close, we were just like sisters," Sarah Lee says wistfully. "We did our nails together every Saturday afternoon, hands *and* feet, and I even read her parts of my diary, the part where I talk about my ex-boyfriend and me sticking our tongues in each other's mouths. She said that was perfectly natural, so I read her the part where he unhooks my bra, and my mom says, 'That's second base and that's natural, too.' And . . ."

Way way way *too much information!* Sarah Lee needs to turn it down a notch, and if Desirée were just a little braver, she'd tell her so.

". . . And after that, well, never mind, I just wanted to say that the best thing about me, Desirée, is that I'm a real good listener and that's why people end up spilling their guts to me. So feel free anytime you want."

Her own guts, thankfully, are still intact, and Desirée resolves to keep them that way. "Thanks, and maybe I'll see you later, then," she says.

"Let me take you over to your room," Sarah Lee offers. "I got nothing better to do, right?"

Fine.

They walk together along the paved path to number 12, and even though Desirée knows that she and the infamous Steve Finely are the only guests, she finds it a little disheartening that there's not a single car parked at any of the units. Sarah Lee unlocks the room for her, swinging open the droopy screen door and the one behind it. Inside it's sweltering, but there's an air conditioner, and the modest-sized, twelve-by-fifteen room looks clean. There are mushroom-colored drapes over a small window, and centered on the wall above the king-sized bed is a shadowy painting of a black cat lounging across the top of a pool table. On the small desk opposite the air conditioner is a cardboard sign that warns: THERE IS A $10 CHARGE FOR ALL PETS STAYING OVERNIGHT. The neatly made bed is covered in a spread patterned with green, black, and gold blocks of color that reminds Desirée of the Rothko print hanging over her mother's dresser. She can't be homesick already, can she? She only left home a big twelve hours ago and needs to suck it up, she tells herself sternly.

"I just have a couple of questions for you," Sarah Lee is saying as she turns on the air conditioner. "One is, did you ever see anyone get pushed under a subway by a crazy person? And the other is, do you know any of those little kids in New York City what got beat to death by their mothers' boyfriends and then maybe thrown away in one of those big trash bins?"

Little kids what *got beat to death?* Funny how a single misplaced word can make you feel as if you're light-years from home.

"God, no, of course not!" Desirée says, and cools her hands at the air conditioner, then bends down and positions her face directly in the delicious flow of chilly air.

"Well, I hope to get to New York someday. And also San Francisco," Sarah Lee says. "Though I hear there's lots of homos in both those places."

"We call them 'gays' in New York," Desirée informs her, surprised at how wounded she feels on behalf of a few people she happens to be well acquainted with back East. "Which is, in fact, what they're called in San Francisco, too."

"Nuh-uh. 'Gay' means happy and 'homo' means homo," Sarah Lee says mildly. "Not a big deal."

You'd think so, but you'd be wrong.

Grinding her teeth, Desirée keeps silent. She's both too tired and too lazy to argue, and beginning to feel jittery, like someone who might not have a clue what she's doing so far from home without even the hint of a plan for tomorrow.

I AM THE WAY, THE TRUTH, THE LIGHT.

But for her the truth lies elsewhere.

Maybe what she really needs is a dentist; in her lower jaw, all the way in the back on the left side, there's a molar that's suddenly killing her. And she's no longer hungry for dinner.

CHAPTER 9

INSTEAD OF CALLING HER MOTHER as promised, Desirée takes two Aleve for her toothache, throwing her head back theatrically and pounding her chest, a big baby who still can't swallow pills with ease like the adult that she is. She manages to fall asleep for an hour or so, and awakens, gratefully, nearly pain-free. After unpacking two weeks' worth of summer clothing into the tacky, plastic, wood-grained veneer dresser, she studies the street map of Honey Creek left for her in the nightstand, on top of the Gideon Bible (whose history harkens back to the traveling salesmen desperate for help in avoiding all those skuzzy temptations encountered on the road—mainly sex, Desirée figures). She isn't someone you'd want to depend on as navigator on a dark night in an unfamiliar place, but this particular map is a no-brainer. Points of interest, denoted by turquoise stars, include the nursing home and mortuary, along with the police station. The population is 1,623, small enough to be tucked into the vest pocket of New York City.

At last she calls home on her cell, hoping her mother will be out, hoping she will be in; back and forth she goes, unable to decide if postponing this conversation is really in her own best interest.

"Please don't do this to me," Nina says the moment she picks up. "Just come home, pussycat."

Why isn't Desirée surprised that the pain in her tooth has heated up again? But the thought of facing a root canal in Honey Creek suddenly terrifies her, as if she might be forced to put herself into the soiled, inept hands of some unlicensed quack—someone who will take one look at her and reach for a pair of needle-nose pliers straight out of his toolbox. As her mother chides her at length for skipping town, Desirée hunts for the phone book on the shelf under the nightstand, pulling out the scrawniest, saddest-looking Yellow Pages she's ever seen. Inspecting the book, she finds ads for two dentists, Dr. Wayne McVicar, DDS, and Dr. Jeremiah Blank, DMD. Dr. Blank's ad displays a smiling tooth perched, inexplicably, on a skateboard; Dr. McVicar's equally jaunty molar is tricked out in a top hat, bow tie, and walking stick. Desirée hopes to avoid seeing either of these professionals in person, but the tooth in the top hat clearly speaks of a more sophisticated sensibility, and Dr. McVicar will be her man if worse comes to worse. Or worst. In the meantime, she helps herself to another Aleve while her mother continues her litany of complaints.

"So have you caught any?" Nina is saying.

"What?"

"Fish. Isn't that why you're twelve hundred miles from home? Because you had the urge to go fishing?" The sarcasm in her voice is unmistakable.

"Oh . . . well, I'm sorry for having been so . . . cavalier."

"Not sorry enough, I'm guessing."

Switching on the TV set with the remote, Desirée tunes in to the motel's closed-circuit channel, where a camera slowly pans three large, circular weather gauges all in a row. According to the thermometer, hygrometer, and barometer, it's hot as hell, miserably humid, and the barometric pressure is steady. The camera continues to pan in slow motion; in the background, a Muzak version of "Bridge Over Troubled Water" plays lugubriously. Desirée contemplates which is more pitiful, Honey Creek's idea of a weather channel or her mother's insistence that she return home immediately.

She clicks away with the remote: coming up next on a program called *Real TV* is a segment about a nine-month-old baby who can read. This seems intriguing, something that requires Desirée's full attention, and she tells her mother that she has to go.

"Please don't hang up on me, pussycat," Nina says. "Let's see if we can work out a compromise."

The nine-month-old on TV is no genius, according to his proud father. No, sir, he's just an ordinary, everyday, garden-variety baby named Hunter. The father holds up a cue card with the word "clapping" on it, and sure enough, Hunter applauds. The next card says "bellybutton," and the baby points to his own. "Toes"? He wiggles them. "Ears"? Hunter sticks his fingers in them.

"You're not going to believe this, but there's a nine-month-old baby on TV here who seems to be able to read," Desirée says.

No response from the other end, not even the smallest gasp of amazement, or a breathy little "wow."

"Come on," Desirée says, "you're not the least bit astounded by that?"

"What astounds me," her mother says, "is your offhand dismissal of the pleasure I take in having you around. And what astounds me further is your dismissal of my desperate need for the pleasure of your company this of all summers, which, I can tell you right now, will go down as the worst summer of my life."

"I do feel guilty," Desirée admits. What she actually feels is guilt shot through with resentment, an unappealing mix that rises up alarmingly in the back of her throat now.

"That's something, at least," her mother says approvingly. "And by the way, did I mention your boyfriend called?"

Desirée purses her mouth. "I don't *have* a boyfriend—we broke up the night you and I picked him up at LaGuardia, I just didn't get around to telling you."

"So *that's* why he was gone so quickly." Nina pauses. "Are you all right? Is now a bad time for me to let you know how disappointed I am that you couldn't be bothered telling me about Nick until this very moment?"

"I don't want to talk about it, okay?"

"Fine, let's just say that someone *pretending* to be your boyfriend called twice today. He said he left you a couple of messages. As did I, in fact. Don't you check your phone?"

Not in Kansas she doesn't. Because isn't this precisely the point in being here—putting distance, geographical *and* emotional, between herself and everyone she's left behind?

"Here's the message he asked me to give you: 'The course of true love never did run smooth.'"

"Oh, for Christ's sake," Desirée says. "I'm supposed to be impressed because he's got some cliché of a line from *A Midsummer Night's Dream*? He's completely crazy. And a liar, as a matter of fact." Even so, the temptation to feel flattered is hard to resist, as is Nick's patently counterfeit, phony baloney love. Just as Desirée is about to go under, to sink into a warm, comforting bath of bittersweet memories, she comes to her senses. "The next time he calls you," she instructs her mother, "tell him I'm working undercover for an FBI sting and can't be reached."

"Will do," Nina says. "Now where would this plum assignment be taking you?"

"Disney World?"

Her mother laughs. "Call me tomorrow?"

Well, maybe.

CHAPTER 10

THINGS COULD, OF COURSE, always be worse, Nina tells herself as she lies awake waiting for the neon digits on her bedside clock to simultaneously hit seven and a pair of zeroes. She might, for example, have been hitched for over two decades to someone who summarily announced he'd always known his true gender was female and now wanted a sex change. Or might have been married, say, to a man like the New Jersey politician who'd been sleeping with high-priced hookers, evidently for years on end. Those are worse scenarios than her own, aren't they? And then there's the worst scenario of all, which she read all about in the *Times* the other day: in 7.59 billion years, the planet Earth will be "dragged from its orbit by an engorged red sun and spiral to a rapid vaporous death." This miserable fate had been predicted by a pair of noted astronomers, one of whom, employing extraordinary understatement, judged it "a touch depressing." *A touch depressing? Why not the most depressing thing anyone could ever imagine? So let's see, in 7,600 million years, the Earth will be no more.* Despite all those soothing milligrams of Lexapro in her system, Nina begins to weep silently, contemplating this disaster to end all disasters. Deeply embarrassed by these tears shed in private, at 7:01 she rises, yanks her vinyl-and-foam-rubber exercise mat from the closet, and completes four sets of twenty-five sit-ups, counting softly from one to twenty-five, first in English, then French, Spanish, and, finally, German.

Several weeks ago, at her yearly checkup with her internist, the doctor casually admired her muscle tone during his examination, though when Nina complained about her slightly pouchy, middle-aged stomach and the ten or so pounds she would like to lose, the doctor laughed out loud at her. Nina is a relatively trim size 6, but there's a noticeable ring of fat around her abdomen that shames her. Like her internist, Patrick had, not long ago, praised that muscle tone of hers. He had, in fact, always taken pleasure in her body, even when she was pregnant with Desirée and looked as if she'd somehow managed to ingest a regulation-sized volleyball. She insists to herself that Patrick is surely the straightest gay guy imaginable. If he walks like a straight man, and talks like a straight man, how can he find himself sharing a bed—never mind *a life*—with Loverboy? She wants so desperately to understand this unaccountable transformation from husband to "partner," thinking that with understanding might come some measure of relief. But Patrick hadn't been able to offer her much in the way of explanation. He couldn't, he told her, envision a life without Jordan, and beyond that simple, straightforward—and for her, heartwrenching—statement, he didn't know what more it would take for Nina to get it. Well, what it would take is for Patrick to admit that it's all been a fucked-up, mistaken notion on his part, just a big fat stupid blunder. *Oh, and here are a dozen roses and his deeply felt apologies.*

In the shower, shampooing her hair, she thinks of herself and Anna Spargo, the future drug czarina with whom she shared the title "Best Looking Senior Girl," both of them innocently smiling for the yearbook photographer, two seventeen-year-olds who could not have predicted what they would become—in Anna's case, a long-term inmate in a federal prison in Danbury, Connecticut; in Nina's, a wife abandoned in middle age, jettisoned in favor of a slightly younger man who, unlike Nina, had completed his doctorate and wore his hair, according to Desirée, in a silly, inch-long ponytail. Nina considers the pitiful possibility that, in retrospect, high school was her heyday, a time when over four hundred of her fellow students actually deemed her the best-looking girl among them. Funny. In part because she had voted for Anna Spargo, to whom, in Nina's opinion, she herself couldn't hold a candle. And in part because, until six months ago, she would have said that by and large, her life on this earth—the more than sixteen thousand days of it—had been blessed by what almost anyone would consider good fortune: a comfortable life shared with a loving, generous-hearted man and a daughter equally loving and generous-hearted, though recently not as forthright as she might have been. And don't forget the succession of teaching jobs that have allowed her to feel useful, if not exactly a star. But the shit has finally, inevitably, hit the fan. And how ingenuous of her to think it wouldn't.

The phone is ringing as the shower door closes behind her and she steps out and then onto the bathmat; clutching a towel, she runs toward the sound of Patrick's voice. He's calling, he explains, to invite her for brunch. Her sopping hair drips onto her bare toes as she hears Patrick say it's high time she and Jordan finally met.

What for? she wants to say. *What good can possibly come of it?*

"It's time," he repeats, and then there she is giving her assent. And taking down his address, as if she didn't already know it by heart.

CHAPTER 11

MARGARET KEATING—THE SUN-DRIED old woman who owns the Bambi Motel—inserts a bookmark into her plump paperback of *An American Tragedy,* and gives Desirée the once-over from behind the front desk. "So you're our guest from New York? I hear from Sarah Lee that you're in town to see the sights."

"That's me," Desirée says. "How are you?"

"Fair to mediocre, thank you. Lived here my whole life, know everybody in town, good people all of them, except for my good-for-nothing grandson Curtis Junior. Went away to college, came back a Buddhist, of all things. He's got an altar in his living room and chants three times a day, and that's a minimum. That's what Buddhists do, dontcha know, they chant. Chant to win the state lottery, chant to get the prettiest girls to go out with them, chant to keep the police away when they're out in the garage getting high on whatever it is they're smoking."

So this is what you get when you ask the three simple words "how are you?" Surely no one would ever accuse these Honey Creekers of being reticent.

Margaret squints at Desirée. "You're not a Buddhist, are you?"

"Me? No, I'm not," Desirée says, and sidles over to the soda machine for her first Diet Coke of the day. She's come to the front desk to find out where she can get some breakfast and is already eager to be on her way out the door.

"Presbyterian?" Margaret says.

"Excuse me?"

"Lutheran?"

"No."

"Don't tell me you're a Catholic."

"Not really," Desirée says, and takes a small, nervous sip from the sweating can in her hands. "Not a hundred percent," she murmurs.

"I just *knew* you weren't a Catholic. Not that there's anything so terrible about Catholics," Margaret adds.

"Or Jews, for that matter," Desirée hears herself say.

"Don't know any," Margaret says. "Never saw a Jew in my life, though there's some in Kansas City. They've all got secret vaults under their basements filled with loads of jewels and cash."

Desirée nearly chokes on her Diet Coke.

Never saw a Jew in my life.

Is this America in the twenty-first century? And what's with the Jews and their jewel-and-cash-filled secret vaults? Where does Margaret Keating get her intel from? The *American Nazi Party Daily Tribune*?

When Desirée asks, Margaret says, "I didn't *read* it anywhere, it's just something I *know*. Like I know the words to 'The Star-Spangled Banner.' Or how to scramble an egg."

Desirée envisions a pair of zebras behind bars in the Kansas City Zoo, along with white tigers, orangutans, and great apes, endangered species all. And a single family of pale, worried-looking Jews—children, parents, grandparents—pacing incessantly in their cage, driving each other crazy, bringing out the worst in each other in captivity, not an Anne Frank among them. Yellow Stars of David sewn above the pockets of their institutional-gray jumpsuits, and just above the stars, the legend "Property of the Kansas City Zoo." She can see it all with perfect, unwelcome clarity. But why not go for broke? she thinks. Wouldn't it be cowardly, an act of self-loathing, not to?

"Actually, you're looking at one right now," she tells Margaret. "A half-Jewish person, that is."

Margaret Keating's mouth falls open, displaying extensive bridgework and several gold fillings. "Hey you," she calls out as Sarah Lee appears, trailing cigarette smoke in her wake. "You got to hear this!"

"Hey Desirée. Get a good night's sleep?" Sarah Lee is in shortalls again, but this pair is shocking pink, and there are perfectly matching pink flip-flops on her feet.

"Never mind about that," Margaret says. "But listen to this: your new friend here is half a Jew."

"Totally awesome!" Sarah Lee says. "Our first Jew or half Jew ever!" She looks at Desirée fondly. "So you must be real smart, huh?"

Desirée squeezes her Diet Coke so hard, droplets of soda fly in her face, instantly proving Sarah Lee wrong. "What do you mean?"

"Well, let's see, Jerry Seinfeld's one of your people, right, and of course Jesus Christ Himself."

Whisking the soda from her eyes, Desirée says, "And don't forget Einstein, Freud, Bob Dylan, Woody Allen, and . . ." She falters a moment, then recalls Harrison Ford cracking a bull-whip in *Indiana Jones* and all those sequels. "And Harrison Ford," she finishes. "He's half Jewish like me."

"Hold it!" says Sarah Lee. "No way is Harrison Ford a Jew. We got a guy named Jimbo Ford here in town and no way he's anything but a Methodist."

"Thomas Alva Edison, wasn't he a Jew?" Margaret asks.

"I'm afraid not," Desirée says.

"You sure Alva isn't a Hebrew name? Anyways, he was smart enough to be a Jew, what with inventing the light bulb and the record player and the TV and the VCR."

"Not the VCR," says Sarah Lee.

"He died in 1931," Desirée says, working hard to suppress her laughter. "The same year my grandmother was born," she adds.

"Well, fine," Margaret says. "But I'm positive he was a Jew." Giving Desirée another swift, appraising look, she says, "Hmm, and I'm supposing you dye and straighten your hair, am I right?"

Now what? Unfortunately for Desirée, her red hair—inherited from her father—is of the stick-straight, baby-fine variety, the sort you can't do much with except allow it to hang in its customary limp way and generally ignore it. She explains this to Margaret, who insists, "Any kind of Jew at all has dark, kinky hair, not as kinky as black folks, but dark and kinky just the same. So you know what I think," she continues, "I think you aren't a half Jew at all, I think you're a fake, especially when I get a nice long look at that nose of yours."

Instinctively, protectively, Desirée's hand goes straight to her nose, as if Margaret Keating is about to throw a power punch in her direction. "What's wrong with it?" she says. And then is remembering a scene from a Holocaust movie she'd watched not long ago; what she recalls so vividly is a classroom filled with uniformed Hitler Youth, all of them listening, rapt, while their teacher delivers a lesson—complete with illustrations and a wooden pointer—on HOW TO RECOGNIZE A JEW. *His nose is hooked, the back of the head flat, his ears stick out, his eyes are shifty, his walk apelike,* the teacher instructs them, with all the authority and assurance of a man preaching the gospel truth. As she listened, Desirée's skin had turned to gooseflesh, and yet . . . she had to laugh, didn't she, at the sheer idiocy, the outrageous dimwittedness of this ignorant clown masquerading as a classroom teacher. And after she stopped laughing, she had to wipe away the tears that came from everything she knew of that unspeakable time in the history of human civilization.

"There's nothing wrong with your nose," says Margaret, a hint of disappointment in her voice. "It's just a regular old nose."

If ever there's been a time for Desirée to be on her best behavior, a model citizen representing half Jews everywhere, this is it, though in fact she longs to sink down into the gutter with Margaret Keating and get her hands good and dirty.

"Come on now," Margaret urges, "tell us who you really are."

"Look, I'm the real thing," Desirée insists. She tells Margaret and Sarah Lee that she and her Jewish mother routinely fast on Yom Kippur and eat matzoh during Passover. These are lies, but at this moment she wishes they weren't, wishes that there were more to her Jewishness than there actually is. Shamelessly, she continues, "I'm so kosher, I can't even eat the inside of a Mallomar, for God's sake." In truth, she is someone whose life is tinged with Jewishness, but just barely. And she doesn't have a spiritual bone in her body—coax her into either a synagogue or church once every seven years and she's anesthetized in nothing flat. But in her heart, she believes, she is authentically Jewish, someone who can't bring herself to drink a glass of milk with a BLT or laugh at a joke about the Holocaust.

Hey, did you see the kid wearing the shirt that said,

MY GRANDPARENTS WERE IN DACHAU
AND ALL I GOT WAS THIS DUMB T-SHIRT

"You can't eat Mallomars? That is just *so* sad," Sarah Lee is saying.

"Or spare ribs," Desirée continues; she can see that she is on a hot streak here and decides to go with it. "Or Jell-O."

"What in the name of Jesus could possibly be wrong with good old Jell-O?" Margaret asks.

"Well, it's made from the marrow of horses' bones," Desirée explains, "and pigs' bones, and the bones of improperly slaughtered cows. Just like Mallomars are."

"That's disgusting!" Sarah Lee says. "Maybe I should be kosher, too. Maybe we should all be kosher."

Matching her palms together, as if she were about to petition the Lord in earnest, Margaret concedes, "I've been thinking that I was wrong to call you a fake, Desirée. You know too much about things like what's not kosher about Jell-O and Mallomars to be faking it. I'm a stubborn old senior citizen but when I'm wrong, well, I'm not too proud to admit it. So look, I'm pretty sure we're happy to have you here in Honey Creek, and even if we're not, at least you're not a homosexual or a woman lesbian. And so I've decided to offer you an extra-special weekly rate for as long as you're here. Now I don't normally offer a discount, but mainly because you're our first New Yorker ever, it's only right that I do something special for you."

Desirée thanks her, though she can't help wondering how swiftly she'd be booted out the door if she were, like her father and Loverboy, one of those homosexuals or "women lesbians."

There's a small, high yapping sound coming from somewhere behind the desk, which prompts Margaret to say, "Ever hear of a dog with irritable bowel syndrome? Well, my poor Goliath's got it. And I need to go take care of him."

Sarah Lee waits for Margaret to disappear into her living quarters in back, and then she says, "Fuck you, you stupid old lady."

"Ignorant, maybe, but probably not all that stupid," Desirée says. "She was reading *An American Tragedy*, one of the truly greats, when I came in here."

Snickering, Sarah Lee says, "That big fat book she's always got with her? That's not hers, that belongs to Curtis Junior. He left it here and for months Margaret's been trying to get through it. She thinks there's some secret message in there from Curtis Junior, like maybe why he became a Buddhist."

"I doubt that," Desirée says, smiling.

"She's gotten even creepier ever since her son Big Curtis hung himself in number eleven, right next to your room, on New Year's Eve. They say he was probably the one what stole the eight thousand dollars from her, but I don't know. He'd lost his job as manager at the Kum & Go, and then not long after that Margaret realizes her money is missing and then Big Curtis turns up dead. At the funeral Margaret and Big Curtis's ex were crying so loud you could hardly hear yourself think."

"Poor Margaret," Desirée says, and despite her horror of the old lady's ludicrous, anti-Semitic notions, can't help feeling a stab of pity for her.

"Maybe, but that's no cause for her to be saying such dumb shit right to your face." Sarah Lee throws up her arms and crosses them over the top of her head. "Damn! Sometimes I get so totally sick of this place and pretty much everyone in it. But you know what, I'm taking a coffee break now, right, so let's cheer ourselves up and get you some breakfast, okay?"

CHAPTER 12

DESIRÉE AND SARAH LEE are sauntering down Minnehaha Avenue, Honey Creek's main drag, that weary-looking street lined with old, two-story, redbrick buildings that are mostly residential on top and commercial below. There are some cars and pickups parked in the sun and five or six pedestrians, not one of whom can resist stopping to talk to Sarah Lee and the unfamiliar woman at her side.

"So this must be our visitor from New York," the first few begin, and the rest ask slyly, "Who's your new friend, Sarah Lee?" knowing perfectly well what her answer will be. They stare at Desirée, dressed in jeans and an ordinary black T-shirt, as if she were an object of utter fascination, and she starts to wonder if she's sprouted those infamous horns—in her case, would a single horn denote half a Jew? Or are horns only found on males, like antlers on a buck? Or perhaps her nose has grown long as an arm because of the lies she's told today.

"What's going on?" she asks Sarah Lee finally, as they make their escape into a luncheonette called the Sweet Tooth. It's shortly after nine in the morning, and already she's weary of shaking hands and answering questions about stabbings on the subway, rapes in Central Park, and "that poor little Nixzmary Brown girl, you know, what got beat to death by someone in her own family." She and Sarah Lee seat themselves at the counter on stools with cracked maroon leather cushions. No one turns to look at them, though this is only because the place is deserted.

"What's going on *where*?" Sarah Lee says.

"It's just that I feel like some sort of weird, D-list celebrity."

"Well, you are," Sarah Lee says. "A celebrity, that is."

Someone dressed in a waitress uniform emerges from under the varnished wood counter and turns her smile on Desirée like a searchlight. Her hair has been dyed a harsh blue-black, and brown roots are already showing, but she is strikingly, head-turning pretty, and looks as if she belongs in the limelight instead of behind the counter at the Sweet Tooth. "So hey, Sarah Lee," she says.

"Hey yourself. This is Des—"

The waitress interrupts her with laughter. "Like I've been living under a rock, right?" She nods in Desirée's direction. "Riley Maxwell. How's it going, Desirée? Actually, I personally am a little tired, and you know why? I had a dream last night that I cleaned out the whole garage, all those cartons full of old magazines, all the kids' ratty old baby clothes, I mean *everything,* and when I woke up I was just exhausted from all that hard work."

"Riley's my sister-in-law," Sarah Lee explains. "She and Wes fell in love in the sandbox in kindergarten."

"Well, Wes is a great guy . . . mostly."

"Great guy," Sarah Lee echoes mockingly. "You're a real forgiving person, Riley. Not everybody would forgive and pretend to forget the way *you* do."

Handing Desirée a menu, Riley says, "So he got drunk and went a little too far with my next of kin, does that have to be the end of the world?"

The menu is a foot-tall card sealed in plastic; Desirée hides behind it, suspecting that Sarah Lee and her sister-in-law have already engaged in this particular conversation too many times in the past and that she has no business listening in.

"A *little* too far? He knocked up your sister, for Christ's sake! How can you forgive either of them?"

"But it's not as if Allison went ahead and had the baby or anything."

"She had a miscarriage," Sarah Lee points out.

"You just watch the way you talk about my sister!"

Desirée peeks out from behind her menu tentatively. "The waffles and strawberries sound good," she says.

"Well, it's *my* brother knocked her up," Sarah Lee says. "I have every *right* to be pissed at him!"

"So are those strawberries fresh or frozen? On the other hand, the black-and-white shake with homemade ice cream sounds good, too."

"Go for the waffles," Riley suggests tearfully. And to Sarah Lee, "Forgiveness is the Christian thing to do, and that's the way I had to play it."

"But Riley, sometimes the Christian thing to do is the exact opposite of what you *need* to do," Sarah Lee says. "You should have done everything you could to make them both feel like the miserable little shits they are."

"I need to have my kids grow up in a two-parent household," Riley says. She plucks a flimsy napkin from the metal dispenser on the counter and blows her nose. "And will you be having the strawberries on the side or on top of the waffles?"

"My brother doesn't deserve her, no way," Sarah Lee whispers to Desirée. "She's way too good for him."

"If you say so," Riley agrees, washing her hands (Desirée is relieved to see) and then setting to work on the waffles, using batter and a real waffle iron.

The sweet perfume of her breakfast fills the room and Desirée thinks of her mother in her aqua-and-white striped seersucker bathrobe endeavoring, one recent Saturday morning, to get a spoonful of rice pudding between her grandfather's stubbornly clenched teeth. She can hear the clatter of a teaspoon hitting the ceramic-tile floor as her mother simply gives up. *You want to starve to death? Fine, be my guest.* And she sees that utterly blank Parkinsonian stare of her grandfather's concealing everything—humiliation, frustration, disappointment. Who knows what he longs to say out loud in that powerful, rough-edged voice that had once been his and is now just one more lost treasure among the endless losses that will never be recovered.

"Miss Lavender says we've all got extra lives coming to us," Sarah Lee informs Riley.

"Miss Lavender's a wack job. She never did tell me one single thing that ever came true."

"That's because you don't believe in her. You shut yourself up like a closed box and she can't get near you, can't get inside you. What do you expect with that kind of lousy attitude?"

"All right, so who's Miss Lavender?" Desirée asks. The waffles are excellent, with a light crunch to them, though the fresh strawberries are rather pale and tasteless. But for two bucks, it's a bargain breakfast, and she's hungry enough to devour every bit of it. Her first meal in Honey Creek, she notes, feeling oddly sentimental, as if she were already back home on the Upper East Side and longing for Riley's waffles.

"Miss Lavender," Sarah Lee says, pouring coffee for herself, "is someone who was struck by lightning years ago. Ever since then she's been psychic, and for twenty dollars she'll sit you down and tell you what you want to know. Before the lightning struck, though, she used to be called plain old 'Lizzie' and no one thought there was anything special about her. But there's lots of people in town who swear by her—they won't go on a trip to anywhere at all without checking with her first to see if it's safe to leave Honey Creek."

"When you tell it like that, you make it sound like this town has got a whole lot of ridiculous people in it," Riley says.

"Well, doesn't it? But not because they put their faith in Miss Lavender like I do. There's other reasons, but I'm not going to take the time to put it in a lecture and explain it to you right now."

"You're wrong. We're just like the rest of the world," Riley says.

"Wanna bet?" Sarah Lee snaps.

Outside the plate-glass window, a couple of boys fly by on silver unicycles, five feet above the sidewalk. It's such an unexpected sight, Desirée is half convinced she's conjured it, and runs to the window; sure enough, the boys are peddling down the street beyond the Bambi Motel, their arms spread like wings for balance. She returns to the counter just in time to hear Riley saying, "If you don't know, don't ask, okay?"

"Okay," Sarah Lee says, though she stares quizzically at Riley, who looks away.

"Those are terrific waffles," Desirée says. "You could probably charge about twelve dollars for them in New York." Riley has turned her back, her hands shoved into the pockets of her bright white polyester uniform. Her shoulders are trembling. "Or more," Desirée says. Though she's only just met Riley, she's tempted to lay a soothing hand on her wrist. "*Fifteen* dollars, I bet."

Sarah Lee wants to know who would be stupid enough to pay fifteen dollars for a plate of waffles.

"You'd be surprised," Desirée says. "In my neighborhood, probably just about everyone."

The door flaps open and a twenty-something customer cruises in and slides into a booth. He crosses his arms over the table, lowers his head onto them, and calls out, sluggishly, for coffee.

"Good morning to you, too," Riley addresses him. "And if you think I'm going to let you sit there all morning nursing your one cup of coffee, you can forget it, Bobby."

"How about a little sympathy?" the guy named Bobby says.

Desirée is instantly taken with the meticulously plaited rope of blond braid that reaches just beyond his shoulders; she is already wondering how he manages it by himself. Maybe there's a devoted girlfriend who stands behind him every morning and patiently does all the work.

"Band's having problems?" Sarah Lee says.

"Seriously. We had a gig at the Longhorn Café in Greenville, but a little while into the first set, some guys who were really wasted started throwing balled-up napkins and lemon rinds at us, and then the chicken bones went flying, and then a chair, and my drummer Sandy ends up with nine stitches above his eyebrow. And he doesn't have health insurance, so we're all going to have to kick in to pay the bill from the ER."

"Oh, Bobby! What a bunch of assholes. I'm sorry."

"So can I ask what kind of music you play?" Desirée says; uninvited, she installs herself across from him in the worn leather booth. It's unlike her to be so forward; later, when she considers this presumptuousness of hers, she will attribute it to Bobby's golden braid, and also to the dismal image of bar food flying as he and his band played their hearts out. And perhaps the no-boundaries conversation between Riley and Sarah Lee gave her a small push, too.

"What kind of music? Well, our own," Bobby says, lifting his head. "Heavily influenced by R.E.M. and Sonic Youth, I admit, but we've got our own take on things."

"Got it," Desirée says, and introduces herself as a New Yorker, adding, "*Huge* R.E.M. fan, by the way."

"Bobby McVicar."

Sarah Lee urges him to tell Desirée his middle name. "Wait till you hear this," she says.

Sitting up straighter in his seat, Bobby nibbles on the corn muffin Riley has placed in front of him. "First of all," he says, "you need to know that my parents are a couple of formerly tie-dyed old hippies. So they combined the *G* and the *R* from the Grateful Dead, and the *A-I-R* from Jefferson Airplane, and came up with 'Grair.'"

"Outstanding!" Desirée says. "And your braid, too, of course."

"No kidding?" Bobby appears surprised by her approval, and confides that other than his bandmates, Honey Creekers seem to regard him as a freak of sorts. "You know, except for the band, I'd never have come back here this summer after school ended. This isn't exactly the most comfortable place in the world for me—not that it ever was—and I swear I can feel it pretty much every minute of every day."

She understands the sentiment, Desirée says. "Of not feeling at home in the very place that's actually home." She doesn't elaborate, though, doesn't tell Bobby McVicar that, in truth, she has always been cool with New York; it's only her family she can't bear right now. But she already feels warmed by a connection she senses with this uneasy rock 'n' roller from the middle of nowhere—and she will do what she can to stoke it, to amplify whatever it is they may have in common. Which of course probably isn't much, she would guess.

"Oh, and catch this, Desirée," Sarah Lee says. "His mother's name is Starshine."

"Starshine!" Desirée says, relishing the sound of the word. "What about your father?" she asks Bobby.

"Just plain, ordinary Wayne."

"But Dr. McVicar's the best dentist," says Sarah Lee. "He has this nice soothing voice and makes you feel like you're just there to have your hair done or something."

"I think there's a root canal in my future," Desirée confesses, though, luckily, so far today she's felt not even the slightest pang.

"I'd be happy to get you over to my father's office," Bobby

volunteers, and seems a trifle deflated when Desirée says she's fine. "Well, how about taking the deluxe tour of Honey Creek this afternoon instead?" he offers. He looks down shyly at the constellation of oily crumbs on his plate. "Unless, of course, you're all booked up."

Perhaps there's no girlfriend to be relied upon to braid his hair for him after all.

"Let me consult my daily planner," Desirée jokes, pretending to check her BlackBerry. And then, a mere heartbeat later, "Guess what, I'm totally free all day."

STANDING OUTSIDE THE Sweet Tooth later, Desirée is aroused by a small thrill, as if she and Bobby McVicar are about to explore a place of bona fide exoticism, one whose culture and traditions she might barely comprehend even with a guidebook in her hand and the guide himself beside her. At noon the town is sleepy, scarcely stirring, and every sound—a truck shifting gears in the distance, a car door slamming, the tires of a pickup rolling over the cobblestones of Minnehaha Avenue—is discrete and easily identifiable. You can't mistake, as you might in New York, the screams of a laughing teenager for the terrified shrieks of someone being robbed in broad daylight.

She stares at a butterfly resting in the cracks between two cobblestones at her feet, a black-veined orange monarch taking a break before it sweeps aloft again. "Pretty," she murmurs. The monarch rises gently, like a petal in a mild breeze, and flutters away.

"Never seen a butterfly before?"

When she looks up at him, she sees, to her surprise, that Bobby isn't joking.

"*Of course* I have, though never out in the street in the city like that."

"Well, I've never seen a homeless person wrapped in plastic bags sleeping over a subway grate. Not in person, anyway." Bobby tells her that his mother and father have a subscription to the Sunday *New York Times* and that he usually takes a look at it every week, and Desirée finds herself touched by this smallest bit of information that, for her, signals something essential about his character, his very soul, even. Because, let's face it, if you're not going to take the time to read the crème de la crème of newspapers, what kind of person *are* you? Certainly no soul mate of *hers*.

"Your parents are happy here?" she asks.

"It's home," Bobby says, shrugging one shoulder. His father's practice has always done well enough, and his mother is busy with the counseling center she runs. And they occasionally drive to Kansas City for concerts and the theater. They seem content, he says—if they weren't, wouldn't they have fled Honey Creek long ago?

"And you?" Desirée wants to know.

"Don't laugh, but I'm hoping my future as a rock 'n' roller eventually includes playing with a band so good it gets to go on tour," Bobby says. "*World* tour," he adds solemnly.

She has to laugh, but only at his gravity. "Don't you know you're supposed to smile when you say that?"

"Why?" Bobby says. "I'm dead serious. Not even the remotest possibility that I'm going to spend the rest of my life in this dried-out, dying place."

"Oh, I believe you." Desirée's on the verge of confessing her own long-nourished dream—to be a writer, teller of all the startling, quirky, poignant, funny stories she sees and hears and feels all around her—but she's overtaken now by shyness, and says nothing of the notebooks she's filled, since high school, with her raw, unfinished narratives.

The first part of their walking tour includes a peek at Krispy Krunchy Chicken and an out-of-business video store where, unaccountably, the only thing remaining in the window is a soiled-looking poster of a colossus-sized, bare-chested Howard Stern rising above Manhattan's skyline, advertising a movie that was released a decade ago. Next to it is a Christian bookstore with a large plaster statue of a mournful Jesus in the window. And next door, A Touch of Class Charm School, where Venetian blinds are drawn over the windows and the propped-open door is chipped and peeling. Accompanied by live piano music, a woman's voice screeching, " 'Start-ing here, start-ing now, hon-eee, ev-ree-thing's com-ing up ros-es!' " can be heard as they pass the school; Bobby and Desirée exchange smiles. And then she finds herself considering the Japanese, Indian, Thai, and Cambodian restaurants all in that five-block radius of her home on the Upper East Side. Not to mention the multiple pizzerias, bistros, hair salons, and nail salons. The pair of Starbucks separated by only a few blocks, the Banana Republic, and the Gap, all of this available to her whenever she steps from the lobby of her apartment house. But how do these Honey Creekers survive with such meager offerings? It's unfathomable, really. A mystery light-years beyond her comprehension. Because even if, say, Sarah Lee and Riley spent half their lives online, sampling the world on their computer screens, it still wouldn't be enough. She thinks of the friends she grew up with, every one of whom, along with Desirée herself, attended Griffin—a richly endowed, celebrity-studded private school— and would, she knows, be hard-pressed to spend more than an hour touring Honey Creek before they'd be itching to hightail it back to New York.

Bobby's beautifully made braid swings slightly as he and Desirée amble on, strangers who have yet to discover what they might actually offer one another. Desirée only reaches to his shoulders—a trifle hunched under the faded cutoff denim shirt he is wearing— and she feels small beside him, dainty, almost. She is, she realizes, accustomed to her ex, Nick Davenport, who, at five seven or so, isn't much taller than she, with hands and feet that nearly match her own. Falling just a bit behind Bobby McVicar now, she studies his broad back, his narrow hips, the backs of his legs fuzzy with golden hair. His blond braid is glossy in the Kansas sun, and out of nowhere she has the crazy idea of snipping it off, of taking it home as a souvenir she can hang from the reading lamp at her nightstand or keep under her pillow, brushing it tenderly across her face late at night as she grows drowsy against the sheets.

"Wait, stop," Bobby says, as if he's read her mind and can see the scissors glinting menacingly in her hand. They're in front of the chamber of commerce, a storefront operation shaded by a limp-looking green canvas awning. "I might as well pick up my father's shirts while we're here."

"At the chamber of commerce?"

"It'll just take a minute," he promises.

Inside, a mutt large as a German shepherd lies with his head between his paws on a furry, avocado-green bath mat, surrounded by his rubber toys and a rawhide bone glistening with saliva. He regards Desirée and Bobby indifferently, as does his companion, a middle-aged woman wearing a baseball cap seated at her desk perusing *TV Guide*. Behind her is a wire stand displaying pamphlets and maps, and shelves filled with ceramic mugs inscribed with the words HONEY CREEK, KS: THE SWEETEST PLACE ON EARTH. A coat rack running the length of the room is shoved against one wall; it holds several dozen garments wrapped in see-through plastic bags—shirts, pants, and jackets. The quintessential chamber of commerce–cum–dry cleaners!

"Sorry to disturb you, Laurene," Bobby says, "but you've got a few of my dad's shirts there." He bends down and squeaks one of the dog toys, a big rubber spoon with a tiny kitten hitched to its bowl. "Oh, and this is Desirée Christian-Cohen."

"Heard all about this young lady from Margaret Keating," Laurene says, trotting out from behind her desk in baggy gym shorts and slip-on Keds, and heading for the dry cleaning. "And that's six dollars for Dr. McVicar's shirts."

"You might want to fill her in on some of Honey Creek's history," Bobby suggests, winking at Desirée. Hearing this, the dog growls disapprovingly. "Be nice, Simon," Bobby warns him.

"History?" Laurene says as she sorts quickly through the rack. "Let's see, Honey Creek was founded in 1859 by John S. Baird, John L. Schmitt, and John D. Baker. Our first school opened in 1874, and we had our fire department organized by 1876 . . ."

It's as if Laurene were a docent in the world's most uninteresting museum, and for Desirée there is no polite way out, not even the front door.

". . . we're 92 miles northwest of Kansas City, 66 miles north of Topeka, and 119 miles south of Omaha. Agriculture's our main source of income . . . Anything I left out, you can get from our informative brochures over there. And that's six dollars for the four shirts, as I believe I mentioned earlier."

"Thanks very much," Desirée says. The dog is on his feet and advancing toward her now; deliberately, with malice aforethought, he shoves his cool, damp nose between Desirée's legs, nearly knocking her over. Though she has never been a dog lover, someone who recognizes the innate charms of every dog, large or small, that comes her way, she has always forced herself to be civil. "Please don't," she tells Simon, and pushes him away with both hands, losing her balance and falling backward into Bobby McVicar, who catches her, his hands at her hips.

"Simon doesn't care much for strangers," Laurene reports without apology.

Bobby's hands are no longer at Desirée's hips; absently, his arms have circled her waist, and the two of them, the rescuer and the rescued, are standing motionless, almost in a trance, Dr. McVicar's shirts sheathed in plastic in a puddle at their feet.

"Still waiting on that six dollars," Laurene reminds them.

"Sorry," Bobby says, and slowly releases Desirée. They both kneel to the floor for his father's shirts, her fingers grazing his, tip to tip, as they reach for the hangers. Oddly, it seems the most intimate of moments, as if they've just stripped down to their underwear for the very first time, the mere thought of which heats Desirée all over.

"Know anyone in New York City by the name of Kelly-Ann Woodrow?" Laurene asks. "I don't think she's a Jew, but I thought there was a chance you might know her all the same."

Before Desirée can formulate precisely the right comeback, Bobby says, "That's *really* inappropriate, Laurene. REALLY inappropriate."

Mind reader, knight suited up in polished armor, card-carrying member of the ACLU—whoever he is, Desirée stares at Bobby worshipfully now.

"I'm pretty sure I didn't mean to insult anyone," Laurene says. "After all, we're the chamber of commerce. And honestly, I've got nothing against the Jews per se. They're a very hardworking people, which must be how they all got to be so rich and powerful, right?"

A shrieking siren goes off in Desirée's head, but she tries her best to ignore it. "*I'm* not rich and powerful," she points out in a tiny voice. "Not in the least."

"Apparently you're not working hard enough like the rest of your people," Bobby suggests. "Or maybe it's just that Laurene doesn't know what the fuck she's talking about."

"I resent that, and also your disgusting language," Laurene says. "I'm a churchgoing woman, I've raised three wonderful daughters to respect all God's children, Christian, Jew, black folks, Mohammedans, what have you. And while I may not be rich and powerful like *certain* people, when I wake up every morning, at least I can—"

Mohammedans? Black folks? What decade is this woman living in? What century? And those gym shorts of hers have got to go, along with those plain white Keds.

"Welcome to the sweetest place on earth," Bobby McVicar murmurs. Ignoring Laurene, he smooths Desirée's hair back behind one ear before kissing her lightly on the lips, then immediately draws back, as if he might have trespassed.

"No, no, hey, come back here, you," Desirée says, placing her hands flat against his ears and pulling him toward her for another kiss. She suspects that all of Honey Creek will hear about this before the end of the day, but now that she's a celebrity—albeit a low-wattage one—why not just relax and fully embrace her fame?

CHAPTER 13

AFTER CLASS, THERE IS, INVARIABLY, at least one student who will want a heart-to-heart with Nina; today it's a slit-eyed, long-faced girl named Elaina Whitacre who approaches her at the seminar table as the rest of the students file out, some with earbuds already in place, iPods up and running. And today Elaina is wearing, not for the first time, a T-shirt that announces,

I AM A DYKE
AND I AM DYNAMIC!!

"Can we talk about the second draft of my essay?" she wants to know.

"Have a seat," Nina says, and gets up to shut the door so they can have some privacy. When she sits down again, Elaina is prying open a large Styrofoam container of a rather extravagant and fragrant salad topped with crumbled blue cheese and bacon, delicate rings of purple onion, and a generous sprinkling of bean sprouts.

"Eeew! You want my black olives?" she asks Nina.

"Sorry?"

"It's just that I hate them but don't want them to go to waste."

Over the years, Nina reflects, her students have grown increasingly informal in the ways in which they regard and address her: she has to laugh when she sees the e-mails that begin "Hey Nina!" On the one hand, she welcomes their informality, their presumption of chumminess and intimacy; on the other, there's a part of her that would like to preserve just a smidgen of respectful distance between her and these twenty-year-olds who, more often than not, feel so free to divulge in their writing the seamiest, saddest details of their young lives. And why not? Why not ape what they hear and see on the ever-growing multitude of reality shows, not to mention the eponymous example of Oprah herself. And so Nina already knows all about the verbal brutality unleashed by Elaina Whitacre's stepfather, her mother's refusal to shield her from it, her sister's incessant mockery of Elaina's clamorous defense of her sexual identity. And surely Nina aches for this young girl and her uneasy life. She cannot, herself, ever imagine discussing publicly exactly what it is that pains her most about her *own* uneasy life. She hates to admit it, but she's undeniably connected to that parade of betrayed women on *Oprah* and *Dr. Phil*—without a doubt there's already been *at least* one hour devoted to episodes entitled "My Husband Left Me for His Gay Lover." What could Nina contribute, shamefaced, to a panel of abandoned wives? NOYB. *None of your business, people.* On second thought, make that *none of your* damn *business.*

"Black olives? No, thank you," she tells Elaina. Though a little bacon might be nice . . . Just kidding—she would never eat from a student's plate! Or, in this case, take-out container from Marquis de Salade.

"So . . . do you really think I'm going to need a third draft? I mean, I tried really hard to clarify why my stepdad is such a bastard and my sister's such a nasty, narrow-minded bitch."

There's a smudge of chalky-white salad dressing on the tip of her student's nose; in an exercise of self-control, Nina refrains from mentioning it or picking up the small stack of paper napkins next to Elaina on the seminar table and wiping it off.

"Yes, I took note of all your emendations," Nina says, "but there's more to—"

"I'm sorry," Elaina says, her face conveying confusion, "but what are emendations? I mean, is this a word I should totally know? Because I never heard it before."

Never? "It just means, well, 'corrections and alterations,' and it's certainly a word you should know, Elaina."

"Do you have a pen I can borrow? I wanna write this down."

"You came to class without a pen?" Nina says, horrified.

"Dumb, I know. My fiancée and I overslept this morning, and we didn't get up until almost eleven, and then I was in such a rush to get here on time and . . ."

Handing her a pen, Nina says casually, "Oh, you have a fiancée?"

Elaina's frequently sullen face is almost incandescent now. "Yeah, we just got engaged a few weeks ago. I have a picture of her on my cell phone—do you wanna see?"

"Of course," Nina says, and is treated to a digital image of Elaina and her fiancée in mid lip-lock, their features mostly obscured. "Very sweet," she remarks.

"Kirsten's a lawyer. She specializes in employment discrimination, most of it relating to issues of gender and race," Elaina says proudly. "We're getting married as soon as I graduate next year. It's pretty much gonna be one of those weddings that's all friends and no relatives, which is sad, but not *that* sad. I mean, I can totally think of things that are way sadder. Like what's happening in Darfur and children dying of AIDS or people being stoned to death for adultery in the Sudan . . ." Elaina's eyes gleam with tears. "Those are terrible, horrible things. Having your mother and stepdad and sister and grandparents refuse to acknowledge your sexuality, well, that's just ignorant and mean, but not horrible, don't you think?"

"Are you all right?" Nina says foolishly, because isn't it evident from Elaina's quiet sobbing that she's not? "Here," Nina says, offering her student a handful of napkins. And then hears herself confessing, "Actually . . . someone very close to me, someone I've known for more than twenty-five years, recently came out."

"Really?" Though she's unaware of it, Elaina has cleaned the salad dressing from her nose, Nina is relieved to see. "Tell me," her student says.

"Oh, just someone in my family."

"Don't worry, you can tell me," Elaina presses. "I mean, who am I gonna tell? It's not like I have even a single friend in this class."

And then, against her better judgment and all her best instincts, Nina whispers the words "my husband."

"Whoa! No shit! How bad does it suck to be *you*?" Elaina shakes her head, no longer weeping.

Distracted, lifting the plastic fork from the Styrofoam container, Nina rakes it through Elaina Whitacre's salad. "It's been difficult," she acknowledges.

"You guys getting a divorce?"

"Not yet," Nina says, because Patrick still hasn't raised the issue, and neither has she, though of course they're merely post-poning the inevitable.

"Well, it's gotta be tough, huh? But, like, look at me, things have been so shitty between me and my family, but I'm engaged to the best person in the world, and we're gonna have a great life to-gether, and if my family can't deal, well, fuck 'em." Half rising from her seat now, Elaina says, "Would it be okay if I gave you a hug?"

Nina smiles as her student stretches awkwardly across the seminar table to embrace her. "You can't tell anyone," Nina says. "Promise me."

"What? That I hugged you?"

"About my husband."

"I would never," Elaina promises. "But does this mean I'm definitely getting an A for the course?"

Beyond the open, second-story windows of the classroom, a girlish voice shrieks, "*What*, are you crazy? Or just out of your mind?"

"Elaina," Nina begins.

"Just *kidding*!" Elaina says. "I would never."

Nina hopes not, hopes that she herself hasn't, in her weak-ness, opened a door that anyone with half her wits about her would have kept securely shut.

CHAPTER 14

BOBBY IS CERTAIN THAT DESIRÉE will get a kick out of meeting Starshine, whose counseling center is all the way at the end of Minnehaha, he says, gesturing past the only stoplight in town.

"I don't mean to sound like a pessimist, but she's probably not going to be happy with me," Desirée predicts, "and I've got to be prepared for that. I struck out with Margaret Keating, and then with the chamber of commerce, and I'm sure your mother's next."

"Starshine's in a different category altogether," Bobby consoles her. "You'll see."

"If you say so." Her tooth has started to nag at her again, signaling that it's time to pop another Aleve or two, and she decides to wait outside in front of the Kum & Go—Honey Creek's supermarket/drugstore—while Bobby gets her a soda so she can swallow the pills.

"Sure you don't want to come in?" he asks.

"I'm safer out here, don't you think? There's no denying I've been alienating people left and right ever since I blew into town."

"Your luck's changing," Bobby says. "I can feel it."

Maybe. But her toothache is worsening, and it isn't hard for Desirée to picture herself in the hot seat in Dr. McVicar's office, begging for nitrous oxide or whatever else he's got in his arsenal, her credit card in one hand, the other clenched so tight it aches almost as much as the tooth itself.

After Bobby opens a small bottle of Diet Coke for her, she gulps down the pills in her showy way, head thrown back so far, she's staring straight up at the sun.

"Starshine used to pulverize my medicine in a spoon and then mush it into some Marshmallow Fluff. And that was until I was sixteen," Bobby jokes.

"Sounds like an exceptionally loving mother."

He nods. "And yours?"

Desirée considers this a moment. "Absolutely," she says. "But she's in a different mode these days, the stressed-out/dutiful-daughter mode. And it sucks for me to talk about it, actually."

"No worries."

No worries? Easy for him to say. But she's determined to turn her thoughts elsewhere, as far from her family as she can manage, as far as possible from everything that's caused her such distress in New York.

Silently she and Bobby McVicar swan past an old-fashioned barbershop where a pair of white-haired, white-jacketed barbers have canted their heads upward for a look at the TV set positioned on a shelf high in a corner of the store. Desirée stops short, then backs up to see what's captured their attention—a Tom and Jerry cartoon, she discovers. It's disturbing to see those two old men so raptly watching a cartoon cat and mouse annoying each other on a perilous construction site, and she wonders briefly what might happen if she were to go inside and gently recommend that they change the channel to something a little more intellectually stimulating. *And here she is pushing her grandfather in his wheelchair down this strangely slumberous street so far from home, the two of them a curious sight as she rolls him by the charm school, the Christian bookstore, the chamber-of-commerce-cum-dry-cleaners. And look at the sign someone's attached to the back of the wheelchair:* HONEY CREEK'S OLDEST LIVING JEW.

Five gleaming, unmarked gravestones are positioned in front of Sullivan's Funeral Home, as if to attract impulse shoppers who just might, as they're ambling along Minnehaha, stop and pick up a few on their way to the Kum & Go. Beside Sullivan's is an empty storefront with a hand-lettered sign displayed in the window that shows an ineptly drawn bumblebee and the words BEE WIZE—IMMUNIZE!

Starshine's counseling center is directly above the abandoned store, and Desirée and Bobby climb, in dim light, the single flight of creaky wooden stairs. On the second floor, the reception area is brightly lit and furnished with a rust-colored corduroy couch, along with a large metal desk that holds a computer, a mouse pad patterned with pink and gray kittens, and a heart-shaped covered glass dish of pastel-colored M&M's. There are glossy posters taped everywhere along the walls, offering hope and hotline numbers to the afflicted—substance abusers; cancer victims; HIV-positive single mothers in need of food stamps; battered wives in need of a safe house; runaway teens in need of shelter and a nutritious meal. If your life is bad news, the good news is that Starshine and her extended network of helpers know exactly what to do with you.

Just as Desirée and Bobby arrive, women begin streaming out of the inner office, some wearing turbans or scarves wrapped taut across their heads, some with little bits of fuzz sprouting poignantly across their scalps, a few with a decent head of hair. They are about ten people in all, and not one of them is what Desirée would consider old. She knows what she's just walked in on and she feels a jolt of compassion and pity for all of them, especially a beautiful pale bald woman who might be Desirée's own age and who is missing her eyebrows and lashes and has three gold teardrop earrings in each ear. It is surprisingly easy for Desirée to conjure up clumps of the woman's hair swirling around the tiled floor of her shower before collecting in the drain, easy to imagine the woman using the heel of her hand to wipe at the steamed-up bathroom mirror for a look at herself, easy to hear her howl of anguish. The beautiful bald woman is approaching the desk now, going for a handful of M&M's, several of which she drops casually into her lipsticked mouth. The woman catches her staring; mortified, Desirée looks away and directly into the eyes of someone with a paisley scarf arranged tightly over her skull and a pair of arched, midnight-blue eyebrows that have been drawn in pencil. She looks no older than Nina, and she is smiling at Desirée and Bobby.

"You're that kid from New York?" she says, stepping toward them. "I'm Louise Ryan, Sarah Lee's father's girlfriend? One look at you and I thought, that's the nice red hair Sarah Lee told me about. When mine grows back, I'm going to dye it your color, even though Sarah Lee's bound to hate it, because to her way of thinking, whatever I do is one hundred percent wrong. But Ron, her dad, is a prince among men. I twist a scarf around my head, put on a little makeup, and Ron looks at me and says, 'You're a good-looking woman, Louise, hair or no hair.'"

"Nice to meet you," Desirée says. She's already backing away from Louise, who, like Sarah Lee, seems to have a natural disposition for oversharing, that urge to reveal too much too soon—and which makes Desirée herself a little queasy.

"Hey Mom," Bobby says as Starshine comes sneaking up behind Louise. Starshine is a tiny woman with delicate features; she's dressed in high-waisted mom jeans (the likes of which, thankfully, Nina and almost every other Manhattan mom are way too savvy to ever wear, Desirée knows) and a T-shirt tucked in and emblazoned with the words THE BREASTCANCERSITE .COM. Her blond hair is threaded with gray and pulled back in a big velvet scrunchie. Her feet are in flat-heeled, brown leather sandals; there are silver rings on a couple of her toes. Perhaps it's the sandals and toe rings, but she still has that look of someone who's been to Woodstock and loved every minute of it. And yet her face resembles, more than anything, the cute, snub-nosed dolls Desirée had played with so indifferently as a child.

"And if you really want to know the God's honest truth," Louise Ryan continues, "sometimes I feel like slapping Sarah Lee across the face would be *just* the thing to raise my spirits a notch or two."

Desirée and Starshine flinch.

"Let's try meditating for fifteen minutes or so every morning like we talked about and see if you can't get rid of some of that hostility, okay?" Starshine suggests.

"I'll see, but I'm not making any promises," Louise says, and heads for the door.

Officially introducing Desirée to his mother, Bobby smiles self-consciously.

"So you're an actual New Yorker? My best friend and I were lucky enough to visit for a week in 1969, and you know, Washington Square was the hippest place on earth in those days," Starshine says, her voice betraying something ardent and hungry and wistful. "There was music everywhere and the smell of incense and pot, and people were out in the streets just grooving to it all. Or at least that's how I remember it. I was seventeen and thought I'd died and gone to heaven."

"No offense, dude, but it doesn't seem even remotely possible that you could ever have been seventeen," Bobby teases.

"Well, believe it. And Desirée, it probably sounds pathetically unworldly to you, but even the traffic in the streets amazed me; it was an endless river of cars and trucks and buses and people hurrying to wherever they needed to be. And I was standing still on Eighth Street while the city rushed by me and I thought to myself, *Everything I could possibly want is right here.* Music and bookstores and hippies selling dangly earrings in the street and . . . Listen, would you mind if I asked you about 9/11?" Starshine says abruptly. "It's just that I've never had the opportunity to ask a New Yorker before. Were you there when it happened?"

She doesn't mind. Or thinks she doesn't.

She was fourteen years old, a ninth-grader, Desirée tells them, and she'd been home sick on 9/11 with a fever, swollen glands, and what turned out to be strep throat (though that wasn't discovered until Saturday, September 15, when she finally went to the doctor, who took one look at the tiny, telltale red spots at the back of her throat and announced his diagnosis). She and her mother had seen it all on TV as it was actually happening, seen the Twin Towers collapsing, like fairy-tale giants falling swiftly to their knees, she and Nina clinging to one another in the middle of the living room as if there were no tomorrow. And who, in fact, knew if there would be? They were five miles from ground zero, and in the hours and days to come, all the rooms of their apartment would reek of burning plastic and God knows what else if they opened the windows just a crack. The lampposts in their neighborhood were plastered with photographs of the missing—so many of them looking not much older than Desirée is now—smiling out at her from some picture snapped at a frat party or a family gathering, smiling as if they just knew, with all certainty, that they had their whole lives ahead of them. It was unequivocally heartbreaking, but why belabor the fucking obvious, and so she falls silent now, listening to Bobby saying, simply, *Wow*, Starshine merely shaking her head woefully. And Desirée herself surprised to discover that the strain of talking of these things six years later has caused her to sweat right through her T-shirt.

"Excuse me a moment," Starshine says, her voice a little thickened, and she makes her way to the door, where she immediately gets caught up in several conversations at once. By the time she returns and the room has emptied, she throws herself down on the corduroy couch, confessing, "Man, those guys wear me out. And of all my support groups, this is the one that just kills me week after week. It's funny to think I ever had faith in a higher power up there. Because if anyone's watching over those poor people, or, say, the ones in my Alzheimer's caregivers group, He or She's obviously doing a lousy job. And who knows, maybe I am, too."

"Might be time to change careers," Bobby proposes. He's perched on one arm of the couch now, while Desirée sits leaning against his mother's desk. "You could go back to law school," he says, explaining to Desirée that Starshine was forced to drop out years ago when her own mother had been in a catastrophic car crash and Starshine was needed to help care for her.

As Starshine crosses her ankles, the little bells attached to her toe rings jangle. "I'm too old for law school," she says. "My memory's shot. The other day I tried to think of the word 'foreplay' and it didn't come to me until hours later. And then just today I was thinking about *A Clockwork Orange* and couldn't remember who directed the movie."

"Stanley Kubrick?" Desirée volunteers.

"You clearly didn't have to think about that for more than an instant," Starshine says. "That's because you're young and carefree. Just wait till those first gray hairs start showing up and it suddenly hits you that you're not, in fact, immortal."

"I'm *not?*" Desirée laughs. She would like to point out that contrary to what Starshine believes, she's hardly carefree, but the lingering image of the bald woman's elegantly beautiful face keeps her silent; after all, by *her* lights, what could Desirée possibly have to complain about?

"Wait a minute, *I'm* not immortal, either?" Bobby says.

"I know it's a difficult concept to grasp, amigos, but one of these days the truth is going to bite you on the behind with its sharp little teeth," his mother says.

"Ouch."

"Is that the same truth that's supposed to set us free?" Desirée asks.

"I *like* this girl," Starshine says. "Where'd you find her?"

"At the Sweet Tooth, chillin' with Sarah Lee and Riley."

Starshine wiggles her toes breezily, setting off her bells again. "So you're the one Louise Ryan heard about from Sarah Lee. The one Margaret Keating said was a fraud."

At Starshine's desk, Desirée helps herself to something from the candy dish. "I am, however, the real thing," she says. "The genuine article, as it were. Well, half the genuine article."

"Well, *I'm* pleased to report that some of my favorite writers are Jewish—Philip Roth, of course, and Joseph Heller, and you know, the guy who wrote *Herzog* and *Henderson the Rain King,*" Starshine says. "The handsome silver-haired guy who won the Nobel Prize . . ."

"Bellow," Desirée says, massaging her jaw; clearly those M&M's weren't the smartest idea. And either the medicine still hasn't kicked in yet or things are worse than she thought. She can see Dr. McVicar's perky molar in its top hat and bow tie and Dr. McVicar himself, greeting her in an outfit matching the molar's, black patent-leather tap shoes on his feet, the Fred Astaire of dentists performing one quick number before injecting her with Novocain.

"I've got to see a dentist," she announces. "It might even be an emergency."

"Then this is your lucky day," says Starshine. "Because the only thing I have to do to hook you up with the best dentist in the county is press my speed dial." In a moment, she is at the phone. "And what, may I ask, is the nature of your complaint?" she calls out to Desirée.

"Pain," Desirée says, though she has the urge to apologize for her use of the word. Because she knows that what she's feeling is nothing—truly *less* than nothing—when measured against what Starshine's support group has already endured.

All at once it's as if someone has set her tooth on fire, and she can nearly believe that if she were to take a look inside her mouth, she would see saffron-tipped flames rising. So this is it, she knows, her punishment for deserting her mother, for brashly taking off for parts unknown while Nina struggles with a wordless old man who can't offer her anything even remotely resembling affection, companionship, or gratitude.

"Pain," she hears Starshine saying into the phone. "Pure and simple."

CHAPTER 15

FORTUNATELY FOR DESIRÉE, Dr. McVicar is able to see her immediately, and so now Bobby is hustling her down the stairs and into Starshine's SUV, which she's generously offered for transportation. In the passenger seat, Desirée leans against the armrest and keeps her jaw cupped in her palm. "Do you mind if I close my eyes?" she asks Bobby.

They are moving along swiftly now and she's missing out on the scenery, but she feels a bit better with her eyes shielded from the light. "You're speeding!" she says as they round a corner and she is almost launched into Bobby's lap.

"This is a dental emergency, right?"

"But if we get killed on the way over, my family won't know how to find me. And they'll be furious with me for all eternity."

"I'm going to get you there in one piece," Bobby promises. "Just relax."

"You know, your mother's some kind of savior. She even had a hotline just for me," Desirée murmurs. Eyes shut against the pain, she daydreams of Starshine sporting a pair of angel wings, pure white, satiny feathers outlined in glittery silver, Starshine swooping above Honey Creek, on the lookout for the sick and the lame and the despairing, filling her office with support groups of every stripe. Desirée's mother, enfolded in those wings against her will, is kicking and screaming, insisting she has nothing in common with a roomful of strangers on Minnehaha Avenue. But even in her reverie, Desirée knows her mother is just being snobbish.

They are no longer in motion; Bobby has cut the engine, saying, "You can open your eyes now."

"Did I miss any of those amber waves of grain?"

"Not on this trip."

She sees that they are parked in front of a two-story white clapboard house surrounded by maple trees, set against a lawn spotted with bald patches. Directly above the front door, on the second floor, is an odd little porch with a circular cutout; within the cutout sits an adult-sized mannequin wearing nothing but Old Glory.

"Welcome to Kickapoo Lane," Bobby says. "And now I'm going to escort you straight into the arms of your *real* savior." He comes around to open the door for Desirée, and as he helps her out of the SUV, she realizes that, miraculously, her pain has subsided to a familiar, blunt-edged ache.

"I'm better," she says. "Turns out it wasn't an emergency after all."

"Well, good," says Bobby. "And no need to sound so apologetic— teeth are like that." He leads her to the side of the house, to a white brick extension. Inside, he waves to the receptionist, a blue-haired woman sealed behind glass.

"Hey Nila," he says.

"Hay is for horses," the woman says crossly, sliding open the glass. She looks none too friendly, and Desirée decides to let Bobby do the talking as she drops into a fake-suede director's chair and tries to keep a low profile. There is one other patient in the room, an old man wearing bleached-looking overalls and rooting through a pile of magazines.

"No *Reader's Digest*?" he complains. "What kind of joint *is* this?"

"You stop your bellyaching now, Lester," the receptionist calls out to the patient. "If you don't like our magazine selection, you can go clear across town to that other dentist, the one who used to be married to that daughter of yours. I'm sure he'd be just as happy to see you as you'd be to see him."

Lester ignores her. "These are all magazines for ladies. Why should I care about thirty-six sexy little love-life thrills, or men confessing why they stay, why they stray? And what's handbag mania, tell me that."

"Let's get you checked in, Desirée," Bobby says, slipping behind the glass partition, where he whispers something to Nila before returning to Desirée's side.

"Desirée Christian-Co-hen!" the receptionist barks. "Doctor will see you now."

"Hey! We all know whose turn it is and it's definitely not hers," Lester says.

"Settle down, mister. This person here is in pain, which is why she's going ahead of you. So don't be a big old spoiled baby," Nila chides him.

"Well, I'm in pain, too. And who's to say my pain isn't worse than hers?"

"You're only here for a checkup and a cleaning, Lester. So let's ask ourselves what Jesus would do. I think he'd let this stranger among us go first, don't *you*?"

Lester runs a hand over his grizzly jaw a few times. "Thing is, been doing pretty much what Jesus would do all my life and where did it get me? My wife's dead, my daughter's carrying on with a married man, and my grandson takes a joyride in the cornfields in a stolen car and ends up spending the night in jail."

"I hear he only got probation. That's a lucky thing," Bobby points out.

"Still, it's a blot on the family name. But even so, you can go on in, miss," Lester tells Desirée. "I'll just sit here and read about handbag mania for a while."

Tentatively, Desirée rises from her seat, prepared to sit down again if Lester changes his mind. "Are you sure?"

"Git!" Lester says, a word she's certain she's never heard uttered before except in movies.

She gits goin', but on her way into the examination room, she stumbles in the narrow hallway and crashes, headfirst, into Dr. McVicar.

"Whoa there," he says, as if she were a rambunctious mare in need of a little more training before venturing out any farther into the world.

"Did I hurt you?" she says. "I'm so sorry."

"Ms. Christian-Cohen, I presume?"

Even with his mustache and graying hair, Desirée can see how strongly Dr. McVicar resembles his son, each of them with that lean face and long, elegant nose. Staring rudely, she dresses him in bell bottoms and a tie-dyed T-shirt, darkens his hair, and arranges a meticulously rolled joint between his thumb and index finger.

"So my wife tells me you're in a lot of pain," Dr. McVicar is saying. "Yes? No? Maybe?"

"Well, I was," Desirée says as he steers her through a doorway and into the hot seat.

"Welcome aboard and let's take a look." He puts on latex gloves and a mint-green paper mask and lowers a mercilessly bright light into her face. The canned music seeping from a hidden speaker is early Beatles; poking around in Desirée's mouth, Dr. McVicar sings, " 'If I gave my heart to yewww . . .' "

"Ahhh!" The pain, momentary, already fading, curls her toes.

"Hmm. Can't tell much without X-rays, Ms. Christian-Cohen. But I do see that there's a temporary crown in there. Do I have your permission to take a couple of pictures?"

"Call me Desirée. Sure, but promise me I won't die of radiation poisoning forty years from now."

"Done. And done." Lowering a lead apron across her chest, he orders, "Now hold this film in place with your right thumb while I skedaddle." He returns, snaps another picture, collects the film, and leaves her with a copy of the *Honey Creek Herald* to peruse while the X-rays develop. The newspaper is about the size and thickness of her college paper, the *Yale Daily News*, and Desirée observes that, pathetically, it's actually less professional looking. The front page reports that Honey Creekers Jody Robinson and Forrest Orton, both age nineteen, had been taken into the sheriff's custody on charges of possession of marijuana and drug paraphernalia. Page 2 notes that there were seven admissions and six dismissals this week from the Community Hospital, and lists all thirteen names. On page 3, Desirée learns that Mr. and Mrs. Douglas Knapp celebrated their forty-seventh wedding anniversary on June 15.

And congratulations to seniors Christina Day, Denise Perkins, Jonothon Allbright, and Matthew "Chewy" Conley on making the High Honor Roll at Honey Creek Consolidated High. All of these students distinguished themselves with 4 grades of 90% or above, and one grade as low as 85%, in the final marking period.

Page 6 carries the vacation column, reported by Mrs. Ona Armstrong:

The vacationing Shipleys returned home late Saturday night after visiting with Pearl-Ellen's brother, Jim Gilchrist, and sister-in-law Annie, in St. Louis. They saw 3 movies, including 2 with the handsome and charming George Clooney (Pearl-Ellen's favorite!), and dined in a French restaurant where the food was prepared at their table for them by a chef from Alaska, of all places!

If this is what passes for news in Honey Creek, Desirée won't be greatly surprised if her arrival in town ends up documented somewhere in the *Herald,* accompanied by her photograph—and maybe even her dental X-ray—one column over from a glowing couple celebrating their nineteenth wedding anniversary. Though perhaps, she considers, she's got it all wrong and is merely—and mortifyingly—puffed up with foolish self-importance.

"Greetings!" Dr. McVicar says when he reappears.

"If the words 'root canal' are on the tip of your tongue I'm going to need some of your very best Xanax," Desirée informs him.

"No, no, the X-rays show nothing's out of order."

"Nothing?"

"The thing is, I'm going to have to yank that temporary crown and see what's bothering you."

"Yank?"

"Gently pull?"

"Got a little Novocain for a big coward?" Desirée says.

"Nah, let's see if we can do without it." Dr. McVicar just can't resist accompanying the Muzak, this time humming along with "All My Loving." "You know, the night John Lennon was mortally wounded I cried like a baby," he confesses as he goes after her molar. "The man was like a god to me." He grunts, pulling hard, then harder. "Pay dirt! You okay?"

"Oom."

"Well, guess what, the nerve seems more than a little inflamed. Let's put some nice sodium hypochlorite in there, cement this sucker back in place, and hope for the best." He works away, all the while lamenting the loss of John Lennon; from time to time his voice actually falters. "I'm a very emotional guy," he admits. "At least when it comes to certain subjects, including, of course, the Beatles."

"Ooomm."

"You can talk now," says Dr. McVicar. "We're through here. You feeling all right?"

"Think so," she says, and thanks him.

Disposing of his gloves and mask, he offers her the standard gifts—a spool of mint-flavored dental floss, and an emerald-green toothbrush flecked with gold and embossed with Mr. Molar in his top hat. "Whatcha doing such a long way from home, Miss Desirée, if I may ask?"

"Long story," she says vaguely, and twists a minty piece of floss around her finger.

" 'New York, New York—a hell-u-va town,' " Dr. McVicar sings.

Desirée smiles, wondering what else is in his repertoire. "You don't tap-dance, do you?"

"Only at weddings and bar mitzvahs."

"What?" she says, startled. "I'm sorry, can you repeat that?"

"Well, *one* bar mitzvah, anyway. Astonished though you may be—I see that dropped jaw of yours—the truth is—and it's a secret I haven't shared with anyone here, not even my wife—I'm actually one-eighth Jewish," he confides. "That one eighth is Great-grandma Elsie, a little round dumpling from Lvov, Poland, who was, by the way, fluent in Polish, Russian, German, and Yiddish, though her English wasn't so hot. So anyhoo, this particular bar mitzvah took place in 1966, in Kansas City, where it was thrown by cousins of Elsie's, people I'd never laid eyes on before or since. Her entire family had written her off for dead for marrying out of her faith, as it were, and for allowing her daughter—my grandmother—to be baptized, but ostensibly some among them decided to let bygones be bygones, and hence the invitation arriving in our mailbox. So . . . we drive all the way to Kansas City in our Sunday best and sit in the back row of this Jewish temple. We listen to the bar mitzvah boy, Ira, this ninth cousin of mine twice removed, singing from his Torah, and out of the blue, Great-grandma Elsie starts to cry. Floods the place with her tears. She's making such a commotion, the bar mitzvah boy loses his place, freaks out, and they have to stop the service."

"No way!" Desirée has wound the length of dental floss so tightly around her finger, she's cut off the circulation.

"It gets worse," Dr. McVicar promises. "So they have to bring up Ira's mother and father to the altar, to calm him down, and then the rabbi says, 'Will someone *please* get that woman out of here?' And poor Elsie is led away to the ladies' room by my mother and grandmother. And of course they're afraid to come out after it's all over, so my father sends in my little sister who's all of eight years old and she brings us the news that we have to go back home to Honey Creek because there's no way Elsie can face these people."

"Perfectly understandable."

"Not to my father, not after he's driven the whole damn way to Kansas City. So while the women are hiding out in the ladies' room, he and my sister and I go to the party they're having down-stairs, where we eat a lot of fancy food, and dance a few dances, the cha-cha being among them, if memory serves."

"Poor Elsie," Desirée laments. "And that poor, humiliated bar mitzvah boy. What a nightmare! Oh, and BTW, that's a *bima*, not an altar."

"Well, the last I saw of Cousin Ira, on that spring day in 1966, his pockets were bulging with envelopes stuffed with checks and cash, and he was dancing the limbo. Which, you'll no doubt be surprised to learn, is actually a sacred funeral rite in the West Indies, signifying, as it does, the soul of the deceased passing from this world into the afterlife. As for my great-grandmother, she was never the same after that."

"She died a broken woman?"

"Hardly. She moved back to Kansas City, where my great-grandfather had met her. Her Jewish family took her back into the fold just like that, as if she hadn't been gone for almost sixty years, hadn't blended in with us Presbyterians and baptized her daughter and all that jazz."

Desirée feels drained, as if she'd just escaped the reception at Cousin Ira's bar mitzvah with the McVicars, heard Elsie's wailing and fled to the ladies' room with her, where she'd done her best to comfort the old lady but failed completely. As drained as if she'd watched Elsie living uneasily among all those Presbyterians, all the while feeling that irresistible pull toward Kansas City and the family that would eventually forgive her. So this ancestor of Dr. McVicar's—of Bobby's—had married a Presbyterian. So she'd taken her daughter to church and looked on as she was baptized. So she'd returned decades later and fucked up a thirteen-year-old during his big moment. Well, despite all of that, she was still family. Desirée *gets* it, even if Dr. McVicar doesn't.

"Elsie went home," she says. "Back to where she belonged, that's all."

"She used to kiss me on the top of the head, never on the cheek, whenever she saw me. She'd put her hands up there and give me the sweetest, warmest smooch," Dr. McVicar says wistfully. "But that's all ancient history. So listen, if you're staying in town a while, will you come for dinner some night? It would be nice to have an out-of-town guest for a change."

Desirée pulls out her wallet and MasterCard. "No idea how long I'm staying, but first I want to make sure I take care of the bill, okay?"

"Oh, just forget it," Dr. McVicar says. "Next time I'll charge you double, if that'll make you feel better."

Smiling, lifting herself out of the hot seat, Desirée says, "Infinitely better." She stands in the doorway of the examination room now, pain-free and profoundly grateful. The alliance she feels with Dr. McVicar and the twelve and a half percent of him that is genetically Jewish seems a touch pathetic, like clutching at straws, but there it is. And if there's a single dentist in all of New York City who would treat her for free, well, she's never met him. (Clearly Dr. McVicar plays by kinder, gentler rules; who wouldn't be seduced by his generosity?)

"I'm so impressed with you," she tells him. "And that's not even taking into account the very small part of you that's unacceptable to the Aryan Nation."

"Miss Lavender, Honey Creek's reigning psychic, once told me that there was a guardian angel hovering over my shoulder—someone who sounded suspiciously like my great-grandmother

Elsie—and don't laugh," Dr. McVicar says, "but I happen to believe that guardian angel of mine is in this very room right now, smiling down on both of us."

"Okaaay . . ." Embarrassed for him, Desirée busies herself stowing away her newly acquired dental floss and toothbrush; she just can't bring herself to look Dr. McVicar in the eye.

"You think it's a crock, don't you?"

"What I think," she says, "is that I can't go wrong keeping my big mouth shut on this particular subject."

"I'm a man of science," Dr. McVicar reminds her. "You should trust me when I tell you what's what. Now go on, git goin', see you sometime soon at dinner."

Under orders, for the second time today, Desirée gits goin'.

CHAPTER 16

NINA IS SAVORING the moment—and who can blame her?—when both her father and Porsha are down for the night, and she can, at last, settle onto her bed, behind closed doors, with the TV remote in one hand and a sixty-calorie Weight Watchers sherbet-and-ice-cream pop in the other. There's a folder full of student essays awaiting her attention and her extra-fine-point red pen, but hasn't she earned some downtime? After class today, she'd raced back uptown to accompany her father and Porsha to his ophthalmologist appointment at the New York Eye and Ear Infirmary—all the way downtown again, not far from her classroom. If Porsha could have managed on her own, Nina would have simply met them at the doctor's office, but maneuvering her father in and out of a cab, even with the willing or unwilling help of the driver, is no easy feat. Later, listening to the ophthalmologist report that Marvin's cataracts had ripened and were therefore ready for surgery, Nina was close to tears. Why subject the crumbling old man to the *Sturm und Drang* of eye surgery when he hadn't read a book or even the front page of a newspaper in nearly two years and not because of the cataracts. He'd been withdrawing, steadily and sorrowfully, from life, ever since the Parkinson's diagnosis, and as much as Nina would like to be convinced otherwise, she knows full well that whether or not he has the surgery, he will never read another word again. The ophthalmologist, a dark-haired hunk in an immaculate white coat, sat behind his desk rudely twisting a Rubik's Cube as Nina talked to him. *Yes, of course he understood her point.* Even so, as he spoke, Nina could see a flicker of distaste for her in his slightly narrowed eyes; *you selfish, lazy, ungrateful daughter—what gives you the right to deny your father perfect vision?* There in the doctor's inner sanctum, Nina turned her head to the empty seat next to her, looking for Patrick and his wise counsel. He happens to possess a gift for dealing smartly with doctors, gaining their interest and respect by asking the right questions in the right order, taking notes, and then making intelligent, informed decisions. Nina has a long history of relying on him, for so many things, but that part of her life is, shockingly, *finito*. Though what's to stop her, really, except her pride, from picking up the phone now and calling for his advice? He would be perfectly willing to help her decide what to do about her father. Whom he has, in fact, come by to visit from time to time over the past six months since their split.

A good son-in-law, a good man, formerly a good husband.

She's paying close attention to last week's *CSI: NY*—one hour in the more than fifty she's stored in the magic computer of her cable box—when the phone begins to ring. The caller ID identifies someone named Daniel Rose, and she almost doesn't pick up, because who's Daniel Rose and why is he bothering her after ten on a night when all she wants is to watch TV, slothlike, and eat her Weight Watchers pop in peace? Her arm stretches out, as if of its own accord, toward the telephone, and Nina says, a touch exasperated, "Hello?"

The voice on the other end apologizes for calling "a little on the late side" and then the man asks if this is Desirée's mother he's speaking to and says that he'd sat with her on her flight to Chicago. "Oh, and also on the plane to Kansas City. And . . . I'm feeling a little guilty for not calling you sooner."

"Calling about what? I don't really understand," Nina says, fear-stricken, and freezes, on the TV screen, the bizarre image of a glamorous young woman drowned in an enormous martini glass. "Is everything all right? Do you have something important to tell me?" she says.

"You must have spoken to her yourself, haven't you? So I guess I don't really have anything much to say, it's just that I promised Desirée I'd call and tell you not to worry."

Thank God! "Sorry, but you're a perfect stranger calling to tell me not to worry about my daughter?"

Daniel Rose laughs. "It does sound kind of lame, doesn't it? But after talking to Desirée and hearing where she was off to, I had the feeling that if I were a parent, I'd be glad to hear from a stranger that, in his professional opinion, I shouldn't be worrying."

"And what profession is that? Are you a shrink? A profiler for the FBI?"

"Apparently I'm an idiot," Daniel says good-naturedly. "And, by profession, an oncologist."

Unfreezing *CSI*, Nina restores it to its former position on her lineup of saved shows. "Sounds all at once both immensely gratifying and deeply depressing."

"Well, it's in my nature not to get too, too depressed about anything at all, not in the professional realm or the personal, either."

"Smart words to live by . . . whether you're a parent or not."

"That's something I've regretted from time to time—not being a parent, I mean—but at least it made my divorce a lot simpler than it would have been if there'd been children to consider."

"Undoubtedly," Nina says. An orangey-pink stream of melted passion fruit and vanilla ice cream is trailing down her bare arm now; with no tissue in sight, she licks it away with the tip of her tongue, catlike, embarrassed at what Daniel Rose would think of her if only he could see what she is doing.

"I hear *you're* divorced, as well," he says.

"Separated, but with no chance of reconciliation," she says, surprised to hear herself admit it.

"I'm sorry."

"Thanks. And thanks for your call." She doesn't mean to sound so impersonal, but doesn't know what else to say to this stranger.

"My pleasure," Daniel says.

You can hang up now if you want to, she almost tells him, but senses that he's not ready yet, though she can't imagine why. The rest of her Weight Watchers pop has melted into a pastel mess on her nightstand; idly, she puts her fingertip into it.

"Well, take care," he says.

"You, too," she offers, hanging up.

She washes her arm in the bathroom sink, sponges off the sticky puddle at her bedside, and returns to *CSI*. When the phone rings again, she's only partly surprised to see on her caller ID that it's Daniel Rose again.

"I don't even know your name," he begins, and those half-dozen ordinary words somehow possess the power to move her.

CHAPTER 17

BOBBY MCVICAR'S SAAB TURBO is a decade old but spotless inside and out, Desirée notes when she gets in next to him for a spin into the countryside. Whizzing past countless acres of corn, she spots a lone brown cow lapping water from a bucket in a parched field, a farmer astride a tractor with a sun umbrella overhead, and the Kickapoo Nation School, a small, flat-roofed building of yellow brick. But now she catches sight of something that astounds her—an official-looking sign of glittery green metal announcing that the sponsor of the next five-mile stretch of road in the Adopt-a-Highway program is none other than the John Birch Society.

"No fucking way!" she says.

"Big surprise," Bobby says, and his humorless laugh reveals all Desirée needs to know. "One of my great-grandfathers was a Grand Dragon in the KKK. How's *that* for a conversation stopper?"

Whoa! What demented, nightmarish place is this? Is she actually traveling through John Birch territory, seated next to a direct descendant of KKK royalty? It doesn't seem possible, and yet it is so. "On the subject of family history," she says, "one of *my* great-great-grandfathers was the recipient of a fatal kick to the head during a pogrom in Russia. And there's more where *that* came from . . ."

Bobby slows down the Saab as they arrive at a sprawling cemetery rimmed in maple trees. He stops the car at the entrance. "Let's take a walk," he says. The place is deserted—no mourners, no visitors, no employees. Just Bobby McVicar and Desirée, strolling among the tombstones, some more than a century old, all of them erected in grass that's sporting a buzz cut. Overhead the sky is a pearly gray, the sun nowhere in sight.

Soon the heavens have taken on a tarnished look, and there is a shower of lightning like modest fireworks, bony fingers of light that flash briefly against the sky. A deep rumbling follows, then the rain, warm, milky-white sheets of it.

"Goddamn it," Bobby says. He seizes Desirée's hand and they run toward a roofed and pillared mausoleum without walls. But a roof is all they need, and each of them slides gratefully against a pillar, chest heaving.

"Something a little more comfortable?" Bobby walks her around to an overstuffed armchair carved in marble. "Have a seat," he offers. The marble is ice-cold but she can't resist. Standing guard on either side of the chair are life-sized figures of an elderly man and woman, beautifully sculpted, delicately detailed, the man in a buttoned-up suit and tie from another era, the woman in a dress with puffy sleeves and a lacy neckline. These are the Kellys, Bobby tells her; they're eerily lifelike, and there are more of them, ten figures in all. As she and Bobby circle the mausoleum, Desirée notes that Mr. and Mrs. Kelly are growing successively younger looking, their faces softer and fuller as they retreat toward their youth. She strokes Mrs. Kelly's icy marble face, draws her fingers across the statue's faintly smiling mouth. It's evident that every bit of this statuary is meant as a tribute to the Kellys' life together, to a marriage rich in love, and it brings out the sentimental geek in Desirée, who feels herself choking up.

"What a marriage this must have been," she says; to her surprise, Bobby laughs at her. She gazes downward at the bronze plaque announcing that Mr. Kelly had erected the memorial in sacred memory of his beloved wife.

"My advice to you," Bobby says, "is not to believe everything you read."

"Not even when it's etched in stone?"

"They say the guy spent a quarter of a million dollars during the Depression—over three million in today's money—to have all of this marble sculpted in Italy, but people who knew him said he'd always been a lousy, unfaithful husband and spent those big bucks just to cheat his heirs out of their money."

"Well, he could have fooled me, the bastard."

"Don't take it so hard," Bobby advises. Returning to the marble armchair, he opens his arms to Desirée; arranging herself in his lap, facing him, she takes hold of his soaking braid, its tip like a wet paintbrush, and sweeps it slowly across her mouth. Bobby lets out a small sigh, and in this extravagant tomb, among restless ghosts, he and Desirée are two people who just can't get enough of each other.

HE DRIVES HER BACK to the Bambi so she can change out of her wet clothes, and by the time they arrive, the air has turned thick and steamy. But the two of them are damp and chilled, and Desirée can't wait to get into a hot shower. First she rummages through the dresser and finds a droopy, extra-large Yale T-shirt for Bobby—in truth, it's not hers but Nick Davenport's, and Desirée, sentimentally attached to it still, hasn't yet been able to toss it out. She offers the use of her blow dryer to warm up the rest of Bobby's clothing, and has to stop herself from asking if he'd like to join her as she heads for the shower; though it seems far too soon to extend the invitation, the reckless side of her longs to speak up. And, while showering, she's well aware that Bobby's a mere fifteen feet away from her, on the other side of the bathroom door.

Afterward, she gets into fresh underwear, wraps herself cautiously in an all-too-thin, plain white towel, and parades back into the room, wondering if the sight of her might stir Bobby just a little.

He's at the foot of the bed in his damp corduroy cutoffs and Nick's T-shirt, reading that puny Yellow Pages, strictly out of desperation, she guesses. "Oh God," he moans, and slaps a hand over his eyes.

"Can't stand the sight of me?"

"It's painful all right," Bobby says. "It's a guy thing, you know?"

"We haven't even known each other a week," she reminds him. "There's probably some sort of official waiting period, don't you think? A month? Two weeks? Eight days?" Her voice grows fainter, as do thoughts of assorted sexually transmitted diseases, along with the fear that she doesn't have an inkling of just what, precisely, she might be getting herself into.

"You've got beautiful legs," Bobby McVicar says sadly.

"They're my mother's. And the nose is my father's."

"I'm not interested in your parents right now," Bobby says, rising from the bed and lifting his arms to her waist. "One kiss and then you can get dressed."

"Too risky," Desirée says. "I don't trust myself."

"Trust *me,* then," Bobby pleads. "One kiss. Ten seconds long. Short and sweet."

He puts a hand under her chin and tilts her head back. She begins to count backward from ten silently, as if an anesthesiologist has arranged a mask over her face, and, obediently, she is following his orders. By the time she reaches eight, whatever Bobby is giving her has taken over, and she stops counting.

They are stretched across the bed, their breathing labored, hands searching everywhere, when the phone rings. Just like in the movies, Desirée thinks, though not the sort that garners any awards at film festivals, but rather the kind that bashes you over the head with a sledgehammer.

"Don't answer it," says Bobby, and returns to licking the knobs of her collarbone.

"But it's driving me crazy."

"Rip it out of the wall," Bobby recommends. "Here, let me do it."

Instead she reaches behind her and grabs the receiver.

"Is this Desirée Christian-Cohen?" The voice—female, unfamiliar, and a bit sharp—continues, "Jane Cowley. I'm a reporter for the *Honey Creek Herald?* I was hoping we could get together for an interview."

"For the paper?" Desirée says. Idiotically, she realizes. She claps her hand over the receiver. "It's a reporter from the *Herald,*" she whispers. "She wants to interview me!"

"What the hell for?" Bobby says into her neck.

"May I ask why?" she says to the reporter. In the background she can hear a man's voice complaining, "I don't give a flying fuck what Humpy Wilson thinks about anything, least of all *that.*"

"Oh, just a little human-interest story. New Yorker comes to town, that sort of thing."

"Human-interest story," Desirée murmurs to Bobby.

"Your breasts are perfect, did you know that?" he says.

"Pardon me?" Jane Cowley says.

"Okay, sounds fine, but I've got to hang up now," Desirée tells her.

"Hold on—I'll be out of town for a while, but let's meet at the Sweet Tooth next Friday at three o'clock, all right? You'll still be here?"

Bobby's face is buried in her breasts, his breath steamy against them. "I'll be here," Desirée says, lifting his T-shirt and tickling his back with the tip of his braid.

"Ciao," says Jane Cowley.

It's the "ciao" that does it, that awakens Desirée, piercing through her fuzzy thinking and hitting her with a severe case of giggles. "Ciao, baby," she tells Bobby, and her whole body twitches with laughter; poor Bobby, along for the ride, can't do a thing to sober her up. It's too late to pick up where they've left off; even while she is laughing uncontrollably, the light of common sense is glowing like a fluorescent bulb in a cartoon. "We've got to stop right now," she wheezes. "There's no way we're going ahead with this, no matter how much we both might want to."

"What's wrong?" Bobby asks, pulling himself off her and flopping over onto his back. "I've never had anyone laugh at me like that in bed before." He sounds offended.

"I wasn't laughing at you. It's that Jane Cowley I was thinking about," Desirée explains. She is in control again, and yanks the bedspread over herself, which seems to be exactly where it belongs. "Maybe it was hearing that word 'ciao' in the middle of Kansas. I don't know, it just seemed so funny. And fake. And more than a little pretentious."

"I don't get it," Bobby says. Then, "I *told* you not to answer the phone."

"You think she'll bring a photographer along with her? Maybe I ought to do something about my hair."

"It's only the *Honey Creek Herald*. I wouldn't get all excited." He tugs at the bedspread. "I've got to have another look at you."

Unexpectedly, she is overcome with self-consciousness, only too aware that here she is, almost naked, on a bed with someone she met in a coffee shop less than a week ago, someone she is drawn to for any number of reasons, but even so . . . Isn't she on the rebound, and more than a little vulnerable? Didn't she sleep with Nick just days ago? Is it possible she's misplaced her self-respect, her dignity, not to mention her common sense, somewhere back in New York?

"We hardly know anything about each other," she hears herself saying to Bobby McVicar now. "Like, for example, I know nothing about what your favorite books might be, your favorite movie of all time, your favorite kind of music besides rock. I have no idea whether you're into drugs or kinky sex. Or why you broke up with your last girlfriend. Whether you've ever had unprotected sex . . ."

"Okay, but you give me your answers first," Bobby says, looking at her hopefully. "I'm all ears."

"Fine," she says. *Crime and Punishment, Women in Love, Portnoy's Complaint*. And others too numerous to mention. *Raising Arizona*. Baroque, especially anything at all by Handel. Occasional pot smoker. Not into kinky sex. Because he didn't love me. And never ever." She lies back against the too-plump motel pillows. "So there you have it. And a little something of my soul, actually."

"Pleasure to meet you, Desirée Christian-Cohen."

"Your turn."

He salutes her snappily from his side of the bed, where his long fuzzy legs are outstretched and crossed at the ankles. His toes are dusted with golden fuzz, too; unaccountably, Desirée, who is generally repulsed by the sight of bare feet belonging to anyone except an infant, finds herself charmed by his.

"All right, here goes, but in reverse order: never ever. Because I was restless and bored. No hard drugs, though I'm an occasional, enthusiastic pot smoker. Not into kinky sex unless you count bondage and cross-dressing." He winks at her. "Just kidding. And actually, I think I've lost my place on this questionnaire of yours."

Scooting down just a bit, Desirée strokes his ankle with her foot. "So far, so good."

"Are you sure?" he says, and she slides back up to kiss him. "Let's see: *Catch-22*," he continues, and licks the curve of her ear. "*Cool Hand Luke,* the original *Manchurian Candidate,* and, um, others too numerous to mention."

"Keep going," she whispers. The bedspread has partially

fallen away; Bobby draws circles around her nipple until she seizes his finger. "Just one more answer," she says.

"Classical, especially Chopin's ballades." They've rolled over and are facing one another now. "Are we there yet?" Bobby says. "Please tell me we are."

Perhaps it's that the answers he's given her are all spot-on. Or perhaps it's that Jupiter's aligned with Mars and it's out of her hands entirely. An insanely romantic notion, and of course she doesn't have an ounce of faith in astrology. Whatever the reason, the next words she offers him are "Kiss me, you fool," something her mother used to say laughingly to her father in happier times.

And so they go forward, tenderly, carefully, a little shyly. The white noise of a vacuum cleaner filters through from the other side of the paper-thin wall, but Desirée Christian-Cohen and Bobby McVicar are conducting their own music, which, like Desirée's favorite Handel concerti, seems to her nearly heavenly.

CHAPTER 18

DRESSING FOR HER DATE WITH Daniel Rose, Nina is all too aware that this is both the first blind date of her life and the very first date she's had in decades with anyone other than Patrick. She's badly out of practice and full of the sort of anxiety that feels a bit like indigestion. And so she considers reaching for another Lexapro, doubling her dosage for the day. What if Daniel's face falls in disappointment at the sight of her? What if there's hair sprouting from his ears and he doesn't know how to hold his knife and fork properly? Worst of all, what if she and Daniel have absolutely nothing to say to one another? Why hasn't Desirée picked up her damn phone so Nina can at least find out whether or not this guy Daniel is some pathetic troll? But she reminds herself that when he called back that night to ask her name, they'd stayed on the phone for over half an hour, two strangers talking mostly about her father's medical history, the details of which incited Daniel's interest and sympathy. His own father had died last year and Daniel still found himself missing him, he told Nina; she'd imagined his rueful smile as he spoke.

She's poised in front of the bathroom mirror now, applying mascara, her hand trembling slightly. It's difficult to keep herself from worrying about Desirée, who, just last night, sent an e-mail from her BlackBerry, all exhilarated over some boy, the son of a dentist and some sort of therapist, "and believe it or not, one-sixteenth Jewish!" A fact Desirée plainly thought would be of some comfort to Nina, who has been regretting—in the wake of the dissolution of her marriage—the flimsiness of her ties to Judaism, newly distressed that she'd never bothered to send Desirée to Hebrew school, even the watered-down, once-a-week version that would have afforded her daughter a smidgen of this particular fifty percent of her heritage. This failure of hers feels shameful now—now that Desirée is fully grown and it's too late. (Though perhaps this whiff of Jewishness in the boy's family means something to Desirée, as well.) Nina e-mailed back, "Call me, pussycat! Please, *please* call me!" but, predictably, there's been no phone call, e-mail, or text message from Kansas. The thought of Desirée falling for this Bobby McVicar is one more worry to add to her litany.

"Oh please!" she says aloud. There's a smudge of black on her eyelid, which she smears clumsily with her finger, only making it worse. Even this smallest of things gone wrong she blames on Patrick. A bad habit of hers, holding him accountable for every imperfection in her life even as she knows he can't *possibly* be held responsible. Dr. Pepperkorn thinks the state of her mental health is improving, but what does *he* know, really? She'd noted a triptych of black-and-white photographs of his three small children on his desk, but when asked about them, all Dr. Pepperkorn did was smile. *None of your business,* that smile said, angering her. If she didn't need Pepperkorn to write her Lexapro prescriptions, she'd dump him immediately. *In a heartbeat.* Who needs a stranger, even a trained professional, to render judgment on her very heart and soul? She'd alerted him to this prospect of a first date with Daniel, and he'd nodded approvingly. *Back in the game! Excellent! Good for you!* The man certainly has a way with words. Probably a C+ English student in college. She laughs, thinking of just how much she would enjoy assigning a richly deserved mediocre grade to his sessions with her every two weeks. C+/B–, nothing higher. And her written comment: *Your work thus far has been* barely *satisfactory—you need to try harder, Pepperkorn!*

Her new skinny black pants, which she could swear were a perfect fit when she bought them several weeks ago, are just a little too tight now, she realizes with disgust. She'll have to wear them to dinner with the top button open and her shirt untucked. A new low point in her middle-aged life.

Her father is snoozing in his wheelchair with Porsha beside him in the La-Z-Boy recliner tilted as far back as it will go, the TV remote in her hand, when Nina steps into their room to check on them. The local cable news is on; a woman, clearly distraught, is shaking her head and saying, "It was a wrong mistake, that's all." *A wrong mistake;* Nina winces at the sound of it.

"We were just resting up a bit before dinner," Porsha says, "me and Grandpa." She lowers the La-Z-Boy to the floor, as if embarrassed to have been discovered relaxing. "And *you're* looking all nice and pretty for your date."

"Really? Actually, I'm a wreck," Nina says. She remains where she is in the doorway.

"Over one little date? What kind of sense does *that* make?"

"I know, I'm an idiot," Nina says.

"You got *that* right, girl!" Porsha says, making Nina laugh. Porsha herself is twice divorced and once widowed; at sixty-four, she is, she's said, "done with all that." *I got my kids, my grandkids, and even one great-grand. What do I need a man for? To mess up my sweet little home and maybe my life? NO, thanks.*

"When did *you* last go on a date, big shot?" Nina teases her, and sees that her father's eyes have opened.

"Grandpa and I have a dinner date tonight, just the two of us, don't we, darlin'?"

There's that Parkinsonian blankness, that ineffable look of her father's that cannot be interpreted no matter how hard you try.

"Plus we've got *Grey's Anatomy* and one of the *CSI*s, can't remember which." Porsha pats Marvin's hand. "We're all set for the night, right, darlin'?"

"And wasn't it our lucky day when you came to us." Nina feels tears of gratitude filling her inexpertly mascaraed eyes; her customary sangfroid (or what she likes to think of as her sangfroid) seems to have deserted her tonight.

"Are those *tears*? Don't you start crying just before your date gets here," Porsha warns her.

But the mascara is already trickling toward the corners of Nina's mouth and the doorman is buzzing from the lobby to say that "Mr. Rose" is here. Rushing to the nearest bathroom, she cleans the muddy streaks from her face and instructs herself to get a grip.

When the bell rings, she hesitates just an instant before opening the door. The man standing outside in the hallway is holding a modest bouquet of yellow and white freesia in his hands. He smiles at her. "Nina?" he says.

"Guilty."

His smile broadens; his teeth are neatly aligned, his face pleasant and open, a face that sets her at ease. He has a paperback tucked under his arm: *Parkinson's Disease: A Complete Guide for Patients and Families.* "Just thought you might want to have this," he says. "Though maybe that's presumptuous of me," he adds as he holds the book out to her and waits for her to take it.

"No, no, of course," she says. She hugs the book to her chest without looking at it; *of course* she's not going to tell him that she already has a copy. "Thank you."

A mensch, her mother would have called him, Nina thinks as she arranges the freesia in a crystal Waterford vase, a wedding gift from long ago that she never particularly liked and might even try to palm off on Patrick and Loverboy. Just as Daniel misses his father, Nina still misses her mother, gone three years now. A woman whose instincts were unfailingly generous. Bitterness and resentment were alien to her; she simply couldn't abide those emotions she regarded as futile and destructive. If her mother were still alive, she would likely be advising Nina to slam the door decisively on her marriage and get a move on. Easy for her mother to say; what would a veteran of a marriage that happily lasted over half a century know about getting a move on? But how crazy is it to be exasperated with your poor dead mother who's no longer here to defend herself?

"Sorry, *what?*" she asks Daniel.

". . . Only if you think he's in the mood for company . . ."

"My father?"

"I'd like to say hello if that's okay."

Her father is already in his pj's at seven-thirty in the evening; his old self would be mortified. But his old self has vanished and won't be making an appearance again in this lifetime.

"I'm glad to meet you, sir," Daniel says, and doesn't hesitate to take Marvin's hand in his own.

"Yas."

"I'm Nina's friend." He shakes Porsha's hand, as well.

"Yas?" Like a pendulum, Marvin's head begins to oscillate back and forth; Nina looks away.

"My father graduated from Columbia Law School in 1955," she says, so that Daniel understands just where he's directing his pity. *And, as you're undoubtedly aware, the cruelty of old age is some-times simply too much to bear.*

"Columbia Law School? Something to be proud of," Daniel says.

"Yas."

"We never expect things to go as wrong as they do," Nina mur-murs. She doesn't wait for her father's response; all she does is wave good-bye before leaving him behind, his head still swinging.

SOMETHING THAT FEELS ODD and unnatural: dinner in a restau-rant seated at a table for two opposite a man who isn't Patrick. She needs to stop thinking this way, to stop placing Patrick squarely—and limned in the brightest neon—at the center of her orbit. *She's* no longer on *his* radar, or if she is, she's merely a faint image, barely visible, reduced to almost nothing. What she needs to do is shrink *him* down to less than nothing, an itty-bitty subatomic particle.

Gazing across the table in the Greek restaurant Daniel has chosen for them, she listens as he talks about his ex-wife, a surgi-cal nurse who left him for a lab tech who was, "get this—a former Hell's Angel."

It's difficult not to laugh, though Nina presumes she's not supposed to. She's supposed to look both shocked and appalled. But nothing, these days, shocks her, not when it comes to mar-riages going swiftly and permanently down the tubes.

"The guy has two sleeves of tattoos, and a prison record. How could a simple oncologist possibly compete with that?" Daniel says, sounding amused. "Especially that three-month sentence in the slammer for failure to pay child support." He's smiling now, shrugging his shoulders. "You know what, after a certain point you just have to tell yourself you don't *give* a flying fuck. It took me one very long year, but I'm pleased to say I'm cured. And in very good shape, really." He cuts into his grilled octopus happily, offers her a bite, and doesn't seem offended when she waves away a forkful of tentacle cooked in olive oil and lemon juice. "How's your bronzini?" he asks.

"Lovely. Delicious." She extracts a tiny fish bone from her

mouth. "So did Desirée tell you why my husband and I had our own parting of the ways?"

"Didn't tell me a word of it. And *you* don't have to, either. Not if you don't want to, I mean. But if you do, I'm all ears."

"Well, I can assure you there's not a single Hell's Angel at fault," she begins, and soon realizes, spilling all those humiliating details, that it's a narrative she neither needs, nor wants, to tell ever again. And this recognition seems like progress, a small miracle, really. By the time she's finished with her story and her bronzini, she feels spent. Their dishes have been cleared away and they're sharing a plate of walnut-and-almond baklava. "I've talked way too much," she says. "I hope you'll forgive me."

At the table next to them, a dark-haired young guy seated alone, dressed in a sport jacket and tie, is on his cell phone. "I love you so much, Delilah," he is saying. "I want to be with you more than anything in the world. But not like *this,* damn you." He thumps his fist against the table for two, and a small spoon goes flying.

"You're joking," Daniel says to Nina. "Why do you need to be forgiven? Do I *look* like I'm bored?"

Her single vodka martini (no sickening, licorice-flavored ouzo for her!) has finally gone to her head. "You look," she says, "like you need a little bit of a haircut, okay?"

Daniel combs his fingers through his hair, which is abundant and unruly, completely gray. "You think the Albert Einstein look has got to go?" he laughs. "If so, you wouldn't be the first."

"I *do* think so."

"Okay then, we'll make ourselves an appointment."

"Is that the royal we?"

"That's 'we' as in 'you and me.' "

Though she instinctively amends the "me" to an "I," she doesn't correct him. Which, she knows, is another good-sized step in the right direction.

CHAPTER 19

"HEY."

Bobby is waiting, behind the wheel of his Saab, for Desirée to say something, but all she can do is echo, "Hey," unable, it seems, to venture beyond that innocuous, uninspired greeting. The fact that they've been intimate has the odd effect of rendering them a little shy and subdued in each other's presence now, as if they might be the slightest bit embarrassed.

The Bambi Motel retreats in the rearview as they drive along Minnehaha, which has begun to look as familiar to Desirée as Third Avenue in Manhattan, where she'd stood waiting on the corner for a taxi to the airport a little over a week ago. Familiar, perhaps, and yet there's still something fanciful and improbable about finding herself (a native Upper East Sider!) cruising a desolate main drag called Minnehaha. "So listen," she says a few minutes later, "what happened, you know, the other day, was actually . . . perfect. It might happen again and it might not, but I don't regret an instant of it. And it's not as if we're linked for eternity, so if you're uneasy, please don't be."

"It *was* pretty great, wasn't it?" Bobby sighs. "And I'm not worried at all. I'm just going with the flow here."

"Yup. No worries."

He has a quick stop to make before they get to dinner at his parents' house, he says as he pulls the car over in front of the Kum & Go.

Inside the supermarket/drugstore, where Bobby soon deserts her, Desirée wanders the fluorescent-lit aisles searching for some sort of house gift for the McVicars; unaccountably, she finds herself beside a jewelry case stocked with diamond engagement rings and gold and silver necklaces and bracelets, glittery in their velvet boxes. An old woman who has just eased herself into a folding chair guards the treasures under glass.

"Ready to get engaged, or just window-shopping?" she asks Desirée.

What? "I thought I was in the Kum and Go," Desirée says in confusion. "But maybe I'm a little lost. And definitely not engaged."

"You're not lost, you're in Mimi's Gems and Jewels. And I'm Mimi. See the sign up there?" She points behind her to a sign stenciled on a sheet of oak tag. "Didn't you come in here with Dr. McVicar's boy?"

"He seems to have disappeared."

"Well, maybe he got cold feet," Mimi speculates. "But don't worry, he'll come around. In the end, nobody wants to be alone. We come into this world alone and we exit alone, but in between we're all desperate for someone to keep us nice and cozy at night. And if we say we're not, well, then, we're just plain lying." She smiles at Desirée. "My advice, miss, whoever you are, is for the two of you to pick out the ring together. You take your time, and when you both feel the moment is right, you and the McVicar boy come back and find me."

"We're not engaged," Desirée repeats.

"Oh, look, there's your sweetheart over there in aisle eight."

Aisle 8, Desirée notices—observing the sign suspended above it—offers a mystifying assortment of products:

BEVERAGES	CANDY/COOKIES
INCONTINENCE	HEARTBURN RELIEF
FEMININE CARE	CONDOMS

"Excuse me," she tells Mimi, and corners Bobby with his hand at the condom shelf.

"Oh hey," he says sheepishly.

"Maybe one of those tins of butter cookies would be all right for a house gift? And you know, I never realized you could actually buy incontinence. You can't in New York, anyway. Maybe it's a regional thing." She imagines her grandfather, his sense of humor still intact less than a year ago, laughing at the marketing genius who arranged the placement of merchandise and designed the sign overhead. Now, though, Marvin inhabits a world where, it seems, nothing is funny, not even those endless repeats of *Seinfeld,* his favorite show, which fails to amuse him when Nina parks him in front of the TV, pretending he still has what it takes to summon up a laugh or two. Someday, Desirée thinks gloomily, it may very well be her mother in those pee-soaked Depends, and someday far into the century, she herself. She can picture this grim future of hers all too clearly, hear the sickroom-whispers of her children and grandchildren, feel their impatience as they pray for her to get it over with and bite the dust already. And who would fault them? Her octogenarian self is pathetic, all bones and wasted muscle, sour smelling, a living corpse with absolutely nothing to offer . . .

"Oh my God, I'm so depressed!"

"What's wrong?" Bobby wants to know.

"Never mind. Pay for that Super Deluxe Pleasure Package I know you've got your eye on, and let's get out of here," Desirée says, and grabs a tin of cookies for his parents.

By the time they arrive at the McVicars', it is, evidently, common knowledge that Desirée and Bobby are "engaged to be engaged," as Starshine puts it when she greets them at the front door, looking bemused. "So what's going on, you guys?" she says. She's wearing a gauzy, faded, Indian-print dress of blue-green and white that in all likelihood must be a personal relic from the sixties, Desirée surmises, or else something purchased from a thrift shop.

"Oh, just another baseless rumor," she tells Starshine blithely, but the truth is, she is mortified. It's hard to fathom the swiftness with which such an absurdly far-fetched rumor could have been broadcast from one end of Honey Creek to the other. Honestly, don't these people have more gratifying ways to spend their time? Obviously not, and that, to Desirée, is both laughable and deeply mysterious.

"What baseless rumor is *that?*" Bobby says. Having been deliberately spared the details of Desirée's encounter with Mimi, he's completely in the dark.

"Not five minutes ago I heard from someone in my Alzheimer's support group that you two were seen shopping for a diamond ring," Starshine explains, ushering them into the living room in her bare feet.

Bobby indulges in some eye-rolling at the news, but says nothing. "When's dinner?" he asks.

He's settled himself on a wicker throne, with Desirée in an identical seat beside him; every bit of the furniture, even the coffee table, is wicker, as if Bobby and his family were living in the tropics, or, more likely, still waiting for that moment when his parents might feel comfortable plunking down some real money and springing for oak or mahogany—solid, grown-up furniture that suggests you've made your peace with the trappings of middle-class life. The room is light and airy; Desirée admires the pots of flourishing violets all along the windowsill, and the rubber tree that nearly scrapes the ceiling.

"So what's up with the engagement ring?" Starshine asks.

"Well, there I was in the Kum and Go," Desirée begins, "and then all of a sudden I'm in a jewelry store, talking to someone named Mimi, and the next minute she's mistakenly convinced I'm in the market for a diamond ring."

Starshine seems relieved. She dusts the rubber plant with the sleeve of her dress, then arranges herself on the rug, some sort of extra-shaggy Berber whose fuzz she twists around her finger as she talks. "Let's not be too hard on Mimi. The poor thing's been a widow since 1953," she says. "Her husband was run over by a tractor the day the Rosenbergs were executed. She's been alone for more than half a century, imagine that."

No wonder poor Mimi's desperate for someone to keep her cozy at night!

"So how's the patient doing?" Dr. McVicar inquires, bursting forth from the kitchen with an ornate silver tray of hot hors d'oeuvres.

"Great. I'm the picture of health. I mean, dental health."

"Wayne, darling, you know you're never supposed to use that hideous tray," Starshine says. "What were you *thinking*?"

Dr. McVicar is dressed for dinner in jeans with shredded knees that reveal a flash of hairy skin underneath; his big, broad feet are in bright yellow rubber Crocs. "I was thinking, actually, that you forgot to take the hors d'oeuvres out of the oven, and since this was the only tray I could find, I might as well go ahead and use it, hideous though it may be."

"What's wrong with me?" Starshine frowns. "What if it's"— she takes a breath—"premature dementia symptomatic of early-onset Alzheimer's?"

Stockpiling three minitacos and two stuffed mushrooms before taking a seat on the floor, Dr. McVicar says, "My professional opinion is that this Alzheimer's support group of yours has got to go, babe. It's making you crazy. I mean, you've got to stop freaking out every time you happen to forget some little thing or other. You're healthy as a horse and you know it."

"I'm telling you, I'm nowhere near as sharp as I used to be," Starshine complains. "I'm fifty-five years old and I could swear I'm losing it."

"Comeer, babe," Dr. McVicar says, but makes the first move himself, pulling her along the fuzzy carpet and into his lap. "First of all, you're still fifty-four. Your birthday's, what, a month from next Saturday, right? So you know what I'm thinking? I've been considering this for a while, in fact. In honor of your fifty-fifth, we should get married. On your actual birthday, I mean. How does that strike you?"

Whoa! At first Desirée assumes Dr. McVicar is kidding, but when she observes that no one is laughing, it crosses her mind that this is the one and only marriage proposal she's ever been witness to. And it seems a privilege to be seated among the bride- and groom-to-be and their son as they contemplate the possibility, at this poignantly (and shockingly!) late date, of a wedding in the family.

"Married parents—awesome!" Bobby says. "And you know, I'd love to be best man."

"Not so fast," Starshine cautions, but from the gentle way she's worrying the frayed threads at Dr. McVicar's knee, it's clear she's intrigued. "What if marriage just whisks away all the romance and mystery from our relationship?"

"*What* romance?" says Dr. McVicar, smiling. "*What* mystery? After thirty-something years?"

"Thirty-four. And keep talking like that, big shot, and you'll wind up in Reno or Costa Rica or wherever it is you can get one of those quickie divorces."

"Joking," says Dr. McVicar. "But if we do get a divorce, afterward we can just go back to living the way we always have."

Starshine has slipped away from Dr. McVicar and is lying flat on her back staring at the ceiling, her arms arranged behind her neck. "A wedding dress and a bridal bouquet do hold a certain allure," she admits. "Though I don't know about a marriage license."

"Just another piece of official paper to add to our already-bulging files?"

"And absolutely no clergy," Starshine says. "That's all we need, some sanctimonious minister mouthing platitudinous bullshit about the holy state of matrimony."

"Well, I guess that leaves Hizzoner Humpy Wilson. We could do worse."

"We could do better. And of course you know he's got to assume we're already married."

"He and everyone else in town," Bobby says.

"Screw 'em," Starshine says cheerfully. "Let's do it!"

"Congratulations!" Desirée calls out. And then, carried away by her own excitement, "Mazel tov!"

Starshine has propped herself up on her elbows, smiling, then looking curiously at Desirée.

"That's 'congratulations' in Yiddish," Desirée explains, and feels a painful spasm of something like homesickness, having just been reminded that she is, in fact, a galaxy away from that place where the words "mazel tov" have been woven seamlessly into the speech of everyday life.

At dinner, the bride-to-be and her intended are toasted with a couple of bottles of wine. Over and over again, until some at the table are legally drunk and others only moderately intoxicated.

"Too bad our respective parents are dead and won't be able to make it to the wedding," Dr. McVicar muses.

"What a shame," Desirée says. "About your dead parents, I mean." She has never, in the course of her life, been totally wasted, falling-down drunk, but she has to admit, as she slings her arm

117

around Bobby's shoulder and gives the back of his neck a friendly squeeze, that being half drunk doesn't feel too bad at all. "So," she asks him, "are you going to miss being a, um, bastard?"

"From time to time, I suppose. But I'll get over it."

"You know, I've got this sick headache all of a sudden," Starshine reports. "And don't quote me on this, but I think it has something to do with Mimi of Mimi's Gems and Jewels, and the depressing fact that she's been a widow since the day the poor Rosenbergs were fried."

"Those Rosenbergs were innocent as newborn babes," Dr. McVicar says morosely. "And even if they weren't, they never should have been killed like that. It was anti-Semitism that done them in. Or at least my great-grandmother Elsie thought so. And if she didn't know, who would?"

Starshine shoves aside her dinner plate of half-eaten corn-flake chicken and sweet-potato fries and lowers her head into the crook of her folded arms on the table. "I wasn't aware we had a great-grandma Elsie in the family. Then again, I'm feeling rather muzzy at the moment."

"Now *there's* a word I know doesn't exist," says Dr. McVicar.

"Fifty bucks says it does. It's 'muddled' and 'fuzzy' blended together and it's just the way I'm feeling right now," Starshine says.

"Get out the *Webster's,* son," Dr. McVicar orders.

"Do I have to?" Bobby says. "I'm feeling pretty muzzy myself."

It's Desirée who volunteers to look for the dictionary. "That way you can have a private family discussion about a certain Jewish relative who had her daughter baptized so she'd fit in undetected with all the rest of you Honey Creekers."

"I hate to contradict you, Desirée, sweetie, but there were never any Jews in Honey Creek," Starshine says. "Except, of course, you, and you're just a half Jew here on a temporary visa, am I correct?"

Tapping his wine glass with a salad fork, Dr. McVicar says, "I have an announcement to make. In point of fact, the man who's about to become your lawfully wedded husband is, I'm sure you'll be amazed to learn, one eighth of a Jew."

"No kidding! Well, it's a shame this allegedly Jewish great-grandmother of yours can't come to the wedding. I take it she's long dead?" Starshine says.

"Oh, she'd be about a hundred and twenty-eight if she weren't," Dr. McVicar calculates.

"That is *so* sad," Desirée says.

Starshine's head is still down and her eyes are closed now. "You know, drunk as I am, you almost feel like family, Desirée," she begins. "Which is why I'm seriously considering asking you to be a bridesmaid. Or junior bridesmaid, whatever."

"Sweet! I'm going to be a junior or senior bridesmaid at your parents' wedding!" Desirée whoops, as Bobby takes her hand. "And to prove myself worthy of this great honor, I'm going to clear the table and do the dishes."

"Hold it right there," Starshine says. "In this house, guests don't do dishes."

"I'm not a guest, I'm a possible bridesmaid." Desirée manages to get to her feet, and once she is upright, is confident she can do the job. But after only a few trips back and forth to the kitchen, she runs out of steam. In the dining room, Dr. McVicar is narrating the long version of the 1966 Kansas City bar mitzvah, and Starshine is snoozing, though every once in a while she murmurs, "I'm awake! I'm listening!" And Bobby is gone.

Pouring herself a glass of ice water from a pitcher in the refrigerator, Desirée begins to load the dishwasher. An old-fashioned ceiling fan whirls overhead but she is hot and a little dizzy and regrets having volunteered for kitchen duty. She drops into a chair at the kitchen table, polishes off half the water in her glass, then holds it up to her forehead and swivels it slowly across her brow. She takes a long, nosy look around the kitchen, a spacious room with countertops, stove, and refrigerator all in a very seventies, very unfortunate turquoise that probably lost its shine decades ago. Lined up above the stove, as if they were statuettes, is a small collection of empty iced-tea bottles, their labels showing graceful cherry trees in blossom, mysterious-looking geisha girls, bandannaed cowboys on horseback. Over the sink, on a narrow ledge of Formica, stand an inch-high Coca-Cola bottle, a plastic set of pink and white teeth and gums a quarter inch in diameter, and a minuscule ceramic chocolate cake decorated with raspberries the size of pinheads. Desirée suspects all of this has been absentmindedly accumulated over time rather than carefully chosen—a sampling from the hit-or-miss school of decorating that she finds endearing. Unlike almost everyone she is acquainted with at home in New York, Bobby's parents evidently have better things to take pleasure in than gleaming stainless steel appliances and granite countertops. What those things might be aren't entirely clear to her yet, but the McVicars are a genuinely together family, the hippest people in Honey Creek—and perhaps even the state of Kansas. And she's more convinced of this than ever the following morning, when, shocked to find herself squeezed next to Bobby in his twin bed, she looks up to see Starshine standing over her, a complimentary cup of coffee in her outstretched hand, a benevolent smile on her face.

Slightly hungover, flustered at having been discovered in a bed she can't for the life of her remember falling into, Desirée immediately takes stock of her clothing, all of which, thankfully, she is still wearing, except for her jeans, which *someone* must have misplaced, presumably last night. Bobby's clothes are on the floor, except for his boxers, the waistband of which is visible above the blue and beige plaid summer blanket lying untidily across his hips. Desirée starts to offer the vaguest sort of apology for all of this, but Starshine waves it away with her free hand.

"You can't be serious," she tells Desirée. "Don't you know you're among friends? I mean, where do you *think* you are?"

In Kansas, far from home, but among friends nevertheless. Friends who, unlike her mother, apparently don't mind in the least in which particular bed their houseguest happens to land for the night.

Beside her, Bobby stirs, yawns, and fastens his arms securely around her waist.

CHAPTER 20

"REMIND ME AGAIN why I would even *want* to meet him?" Nina asks Daniel Rose in the cab that is carrying them through the park to Riverside Drive, to the brunch she's been alternately dreading and anxiously looking forward to ever since Patrick extended the invitation.

"Jordan? How about because he's Desirée's stepfather of sorts?"

"That's a little hyperbolic, don't you think? At this point, anyway."

"Okay, how about because it's smart to accept a friendly invitation from the man you spent more than two decades of your life with?"

"Fine."

"I'll be with you every step of the way," Daniel says, depositing a soundless kiss on her cheek. "Relax."

She is grateful for his nice, modest self-confidence, a distinct contrast to the overweening self-assurance she's observed in so many of the doctors she's dealt with these past few years of her father's illness. (Though she doesn't, of course, know what they're like in their private lives, she thinks she has a pretty good idea.) She's grateful, too, for Daniel's all-around menschy-ness—for the way he makes a point of addressing Marvin as "sir," and spending a few minutes talking with him whenever he comes to the apartment to pick her up. She and Daniel have seen each other two or three times a week for several weeks now; she looks forward, with a youthful eagerness, to the sound of his voice on the phone and the feel of her hand clasped in his as they cruise along the street together after dinner or a movie. She hasn't yet been to his apartment in downtown Brooklyn, but suspects that even greater pleasures await her when she eventually finds her way there. And all thanks to Desirée, her exasperated and sometimes exasperating daughter, who just *had* to skip town in a blatant effort to escape—at least in part—from *her.* Desirée's calls from Honey Creek have been brief and not very informative—two minutes one day, three minutes the next, her voice a little breathless as she reassures Nina that yes, everything's cool, and no, she hasn't given any thought at all to when she can be expected home. Every so often Desirée reminds Nina that she is twenty years old, that it's the twenty-first century, and that Nina herself needs to lighten up. Perhaps so. And Desirée has happily taken credit for the role she inadvertently played in bringing Nina and Daniel together, trying to underscore the notion that this trip of hers to Honey Creek was clearly an inspired idea. But the jury's still out on that one, Nina thinks.

Stepping out of the cab, she sees an Asian mother and daughter crossing Riverside Drive, the thirty-something daughter clutching the last two fingers of her mother's right hand as they walk together under the scorching sun. Nina looks at them wistfully, imagining the outrage in Desirée's incredulous voice: *What? You want me to hold your hand? Am I five years old?*

And now Nina and Daniel are entering Patrick's new home and his new life with Jordan, who, unlike Nina, managed to earn his Ph.D. and a tenured position at Columbia, a university that declined to invite her to return after a single semester teaching there years ago. There are handshakes all around, and for Nina, a fervent hug and a soft massaging of her shoulders from Patrick. For a moment it feels, to Nina, like a momentous occasion and then it doesn't; they're just a quartet of civilized adults standing in a large, high-ceilinged living room with a truly spectacular view of the Hudson, and, beyond it, the undistinguished skyline of Fort Lee, New Jersey. She hears Patrick describing to Daniel the courses he teaches in the School of Engineering and Applied Science: Polymer Surfaces and Interfaces; Theoretical Methods in Polymer Physics; Intro to Surface and Colloid Chemistry. After all these years, she still doesn't understand exactly what a polymer is. And, moreover, still doesn't care; a failing, perhaps, but one that she can finally overlook.

"You know, I hope, that you're a gorgeous woman," Jordan offers. He's next to her with a plate of homemade steamed vegetable dumplings; gripped in his hand are four pairs of ivory chopsticks.

What? "Even the dumpling skins are made from scratch?" Nina says, hoping to change the subject.

Jordan nods, almost bashfully. He gestures for her to take a seat. "Patrick told me you were voted 'Best Looking' in high school and I can certainly understand why."

Daniel is smiling at Nina. "No kidding!" he says.

"High school," she says. "We all know how stupid high school was. And beyond the obvious superficiality, there's something almost demeaning at the very notion of being voted 'Best Looking.'"

"Excuse me?" Jordan says, and all three men are staring at Nina now.

"Why can't you just accept a compliment," Patrick says, "and the generous spirit in which it was offered."

"Have some chicken satay," Jordan says loudly, frowning at Patrick. "You like those professional-looking little skewers they're on?"

"The satay is homemade?" Nina asks, already knowing the answer.

"I love to cook, that's all. No big deal."

Gazing around her, Nina takes in the gleaming, beautifully set glass dining table, the immaculate Persian rugs, the glass display case filled with Oriental ceramic pieces, the elegant, ultra-modern, carefully placed stainless steel lamps. And not a mote of dust anywhere. She envies Jordan's good taste, along with the high ceilings and the magnificent view of the river. Face it: Jordan is a better cook, housekeeper, and decorator than she will ever be. She can't possibly compete with this man of many talents. In addition, she can see that he is affable and gracious, not to mention an expert on Flaubert. *Foolish little ponytail aside, it's no fucking wonder Patrick fell for him.* The wonder is that Patrick's a gay man and that it took him a lifetime to accept that this is what he was all along.

As Nina herself has not accepted it.

And never will, not entirely.

She would desperately like to do the civilized thing and wish the two of them well together, but instead feels the urge to grab Loverboy/Jordan and shriek, *Give me back MY HUSBAND, YOU BASTARD!* And yet seeing the two of them together in their lovely home goes a long way toward convincing her that she and Patrick are done. Finished. The fat lady has sung, and *fortissimo*.

The unpredictability of life is a given, Nina knows; bombshells are dropped by our loved ones and we are rendered speechless. She's been blindsided by Patrick, but she will recover. She will sit down at the table with him and his beloved, and of course Daniel, and eat the food that has been so meticulously prepared for her, the guest of honor—cellophane noodles with pork, spinach, and peanuts; vegetable moo shu; foil-wrapped ginger chicken. Every mouthful of which is delicious. Irresistible. She will try her best to keep up with the conversation, which includes those damn polymers, nineteenth-century French literature, and the newest advances in breast cancer detection. And *her* contribution—the astonishingly lucrative take-home pay of exotic dancers.

There will be homemade green tea ice cream for dessert, and then she will announce that she's too stuffed to move. When Jordan lifts her hand to his mouth and kisses it—in a manner that seems partly sincere and partly campy—and tells her they *must* do this again sometime soon, she will agree, and then fall sorrowfully into Patrick's farewell embrace.

In the elevator ride down to the lobby, she will be stricken by mild nausea, which will only worsen in the cab homeward. Miraculously, and through sheer force of will and a little luck, she will manage to make it home only moments before puking her guts out. On her knees in front of the toilet in the master bath, her hair yanked out of the way with one sweaty hand, she will purge herself of every bit of Loverboy's impressively good cookin'.

Food poisoning, maybe? Though, inexplicably, she will be its only victim.

And thank God for Daniel, who will stick around to feed her ice chips and lay his palm so professionally across her damp forehead.

CHAPTER 21

EYELIDS SHADOWED IN SPARKLY BEIGE, hair as sleek as she can manage it, Desirée ventures alone to the Sweet Tooth, where Riley Maxwell greets her with visible excitement.

"I am *just* thrilled for you!" she gushes. "Love those black jeans—all in black for the big interview, right? Awesome." And then, to Desirée's embarrassment, Riley calls out, "Hey, guys, Desirée's being interviewed right here by Jane Cowley for a feature in the *Herald*." "The guys" are a quartet of middle-aged men in overalls lingering over their coffee at a table up front. All four raise their hands in mute greeting, staring at Desirée briefly in her seat at the counter.

"Hey, how *are* you?" she says, and waves back.

"Best to watch what you say to Jane, young lady," a bearded blond guy warns. "She's smarter than you think. Crafty, like a fox."

"A wolf, Eugene, not a fox," says one of his pals.

"Crafty like a wolf in sheep's clothing?" Desirée says, smiling, but no one offers her anything beyond a stare.

"Same difference. Both carnivores, both members of the dog family. So a fox is a little smaller, he's got shorter legs, a pointier muzzle, so what?" Eugene says.

Waiting for the grilled cheese she's ordered, Desirée sits at the counter and wonders, uneasily, if there's the smallest chance she's waltzing into a trap cruelly set for her by Jane "Crafty Like a Wolf" Cowley.

"Oh, Jane's no genius," Riley says. "But she uses a lot of foreign words and likes to make you feel stupid for not knowing what they mean."

With seven years of French, three of Spanish, and one year of intensive German under her belt, Desirée is somewhat confident she can hold her own.

"It all started," Riley explains, "when she went to KU and met this French guy, he was her professor, I think, and they were hot for each other for a while but then he moved on to someone else and Jane came back to Honey Creek all depressed and druggy and I guess you could say suicidal because they had to pump her stomach in the emergency room. But then after that she pulled herself together and got herself a job over at the *Herald*."

After serving up Desirée's lunch, Riley sets her elbows on the counter, leaning in for a tête-à-tête. "So where's your friend Bobby McVicar?" she says casually.

Desirée shrugs.

"Well, I hear his car's been parked over at the Bambi a whole lot recently, like just about every night."

"Did you use more than one kind of cheese on this?" Desirée asks, biting into her sandwich, which is memorably, deliciously, rich, soaking her fingertips in butter.

"What I'm trying to tell you, Desirée, is that you can't do anything in this town without at least *some* people finding out. There's kind of a network out there and it works real well. Like, for example, if you were to go to Dr. McVicar and he were to fix up that inflamed tooth of yours and not charge you a cent, before you know it, *some* people—not me, obviously—might be wondering why he wouldn't take your money. And then they're thinking, hmm, maybe there's a connection between this free dental care and the fact that Bobby McVicar's car is parked in front of your motel room night after night after night—"

"Oh, for Christ's sake! How can you stand living in this fishbowl?" Desirée says indignantly.

"It may be a fishbowl, but it's home and it's generally quite comfy. And don't you shake your head at me like that, Desirée. I'm twenty-three and I've got two kids and a husband and a job. It was all settled a long time ago, the moment I found out I was pregnant with my first. So I'm not going anywhere, and most days it suits me fine." Riley straightens up suddenly, pulling back from the counter in a hurry. "Super," she says grimly as another middle-aged man arrives, this one dressed in jeans, work boots, and a clerical collar. "Reverend Billy Lee Ribbs, Desirée Christian-Cohen," she says. "And vice versa."

"A real true pleasure meeting you in the flesh. I mean, I've heard all this and that about you and here we are, together at last."

The Reverend Ribbs smiles pleasantly at Desirée. "You're the first New Yorker I've ever met," he confesses, "believe it or not. Someday I hope to get to New York, and would like nothing better than to see a show like *Oklahoma!* on a real Broadway stage. Yup, that would be my dream."

"And believe it or not, you're the first, um, man of the cloth I've ever had a chat with," Desirée says.

"Really? But how's that possible?"

Desirée just can't resist temptation. "Well, I was raised by heathens," she says.

"Then let me tell you—and I don't mean to sound presumptuous here—but sooner or later, we all need a little help from Jesus. Even you, Desirée Christian-Cohen, may someday find yourself looking for help from the right place. And when you do, He'll be there for you, I guarantee it."

"And *I* don't mean to sound dismissive, but I'm actually getting along fine without Him," Desirée says. "Trust me."

"Trust in *Him,*" the Reverend Ribbs urges, "for He is the way, the truth, the light. You might want to think on that a while, Miss Desirée."

The man is simply doing his job, but even so, Desirée feels reduced to the size of an insect, a cockroach the Reverend Billy Lee Ribbs might squash beneath one of his clunky, mustard-colored work boots any moment now. She opens her mouth and hears herself say, "The thing is, we heathens are happy just the way we are."

The Reverend Ribbs raises both hands in surrender. "I wouldn't touch that with a ten-foot pole," he says, "much as I'd like to. God willing and the creek don't rise, we all have to live our lives as we see fit. But I like to put in a plug for Jesus whenever and wherever I can, that's all."

"Understood," Desirée says. "It's only that—"

"Don't look now," Riley interrupts, "but your new friend Jane Cowley is on her way over here. And she's all dressed up for the occasion."

Striding toward them is a tall woman in cowboy boots that are clomping against the wood floor all too decisively, Desirée observes. And Jane Cowley is actually a commanding figure despite her oddly chosen wardrobe, which includes jeans with the bottoms rolled up in big, graceless cuffs, and a T-shirt adorned with the image of a girl wielding a hockey stick; underneath the hockey player is the legend IT'S ALL ABOUT ATTITUDE. Jane is what Desirée's mother would call "a big girl"—broad-shouldered and bosomy. Her cool blue eyes lock with Desirée's as she approaches. Her handshake feels bone-crushing; it's nearly impossible to believe this is a woman who'd wanted to kill herself over a washed-up romance. Desirée tries—and fails—to imagine her lying on a gurney in the emergency room, her skin grayish and clammy, her breathing shallow. In her mind Jane Cowley is, instead, the college roommate hovering over the gurney, urging, "Snap out of it, girl, you know he's not worth it!"

They settle across from one another at a table in back with a small tape recorder between them. "Don't be afraid of this thing," Jane says. "Forget it's even here."

Desirée confesses that she's only been interviewed once before.

"Great!" Jane switches on the tape. "Testing, testing, *un, deux, trois,*" she says, then plays back her voice.

"It was the *New York Times,* actually."

"Really."

Though that deadpan reply reflects not a flick of surprise or interest, Desirée can't let it go. "One of my high school classmates was arrested for attempted *murder,*" she says, "and the reporter from the metro section wanted to know my impression of him."

"Whatever. Let's get started here."

Whatever? Determined to evoke a more impassioned response, Desirée tells her the story of Jake DeMaria, who, in their senior year, decided to kill his grandmother as a favor to everyone in the family, who hated the nasty old lady's guts. "So he tried to stab her to death with a carving knife at Thanksgiving dinner," Desirée says. "It was all a misunderstanding on his part, obviously. And luckily the wounds weren't deep enough and she survived the attack."

"Is that supposed to surprise me?" Jane Cowley says. "I mean, look, New York is teeming with people who need just the smallest something to send them over the edge, right? So what's new about *that?*"

"Come on, that's the broadest sort of generalization. What kind of journalist *are* you?"

"Okay, okay, mea culpa. That's Latin for 'my fault.'"

"Funny, I thought it was Latin for 'I'm pretty obnoxious,'" Desirée snaps, and it's a revelation to her that she herself is capable of boorishness, the intentional sort you just can't rein in even though you know you should. Instantly she wises up to the possibility that she may have made a serious error here—she who'd planned to be nothing less than charming and accommodating at every turn. But why is the insufferable Jane Cowley making things so difficult for her? The thought of exactly what this misbegotten interview is going to look like in print sends a quiver of fear through her. Maybe she should make her escape now before things deteriorate even further . . .

Mercifully, Jane shuts off the tape recorder. "Okeydokey," she says. "Let's get something straight—you and I are working together as a team here. So let's try our best not to alienate one another, all right?"

"I'm really a perfectly decent person," Desirée claims, realizing, to both her surprise and disgust, that she sounds just like her mother. But, like her mother, isn't she telling the truth?

"Well, so am I," Jane Cowley says.

"So we have something in common, then?"

"Absolument."

"Généralement, les gens qui savent peu parlent beaucoup, et les gens qui savent beaucoup parlent peu," Desirée says. *"Tout comprendre c'est tout pardonner."*

"Are you finished?"

But once Desirée gets in the groove, it's difficult to stop. *"C'est plus qu'un crime, c'est une faute."* And, finally, triumphantly, *"La critique est aisée, mais l'art est difficile."*

"You call that doing your best not to alienate *moi*?"

This interview may be going down in flames, but perhaps there's still a chance for Desirée to redeem herself. "Look, I think we can both agree we need a fresh start," she says.

"Whatever. I'm going to switch the tape recorder back on."

"Fire away."

. . .

LESS THAN AN HOUR later they are wrapping it up, and Desirée has hopes that, on the whole, she's come across as personable and open-minded; in short, a model tourist. She never mentions any of the unenlightened (*outrageously* unenlightened, come to think of it!) comments she's been treated to along the way these past couple of weeks, and speaks glowingly of Starshine and Dr. McVicar, describing how impressed she's been with their kindness and solicitude. "This may be a small town," she finishes, "but, um, there are some big hearts here." Though she nearly chokes on this shovelful of sentimentality, it sounds, to her ears, like something every Honey Creeker would be more than happy to hear.

"Fabulous," Jane says—in a chilly way that worries Desirée—and tosses the tape recorder into her bag.

All the sweet-talking Desirée's done has parched her throat, and her fingers have stiffened from being clenched for so long. "Jane," she says, "if you screw me in this article I just know we'll both end up sorry."

"Screw you?" Jane says. "Come on, don't get all paranoid." She pats Desirée's hand. "A little human-interest story is all I'm after. Oh, and BTW, the one thing I forgot to ask is why you decided to travel all the way here to Honey Creek."

"Well, to be honest, it just sounded like the sweetest place on earth," Desirée says shamelessly, astonished at the simpering suck-up she's become.

"Right. And are you disappointed?"

"Not in the least. Here, you can quote me: 'Honey Creek lives up to its name and then some.'"

Jane Cowley's eyes are narrowed in suspicion but she quickly gives way to laughter. "What is that, an ad for the fucking chamber of commerce?"

"What, you think New Yorkers are all big-city cynics? You have to know that's not true."

"Do I?" Jane Cowley says, then offers another of those bone-crushing handshakes before she heads for the door.

And Desirée, someone who has never basked in the limelight before, suddenly can't wait to find her way out of it.

CHAPTER 22

KINGSLEY THE STRIPPER has been falling asleep in class; not those little power naps people are so fond of these days, but for extended half-hour periods where she somehow manages to stay erect in her seat at the seminar table, while at the same time snoring lightly, her eyes firmly shut. Nina hasn't yet found the heart to wake her during these minicomas of hers, though of course this simply cannot go on. Rummaging around in her carryall bag one afternoon several hours after class, she discovers an anonymous, handwritten note—no doubt slipped there while she'd been preoccupied critiquing someone's essay.

> Anyone who sleeps in class should be
> THROWN OUT ON HER ASS.
> With the door locked behind her!

Nina can guess that the anonymous author is Davis, the student so admiring of Kingsley's descriptions of the bruises she suffered while learning to pole-dance. Admiring though he may be, he's the sole member of the class arrogant enough to have written the note, which Nina tears into pieces and pitches into her kitchen garbage, sprinkling the shreds of paper along the length of a still-fragrant, discarded banana peel. And then she sighs, because it's clear that confronting Kingsley is now absolutely unavoidable.

"GOT A MINUTE?" she asks as Kingsley rouses herself at the end of class today. "We need to talk."

"Uh-oh, are you breaking up with me? I mean, that's what my most recent ex said just before he dumped me."

Nina closes the door after the last student, and, stalling, clears the seminar table of Starbucks cups, soda cans, a crumpled, oil-smeared paper bag from Burger King, abandoned packets of duck sauce that accompanied someone's $4.99 luncheon special from Hong Kong Kitchen.

Watching her, Kingsley says, "Don't you just feel like a waitress? Really, those guys are total slobs. You should make them clean up after themselves."

She's right, but Nina doesn't say so. "You and I need to have a conversation about something important," she says, still standing at the small trash can in the corner of the room, still procrastinating; as if, in doing so, she will somehow render unnecessary what is about to become an uneasy heart-to-heart between teacher and student.

"Aren't you going to sit down, at least?" Kingsley asks her.

Perching herself at the edge of the seminar table, one leg arranged over the other, Nina finally summons the moxie to look directly into her student's sleepy, cerulean eyes. "I don't want to sound like someone's annoying mother, but you've got to get more rest, Kingsley. You just can't keep coming here and nodding off during class. You're one of the very best students I've got, and I need you awake and alert. And, by the way, it's demoralizing to all of us to see you like that."

"Hate to say it, but don't you think a lot of those guys are pretty lame?" Kingsley says. "They're what any intelligent person would have to call 'clueless.' Sometimes my roommate and I read their essays out loud to each other and it's too funny. I mean, how can you *stand* it?"

Time to put an end to the inappropriate turn this conversation has taken. But wouldn't Nina just love to agree, out loud, with much of what she's heard? "This is about *you*, Kingsley," she says. "Never mind about the rest of them. And please, *please* don't force me to ask you to officially withdraw from the class. Which I'll have to do if you continue to sleep through it."

"Look," Kingsley begins, "I work at the club from midnight to five A.M., four nights a week, and more on the weekends. I can't stay in school without the money I earn. And it's not as if I'm falling asleep because I'm bored, it's just that I'm exhausted. So don't be offended, okay? I mean, don't take it personally."

She's gazing at Nina so earnestly, so appealingly, it's impossible not to have all the sympathy in the world for her. "Can't you change your hours?" Nina says. "For at least a couple of nights a week?"

"You're kidding, right? Those are prime hours, the time when the club is really jumping. Don't you understand that I'm *lucky* to get them?"

Lucky? "What about a different sort of job altogether?" Nina says. *A job with a little more dignity.*

Now Kingsley is laughing at her. "If you can name one job besides this one where I could make seven thousand dollars on a good night, I'll quit the club in a minute." Waiting a beat, she says, "I didn't think so. And you know what else, this is the best job out there for me right now. Tons of money and lots of guys telling me how beautiful I am and how good it makes them feel just to see me. So I have to take my clothes off, so what? Big deal."

"It's *not* a big deal?" Nina says in disbelief, though she knows from Kingsley's essay exactly the way this goes.

"Fuck, no. I just think about other things while I'm dancing on the pole or sitting in some guy's lap pretending to listen while he complains about how shitty his wife is to him, how she'll only have sex with him one Saturday night a month. Every guy that comes in has some crappy, depressing story that I don't want to hear, so I just nod my head and say, *Uh-huh, baby, that's too bad,* and all the time I'm thinking about the paper I'm going to write on *Sister Carrie,* and the dry cleaning I forgot to pick up, and how much I'm looking forward to crashing in my nice cozy bed when I get home, and before you know it, the guy's hour with me in the Champagne Room is over, and he's giving me an extra five-hundred-dollar tip in cash, in addition to what he's already paid up front on his American Express, and you know what, it's a win-win situation—*he* gets what *he* wants and *I* get what *I* want. Comprende?"

No, she *doesn't* comprende. She's a little sickened and pretty dejected, worried that Kingsley's young life may already be well on the proverbial road to ruin. And she reminds herself, yet again, that Kingsley is not her daughter, that *she's* not her mother, that all of this is another family's problem, and doesn't *her* family have enough problems of their own? But she's not going to retreat, not when she's sitting here with the perfect opportunity to convince this twenty-year-old that she deserves better.

"You're very sweet to care about me," she hears Kingsley say. "And I appreciate it, but there's nothing that's going to make me change my mind. It's a business decision, you know? When I'm finished with school here, I'm going to walk away from all of this, and it'll just be one small part of my life that's over and done with. I'm not ashamed—it's just a job, right? A means to an end. I'll have socked away enough money to go on to grad school and get a doctorate in English. I'm thinking early-twentieth-century lit—James, Wharton, Dreiser. Sounds great, right?"

"Sounds great," Nina agrees. "Your wanting to pursue a doctorate, that is. As for that means to an end, Kingsley, I think it's an exercise in self-deception. What you're doing—and this is exactly what I would say to my own daughter—is unbecoming; it's beneath you. You're far too smart to be dancing naked at four in the morning for men who can't wait to stick money in your G-string."

"Can you please not insult me like that?" Kingsley's out of her seat now, gathering her backpack and bag, slipping the earbuds of her iPod in place. "Don't tell me I'm too smart. What I really am is smart enough to know a good gig when I see one."

"Enjoy your weekend," Nina calls after her vainly, disgusted with both of them, but mostly with herself for failing to properly illuminate the path Kingsley seems so hell-bent on avoiding.

CHAPTER 23

BLAME IT ON THIS DAMN headache of hers, Starshine confides, but she isn't much in the mood to take charge of her support group tonight. She does, however, have a contingency plan—one that stars Desirée, who she hopes will consider coming with her and helping out if necessary.

"Me?" Desirée's lolling on Bobby's bed listening to him play a pensive new song on his Stratocaster. Hanging with Bobby day after lazy, desultory day, she's surprised at how serene she feels, how utterly lacking in the sort of guilt that would normally plague her if she were back home and doing very little but taking pleasure in the company of someone new.

"You're perfect for the job!" Starshine shouts over the music, and gestures to Bobby to lower the amplifier on his guitar. "You've got firsthand experience with an advanced Parkinson's patient and you've got a close, personal relationship with one of his primary caregivers, i.e., your mom. If you don't know my group's aches and pains, who does?"

"Isn't this is an Alzheimer's group?"

"Even though we call it that, we've got Parkinson's caregivers, too. The day-to-day grief everyone deals with is the same, believe me."

"But you're a trained professional and I'm—"

"And you're a visiting dignitary. It just may be that you've got some new perspective we could all benefit from. And don't forget, a bridesmaid's got to be there for the bride, right?"

"You two finished?" Getting the signal from his mother that he can turn the amp back up as she leaves the room, Bobby sings, soulfully, "Hey man / there's a Post-it on the fridge / for yewww. / It says / all your rock 'n' roll dreams caaame through. / Caaame through."

Oh, that ache of longing in his voice! Desirée is actually near tears, thinking of an artillery of dissatisfied customers at the Longhorn Café in Greenville mounting a barrage of chicken bones and lemon rinds in Bobby's direction, a chair heading straight for his drummer's tender brow.

"I REALLY APPRECIATE your coming," Starshine says as she and Desirée negotiate their way up the darkened staircase to her office on Minnehaha. "I know it's a lot to ask."

They flick on the lights and Starshine hurries into the outer office while Desirée lingers in the doorway, wondering what she's got herself into. She already misses Bobby, misses the melancholy sound of his singing, that surprisingly expressive baritone of his.

"Don't be shy, Desirée. Grab a seat and start acting like you own the place."

There are a pair of vinyl couches in Starshine's inner sanctum, arranged perpendicular to each other, one inexplicably tangerine colored and the other, dark green; squeezed between the two is a cane-backed rocking chair, on its seat a black needlepoint pillow with silver stars spelling STARSHINE ROCKS!

"You can have any seat in the house except mine," Starshine says. "You like the pillow? My husband-to-be made it for me. Without help from anyone, I might add."

"Nice. What a pair of hands on the guy."

"All well and good, but what if we're not the marrying kind?" Starshine says, looking stricken. "What if we start to feel like we're suffocating, like we're literally cutting off each other's oxygen? Then what?"

"You two have had a thirty-four-year-long love affair, right?" Desirée says. "You can't possibly believe a ceremony and a marriage certificate will spoil it."

"Then what's this sick feeling in the pit of my stomach? You know, I'm just not sure I can go through with it."

"But I already have my bridesmaid dress picked out," Desirée teases, though in fact she hasn't.

Starshine smiles at her—gratefully, Desirée thinks—and settles into her rocker. Three women, fiftyish, troop in, two of them identical twins, the third looking so much like the other two that she's unmistakably their sister. All three are similarly overweight—

136

twenty pounds or so—and outfitted in pastel-colored sweatpants and white canvas Keds; their hair has been dyed the same unfortunate, overly bright shade of gold.

"Meet the Beaudine sisters," Starshine says. "Even though they've all been married for years and years, we still think of them as the Beaudines. So that's Georgia and Olive, and their older sister, Frances. Their dad's been suffering from Alzheimer's for a long while now."

"*We've* been suffering for a long while now," Frances says. "Most especially me, because I'm the one he's bunking with."

"You always have to suffer the most, Franny," one of the twins says accusingly. "Your whole life. Your kids have to be the worst in creation, your husband the laziest, your house the smallest, your—"

"Zip it, Olive. We haven't been here but one minute and already you're attacking me like the vulture you are."

"Come and sit down, ladies," Starshine says. "And meet my temporary assistant, Desirée. She's here visiting from New York City, where she . . . helps run a Parkinson's group with her mother, don't you, Desirée?"

"So they say," Desirée murmurs, amused by, and admiring of, the ease with which Starshine has fashioned a fake résumé for her and her mother.

"Welcome," Frances says. She joins Desirée on the tangerine couch while the twins pointedly choose the other one. "I saw on CNN where a little girl in New York City was killed by her stepfather—who, mind you, was also her uncle—all because she accidentally broke a glass on their kitchen floor. The stepfather-uncle smothered her with Saran Wrap and then tied shoelaces around her poor little throat just to make sure he choked the life out of her. He was, I believe, a member of the Spanish-speaking race."

"That's a tragic, sickening story all right," Desirée concedes, "but you have to know that it's an anomaly. That the city is filled with millions of law-abiding citizens, not to mention some of the world's greatest museums, the Metropolitan Opera, the—"

"Saran Wrap and shoelaces for murder weapons—what will they think of next?" Georgia interrupts.

"I'm still working on how her stepfather could be her uncle. Sounds like incest to me," Olive says.

"Sleeping with your husband's brother isn't incest," explains Starshine. "It's just sleeping with your brother-in-law. And you know what, you ladies are making my headache worse than it already is."

"You have a headache? So do I," Frances says.

"That's because you're just a big old hypochondriac," says Olive.

"Well, *you* try living with an Alzheimer's patient day in and day out for three years and seven and a half months and see how healthy *you* feel," Frances says bitterly.

The twins exchange a look; apparently they've heard it all before and remain unimpressed. "How many times do we have to tell you," Georgia says, "if you can't stand the heat, put him in the nursing home."

"Two, three weeks in that nursing home and he'll fold up and die," Frances says. "Is that what you girls want?"

"Now, what I'm gonna say isn't pretty," Georgia begins, "but it's the truth: if he dies, he dies, and so be it. He's eighty-six years old, he's got no mind left to speak of, he drinks Sunlight dish detergent straight from the—"

"Hold that thought," Starshine says as the outer door opens and shuts. "Here's the rest of our little group and not a moment too soon."

"Sorry we're late," says the younger of the two men, who has a graying crew cut, and a heart-shaped tattoo on his upper arm with the name "Tuffy" inscribed in it.

"I wasn't ready when he came by for me," his friend confesses. His eyes look troubled and his slender shoulders appear permanently slumped. Around his neck is a bolo tie fastened with a polished turquoise-and-silver clasp, worn, perhaps, to brighten that Sad Sack look of his.

"Introductions," Starshine says, and then Desirée is shaking hands with Rusty Wallis, the older man, who tips an imaginary hat and takes a seat next to her; Jimmie Johnson simply nods in her direction.

"I got a cousin living in West New York, New Jersey," Jimmie says. "A gravedigger, as a matter of fact."

"Any man what digs graves for a living has got to be a funny duck. Gives me the shivers just to think of it," Rusty says.

"I'd rather be digging graves than packing paper sacks like you do at the Kum and Go, Rusty."

"That's just part-time," Rusty says. "After I sold the farm and Helen took sick with the Parkinson's, I had to do *something*, had to spend time with people who could at least answer me when I talk to them."

"Why don't you tell us how you've been coping lately, Rusty," Desirée is startled to hear herself say. As if she's some budding young therapist or social worker, someone who knows just how to encourage a distressed old man to unburden himself.

Rusty stares hard at her. "Am I supposed to know who you are, young lady?"

"She's my assistant tonight," Starshine explains.

But this doesn't quite satisfy Rusty. "She's a stranger," he says. "I don't tell strangers my personal private business. And besides, she's too young to hear what I got to say."

"She's a dear friend of mine," Starshine says. "She's going to be a bridesmaid at my wedding. You can speak freely in front of her, Rusty. Let's not forget that anything that's said in this room by any one of you is regarded as absolutely confidential."

"Your *wedding*?" the Beaudine twins chorus.

"You and Wayne are getting a *divorce*?" Frances says.

"And here I thought the two of you made such a beautiful couple," Georgia says.

"So who's the lucky guy?" Olive asks.

"And what about poor Wayne?"

"It's poor Wayne and I who are getting married," Starshine says, smiling.

"You're renewing your vows?" Frances says. "After all those years? That's *so* sweet!"

"Nope, we're not renewing anything. It's a first for us."

It takes a long moment for this to sink in, before Frances says,

"I have to tell you I can hardly believe what I'm hearing, Starshine! It's a huge shock, is all."

"You think they'll go to hell?" Rusty muses. "And if Dr. McVicar has been dipping his fingers in sin all these years, I don't know if I want him working on my fillings and such."

Ah yes, SIN IS A CANCER TO ALL PEOPLE! *And don't you forget it,* Desirée thinks.

"Oh, don't be a jerk, Rusty. He's the best dentist in town," Jimmie Johnson says. "And what's a marriage license, when you get down to it, but a piece of paper?"

"Well, you're all invited to the wedding," says Starshine. "A couple of weeks from now in my backyard, weather permitting."

"What kind of food you serving? I could make my five-layer salad," Olive volunteers. "Even if it's for the wedding of two people who've been living in sin right under our noses."

"Living in sin"—to Desirée, these words are from an alien and mystifying vocabulary. The very notion is laughable, really, or would be, if it weren't so chilling. She can well imagine the horror with which Olive would recoil if she knew of her father's living arrangement with Loverboy. Not that Desirée herself has offered them her warmest wishes. But hasn't that ice-cold bit of her heart finally begun to thaw? She doesn't want to be thought of as a person, a daughter, who will not give an inch. Maybe the time has come, at last, to give her father the call he's been waiting for. Maybe later. Tonight. Tomorrow. Soon.

"Oh, quit being such a drip," Frances chides her sister. "I've been thinking who cares, really, after all this time?"

Rusty's hand shoots up. "*I* do," he says. "You read your Bible lately? Two unmarried people lying together is fornication, right? Well, you can't argue with the Bible, not if you want to be a good Christian, anyway."

"I'm quite sure," Starshine says, "that Helen wouldn't be proud to hear you talking like that, Rusty."

"The truth is, they're warming up a seat in hell for me, too," Rusty reports, his voice all at once impassive, his eyes, as Desirée turns toward him, glassy.

"Oh?" Starshine says.

"Sometimes doing something very, very bad, something *terrible,* is the only way to make things right."

Sliding to the edge of her chair, Starshine leans forward, and clasps her hands together on the old man's knee. "What's going on, Rusty?" she says gently.

"I'm probably going to have to tell the sheriff, anyway, so I might as well tell you, too." There's a bit of throat-clearing, and then he begins, "Well, you know Helen and I got together all the way back when we were eighteen. I promised to be a good husband and I was. Maybe I made her cry now and again, but I never did say or do anything I was ashamed of. Not even tonight, you got to understand that. And today was Helen's birthday, her seventy-seventh. But her whole body was so rigid from the Parkinson's, she couldn't move from the bed. We had store-bought birthday cake and it was a little dry, so I mixed some water in with a teaspoon of cake for her since she couldn't swallow anything anymore." Rusty seems submerged in a trance now, his body inert, except for his mouth, which, like a ventriloquist's, appears to scarcely move at all.

"There were crumbs on her lips," he continues expressionlessly, "and I wiped them off and kissed her. And then I helped her swallow down a whole lot of her pills all mashed up and that took a long, long time. And after that I tied a plastic bag around her head, just to make sure."

The room has fallen into a silence so vast, Desirée can hear the ticking of her pulse, the blood in her veins rushing toward her heart.

"Just like that animal in New York," Frances murmurs. "The member of the Spanish-speaking race."

"I stayed with her until it was done. I took away the plastic bag and held my hand up to her mouth and then I knew for sure she'd stopped breathing. Afterwards I brushed her hair because she wouldn't have wanted anyone to see it mussed up, not even me."

"You're a good husband," whispers Starshine, patting his knee encouragingly, as if he were a very young child who has completed the simple task assigned him.

The twins are weeping quietly; Jimmie Johnson's mouth flaps open in pure astonishment.

Over the course of a fortnight, Desirée has borne witness to a marriage proposal and the confession of a mercy killer; it feels as if she's been sitting in the audience of a TV talk show where one guest after another is so easily persuaded to bare his soul to twenty million unseen viewers.

Her arm finds its way now across Rusty's sagging shoulders and he makes no effort to shake her off.

"I'm going to jail, aren't I?" he says in that eerily detached voice.

"Not if *I* can help it," Starshine says. "But I do have a legal obligation to call 911 to report the death, Rusty, and to have someone from the funeral home come for her."

The room is starting to return to life; people are shifting in their seats, skimming their fingertips along the damp planes of their cheekbones, blowing their noses, some delicately, some vigorously. Rusty's shoulders have warmed under Desirée's arm. She's afraid to move, fearful that if she lifts her arm, Rusty will slip away from her and into danger. Under the fluorescent light fixture resembling an old-fashioned metal ice-cube tray, his white hair looks tinged with a pitiful yellow.

"We're coconspirators. We're sitting around here doing nothing when we should be doing *something*. Jesus, we could all go to jail!" Olive warns.

"Like I said, zip it," Frances tells her sister.

"He KILLED her, for God's sake! Am I the only one here who's heard of a little list called the Ten Commandments?"

"'On Christ the solid Rock I stand / all other ground is sinking sand,'" Georgia, the other twin, sings sweetly.

"Seems to me," says Jimmie Johnson, "that if Rusty didn't exactly do the right thing, he didn't exactly do the wrong thing, either. He did what he had to do, and he did it for Helen."

"Some birthday present. Death by overdose and suffocation," Olive notes.

"Maybe they'll let him off with a suspended sentence and a hundred hours of community service," Desirée says hopefully. Though she wonders if she's fooling herself with misplaced optimism here in what is evidently the Bible Belt. *And evidently no place for a Jew. Or even half a Jew.*

"Without an autopsy they can't prove a thing," Starshine points out. "Look, she was a sick, elderly woman who died at home. What's so suspicious about that?"

"It's what-do-you-call-it, euthanasia, and it's plum wrong," Olive says. "Do you really think it's okay to go around killing all the sick people we feel sorry for?"

"It's not your place to be passing judgment. What he did is between him and Helen," Frances says. "And what *you* think counts for less than nothing, Olive."

"My conscience tells me I need to speak up."

"Well, tell your conscience to mind its own goddamn business, how's that?"

"Excuse me," Starshine says. "Remember the confidentiality rule here, folks."

"If I go to jail," Rusty says, "I won't have to cook for myself. I'd sure appreciate that."

"You're not going to jail," Jimmie Johnson tells him. "Because no one in this room is going to rat on you."

"Don't count on it. All I need is to whip out my cell phone and I'm on my way," Olive says. And short of a miracle or natural disaster, Desirée sees, she's going to make that phone call.

Underneath Desirée's outstretched arm, Rusty's shoulder twitches, a small shudder of fear, thanks to the zealousness of his civic-minded neighbor. Desirée imagines flying home to discover that her mother has taken a page from Rusty's book and put an end to her grandfather's suffering. And consequently, Nina's own—on *that* score, anyway—as well. But it's a grotesque fantasy that her imagination just can't sustain. And yet isn't it perfectly understandable for her mother to occasionally indulge in this sort of daydream? Though even if her grandfather begged them to hasten his death, Nina is far too much of a coward, she's willing to bet, as is Desirée herself. But here's Rusty, brave as can be, convinced he's going to hell one way or another and wholly willing to pay his dues.

Olive's cell phone is fired up now, her stubby thumbs tapping the key pad.

"You're shaming the Beaudines forever!" Frances calls out, followed by Georgia, who yells, "You always *were* the biggest tattletale, Olive, even when we were kids!"

"Yeah, Olive, can't you show a little compassion?" Starshine adds.

"Everyone shut the fuck up right *now*!" a man's voice says; clearly he means business.

Desirée knows it has taken less than an instant for everyone present to recognize that this is one of those heart-stopping moments where a condensed version of your life is about to pass before you as you silently impart a few desperately quick, but deeply felt, good-byes to your loved ones.

"Oh shit," Jimmie Johnson says.

The intruder, tall and beefy in jeans and an army-green T-shirt, a backpack drooping from one shoulder, has a *Silence of the Lambs*–inspired Hannibal Lecter mask pulled over his face, and a pistol in hand, which he aims in the general direction of his audience as he moves toward the center of the room. "Saw your light on and thought I'd stop by for a visit," he explains, sounding almost sociable now, despite the horrifying face he presents—beneath thick brows, and marble eyes set into wrinkly latex flesh, there's a face guard with a metal cage over an ugly, open mouth.

"This is a support group," Starshine says. Her voice is a tremulous, high-pitched chirp. "Specifically for caregivers of Alzheimer's and Parkinson's patients. Is there something we can do for you?"

"Kinda running low on cash," the man says. "Otherwise I'm good, thanks."

"And have you . . . engaged in this sort of . . . activity previously?" Starshine asks.

"What's it to you?"

"Can't help wondering if you have a long history, or if this is a one-time thing."

"What are you, a shrink or something?" the guy says suspiciously. "Just hand over your wallets and cell phones and I'll let you get back to your sweet little support group."

"Are you going to shoot us afterward?" Rusty says.

"Quiet!" Desirée hisses. Her heart is going at warp speed and she can hear her mother's voice saying, *See what happens? See what happens when you leave home for no good reason at all and go someplace where you simply don't belong?* Oh, she hates to think of herself lying lifeless in a dark pool of her own blood so far from home, the stories in her notebook still raw and in need of burnishing, her books yet to be written, her budding relationship with Bobby McVicar a big question mark. All that unfinished business and her parents arguing over the appropriate cemetery plot—his place or hers?

"Why? Do you *want* me to shoot you?" the gunman is saying to Rusty.

"He just lost his wife and he's terribly . . . disoriented," Starshine explains.

"Sorry to hear it. Wallets and cell phones, people. Any of you got fourteen-carat gold jewelry on you?"

"Here's my earrings," Georgia offers; her twin does the same.

"Toss it right this way, fat stuff," the gunman addresses Frances.

"If you shoot me I won't hold it against you. I'm going to jail anyhow," Rusty says.

"Huh, whadja do, cheat on your taxes?"

"He killed his wife," Olive volunteers. "Though of course it was one of those mercy killings."

"No shit!"

"Could you *please* put that gun away," Starshine says. "It's making us all very, very nervous."

"Well, that's kinda the point," the guy says, but he shoves the gun into the waistband of his jeans, the pitch-black hand grip sticking out prominently.

Starshine thanks him, then adds, "I'd really like to know your name, sir. Not your real name, of course, I wouldn't expect that."

"That's good, because you're not gonna get it. You can call me Angel, though."

"I bet armed robbery isn't really your thing at all, Angel," Starshine says, wooing him. "I bet that right now you're wishing you'd asked your family for a loan instead, am I right?"

Apparently Angel doesn't feel the need to dignify with an

answer what he regards as an idiotic question. "Will you hurry up with those wallets and cells? I don't have all night," he says.

"So tell me about your family," Starshine urges.

"I want to know why that poor old bastard over there killed his wife."

"She was sick with the Parkinson's," Rusty says, while the group pitches their wallets and phones into the center of the woolly, tasseled rug. "Couldn't walk, couldn't talk, couldn't eat, couldn't move."

"You're messing with the Lord's business there," Angel says disapprovingly. "You know, what the Lord giveth, the Lord taketh away? You got no call to take a life like that, dude. You're going to the slammer for sure."

Hearing Angel quoting from the Scriptures, the support group seems to relax a bit; Angel is unlikely, Desirée senses, to mess with the Lord's business himself. And now she has a free moment to mourn the loss of her all-important, candy-bar-sized BlackBerry, upon which, in addition to making and receiving phone calls, she checks her e-mail, listens to music (arrgh—the thought of the dozens of songs she'd downloaded!), takes pictures, and, of course, surfs the Web. Robbed of all of this, how is she going to survive?

"My wallet's got but five dollars in it," Rusty apologizes. "You going to be mad at me for that?"

"The thing that makes me mad, dude, is that you offed your wife. You shouldn'ta done that." Kneeling to the floor, Angel sorts through the wallets in an unaccountably leisurely way, examining family snapshots and commenting on them as he tosses them at his feet. "Cute kids," he says. "Especially this one in the cowboy hat."

"That's my grandson," Frances says. "He's six this past May."

"Well, better keep an eye on him so he doesn't turn out like *me*," Angel recommends, and snickers. But he begins cruelly tearing up the pictures as soon as he looks them over, ostensibly unhappy with the measly bucks he's collected and which he is now busy stuffing into his backpack along with the cell phones. He's hit the jackpot, though, when he picks up Desirée's wallet, which has nearly two hundred dollars remaining in it, pristine twenties straight from the ATM across the street from her apartment in the city. "Excellent!" Angel says, and ostentatiously shows off the bills in his fist. "Hey, who's the one with all the dough? Raise your hand so I know who you are."

"Me," Desirée squeaks, and raises a trembling index finger in the air.

"So how come you're the only one with the big bucks?"

"She's from New York City," Frances says helpfully.

"Yeah? So what's it like living in a godless place overflowing with hookers and pervs and murderers?" the armed robber wants to know.

"Why would you say something like that?" Desirée asks, as if she were addressing anyone at all and not the one person in the room equipped to blow her to bits. "I don't know where you're getting your information from, *Angel,* but that's just the grossest distortion."

"Desirée?" says Starshine, frowning. "Let it go."

But she can't; she's heard this sort of talk all too frequently over the past few weeks, and she's had it up to here with diplomacy, with employing every ounce of tact and savoir faire she can manage to summon. And if there is any possibility she's going to get it between the eyes right here and now, why not go down defending her home? "I'm sick of people badmouthing what's arguably the greatest city in the world," she says, recklessly mounting the soapbox she's tried so hard to avoid ever since her arrival in town. "Where, for your information, I've never been robbed at gunpoint. So what would you think if I went back East and started a blog just to let everyone know that Honey Creek is nothing but a two-bit town of small-minded, Bible-thumping, self-righteous, Jew-hating John Birchers? Would that be an accurate picture or a gross distortion?"

"Gee, I don't know," Jimmie Johnson says. He scratches absently at his "Tuffy" tattoo. "I never gave it much thought, but now that you mention it . . ."

"What's a blog?" Olive says.

"Yeah, what is it?" her twin asks. "Whatever it is, it sounds real ugly."

Angel yanks the pistol from his pants, rising from the floor and aiming the gun at Jimmie Johnson. "You with the big mouth, shut it, and you, the chick from New York, if you don't like it here, leave. But don't go telling folks back home nasty shit about the people here. Because mostly everyone here's good people. Or good enough, anyway."

"And that would include *you*?" Starshine says.

"Fuck yeah! At least most of the time."

"So what went wrong today?"

"Today's been kind of sucky all day," Angel reflects. "You know, you get up, you look in the mirror, you don't like what you see. Then it turns out your roommate used up the last three eggs in the fridge, the ones you were counting on to make an Egg McMuffin. And then your boss at Business Cards Tomorrow calls you an incorrigible slacker and tells you to take a hike. And your girlfriend hasn't had sex with you in four days because she's . . ."

So hidden behind the creepy, terrifying Hannibal Lecter mask is one more ordinary loser, albeit one desperate enough to brandish a semiautomatic before a roomful of frightened people. Desirée feels, momentarily, something approaching pity for him; as he turns his head, she notices the smooth, pale skin at the back of his neck left unconcealed by the mask. For the first time she considers how old he might be—twenty-five? Thirty? Even older? She wonders, too, if he is already feeling a pinch of guilt and remorse, or if he's high on the near-certainty that he's about to successfully pull off a modest little robbery. And now she's moving past that split second of empathy, offering up a prayer that he take his sad, dangerous self along with her two hundred bucks and disappear.

"We've all had days like that," Starshine is saying. "Haven't we? Put your hand up if you've had a day like that recently." This isn't a request, it's an order, and obediently everyone raises their hands. Save for Rusty, who seems to have nodded out in all the excitement. "Now that ought to be of some consolation to you," Starshine says soothingly. "Am I right, Angel?"

"Yeah, yeah, whatever."

"My advice to you is to put the gun away, gather up your loot, and make a run for it."

"Yeah, I'm out of here," Angel says, shouldering his loaded backpack.

"One more word of advice, if I may?" Starshine says. "The next time you feel the urge to commit armed robbery, think how you'll feel about it the morning after."

"Happy as a pig in shit?"

Starshine sighs. " 'Guilty and deeply ashamed' is more like what I had in mind."

"Sorry to disappoint you." And then Angel is gone, thumping down the wooden stairs and into the getaway car, which the support group can hear squealing sharply in the warm, still night beyond the windows of Starshine's office.

It is only now that he has vanished that Desirée allows herself to acknowledge the sheer terror that has transformed her into such a sodden mess—sweat-drenched, sticky, her pulse out of control, her mouth parched and sandy, her bare feet swimming in perspiration in her leather flats, her thong pasted to her flesh as if fastened with liquid adhesive.

"I don't know about the rest of you, but I almost peed my pants," one of the twins confesses.

"Somebody has got to call 911," Starshine says. "There's the phone on the desk in the outer office."

"I have to tell you I'd been thinking about quitting this support group of ours," Jimmie Johnson admits. "But now we've finally got something interesting to talk about, so I ain't goin' nowhere."

"Say again?" Rusty requests.

"I said, WE FINALLY GOT SOMETHING INTERESTING TO TALK ABOUT!"

"And I've got to get me a lawyer."

It's this that propels Desirée out of her seat and over to the landline that Angel had carelessly overlooked. She dials 911 for the first time in her life and it feels momentous; even without the improbable news of how Rusty has spent his wife's birthday, the operator at the other end is spellbound. Desirée has made her day.

"Post-traumatic stress disorder?" she hears Starshine say. "Oh God, as if we don't have enough to worry about."

Hanging up the phone, Desirée has, she discovers, an honest-to-God desire to speak to her mother, to tell her that there's nothing that can set you straight like having a semiautomatic waving nearly in your face. Nothing that can more powerfully inspire you to be a sweeter, kinder, more loving and compassionate version of yourself—to be, in fact, the sort of devoted daughter who might even go so far as to accept that the love of her father's life is a forty-something guy with a gold hoop suspended stylishly from the tip of his ear, a guy who deserves better than to be called "Loverboy" behind his back. Hard to say what her mother will make of this new, improved daughter of hers. And whether Desirée herself can get with the program and actually stick with it. Or whether, like her mother on the low-fat, low-salt diet she dispensed with after a couple of months, Desirée's good intentions will come to nothing at all.

CHAPTER 24

NINA IS DEEPLY IMMERSED in a dream whose meaning is so apparent, even her dream-self understands it perfectly: she's driven alone to the house in which she and her younger (and perhaps smarter, or at least more ambitious) sister were raised on Long Island, but the house is no longer there. The generous-sized colonials adjacent to it, left and right, are still standing, but her family's home has vanished. In its place is an empty half-acre lot with wildly overgrown grass and a solitary poplar tree drooping forlornly. Nina thinks of calling her sister, Caroline, in Santa Monica to tell her the news, but when she digs into her bag beside her on the front seat of her parents' sleek, '72 Buick Riviera—the car in which her mother had ferried her and Caroline to their piano and tennis lessons—she discovers her cell phone is missing. And yet there's a phone ringing, loud and insistent; she can't figure out where the sound is coming from. Rising through what feels like endless depths of water, she reaches a state of half wakefulness, and extends her hand to the landline at her bedside. "What?" she says into the phone, and it occurs to her, but only in the vaguest way, that she should be worried, terrified, even, by the middle-of-the-night sound of a ringing telephone. Though when she studies the numbers on the clock radio, she sees that it is, in fact, early morning; 5:32, an ungodly hour any way you look at it. And though the voice she hears speaking to her now is vaguely familiar, it does not, thankfully, belong to her daughter.

"*What?*" she repeats. "Slow down, I can't understand a word you're saying."

"It's Kingsley," the voice says. "Your student?"

"But how did you get my number?"

"You gave it to us on the contact sheet for the class. Don't you remember?"

Ah, the all-important contact sheet listing the cell phone

numbers for every one of her students, so Nina can hunt them down when they fail to respond to her e-mail messages inquiring about absences and missing and late assignments. "I'm pretty sure I didn't mean for you to be calling me at five-thirty in the morning, Kingsley," she says, but is so relieved this isn't Desirée at the other end, she's actually smiling.

"I'm at the ER at Lenox Hill," Kingsley explains, "waiting for them to take a look at what I'm pretty sure is my fractured nose."

"Oh, Kingsley!" Sitting up in bed now in the dark, Nina says, "What happened? Are you all right?"

"Yes. I mean, no." She sounds weepy as she says, "I can't talk about it, okay? Not now, anyway."

Nina thinks for a moment, then realizes that she's been summoned. "You're alone, aren't you? Do you want me to come to the ER?"

"I wish I didn't, but I do," Kingsley admits. "You can take a cab and I'll pay you back, I promise."

As if she would ever take money from a student. Even a student who, like Kingsley, might just happen to pull in a cool seven thousand on her best night.

"Thank you soo, soo much, Professor Cohen," Kingsley is saying, sounding like an ordinary girl as her gratitude gushes sweetly through the phone.

SLUMPED IN A PLASTIC CHAIR, both her eyes blackened, her nose a swollen mess, nostrils encrusted with russet blood, Kingsley greets her with a simple "Hey."

Nina takes a seat beside her, close to tears at the sight of her poor battered student. "What *happened* to you?" she says. There are only a handful of other people in the ER's waiting room, a surprisingly small area with a TV screen suspended from the ceiling and a woman in hospital greens installed behind a glass partition.

"I did something totally stupid," Kingsley confesses.

"Oh my motherfuckin' God!" a man seated nearby says gleefully, cell phone held to his ear. "She definitely know the meanin' of the word 'tube top,' that for sure."

"You can tell me," Nina says, and strokes Kingsley's thin, bare shoulder exposed by her flimsy tank top. "You're freezing," she says. "Here, take my sweater."

"Don't you be tellin' me she wasn't there, Jayden," the man on the cell phone says, the inflection of his voice darkening. "I watched her ass goin' in and I watched her ass goin' out."

Nina arranges her shapeless, stretched-out black cardigan around Kingsley's shoulders. "Who did this to you?" she says.

Across the room, a little boy, asleep with his head in his mother's lap, stirs.

"Well, there was this totally cute guy in the Champagne Room with me tonight. Younger than the usual customers. And so cute—he looked like, um, Jake Gyllenhaal. And he was wealthy, too, he was wearing a Patek Philippe watch, it cost, I don't know, maybe thirty-two thousand dollars, and we had such a good time in the Champagne Room that when he asked me to meet him at his apartment after work, I said yes, something I've never, ever done before. And he sent his driver for me, just like he said he would."

"Oh, Kingsley," Nina says for the second time.

"Park and Eighty-third Street, luxury neighborhood, right? And he's a lawyer in a Wall Street firm, he gave me his business card. His apartment was a duplex, with a spiral staircase, and a hot tub in the bathroom. He did a line or two of coke, but drugs aren't my thing, so I didn't, I just watched him snort. And that's when he tells me he's into S and M, which I completely had no idea about, because when we were in the Champagne Room, all I did, of course, were some lap dances, and then some regular slow dancing with him, nothing kinky at all. So obviously I told him I wouldn't do that shit, and that I had to leave, had to go home, and he totally freaks, he punches me in the face, really hard right there in his amazing bedroom with a hidden TV that you push a button, and it rises up out of a credenza and onto the wall. And after he punches me, he *spits* at me. In my face, which was horrible, the biggest fuck-you there is." Despite her battered face and stricken look as she recalls the warm saliva clouding her eye, Kingsley is still, Nina sees, unduly impressed with that fancy television set. "And so I ran out of there, and the doorman was very sweet and gave me some paper towels for all the blood and got a cab for me, and told the driver to take me to the closest hospital."

If this were Desirée, Nina would be embracing her now, horrified, anxious, disgusted, mystified. And guilt-riddden, because how could a smart young girl like Desirée, raised so lovingly, end up like this? And what Nina actually feels at this moment is all of these sentiments, minus the guilt, when she casts her arm across Kingsley and says, "You're finished with this business, do you understand me?" But beneath her arm, she can feel Kingsley shrug, a shrug that says, *Maybe, maybe not.*

"I can't allow you to ruin your life," Nina says, but even *she* knows that she's gone too far, that she's trespassed into territory she has no business crossing.

WHEN, AN HOUR OR SO LATER, Kingsley reappears in the waiting room after being treated, Nina is watching, fascinated, as a clip from CNN shows a middle-aged Indian woman named Mata Amritanandamayi, dispensing hugs and Hershey's Kisses to fifteen thousand of her followers in a Manhattan convention center. "Amma the hugging saint," as she is fondly known, has, in fact, hugged twenty-seven million of her followers, the CNN anchor reports briskly. Donations, plus sales of DVDs of Amma chanting, have raised millions of dollars for her charities.

"So even saints have their own DVDs," Kingsley observes. "What the fuck is *that* all about?" There's a single, Band-Aid-sized piece of adhesive tape fastened across the bridge of her nose, and white packing plugged into her nostrils; one eye is now swollen shut, the other only partially closed.

"Let's get you home," Nina says, rising from her vinyl seat and taking Kingsley's arm. But immediately she corrects herself, adding, "I meant, *my* home. You'll stay for a couple of days, all right? Just until you're feeling better." She's expecting an argument from Kingsley, perhaps a halfhearted one, but Kingsley simply nods, offering a whispery "thank you."

They take a cab downtown to the Village; Nina waits in the

backseat while Kingsley collects clothing for the next few days from her apartment. She lives above a place called Dean's Doggy Day Care; Nina can see, in the storefront, signage promising customers cardio workouts for their dogs, along with a course teaching basic manners and a cure for "seperation" anxiety.

"Do you have a dog in day care?" she asks when Kingsley gets back into the cab.

"What? Oh, *that* place? Assholes—Dean himself especially," Kingsley says, and then is silent. A few blocks later she is asleep, her head occasionally bumping against Nina's shoulder.

At home, Nina leads her—without introduction or explanation—past Marvin and Porsha having their breakfast in the kitchen, and gets her settled in Desirée's bed. Then she walks across the street to CVS, where she fills Kingsley's prescription for Percocet, charging it to her own MasterCard. Despite the four hours of sleep she'd racked up before being awakened by Kingsley's phone call, she's dead tired, and can scarcely grab hold of the plastic stylus to sign her signature on the credit card screen. She thinks of the saintly Amma; the mere notion of the effort expended on those twenty-seven million hugs makes Nina herself feel close to collapse.

But upon her return from the drugstore, learning that Desirée called just a few minutes earlier from her motel room, Nina phones her back immediately.

"Mommy!" Desirée says, and because she hasn't been addressed this way in years (just plain "Mom" being Desirée's preference), Nina instantly knows that something is wrong.

"Talk to me, pussycat," she says. Even though what she hears from the other end is terribly disturbing, how heartening it is, how deeply gratifying, to know that when things took a sorry turn, her daughter reached for her, wanting the simple consolations of that old standby, good, old-fashioned maternal love.

"Just come home, pussycat," Nina says, hearing about that brandished pistol, the stolen wallet and BlackBerry, and, as an afterthought, an ugly little something about the John Birch Society. "Come home," she repeats.

Come home? No way.

It's love, apparently, but not the soothing kind that flows so naturally from mother to daughter. It's that other kind—torrid, scorching, and not to be denied.

"PLEASE DON'T GO," Daniel is saying, coming up behind Nina, embracing her gently as she admires the view of the Empire State Building from his bedroom window high above downtown Brooklyn. Both she and Daniel are naked in the dark; Nina savors the icy breeze of the air conditioner on her thighs, and the feel of Daniel's arms at her waist, his bony knees at the backs of her legs, his chin resting on her shoulder. He's only the second man (and the first completely straight one!) she's ever slept with; having done so for the very first time tonight, she can't help but regard the act itself as something momentous. And yet she can't really say that he's a more skillful, more attentive, or more desirable lover than Patrick, who, in his gentle way, knew well how to satisfy her. What her memory has come away with tonight is the citrusy smell of Daniel's deodorant (whose silly, long-winded name—"Gillette triple protection system cool wave"—she knows because he'd carelessly left it on top of the toilet tank) and also the faint cinnamon aroma of his breath as he ardently explored her mouth, her neck, her cleavage, her breasts.

She's forty-five years old, but feeling, if not exactly adolescent, well, not exactly middle-aged, either. Not a day over thirty!

"I *have* to go home," she tells Daniel. "What will Kingsley think when she wakes up tomorrow morning and I'm not there? I mean, she knows I had a date tonight."

Daniel is laughing at her, swiveling her around so that they're face-to-face, his thick, out-of-control hair backlit by the lights beyond the window. "You're out of your mind," he says. "You're worried about what a *stripper* thinks of you?"

"I'm worried about what one of my *students* thinks of me," she corrects him.

"Shouldn't have taken her in, then. Not that I blame you for having a tender heart and all that."

"You should have seen what she looked like that night in the ER."

Sushi, Daniel's Siamese cat, takes a flying leap toward the windowsill, his tail skimming the side of Nina's neck mid-flight. While she and Daniel were making love, Nina had opened her eyes to see Sushi at the foot of the bed, licking his paw industriously and, perhaps, passing judgment. She'd wondered, just for a moment, exactly how many women the cat had seen and heard in Daniel's bedroom since his divorce. And how she herself might have measured up to them. And then thought, *What does it matter?* She may be one of many Daniel's had here, but she's here now and happier than she's been in a long while.

"Come back to bed," Daniel says, and leads her there by the hand.

IN THE MORNING, she squeezes toothpaste onto the tip of her index finger and slides it across her teeth, top and bottom. She declines Daniel's offer of frozen waffles and microwaved soy bacon, but is happy to accept his juicy, impassioned farewell kiss at the elevator.

"We'll see each other soon," he promises. "Tomorrow night? Maybe another movie?"

"Maybe," she says with a smile, and on the subway ride back to Manhattan, finds herself smiling at everything and nothing.

An ordinary-looking guy holding on to the pole in front of her suddenly leans forward and says, conspiratorially, "You know, they've got light bulbs that can cure every kind of cancer. I saw them advertised on late-night TV, I swear." A teenaged father, jeans sagging nearly to his knees, clutches what looks like a newborn in a plastic baby carrier. His eyes meet Nina's, and he winks at her, amused, no doubt, to contemplate the possibility of those cancer-curing light bulbs.

Nina's in such good spirits, in fact, that when she arrives home and discovers that Kingsley has taken her father to the park so that Porsha can catch up on a couple of loads of laundry, she lets it go. And doesn't say to Porsha, as she might have, *What were you* thinking?

"She's a nice smart girl," Porsha says, "and when she offered to take Grandpa, I just ran and got the laundry together."

"Not to worry," Nina says lightly, even a bit cavalierly, enjoying the unlikely image of her septuagenarian father sunning himself in Central Park under the watchful gaze of a high-priced stripper.

HELPING NINA WITH THE DISHES after dinner tonight, drying a skillet, a colander, and a brightly colored plastic mixing bowl at the sink, Kingsley announces that she's going home. "It's been almost a week," she says, "and really, I'm fine."

Nina is going to feel her absence, she realizes; not that Kingsley has temporarily taken Desirée's place, of course, but still Nina has been warmed by her company—their nightly Scrabble games, their discussions about David Foster Wallace and Jonathan Franzen, Kingsley's favorite contemporary authors, and about *Sister Carrie*, a subject she missed during the days she took off from school to recuperate. And Nina will not forget the sight of Kingsley shuffling off to the bathroom in her flip-flops and boys' long-sleeved, tattersall pajamas, toothbrush in hand, looking remarkably ordinary—unworldly, even—for someone who earns a damn good living performing at a midtown strip club.

"Are you sure?" Nina says. "Because you're welcome to stay longer."

"I even think I look okay enough to go back to work," Kingsley says, examining her reflection in the skillet's gleaming silvery cover before placing it in the drying rack.

Nina shuts off the faucet, sheds her rubber gloves. "You can't be serious."

"Why? The black and blue is basically gone, my face is hardly swollen anymore. A little bit of concealer and I'm good to go."

"Sit down," Nina orders. And half expects Kingsley to bolt from the room.

"Can I smoke?"

"Pot?"

Kingsley smiles. "Just a stupid cigarette," she says, and tosses a pack of American Spirit and a zebra-striped plastic lighter onto the kitchen table.

"Don't tell anyone," Nina says.

"What? That you let me smoke at your kitchen table or that you let me stay here for almost a week?"

"Both," Nina says.

Holding up one hand, palm facing forward, Kingsley says, "I do solemnly swear to keep my mouth shut. And I'll do a better job of it than Elaina Whitacre, who told me something she promised you she wouldn't tell anyone." She sits down, slings her arm across the back of her chair, cigarette courteously aimed toward the floor to keep the smoke away from Nina. "You know, the thing about you and your husband?"

Nina's face floods with heat. She considers asking if Elaina has told anyone else, then realizes she doesn't want to know the answer to that.

"But Elaina swore to me she didn't have any friends in the class," she says stupidly.

"Oh, she doesn't. She e-mailed me about an assignment, and then, after I helped her, sent me a P.S. that said, 'BTW, did you know Cohen was married to a gay guy?' I didn't bother to respond. I mean, why would I? And who cares, really? You want to know about shitty marriages? My father's been cheating on my mother in an insanely big way for years—he has a girlfriend he bought a condo for in Beacon Hill, but guess what, he cheated on the girlfriend, too." Smoke shooting in an acrid stream from the side of her lipsticked mouth, Kingsley says, "Like I care, right?"

"Your father paid for his girlfriend's condo but won't pay your tuition? What kind of family do you come from?" Nina allows herself to finally ask.

"He wanted me to go to Stanford, his alma mater, but I wanted to be in New York, so no deal. Do you have an ashtray for me?"

"Do you really need to smoke?" Nina says, but takes a saucer out of the cupboard for her to use. "What about your mother? Couldn't *she* try to convince him?"

According to Kinsgley, her mother suffers from clinical depression and has spent time in some very expensive mental health facilities in the suburbs of Boston. "Oh, and she doesn't let me call her 'Mom.' I have to call her 'Grace' instead."

"Grace? Even when you were a child?" Nina says, aghast.

"No, no, only after I went away to Exeter. That first year, when I came back for Thanksgiving, she told me I had to stop calling her 'Mom,' because it was just too depressing for her. No biggie— it's just a word, a name, right?"

Nina can't even look at her. She thinks about Dr. Pepperkorn, about what he would say if Kingsley were sitting in his small, no-frills office right now. *And has it occurred to you that your mother's and father's grievous failures as parents have damaged your sense of self? And led you to seek attention and admiration from inappropriate sources— from strangers who only want to see you in your G-string?*

"It is what it is," Kingsley says. "And I can deal with it."

"Would you like some ice cream?" Nina hears herself ask. As if Kingsley were a weepy child with a skinned elbow. *Let Mommy make it all better, baby.*

"Sure," Kingsley says, so eagerly that Nina suspects it's been a long while since her parents have offered her even something as small and insignificant as this. What are the chances that *she* might offer just the sort of wise counsel that Kingsley would accept as readily as she has this bowl of modest, low-fat Chocolate Fudge Chunk?

One in a million?

For the third or fourth time since taking Kingsley home from the hospital, Nina says, "You know you can still bring charges against that creep who assaulted you. Or even a civil suit. Can't you at least give it some serious thought?"

"Hey, you've been great," Kingsley says. "So good to me in so many ways. And I appreciate all of it. But you've got to understand that I made a single mistake—admittedly a really bad one, one that nobody needs to know about—but it's the kind of mistake I'm never going to make again. And I've got to get back to work tomorrow, and I'm as sure of that as I've ever been of anything. So don't sweat it, okay?"

This isn't her daughter sitting here and speaking to her with such misguided confidence, but somehow, for Nina, that's little consolation.

CHAPTER 25

FOOLISHLY, DESIRÉE KNOWS, she has left her search for a brides-maid dress for nearly the last possible moment. The days have whooshed by, one after another, as they will when you're doing nothing at all but plunging headlong into love, your feet barely skimming the ground beneath you. She and Bobby McVicar have spent much of their time at the cemetery, where he tries out his newest songs on her on one of his acoustic guitars, and where their picnic lunches are simply containers of yogurt with mini M&M's mixed in, their low-budget dinners bags of pretzels, a cou-ple of peaches, and bottles of beer and Diet Coke. They're lazy and slow-moving in the late-summer heat, and interested in exploring only each other. What Desirée has found in him is someone just edgy enough, just disaffected enough, to be sweetly intoxicating, but also someone who will instinctively offer her the bigger, better, juicier half of whatever they happen to be sharing. His voice is sweet, too, his songs mostly rueful though occasionally there's a harder, grittier edge to them that makes her sit up and pay even closer attention. As she listens to him sing late one night, the enormous slate-blue sky patterned with more stars than she's seen in a lifetime, she and Bobby with their backs against the cool marble pillars of the William R. Kelly mauso-leum, she knows that this is the happiest she's been. Or might ever hope to be.

With a credit card borrowed from Starshine in hand and Sarah Lee as her guide, Desirée is browsing now through the disappoint-ingly meager offerings at the Just for You Shoppe, the single store in Honey Creek where clothing is sold. There are exactly three cocktail dresses in Desirée's size, painfully unstylish, matronly-looking things in coral, aqua, and the palest yellow, dresses she wouldn't, frankly, be caught dead in. Presiding over the cash regis-ter, the owner, Pearl-Ellen Shipley, says, "Imagine Starshine and Dr. McVicar living together like that for so many years, pretending to be husband and wife when all along they were just a couple of hippies shacking up." She's a thick, middle-aged woman with an upswept hairdo, a tape measure hanging off a loop of the elastic belt at her waist, and ugly ugly *ugly* army-green rubber Teva-like sandals that display her long, bumpy toes and unpolished nails. "I could have fainted when one of the Beaudine twins told me, and I've been thinking I may just find myself a new dentist, actually."

"Hey, they're terrific people," Desirée says. "And there's no better dentist in all of Kansas," she adds extravagantly.

"Well, if they're about to become your in-laws, I suppose you'd *have* to say that."

Not this again! Jesus Christ!

"*What?*" Sarah Lee says. She seizes Desirée's arm excitedly. "What's going on?"

"Oh, for God's sake, it's just another ridiculous misunderstanding," Desirée tells her.

"Suit yourself," Pearl-Ellen says, "but there are rumors flying left and right these days about a double wedding. Plus I still can't believe that old Rusty Wallis poisoned his poor wife. Put weed killer in her birthday cake, Betty Crocker devil's food what he baked himself."

"Weed killer? That's ridiculous," Desirée says, as outraged as if Rusty—who, so far, hasn't been charged with any crime—were entirely innocent, Pearl-Ellen's accusation against him entirely unjust.

"That's what *I* said," Pearl-Ellen agrees. "I'm betting the man has trouble making himself a peanut butter sandwich, so forget the birthday cake."

"So Rusty Wallis is a murderer and Desirée's getting married to a guy she met, like, four minutes ago," Sarah Lee says. "Go figure."

"Suit yourself," Pearl-Ellen repeats. "I'm only telling you what the word around town is."

The word around town . . . So what's that about a tale told by an idiot, signifying nothing?

Out on Minnehaha, Sarah Lee lights up a Marlboro while

Desirée explains the origin of the far-fetched rumor about her alleged impending marriage to Bobby McVicar.

Nodding, Sarah Lee says, in that direct manner of hers that verges on rudeness but intends no harm, "Well, I'm assuming you guys have been sleeping together, right?"

At college and at home, Desirée has more friends than not who, if asked, would answer that question willingly, but this sort of frankness—on this particular subject—does not come easily to her, and she prefers, instead, to focus on the question of where to find a dress for the wedding; thankfully, Sarah Lee doesn't press her. "Well, I can lend you something of mine, which obviously won't fit you great since I'm way taller, or we can drive forty-five miles to St. Jo, Missouri," she says, pronouncing it "Missourah." "There's plenty of shopping there, but of course that's ninety miles there and back, a real drag if you're not used to it."

Ninety miles! Instantly Desirée finds herself considering the elegant boutiques within walking distance of her apartment on the Upper East Side, to say nothing of the enormous, high-rise department stores that are almost cities in themselves and a mere cab or subway ride away. To live, as Sarah Lee does, without Manhattan's immeasurable, dazzling offerings, seems a great deprivation, a reflection of an underprivileged, diminished life. (So what if Sarah Lee has access to all those stores online? They can't provide that same small thrill that Desirée always feels running her hands across the racks and racks of pricey jeans on the second floor of Bloomingdale's with her friends on a drizzly Sunday afternoon.) And the stores and their boundless merchandise are the least of it. For Desirée, the greatest deprivation of all would be to live without access to the New York Public Library and its acres of books—the Mid-Manhattan branch on Fifth Avenue a favorite haunt, one of the places in the world she loves best. And one she cherishes as passionately as she does the city's museums, theater, opera, the Philharmonic, all of which her parents made sure she had her fill of growing up. In truth, she knows it's wrongheaded to pity Sarah Lee, because wouldn't that pity smack of a kind of superciliousness, a loftiness she simply doesn't feel? (Well, to be *entirely* truthful, maybe she feels juuust the teensiest bit of disdain.) But it's her strongly felt regret that Sarah Lee has been denied what has always been at Desirée's own fingertips.

"Yup, that's how far you'd have to drive for a decent pair of jeans." Sarah Lee sounds patiently resigned, and smiles at the sympathetic look Desirée casts in her direction. "Don't feel too, too sorry for me," she advises. "This is what I'm used to and I'm pretty sure it's not gonna kill me. But maybe I'll come visit you in New York someday," she says dreamily, and it might as well be Tokyo or Budapest she's talking about. She's never seen a city crammed with skyscrapers, Desirée marvels, or a solitary home-less woman making her way desolately through bumper-to-bumper traffic on the approach to the FDR Drive, brandishing a paper cup from a coffee shop, its bottom weighted with silver coins, a poorly lettered cardboard sign hanging from her neck explaining that she has AIDS and two young children to worry about and God bless you for your help. Desirée can just picture Sarah Lee seated next to her on the subway to Times Square, sharing space with a man reading a newspaper in Mandarin; a couple of Haitians conversing in Creole; a bevy of college stu-dents sporting septum rings, streaks of fluorescent purple in their hair; a smooth-faced transvestite in black patent-leather fuck-me pumps. And what would Sarah Lee think, Desirée muses, of the near-chaotic bustle of activity at Times Square at any hour, sky-high electronic billboards shrieking for your atten-tion, the streets jammed with traffic, gridlocked, the progress of taxis, cars, and buses measured in inches, their drivers desperate to get wherever it is they are heading. A far cry from paradise and yet, to Desirée, at this moment, absolutely alluring. She's stricken, suddenly, with a potent, dizzying strain of homesick-ness. The feeling passes over her like a wave of acute nausea; her eyes sting and her palms are clammy and possibly she's gone greenish around the gills. She slumps down on the curb, resting her head on her knees. Honey Creek is a weary ghost town this noon, a perfect slice of small-town USA that makes her heart sink.

"What's wrong?" Sarah Lee asks. "Is it your tooth again?"

Desirée knows what it is to have been robbed at gunpoint but somehow this, in its way, is almost as disturbing, this unnerving stillness, this absence of people, of motion, of life being lived in all its complexity or simplicity or just somewhere in between.

"It's not my tooth, it's *this* . . ." she says, raising her head and gesturing lamely with both arms at nothing in particular, at everything, really.

"Poor little big-city girl," Sarah Lee says. "I know what we'll do with you. We'll go to my house and find some dresses for you to try on, but first there's someplace I've got to take you," she says mysteriously.

Wherever it is they're going, Desirée hopes it won't cost too much; she's got to convince one of her parents to make another deposit into her checking account. "They're still having trouble believing I was robbed at an Alzheimer's support group," she tells Sarah Lee.

"We're always bragging this is one of the safest places in the universe," Sarah Lee says as they climb into her father's Chevy Silverado pickup. "Maybe we were bragging just a little too loud."

"Wonder what Angel the stickup guy spent my two hundred bucks on," Desirée says bitterly. She thinks of him cruising the mall in St. Jo, Missourah, stocking up on new DVDs, and maybe a pair or two of inexpensive jeans. Or perhaps he's the generous sort who spent it all on a necklace or bracelet for the girlfriend who recently refused to sleep with him. Is it possible he's dumb enough to have flashed Desirée's credit card the day following the holdup—unaware that it had immediately been reported stolen and that he was about to find himself in deep shit? It gives Desirée a jolt of pleasure to envision Angel captured at the mall, profoundly humiliated as he's dragged away in handcuffs en route to the slammer. It takes the worst variety of scum to rob an Alzheimer's support group, she reflects, or maybe just a certain kind of desperation. And then it crosses her mind that she can put a positive spin on that crazy, terrifying episode in Starshine's office and employ Angel for her own purposes—as the central character in a story she might, if she's lucky, be able to pull off successfully. She can delineate him any way she pleases, sympathetically or not, and, God-like, create a past and future for him. She can render him a descendant of trailer trash or the son of lawyers in a prominent Kansas City firm, two coolly distant parents who'd neglected him emotionally from the day he arrived on this earth.

She truly can't wait to get her hands on the fictional Angel and yank him this way and that until he finds redemption. Grabbing the pocket-sized spiral notebook she keeps with her at all times, she uncaps her Pilot Rolling Ball now, and, for the first time since her arrival in Honey Creek, actually puts pen to paper. She doesn't look up until Sarah Lee steers the Silverado into the two-car driveway of a small house sheathed in aluminum siding. Rising above a patch of pink dahlias is a silver-and-white metal sign that announces HARRIETTE'S HAIRPORT. There are plastic tricycles tipped over and lying abandoned in front of the garage door, along with a Barbie lunch box and Barbie herself, stark naked and showing off an impressive pair of D-cup breasts.

"Who's getting their hair cut?" Desirée asks.

"Oh, no one. This isn't exactly about haircuts."

"Just a social call?"

"Nope."

"Wait, this looks like Kickapoo Lane. Isn't this the McVicars' street?"

"Nope, this is Chippewa Drive. And you'll never guess who lives here. Besides Harriette, that is."

They approach the front door, where two more Barbies lie, flat on their hard plastic backs and tied together by their long, blond, synthetic hair.

"Conjoined-twins Barbie," Desirée murmurs.

"Is that the same as Siamese twins?"

"I can't tell you how important it is to be politically correct," Desirée cautions her. "You've got to be careful."

"Even when it comes to a stupid doll?" Sarah Lee rings the bell and a pair of little girls come to the door, pressing their noses against the screen.

"We don't know you," the taller one says accusingly. "We can't talk to you."

"You do too know me," Sarah Lee says. "And this is my friend Desirée. Go get your mom, girls, come on."

"She's busy!" the girls shriek.

"You're not cooperating, Roxy, and neither are you, Kayla."

"*You're* not cooperating."

"If you let me in, I'll play Barbies with you," Sarah Lee promises, and presses the bell again. This time Harriette, a woman in short shorts and with long legs, appears, and invites them inside.

"Hey Sarah Lee. You're not here for more highlighting, are you? Because your hair looks pretty damn good to me."

"Actually . . . we're here to see Miss Lavender. Or at least my friend Desirée is."

The door opens directly into the living room; a phalanx of half-dressed Barbies is sprawled lifelessly across the moss-colored carpet, like fallen soldiers on a battlefield. "Sorry about these damn dolls everywhere," Harriette says. "It's just that I've been busy all morning with a couple of customers and their perms."

"Wait, why do I know the name Miss Lavender?" Desirée says.

"The psychic I was telling you about?" Sarah Lee reminds her.

"Right," Desirée says, her enthusiasm muted. "*That's* why you brought me here?" she hisses at Sarah Lee as Harriette goes off in search of her aunt.

"Ever been to a psychic before?"

"You can't be serious."

Roxy and Kayla are at the electric piano now, one that reproduces the sounds of an assortment of instruments—harpsichord, drums, cymbals, clarinets, and violins—all at the touch of a button. The girls have a whole orchestra going, and the volume tuned to a nearly deafening pitch.

"You just look like someone who could use some good news!" Sarah Lee hollers.

Arriving with her aunt in tow, Harriette pulls the plug on the music and banishes the girls to the backyard. "Go dig for worms or something," she suggests.

"Can we have a manicure after?" Roxy asks.

"Go outside and I'll think about it."

"I want Pookie Pink on one hand and Dusty Rose on the other, okay?"

"Go!"

Miss Lavender and Desirée make eye contact; in a mortifyingly clichéd moment, Desirée shivers, convinced that an ice-cold hand had touched the back of her neck and was then instantly withdrawn. A slight figure, her face sharp and birdlike, Miss Lavender has the smooth skin of a youngish woman, but if she'd lost her fiancé in World War II, as Desirée now remembers, Honey Creek's reigning psychic must have hit eighty a while ago. Her wispy hair is ginger colored, and she is wrapped in what looks like an authentic kimono, patterned in dragons with long, unfurled tongues resembling flames. Her wrists are loaded down with thin silver bangle bracelets, her nails tipped in maroon polish. Very exotic looking for Honey Creek, but perhaps that's the point, if her ambition is to stay in the fortune-telling business.

"Welcome," she greets Desirée. "You've come a long way."

"All the way from New York."

"And now you're coming into the kitchen with me."

"Sarah Lee?" Desirée says. "Aren't you coming?"

"No, no, just you," says Miss Lavender.

"Sarah Lee's going down to the basement to the Hairport for a conditioning and a trim," Harriette says. "I see now that she's got some serious split ends."

"See ya!" Sarah Lee says blithely, and vanishes down an oddly placed flight of stairs at the back of the living room.

"You don't need your friend," Miss Lavender assures Desirée. "We'll have some tea together and then we'll see what's in store for you."

When Desirée reveals, in hopes of being dismissed, that she doesn't have any cash to pay for a peek at her future, Miss Lavender says, "Freeloaders welcome today. Not to worry."

It's warm and close in the small kitchen; through the open window above the sink they can hear the little girls screeching delightedly—perhaps at the sight of the worms they've dug up—and, from next door, the uninflected voice of a radio announcer broadcasting the current market prices of wheat, corn, beans, oats, and something mysteriously called "milo," which Miss Lavender explains is "just grain sorghum."

Uh-huh. But doesn't "sorghum" mean "cloyingly sentimental"?

"Lemon and sugar in your tea?"

Desirée chooses a seat at the white Formica table, where someone, presumably one of the little girls, had written the name "Kayla" in a reddish ink that evidently survived all efforts to scour it away. "So . . . you must enjoy living here with Harriette and her family," Desirée remarks, just making conversation.

"What makes you say *that*?" Miss Lavender places a drinking glass patterned with faded maple leaves in front of Desirée on a paper towel. There is a worn-looking deck of cards in her other hand and she positions it next to Desirée's glass before settling herself beside her.

"No reason in particular."

"Well, these living arrangements aren't exactly what I would have wished for myself. *That* would have been a different life altogether. But the one great love of my life died on the beach at Normandy, and after that I was never able to find that kind of love ever again. We were meant for each other, Donald Kiernan and I, but fate intervened and I simply had to accept it. There were a few other boys along the way who were interested in me, but what would have been the point of that, settling for less when I'd already known the kind of love that comes along but once in a lifetime and just sets you on fire."

Next door, the radio that had been broadcasting grain prices is now blasting, at high volume, "Stand by Your Man," with Tammy Wynette lamenting, "Some-times it's hard to be a wuh-man . . ."

"That must have been quite a romance," Desirée says.

"And you're in the midst of one yourself, aren't you?" Miss Lavender winks a green eye at her. "Don't try and keep any secrets from me, young lady, it won't work. And by the way, you have a history of unrequited love written all over you, but that's another young man, someone who's not to be trusted. He's a big talker, but where's the proof? I don't need to tell a smart girl like you who to trust, do I?"

"So who's this untrustworthy guy we're talking about?"

"Who? I can't see his name or even his initials, but I do know he's either going to be some kind of doctor or already is one."

There's that chilly hand at Desirée's neck again.

"Don't look so surprised—he's somewhere at the back of your

mind, that's all," Miss Lavender explains. "An ugly thought that can't do you any good. And I'm reading you loud and clear, aren't I?" She gestures toward the deck of cards, saying, "Shuffle those for me, okay, and we'll see what else I have for you."

Desirée shuffles the cards like a pro, making a perfect bridge, thanks to a canasta-obsessed roommate who'd taught her all her tricks before taking a forced leave of absence from Yale two semesters ago. "Full disclosure? You frighten me," Desirée says. She watches as Miss Lavender flips over twelve cards, each with an impressively crisp snap, and arranges them meticulously in three rows across the kitchen table.

"Well, sometimes I frighten *myself,* if that's any consolation." Nibbling at her upper lip, Miss Lavender studies the cards in silence, and after a few minutes, she sweeps them gracefully to the edge of the table and into her lap. "Show's over," she announces.

"What?" Desirée says, worried and relieved all at once.

"Let's just say I make it my business not to give out certain kinds of news to certain kinds of people who are poorly equipped to handle it. It's a good, sensible policy and I have to stick with it."

"My flight home's going to crash?" Desirée says, unable to suppress the first horrific thought that comes barging into her imagination. "You can't keep that kind of information to yourself!" The hysterical pitch of her own voice frightens her almost as much as her dark future. And what about the irony of having survived an armed robbery only to go down on a doomed aircraft in the middle of God-knows-where!

"Calm down, will you please? Did I tell you it was going to be something terrible?" Miss Lavender is saying. "No, I did not. Just have some of your tea and relax."

"I can deal with anything you tell me," Desirée insists. "Especially now that I know I'm not going to die."

"At least not in the foreseeable future . . . Look, your aura is very strong, very positive," says Miss Lavender cheerfully. "You're in good shape, believe me."

"I didn't expect to believe *anything* you said. I'm not into New Agey stuff at all," Desirée confesses. "Which is more than a little ironic, given that I've had this freelance job editing horoscopes, and I—"

"Not anymore you don't," Miss Lavender reports.

"I don't?"

"Whatever job you had, you've lost it, but don't ask for details, because I don't have any."

"That was the news you were going to keep from me? That's fantastic! Compared to a fiery death in a plane crash, I mean."

"All I can tell you is that certain things are meant to be and can't be avoided."

"Wait, are you saying free will doesn't exit?"

"Free will, my dear, is a beautiful thing, that's what I tell everyone who comes to see me. And of all the things I know—and I know *plenty*—that's the most important." Miss Lavender smiles. "I have to say, Desry, you're no challenge at all. It's like you've opened a window and let me take a nice long look inside."

Affronted, Desirée says, "I'm transparent as a sheet of glass?"

"Yes, ma'am, and it's been a real treat for me." Gathering up her cards, Miss Lavender says, "And now I've got to go watch my soaps, if you don't mind."

Dismissed, Desirée takes one more sip of dishwatery iced tea and carries the glass to the sink. "Well, thanks very much," she says. "At least it's nice to know my aura's so strong and positive. The rest I'll try not to think about."

"Thank *you*. I haven't had this much fun since the Beaudine twins came out here for a reading and their auras kept getting in each other's way and finally I had to put them in separate rooms. But you enjoy your visit to Honey Creek, Desry, and don't worry too much about getting fired. You'll find something else soon enough."

"Something that pays thirty dollars an hour?"

"The details elude me, hon. Now that I'm getting on in years, they often do. In the old days, when I was at the height of my powers, I could give it to you almost down to the last detail. But the truth, then and now, is that I don't know everything." Waving her little manicured hand, Miss Lavender says, "Bye now."

Desirée follows the stairway down to the basement, which is paneled in knotty pine and exudes that familiar salon smell—a sweetish, not entirely benign mix of chemicals and blow-dried hair. The walls are plastered with posters of long-necked models displaying a variety of hairstyles, and there is one poster unrelated to all the rest: lettered in gold against a white background, it reads,

DO IT GOD'S WAY!

Sarah Lee is seated in one of the three barber's chairs facing a mirrored wall; she's wearing a brown vinyl cape and sobbing vigorously, her formerly waist-length hair cut to her shoulders, blond ribbons littering the linoleum floor beneath her.

"Oh, in a year or so it'll be back where it used to be," Harriette consoles her. "Eighteen months, tops."

"Why did you listen to me?" Sarah Lee weeps.

"You're the one in the driver's seat, girl. You tell me to cut, I cut. But listen, your eyes are swelling up from all that crying," Harriette says reproachfully. "I can't have you leaving here in tears, it's not good for business."

Sarah Lee's face darkens furiously; she's about to go on the warpath. "Listen, you scissor-happy bitch, if you think I give a rat's ass about what's good for business, then you're a bigger idiot than I thought."

"Okay, that's it," Harriette says. She unfastens the Velcro snap at the back of Sarah Lee's neck, and whips off the cape, scattering snippets of hair across the room. "Get the hell out of my chair, out of my house! And by the way, maybe if your mother hadn't run off with Buzz Emerson to Disney World and left you just at the time when a girl needs her mother most—and I'm talking about the teen years, of course—maybe you wouldn't have turned into such an asshole. Unlike *your* mother, I personally would sooner cut off my right arm than desert my precious children."

"For your information," says Sarah Lee, all choked up again, "my mother loves me more than life itself. And it breaks her heart that we can't be together. So don't you go judging my family when you don't know the first thing about us."

Harriette is shaking her head grimly. "I'd die without my little girls. Too bad *your* mother never felt the same way about you."

Sarah Lee leaps, growling, from her seat, and collars Harriette. "You shut the fuck up," she orders, and Desirée has to pry her hands off the startled Harriette, who topples into the barber's chair, fingertips against her windpipe.

"Are you out of your mind?" Harriette croaks. "You'd like to choke me to death, wouldn't you? Well, what if I weren't the decent Christian that I am and decided to have you arrested, then what?"

Abruptly, Sarah Lee, and Desirée right behind her, make a run for it up the stairs; sitting in the pickup alongside her friend as they speed away, Desirée does her best to calm her. *What were you thinking?* she can hear herself asking Sarah Lee's mother. *You traded away your beloved daughter for a husband named Buzz and a job in Fantasyland?* Just why *is* it that people are so disappointing? The longer she's lived, the more clearly Desirée's seen that this is too often true—that mothers and daughters, wives and husbands, friends and lovers, fall short of what those who love them need them to be. She herself had veered off course this winter, unable to rouse any generosity of spirit toward her father, sinking, instead, into disaffection, a sullen, adolescent resentment. What she hopes for now is to be forgiven. And forgiving.

She still hasn't been able to tell her father any of this. And yet she believes she's making progress, though with an excruciating pokiness, it sometimes seems, like a slug making its halting way across a vast green lawn, vast as the world itself.

CHAPTER 26

THE DAMAGE IS DONE, and there is, it seems, no repairing it. Nina is humiliated; she can't bear to think that she's lost Porsha over nothing more than a late-night argument about something as laughable as a single Weight Watchers Chocolate Chip Cookie Dough Sundae, she and Porsha shrieking at each other like a pair of madwomen inextricably caught up in their extravagant folly. And all the while her father staring from the safety of his wheelchair, his eyes widened in disbelief, his mouth working occasionally, forming sounds neither she nor Porsha could decipher.

You want to know why I'm pissed off? There were only two in the carton and you took the last one without asking, that's *why!*

Since when do I have to ask before eating anything in this house? Since when?

You can't possibly understand, Porsha, how much I wanted that sundae!

So why didn't you say something? How else would I know? You think I'm a mind reader?

But I shouldn't have *to say something! You should know that if there's only one left you need to ask first. It's common courtesy.*

And I shouldn't have to tell you *I deserved that sundae after my day today in this house, not one, but two dirty diapers, a big, big load of laundry, a bath for Grandpa, his dinner, and I'm bone-tired and just want that one nice thing for myself at the end of a long day and you're telling me I shouldn't have it? I'm telling you that nice little sundae was* owed *to me!*

Owed to you?

That's right, owed *to me!*

This was when Nina made the mistake of allowing herself a small, bitter snort of laughter—born of exhaustion after her *own* long day at school, where she'd held individual, half-hour-long conferences with one student after another, almost all of whom strayed from talk of literature and writing and only wished to discuss what had gone wrong in their very young, very confused lives.

I have news for you, Porsha, nothing is owed to any of us.

She realized, to her surprise, that they were no longer screaming; in the aftermath of that painful, embarrassed silence Porsha immediately made her escape, marching down the long hallway that led to the bedrooms, allowing Nina to see and hear the fury in the determined swivel of her hips and slap of her bare feet against the parquet floor.

Please don't go. Please.

I got nothing more to say to you.

And now Nina finds herself alone with her father, whose head is shaking either in dismay and sorrow, or simply because the Parkinson's insists upon it. It seems to take all her strength, but Nina manages to ease him onto his bed, then draws the sheet to his shoulders and lies down beside him, holding his hand under the sheet and promising that she will get his beloved Porsha back for him.

Her father says nothing, not even when, feeling sorry for herself, she lists the people who have left her—Patrick, Desirée, and now Porsha. When she adds Kingsley, the last in her brief litany, her father turns his face to the wall, wanting nothing more to do with her.

And who, she thinks, can blame him?

CHAPTER 27

BIG SURPRISE—HER MOTHER IS none too thrilled when Desirée calls on Bobby's cell phone to report that she's run out of money again.

"Who gets robbed in the middle of Nowheresville, Kansas?" Nina says. "I just can't wrap my mind around it."

"I know," Desirée says. "And I'm sorry to have to ask again." Beside her in bed at the Bambi Motel, Bobby tickles her with the tip of his braid. After a couple of hours of the kind of rapturous sex she'd never before had the faintest taste of, she and Bobby are giddy with exhaustion, sunk deep in a kind of postsex hangover.

"What's so funny?" her mother says, sounding irritable. "Why are you giggling like that?"

"It just occurred to me," Desirée says, "that I've never even had my pocket picked on the subway."

"That's hilarious all right. I only hope your stay in the wild West has taught you a thing or two."

"Wild *Mid*west. And did you know that Thomas Edison was Jewish? And that he invented the TV and the VCR?" Desirée hears the unmistakable clicking of computer keys, and then her mother's protracted sigh.

"Live and learn," Nina says. "But I'm not going to deposit any more money into your account, pussycat."

"What do you mean? I'm pretty much down to my last penny. So what am I supposed to *do*?"

"You're supposed to come back home where you belong. Come back and I'll give you a thousand dollars for a welcome-home gift," Nina offers. "And you'll need it, as it happens. I keep forgetting to mention that magazine you work for sent a messenger to pick up your assignment and then left a voice mail saying you'd been dropped from their staff of freelancers. What did you do, get a little reckless with the semicolons?"

"I knew it!" Desirée says excitedly. "A psychic already broke the news to me." She doesn't, of course, tell her mother about the liberties she'd taken that one afternoon while copyediting under the influence of some kick-ass weed.

"You leave New York for half a summer and all of a sudden you believe in fortune-tellers?"

"Only in Miss Lavender."

"All right, look," her mother says, and pauses. "I hate to bother you with this, but Porsha and I had a terrible fight a few nights ago and, actually, she quit . . ."

Desirée clucks sympathetically: Porsha is her mother's savior and the only bright spot in her grandfather's cruelly diminished life. Without her, they're screwed. "Whatever happened, no matter whose fault it was," Desirée says, "you've got to get her back."

"Come home and help me, pussycat. I've called and left so many messages on her machine, it's way beyond humiliating."

"So what was the big fight about?"

"Oh, one of my Weight Watchers sundaes," Nina says, sounding embarrassed. "I'd bought a box of them for myself as a special treat of sorts, but Porsha got to the freezer first and ate the last one."

"No biggie."

"That's a rational person talking. In order to understand this, you have to think like a lunatic, which, I hate to admit, is exactly what Porsha and I were like that night."

"You don't need me," Desirée says. "All you need is Craigslist. Or call a couple of employment agencies. If you can't get Porsha back, you can get someone just like her." This is wishful thinking and she knows it. Though it hurts to imagine her grandfather deprived of Porsha's magic touch, she's not going to dwell on it. Sex, she's discovered, is the anodyne for a whole range of troubles, even guilt, even the massive kind embedded in her DNA—Jewish on the one hand, Catholic on the other.

"I got someone's part-time babysitter in the building to take over, at least for a few hours every day this week. But I'm truly lost without Porsha," her mother acknowledges.

Desirée looks over at Bobby, who's dozed off without her noticing. She picks up one of his warm, long-fingered hands, feels the calluses on the fingertips he uses to play his guitars. He and his band, Private Lee, will be performing at his parents' wedding next week, and Desirée will be his number-one groupie, woo-hooing appropriately and applauding like crazy. But what if the life span of this romance is doomed to be a brief one, like that of the butterfly she saw resting on the warm cobblestones of Minnehaha Avenue? Sometimes she imagines herself and Bobby months from now, e-mailing each other obsessively, their longing heightened by the knowledge that, in essence, they are a couple in cyberspace only, their bodily selves an impossible distance apart. Unless, of course, she decides to leave Yale behind her—a notion that just a month ago would have been unthinkable, but is now center stage in her daydreams.

"I miss you, pussycat," she hears her mother saying.

"Miss you, too," Desirée says, because what does it cost her to offer up the most soothing and harmless of white lies?

"Come home and help me out? Keep me company?"

Desirée is silent.

"Fine," Nina says. "Obviously you're no longer the mensch you were raised to be."

While Desirée is contemplating the least painful route back into her mother's good graces, Nina hangs up on her.

A mensch, Desirée reflects, has certain high standards to uphold, but anyone who falls far short of menschy-ness—anyone who can't be counted on for a generosity of spirit and an unfailing impulse to do the right thing—is free to indulge in sex, drugs, rock 'n' roll, and whatever else is out there for the taking/sampling/savoring. Her mother's newly lowered opinion of her has, in fact, left Desirée a little teary eyed. She is twenty years old and a free agent, and under no legal obligation to think twice about those flawed parents of hers back in New York who seem to ask too much of her. So why is she crying?

"She hung up on you?" Bobby says.

"She's extremely disappointed in me," Desirée says, sniffling.

"Stop crying and call her back," Bobby says. Now *here* is a mensch talking, a blond, blue-eyed one from northeast Kansas, great-great-grandson of the old lady who'd wrecked Cousin Ira's bar mitzvah and was never the same again. Desirée rests her head on his bare chest, glides her fingers through the mat of pale hair. She can feel her love for him intensifying at this moment and when she closes her eyes it's as if she is drifting along on her back in the gentle current of the sun-warmed Caribbean, where, in her childhood, she'd vacationed with her mother and father. *Don't be an idiot; go with the flow,* she tells herself.

"Call her back," Bobby is urging her. "You'll both feel better."

"You," Desirée says, "are your mother's son. So how about starting a support group for, let's see, oh yeah, guilt-ridden offspring of single mothers who've been left by their gay husbands?"

"Maybe there's one in Kansas City," Bobby jokes. "Want me to drive you there?"

"Not me," Desirée says. "I'm happy right where I am." She and Bobby sigh blissfully, happy as a couple of furiously purring cats.

BY THE TIME she peeks past the drapes and discovers the sky has fully darkened, it's well past eight o'clock, and it occurs to her that dinner is probably not a bad idea. They order in from Bonnie Lynn's Carry-Out Pizza, and when the delivery guy shows up, Desirée sees how he takes in the unmade bed, the blankets half on the floor, the pillows kicked over to the wrong end of the mattress. And Desirée herself dressed in nothing but a billowy, knee-length T-shirt.

"Hey," he says from the doorway, eyes lowered bashfully now.

"How's it going, Levi?" Bobby says.

Stepping beyond the threshold and into the motel room, Levi hands the pizza box over to Bobby. "Six-fifty," he says. "Oh, and two bucks for the pop."

Pop, Desirée thinks; hearing the folksy name given to something that, where she comes from, is just plain soda, she feels a mild case of homesickness kicking in.

"Levi's the captain of Consolidated High's basketball team," says Bobby as he forks over a twenty-dollar bill. "And also the president of the Fellowship of Christian Athletes."

Levi, a skinny guy with a small head and closely cropped hair, studies his enormous basketball sneakers, afraid even to look at her, Desirée observes.

"The thing is, Levi," Bobby begins, "it's nobody's business that you saw me here tonight. And that's the reason I'm going to give you a nice big tip, okay?"

Levi nods, and begins backing up to the door. "You really don't even have to tip me."

"Just keep the change from the twenty," Bobby says. "Take it and promise to keep your mouth shut, all right?"

"Swear to Christ," says Levi fervently.

"Well, time for you to get going, dude."

"Slow night at Bonnie Lynn's," Levi says, suddenly, it seems, reluctant to leave. "*Real* slow."

Desirée sidles over to the dresser, where Bobby has set down the pizza box and is helping himself to some mushrooms off the top. "Can't you get rid of him?" she murmurs.

"You know, Bob's gonna be a big success," Levi tells her. "I just bet Private Lee's gonna be huge. When they go out on their first world tour I might just get myself hired as a roadie or maybe even their manager. What do you say, Bob?"

"Can you get us a recording contract?" Bobby kids him.

"Well, Jesus, I'm not God," Levi says.

"Wait, I'm confused—only God can get them a recording contract?" Desirée says.

"See, the way it works is, if the Lord sees fit to have them sign with a major label, it'll happen. But maybe He has other plans for them."

"Now I'm *totally* confused. I thought you said Private Lee was going to be huge. Now you're saying God may have something else in mind?"

"I may have spoken out of turn," Levi admits. "But tomorrow, at the Youth for Christ prayer meeting, I'm gonna put in a good word for Private Lee."

"Awesome," Desirée says, but can't control the eye-rolling that gives her away.

"So you're not a believer, are you?"

"She's the Antichrist," Bobby mumbles, his mouth full of pizza. "Live and in person."

Levi pales; he puts a hand up against the door frame for support. "A cold wind just swept through here, now that you mention it."

"Oh, that's just the air-conditioning cycling in," Desirée says. She doesn't like the way Levi is staring at her now, so piercingly, it's clear he is hoping for nothing less than a look into the pitch-darkness of her soul. "Oh, come on, Levi," she says. "Can't you tell Bobby's joking around?"

"Hold it," Levi says. "So you're that girl from New York? But you know, even though you're a half Jew, you can still be saved." He smiles at her expectantly. "Come to the prayer meeting tomorrow. And there's an ice cream social afterward. First Baptist Church at three o'clock."

When hell freezes over, perhaps. "Thanks for your interest in saving my soul," Desirée says, "but I'm afraid it's beyond redemption."

"Oh, no one's beyond salvation, not even the greatest sinner among us," Levi informs her.

"I promise to keep that in mind," Desirée says politely.

"Super! And you know what, I saw *Swindler's List* on TV a couple years back. I cried at some of the sad parts, but that's a secret, okay?"

"Why don't you go save some souls and leave us heathens to our pizza," Bobby suggests.

"You could come to the prayer meeting, too, Bob. It wouldn't hurt."

"Don't count on it."

Having given it his best shot, Levi studies them both now with what appears to be undeniable sorrow. "Come Judgment Day, the two of you are gonna be waist-deep in some serious shit," he predicts.

"Thanks for the warning, man," Bobby says in farewell. He settles his arm around Desirée, and it isn't until Levi gets into his delivery truck and drives off that either of them says a word.

"The world's full of dickheads," Bobby says. "The smartest thing is to ignore them."

Maybe so, but for the first time in her life, Desirée longs to be one of the faithful, someone who willingly sinks to her knees and asks the Big Guy Up There for a few words of consolation when needed. Unfortunately, she is still her old faithless self, completely earthbound, disconnected from whatever it is that most people seem to just naturally latch on to.

"The pizza's cold," she says as she takes a bite. And when she sees that Levi neglected to bring her Diet Coke and left them with two cans of Dr Pepper instead, she breaks down and cries. It's just too much—first another Honey Creeker wanting to save her soul, and now this icky, undrinkable soda.

"What is it?" Bobby says, looking worried. "What's wrong?"

He wipes her eyes tenderly with official Bonnie Lynn Carry-Out napkins and sets off to the soda machine in the lobby. When he returns, it is with Nick Davenport in tow, and Desirée, wonderstruck, nearly has a heart attack at the sight of them together.

CHAPTER 28

SHE WOULD NEVER have predicted it, but it seems she is something of a sucker for anyone willing to drive five hundred miles just for an opportunity to talk with her face-to-face. Nick is dressed up in khakis and polished loafers and a pale blue buttoned-down shirt with the sleeves rolled past his wrists, looking self-possessed, a guy to be reckoned with. In a homely, extra-large T-shirt, her hair a bit disheveled, her face shiny, Desirée isn't prepared for company. She is, in short, someone who'd had marathon sex and then a cozy nap, followed by insults from a teenaged evangelist who somehow managed to get the better of her.

She stares at Nick coolly, pretending—for Bobby's sake—a stone-heartedness she doesn't feel. "Look who's here," is all she can manage.

"Your friend and I met at the front desk," Nick explains, his voice neutral.

"Yeah, and I've got to get going," Bobby says, handing Desirée the Diet Coke he scored for her. "Right this minute, actually. Private Lee needs a lot more practice sessions before the wedding."

"Take care, dude," Nick says.

"Right." Bobby's hand is already on the doorknob.

The two of them are remarkably civilized, Desirée observes, but all she wants is to fling herself facedown onto that unmade bed, pull the sheet over herself like a shroud, and play dead.

"See you tomorrow, Desirée?" Bobby says.

"You don't have to go," she tells him, though how can he possibly stay?

"The band really does have to practice. You wouldn't want us to make fools of ourselves in front of all those people . . ."

Fools? "No, of course not."

"Well, guh-bye."

"Wait!" His back is toward her, and as he freezes, she sees the sorrowful hunch of his shoulders.

"What?" he says.

"Did you know that 'good-bye' is actually a shortened form of 'God be with you'?" Desirée says inanely. *You have absolutely nothing to worry about,* she means to whisper in his ear, but he is already shutting the door quietly behind him, and what she hears is the distinct sound of his disappointment.

"So," Nick says, as she turns to face him, "do I at least get a hug?"

"Not necessarily. I thought it was clear there'd be no phone calls, no e-mails, no nothin'."

"True, but who said I couldn't call your mother?" Nick smiles. "I gave her the unvarnished, uncomplicated truth—which is that I'm in love with you—and after that, getting her to tell me where you were was a piece of cake."

"Arrgh!" Her own mother, a *traitor*. "She was supposed to tell you I'm working undercover for an FBI sting," Desirée says, refusing to acknowledge what she knows to be Nick's mistaken use of the word "love."

"And I can see this is quite a sting you've got going here," Nick says. He looks around him at the room's untidiness, frowning at the unkempt bed. "*Veeery* professional," he says.

Desirée approaches the tepid pizza and attacks a strip of crust. "Not that it's any of *your* business who I'm spending my time with."

Joining her, Nick folds his arms firmly around her middle, touches his lips to the bridge of her nose, working his way down to her mouth. It's the faintly sweet, familiar scent of his hair—still dear to her and somehow possessing the power, like some favorite piece of music, to carry her off—that, if not for Bobby, might have been her undoing.

The knock at the door is briskly cheerful and couldn't have come at a more opportune time. "Fresh linens!" Sarah Lee announces, making her entrance like a supporting actor in the creakiest of stage plays. "Can I?" she says, and gestures toward the bed. "Sorry to come so late, but, uh, you know how it is."

"No, I *don't* know how it is," Nick says. "Can't you come back later?"

"Nope. And by the way, any friend of Desirée's is a friend of mine."

"Not just any friend, her *boy*friend."

"Ex," Desirée corrects him. "Please."

Sarah Lee begins to strip the bed, and Desirée extracts herself from Nick's embrace to help her, shucking off pillowcases, yanking back the top sheet, praying that she and Bobby have left behind nothing noteworthy.

"Oh, did I tell you that I've been thinking about taking a trip down to Florida to see my mom?" Sarah Lee says. "I called her and we talked for a while and then she gave me a whole list of dates that wouldn't be the best time for me to come. Turns out she and Buzz are having a baby around Christmas."

"Sweet," Desirée says warily.

"Maybe for *them*." Sarah Lee smooths out the fresh fitted sheet, absently stroking the surface with the flat of her hand, again and again, as if she were caressing the fur of a beloved pet. And then, exhaling a weepy-sounding sigh, she curls up on top of the bed.

"Hey!" Nick says. "What kind of maid service *is* this?"

Desirée sits at the side of the bed and massages Sarah Lee's back. "Can I get you anything? Cold pizza? A cold drink?"

"How about a new mother?" Sarah Lee says. "Check this out." She reaches into the pocket of her Umbros and hands Desirée a piece of paper torn from a Bambi notepad imprinted with the legend THE BEST LITTLE MOTEL IN THE SWEETEST PLACE ON EARTH. "Read it," she orders. "Out loud."

" 'September the first through September the sixth—no good. September the tenth through October the second—no good. October the fifth through October the eighteenth—even worse. October the twentieth through Thanksgiving Day—terrible.' "

"Well, there does seem to be a window of opportunity between September seventh and September ninth, and October third and fourth," Nick observes.

"And as if I didn't feel bad *enough*, Harriette's been telling everyone I tried to kill her over at the Hairport, if you can believe that. And Margaret Keating says it's bad for business having a would-be killer working at the front desk, so I may get transferred to maid duty permanently. The thing is, Harriette made me feel, I don't know, small. Teensy. Like if my mother could leave me behind like that, what was I worth to anybody? I mean, what was I thinking, that she actually cares about me?"

"Of course she cares about you," Desirée says reflexively. "Doesn't she always say that it breaks her heart that you can't be together?"

"She just needs to find a way to fit you into her calendar," Nick adds.

Support groups for one and all, Desirée thinks—one for Sarah Lee, one for Nina, and maybe even one for herself, especially after she'd been a victim of an armed robbery while sitting in on a support group. But really, this is bullshit: when you get right down to it, shouldn't you navigate your own way, guided by your own best instincts? Particularly when it comes to love. Or the lack thereof. And it's her own good sense that instructs her to say, in the next moment, "Time for you to be heading back home to Wisconsin, *Nicholas.*"

"Jesus, Desirée. He drove all the way here from Wisconsin and you're already sending him home?" Sarah Lee says.

"And let's not forget that she's in love with me," Nick points out.

"Excuse me?" Desirée says. "Do you remember meeting someone named Bobby McVicar right here in this room only a few minutes ago?"

"And are you in love with *her*?" Sarah Lee asks, ignoring Desirée.

"What do *you* think?" Nick says. "You think I'd make a ten-hour drive all the way down here just for the hell of it?"

"I'm so totally impressed," says Sarah Lee.

"Don't be, because he doesn't love me, that ten-hour road trip of his notwithstanding," Desirée says, in a voice so small, it's as if she's talking to herself. She knows, in the most visceral way, deep in her marrow, once and for all, that this is the irrefutable truth, as it has always been. Though Nick might insist otherwise now, it won't make the slightest difference. Because she *knows*. And is savoring the relief that comes with the knowledge that none of this matters to her anymore; after all, isn't it true that her heart pumps faster, harder, louder, at the thought of someone else?

And doesn't Nick need to know that he's been left far behind, facedown in the gritty Kansas dust?

"Well, I'm not giving up," Nick announces. "I'm not moving an inch until I've convinced you."

"Me?" Sarah Lee says. "*I'm* convinced."

"Really? Did you know that Miss Lavender warned me he's not to be trusted?" Desirée says.

"No way."

"Who the hell is Miss Lavender?"

"She's a psychic, and apparently a very reliable one," Desirée says, able to predict Nick's laughter an instant before she hears it.

"Give me a break, Desi."

"No, Desirée's right," Sarah Lee agrees. "If I were her, and Miss Lavender told me not to trust you, I'd send you packing, too."

"Even so, I'm not leaving."

So what is Desirée meant to do—dial the sheriff's office and have Nick forcibly removed from this commonplace little motel room, listen to him proclaiming his undying, fraudulent love for her as the deputies hustle him away in a squad car? She watches him holding his ground next to that now thoroughly unappetizing pizza, arms crossed against his waist, eyes behind his tortoise-shell glasses trained on hers so hopefully. Without question, a cutie pie who's impressively smart even among Yalies, happily premed despite all that dreary calculus, fractal geometry, and inorganic chemistry—a world Desirée doesn't have a taste for. Was there really a time when she'd been intoxicated by almost everything he did and said, by his unfailing sunniness, by the sight of his deeply etched dimples and his myopic hazel eyes? But now she is immune to him, every cell resistant to his alluring optimism and confidence.

I like you veeery much. Veeery, veeery much. Oh, the crushing, never-to-be-forgotten humiliation of having lost her virginity and received *that* in return!

"Let's go over this one last time," she says. "Love, you don't seem to understand, is not an afterthought. You don't sit around mulling it over and then after a few hours of deep contemplation come to the conclusion that, hey, you're really in love after all."

"You don't?" Nick says. "Why not? I mean, what's so terrible about addressing it analytically?"

"Jesus, how dumb are you?" Sarah Lee says.

Unfolding his arms, Nick shoves his hands into his back pockets. He rocks back and forth in his glossy loafers. "Look, just make me happy and tell me we're back together, okay?" he addresses Desirée.

"What I'm telling you, *Nicholas,* is the very opposite. The polar opposite. The antithesis, the—"

"Stop!"

"—inverse, the converse, maybe even—"

"Maybe we could put our relationship on probation," Nick muses. "You know, kind of a trial period starting right this minute?"

Desirée stares deliberately at him; is he for real? "What we have here is a failure to communicate," she points out.

"I'm sorry, what?"

But of course it's Bobby McVicar who loves *Cool Hand Luke.* Bobby who tiptoed sweetly out of the way to afford her and Nick a modicum of space, Bobby whose body is so miraculously in tune with her own that she aches at the thought of it now.

"How'd you make Phi Beta Kappa junior year? No offense, but you're clueless, dude," she tells Nick.

"Obviously I must be. I mean, I just can't get it through my head that we're never going to, um, hook up, ever again."

Clearing her throat, reminding them that she, too, hasn't moved an inch, Sarah Lee says, "So will you be needing an extra blanket or pillow or whatever, tonight?"

He'll be driving back to Wisconsin tomorrow, Nick announces, slamming the knuckles of his right hand several times against the palm of his left. And then he shoots Desirée an imploring look that says, *You're not going to make me get my own room tonight, are you?*

In fact, her bed is king-sized, almost large enough for a family of four. She tells herself that in the morning Nick will be gone, possibly even before she awakens, like a bad dream that loses most of its vividness and detail the instant you open your eyes.

"Maybe a toothbrush?" Nick tells Sarah Lee. "I forgot to pack one."

In the old days he simply would have used Desirée's.

She thinks now of her mother and father and the weight of their lost intimacy. How bewildering, after so many years, to grow cold in the presence of the one person with whom you'd counted on spending a lifetime. How strange to feel shockingly ill at ease in the company of someone who knows you inside and out.

All the misery between her and Nick had been, on her end, at least, a stinging disappointment that had already begun to pale in memory ever since she set foot in Honey Creek. And now here he is at the Bambi, invading her space, causing her temples to throb and her stomach to churn queasily. If she looks forward to anything at this moment, it is the day—rapidly approaching, she senses—when even the memory of Nick Davenport will have lost all meaning for her. Until then, there is this one last night to endure, and she will have to rise to the occasion. Because it just seems cruel, after his ill-advised, ten-hour road trip, to boot him out the door.

"So why don't you and Sarah Lee get you that toothbrush," she tells him.

"I'm veeery, veeery grateful to you," he says, though it's not at all clear whether it's Desirée or Sarah Lee he means.

SHE CALLS BOBBY from the landline on the nightstand as soon as she is alone in the room, hoping for the opportunity to apologize and to be restored by his lovely, calm voice. But it's his mother who picks up his cell and she is, Starshine explains, "in a state."

"Oh, Desirée!" she says. "The wedding's only a week away, right, and I've got the coldest feet in the world. And I've got Rusty Wallis for a houseguest until God knows when. He finally went and turned himself in and then they released him, you know, on his own recognizance, since of course he's not a threat to anyone, and then he seemed so disoriented they called *me* of all people, and frankly, I don't know what to do with him except stick him in front of the TV, which is where he's been for the past couple of hours. And . . . I just discovered that the dress I was planning to wear to the wedding has a small stain right up front."

Desirée is worn out merely listening to this litany of woes and can just about manage to ask, "Is Bobby around?"

"Bobby? I thought he was with you."

"He was, but then he went off to practice with the band, which I thought might be in your basement . . ."

"Should I be worried that he left his cell phone home?"

"You're having a bad night, aren't you?" Desirée says. *That makes two of us,* she almost adds.

"Well, I'm getting married, I'm turning fifty-five, and an old man who euthanized his wife is sitting in my den watching *Hannah Montana.* And my feet are so cold I think I may have frostbite."

"Why don't you get Dr. McVicar to defrost them for you," Desirée suggests.

"You'd think by my age I'd finally be ready for something like this. Wayne and I have been together practically forever, my son is grown, so really, what am I waiting for?"

"I have the best kind of vibes about this wedding," Desirée says, though actually she has no vibes at all but has decided to ignore her customary inclination toward cynicism. "I think you should get that stain off your dress and put your best frostbitten foot forward," she recommends.

"Good vibes, huh?" says Starshine. "I've got a grief-stricken mercy killer as a houseguest, you know. I'm absolutely certain he's completely harmless, but even so I'm locking our bedroom door tonight."

"Better to err on the side of caution," Desirée says, wearily tossing off one of those old saws she's always been a little suspicious of. "Oh, and if you happen to see Bobby, please tell him I'm so . . ."

"So *what?*"

"No, no, never mind, I'll tell him myself."

SHE AND NICK STAY UP most of the night watching movies from the nineties on a Kansas City cable channel. There's one with

Al Pacino as the devil incarnate, one with a fleshy Sylvester Stallone as a conscience-stricken sheriff, and one with Richard Gere falsely accused of murder in Hong Kong. Eventually Desirée falls into an exhausted, dream-riddled sleep. Clear as day, she sees Rusty Wallis on trial in Hong Kong, with Al Pacino as unsympathetic judge and jury, and Stallone as the bailiff. Unfortunately, they are all speaking in Mandarin, and even though this is *her* dream, no one provides a translator for her. She awakens frustrated and bewildered, and seeing Nick asleep beside her only adds to her confusion.

"What are *you* doing here?" she says grumpily. For a moment she mistakenly thinks they're back in her mother's living room on the Upper East Side, and then it hits her that they are in Honey Creek, and that for two people who are no longer a couple, they're spending way too much time together.

Nick yawns sourly in her face. He's slept with his glasses on, along with his pants and shirt, she's relieved to see. Slipping an index finger under the lenses of his glasses, he rubs first one eye and then the other. "I sounded pretty desperate last night, didn't I?" he says sheepishly. He reaches over with his small, boyish hand, and traces the arc of Desirée's eyebrow. "Irregardless, I really hate to lose you, Desi."

"Regardless or irregardless, you'll be fine," she promises. "And please don't touch me. Ever again."

"Don't tell me I'll be fine—how can I possibly be fine knowing you and I are done?"

"Finished," she agrees, and even the word itself feels deeply satisfying. "You'll be perfectly fine," she repeats. "Especially once you're up and out and on the road again."

"Can we at least have breakfast together?"

And hard as she tries, she just can't come up with a way to weasel out of one last meal with him.

CHAPTER 29

WHEN NINA EXPLAINS TO Daniel Rose that Porsha is gone, that Satyra, her part-time replacement, is signed out for the day, and that she herself has to babysit for her father tonight, he tells her not to worry. An hour and a half later, he arrives at her door with egg drop soup with seaweed and tofu, scallion pancakes, sautéed baby shrimp with cashews, and Buddha's Delight. And a couple of DVDs he'd ordered earlier in the week from Netflix. She is so happy to see him, so choked, really, with gratitude, that, for a moment, it's difficult to summon the voice to speak to him.

"It's just me and some Chinese food," Daniel says, putting down the plastic bag fragrant with their dinner, so that he can embrace her. "Honestly, I'm not the messiah."

"Coulda fooled *me*," Nina says.

In the kitchen, her father sits captive in his wheelchair, an apron fastened around his neck, one sunken cheek marked by an errant bit of rice pudding.

"How are you, sir?" Daniel says, and, as always, clasps Marvin's hand.

"You remember Daniel," Nina says optimistically, though, in truth, she has no idea whether or not this is so. Occasionally, she's convinced her father is afflicted with Parkinson's-related dementia, while other times, when he seems absorbed in watching CNN or in listening to her read from *The Portrait of a Lady*, she's sure he is fully sentient. She knows, too, that if Porsha were to demand, as a condition for her return, that Nina stroll barefoot through a glittery field of broken glass, she'd agree to it instantly. How she wishes she could take back her foolish accusations about that Weight Watchers sundae, her insistence on making an issue over something so utterly trivial, her refusal to just let it go. Every morning since Porsha's departure, Nina has awakened to the soul-sickening knowledge that what awaits her is a drenched diaper, along with a struggle to get her father to swallow down a few mouthfuls of applesauce, a few sips from the first of three daily cans of Nutrament that he has little interest in drinking. He has so little appetite for food, drink, or life itself, and, frankly, sometimes it feels as if it's killing her. She suspects he wants to die, though of course he hasn't been able to say so and she would never dare to ask. If she were in his shoes, in his wheelchair, in his skin, she thinks she would beg for a lethal cocktail, a bullet to the back of the head, a pistol shoved into her mouth. Perhaps her father feels otherwise. Unable to speak his mind, he's loaded with secrets, and not likely to unburden himself anytime soon. She tells herself that she loves him, that if she didn't, she'd never have been able to get past that very first diaper, warm and heavy in her hand and reeking of ammonia. Her sister, Caroline, safely installed in her condo on the beach in Santa Monica, doesn't know what she's missing. A real estate attorney who shares a successful practice with her husband, she's sympathetic, but not sympathetic enough.

What do you want me to do, move him to California, three thousand miles from the city where he's spent almost his entire life? I don't think so, Nina, do you?

Can't her sister at least come to visit him more than once a year?

Can't she make a lousy phone call once a week just to check in?

She could, but she chooses not to. She's not a bad person; she's simply at a distance and doesn't quite understand the prickly texture of Nina's daily life.

And so Nina just has to suck it up. Every single goddamn day.

In addition to the messages she's left on Porsha's phone, Nina sent an e-mail apology—complete with sound effects—through an online greeting card company. If Porsha had clicked on the link, what she would have seen and heard was a goofy-looking royal-blue hound emerging from a body of water and weeping like a baby. And on the screen, she would have seen the words *I've cried me a river / Won't you please please forgive me?*

Evidently she, Nina, remains unforgiven, because she still hasn't heard a word from Porsha.

. . .

"UP HIGHER, HONEY," Daniel groans, and Nina has to shush him, trying not to laugh. Fooling around with her boyfriend in her bedroom while, next door, her father is sleeping makes her feel like a teenager. And what's sillier than a middle-aged woman feeling like a seventeen-year-old?

"Shush!" she says. "You'll wake my father."

And now Daniel is laughing, too, as she draws circles along his inner thigh with her tongue.

AFTER DANIEL HAS LEFT FOR WORK, and Satyra, Marvin's new caregiver, has arrived for a couple of hours, Nina takes the subway to Brooklyn, Porsha's address in hand. The neighborhood is unfamiliar to her; descending the stairs of the elevated train, she walks along a commercial street of downscale shops, passing halal butchers, a Bengali restaurant, a couple of hole-in-the-wall falafel places, and a small grocery, its name printed in Cyrillic letters. Porsha's street, a few blocks away, is lined by modest, two-story homes set on tiny lawns behind chain-link fences. At the very end of the street is a single four-story apartment house with an untidy courtyard strewn with empty plastic bags and forgotten beer bottles; a pair of South Asian teenagers (Pakistani? Indian? She can't tell which), a boy and a girl, are seated on the broad stone steps leading up to the building, both of them wearing jeans and busy on their cell phones. A nun dressed in full habit walks by, pulling a child's red wagon occupied by a sleeping Dalmatian.

Nina makes her way around the teenagers, who are checking their messages now, and enters the building's foyer, where a directory sealed in cracked Lucite and a set of buzzers are mounted on the wall. Behind the locked glass doors, a deserted lobby is visible, with its black-and-white mosaic tiled floor and what looks like a fireplace that has been painted over in pea-soup green. She finds Porsha's name on the directory and presses the button gingerly. There's no answer; she checks to make sure she has the right apartment, and presses again. How senseless to have come all the way to Brooklyn without calling first! But if she *had* called, she's certain that Porsha would have hung up on her.

Claiming a seat for herself on the steps, as far from the teenagers as she can manage, Nina hears the girl say, "I really like people . . . but not really."

"Yeah," the boy says. "I get that. I mean, most people actually like me, but the ones who don't, well, fuck *them*."

Amen to that, dude.

It's a steamy August day and Nina regrets having forgotten to bring a bottle of water with her. All she has is a copy of today's *Times,* where, if she likes, she can find all the bad news that's fit to print. She reads about a twenty-eight-year-old mother who put her newborn baby in the microwave and cooked her to death following an argument with her boyfriend. According to an unnamed source, the woman worried that her boyfriend would abandon her if he discovered the truth—that the baby wasn't his. *Of course—what better way to assuage your anxiety than to microwave your daughter?* Sickened, Nina folds the paper in half and slips it back inside her canvas carryall. At the curb, a squirrel wrestles with a squashed Poland Spring bottle. A young woman strolls past in a T-shirt that says, SKINNY-ASS BITCH.

"What up, Tanquasha?" the teenaged boy calls out, waving to her.

Tanquasha waves back, and continues walking.

And here comes Porsha, carrying two supermarket bags from Key Food in each hand.

Nina rushes through the courtyard toward her. "Let me help you," she says. "Please?"

"Go on home," Porsha says, her face registering no surprise at all at the sight of Nina, only disapproval.

"Come on, Porsha, don't be that way."

"I'll be any way I please."

"You've got four bags there. At least give me *one,*" Nina says. "I can see how heavy they are."

"I'm mad at you, girl."

"I know," Nina says. As Porsha tries to move past her, Nina blocks her way. "Just one bag, that's all I'm asking."

Porsha lowers the bags to the pavement. "How's Grandpa been?"

"Well, he misses you. So let me bring these bags upstairs for you and we'll talk about it," Nina says hopefully.

"You think I'd let you upstairs into my home after you disrespected me like you did?"

I'm *telling you that nice little sundae was* owed *to me!*

"That sundae *was* owed to you, Porsha. And I apologize. Profusely."

"Oh, I know all about your apologies," Porsha says. "You cried yourself a river apologizing."

While Nina waits for absolution, a small flock of pigeons congregates nearby, fighting over a lone hot dog bun.

"A good cry clears the air, just like a good spanking," Porsha says finally.

"What?"

Porsha sighs; the impressively large shelf of her bosom falls, then rises again. "Oh, for heaven's sake, come on upstairs with me."

"Really? Thank you! *Thank you!*"

"Don't you be thanking me so quick. One cup of coffee and I'm sending you home."

Nodding, Nina picks up two of Porsha's bags.

"One cup of coffee for *Grandpa's* sake, not yours."

The apartment house has no elevator, Nina learns, when Porsha points to the stairs in the lobby. "Four flights up. You still coming?"

Marching laboriously up the stairs to Porsha's apartment, Nina sniffs the warm, moist air, whose scent reminds her of an Indian restaurant. "Curry!" she says.

"Those are my Bengali neighbors," Porsha explains. "Debjani and Gopal, Shruti and Sanjay, Joyeeta and Mukundaram. We've got neighbors from Senegal, too. We're a regular United Nations here," she says, and shrugs, then unlocks a steel door painted an ugly maroonish brown. "We need to catch our breath a minute." They deposit the supermarket bags on the table in the small, stiflingly hot eat-in kitchen.

"Oh, you have a window in here—nice!" Nina says. "And I see you have a new refrigerator." It occurs to her that this might sound patronizing, and she instructs herself to keep quiet.

"Come on with me and we'll have ourselves a little rest," Porsha says. She steps out of her bejeweled white leather sandals, and leads Nina into the living room, which is just large enough to accommodate a love seat, an armchair, and, resting on a white plastic cube, a TV set with rabbit ears. The linoleum floor is partially covered by a rug made of industrial carpeting; on the walls hang framed studio portraits of children and grandchildren, most of them in graduation caps and gowns. Nina smiles at a photograph of an infant—three months old, she knows—dressed in jeans, and a T-shirt adorned with a fire engine and a trio of duckling firefighters. The baby's feet are in tiny sneakers, and there is a terry-cloth Big Bird doll clutched in the crook of one arm. Underneath the picture is a hand-lettered sign on a strip of construction paper that says, THINKING OF YOU.

"That's Tyrell, your great-grandson. And that's the outfit I gave him," Nina says, touched to see that her gift had actually pleased Tyrell's mother—a young girl close to Desirée's age.

"Don't you get all excited just because the baby's wearing the nice clothes you bought him. Don't you start thinking I'm coming back home with you just because he's holding the Big Bird you gave him. Because I'm NOT."

"Oh, I'm not here to ask you to come back with me," Nina lies. Afraid to look at Porsha, she studies her fingers laced together in her lap. "Honestly, I wouldn't want to burden you with that."

"So . . . you came all the way to Brooklyn for a cup of instant coffee, did I get that right?" Porsha says. "And maybe you'll have some ice cream? Because guess what, I bought me my very own Weight Watchers sundaes—two boxes of them—and if you were to ask me for one right now, I would go straight to the fridge and get it for you. Because it's just ice cream, don't you know? Ice cream, not gold or diamonds or rubies."

"I know," Nina says meekly. "And is it all right if I say I'm sorry one last time?"

"No more of that. Let's have us some ice cream for breakfast."

"Nothing for me, thanks," Nina says.

But Porsha isn't listening; she disappears into the kitchen, returning with two sundaes, some napkins, and spoons. "*Sit,*" she says as Nina rises from the love seat.

Nina displays her palms to Porsha. "Subway hands," she says. "Got to wash them."

"What language are you talking, girl?"

"It's what Desirée used to say to me, to Patrick and me, when she was three or four, and we wanted to hug and kiss her the instant we came home from work. She must have learned it in preschool."

"So you want to wash your dirty 'subway hands,' is that what you're saying?" Porsha asks, smiling at Nina for the first time today.

Nina smiles back.

"Don't you smile at me like that," Porsha says sternly, but Nina wants to believe her resolve is melting, that Porsha, at least, will come back to her, if not today, then sometime soon.

In the narrow bathroom where she washes her hands, there's an alcove above the sink with a tall wire shelf full of canned goods—okra, carrots and peas, SpaghettiOs, whole peeled tomatoes. And wedged in on its side, an old-fashioned, hard-shelled Samsonite suitcase. The thought of her own spacious apartment shames her now; surely she is no more entitled than Porsha to inhabit a comfortable life. (Isn't it a mere accident of birth that Porsha was born into a family of South Carolina sharecroppers, Nina herself into one of relatively prosperous attorneys?)

Porsha has, at last, turned on the air conditioner projecting from the living room window, Nina observes gratefully. She digs into the drizzle of chocolate syrup ornamenting her sundae, plunges the tip of her spoon all the way to the cookie crumble crust, thinking she will offer Porsha a raise, but not now, not when Porsha isn't yet prepared to give in to her.

"So what do you hear from your baby Desirée?" Porsha is patting her mouth daintily with a folded napkin.

"Not much. She has a new boyfriend out in Kansas," Nina says, as if this were an adequate explanation for Desirée's failure to keep in close touch. "Oh, and her wallet and cell phone were stolen in what sounds like a pretty frightening robbery."

Porsha frowns. "Well, you got to let them live their own grown-up lives," she says, pointing to the wall of photographs behind her. "My grandkid Shamina, you know, Tyrell's mama, she does what she likes and pays no mind to anything I say to her. And her mother was just the same. I had plenty of good advice

for my daughter, but after a time I stopped giving it to her because, see, she was only *pretending* to listen."

"You love them so much," Nina says, "but that only goes so far."

"Never as far as we'd like."

They fall silent, both of them, Nina knows, into their own
well of worry over their wayward girls.

As she prepares to leave, standing in the doorway now, she
comes close to surrendering all dignity, to casting herself at Porsha's bare feet with their polished vermilion toenails, and begging, *begging* her to reclaim her job, her place in Marvin's life.
Not to mention Nina's own.

"We miss you," she hears herself say. Hoping this will be enough.

Porsha keeps her waiting just a beat. "Well, I'll think about it,"
she says, and it's difficult to gauge the expression on her face—
which, Nina is pained to see, is absolutely impenetrable.

CHAPTER 30

DAY OR NIGHT, Minnehaha Avenue remains hushed and forlorn, as if, like the inhabitants of Honey Creek, the street itself were resigned to what Desirée can only regard as the truly lamentable limitations of a small-town existence. *Wake up!* she wants to bellow as she looks ahead toward the Touch of Class Charm School, the Kum & Go, the abandoned video store where Howard Stern still reigns supreme in the window. She just can't help herself: born and bred in the greatest city in the world, she has, well, expectations. *How can you Honey Creekers be satisfied with so little?* she imagines herself howling through a megaphone as she and Nick Davenport approach the Sweet Tooth now. Not that she doesn't understand what it is that Honey Creek has to offer: a comfy sense of security. And more security. Minnehaha will, she suspects, always look much as it does now, its shops staffed by the same array of familiar faces, people you went to school with, went to church with, and, in the end, were buried with. The population is essentially unchanging, a handful of deaths here and there, a handful of births to counter those losses; rarely, if ever, will you be treated to the sight of a person you don't know, a stranger whose accent is unfamiliar, whose skin is surprisingly dusky, whose very walk down Minnehaha arouses suspicion.

So why isn't all this constancy absolutely suffocating to Honey Creek's natives? (The one and only way Desirée can perceive it, even though she is uncomfortably aware that this speaks to a narrow-mindedness she can't quite believe is hers.) How is it that, deprived of the vivid color, the infinite variety, the exhilarating hum of big-city life, everyone here continues to thrive nevertheless? She's tried, hard as she can, since the moment she arrived in Honey Creek. But . . . She. Just. Doesn't. Get. It. And this inability to grasp the pleasures of small-town life feels like a shameful failure to her.

She ushers Nick into the Sweet Tooth, where the two of them

take their places at the empty counter and are greeted quietly by Riley Maxwell, who isn't offering that blinding smile Desirée recalls from the first time they'd met.

"Menus?" she says, her face turned away from them.

"Hey, Riley, remember me?" Desirée says, teasing. Because isn't she still the talk of the town, the city slicker who'd stepped off a bus and directly into the swirl of gossip that keeps Honey Creek whirring?

"Waffles and strawberries?" Riley says in a whispery voice.

"I'll have the French toast and bacon," Nick says.

Riley grunts.

"Pardon?"

"I *said*, there's no bacon." Although she's turned only partially in their direction, Desirée and Nick see it all; the gruesome, blackish-purple, half-closed eye, the cut at the bridge of Riley's nose, the upper lip swollen out to here. And now they're listening to the uninspired, overtly bullshit narrative of how Riley rose in the middle of the night to tend to one of her kids, tripped over a Dora the Explorer doll, and smashed her face against the edge of a partially open dresser drawer.

This is a face from the eleven o'clock news and made-for-TV movies, as painful and unreal a sight as Desirée has ever seen, and she finds herself staring dumbly.

"Don't look at me," Riley says. "Just order your damn breakfast and leave me alone."

"It's Sarah Lee's brother, right? It's Wes who did this?"

"He'll say he didn't, and guess what, I'll say the same thing."

"And you'd both be lying," Desirée says.

"It's like Sarah Lee says, I'm a very forgiving person. And you know, it's what Jesus would do."

Arrgh! "This isn't one of those things you forgive someone for," Desirée says cautiously. "Not that it's any of my business," she adds, "but Riley, how can you give him a pass on this?"

"So does your friend want ham with that French toast instead of bacon?"

"You should have Wes arrested for assault and battery," Desirée says. "You have to."

"Right, and it'll end up on page two in the *Honey Creek Herald* under the sheriff's report, and my parents can read all about it and tell me I've brought shame on Wes and the kids, and of course on them. So yeah, I'll be sure and make that phone call to the sheriff."

"Forget the ham," Nick says. "Would you like Desirée and me to drive you over to your doctor or the ER?"

"I don't even know who you are and I'm supposed to let you drive me somewhere?"

"He's just my ex," Desirée says, deliberately dismissive, then feeling a pang at the aggrieved look on Nick's face.

"So what's he doing in Honey Creek?"

"Trying to win her back," Nick says. "Unfortunately, she won't give me the time of day."

"Oh well." Riley pours them coffee, though they haven't asked for any. "If Wes had given *me* the time of day instead of my sweet baby sister, I wouldn't have punched him in the mouth, which made him so mad he just couldn't help himself and had to punch me back."

"Pretty good coffee," Nick says. "Got any Sweet'N Low?"

"Why don't you come around here behind the counter and get it yourself," Riley instructs him. "And you know what, you can forget about your breakfast. I'm sick of serving you people. But I'll make you those waffles, Desirée, if you still want them."

"So I'm not one of those people you're sick of?"

"It's men I'm talking about. If any of them come in here, they'll have to serve their own damn selves. That's my new policy."

"That's discriminatory," Nick complains. "But give me half a dozen eggs, some bread and butter, and a frying pan, and I'll make us all some French toast."

Riley says, "Help yourself. And I'll have mine extra well done, almost burnt, okay?"

"Got it," Nick says cheerfully. He and Riley exchange places; she and Desirée seat themselves at a booth where they can keep an eye on him. And then, because it hasn't become any easier to look at her, Desirée takes out her oversized Prada sunglasses (an expensive birthday present from her father) and passes them across the table to Riley.

"I'm not going to the doctor," Riley says. "And anyway, Wes got the worst of it, actually. One of his front teeth is dangling by a thread."

"Sounds as if he deserved it," Desirée says, though the thought of fists flying and making contact with bone and flesh—in Riley's household or any other—turns her stomach.

Riley shrugs, drains her coffee. "You know, Sarah Lee says she's seen you writing away in that little notebook of yours, Desirée, and what I'm praying is that you're never going to write about *this*," she says, pointing to her blackened eye. "Because I'd die of embarrassment."

Concealing that sharp prickle of excitement she's savoring now—knowing that for the first time in her life, there is, in fact, someone who regards her as a writer—Desirée says, "Of course I won't."

"Tell me I can trust you."

"Oh, absolutely," Desirée promises. But she knows that Riley is on to something here. That Riley already views her as the person she may very well be on the verge of becoming: one of those greedy souls who observes the lives of others and ruthlessly picks them clean, cannibalizing them for her art. One of those who would sell her own family down the river for a couple of especially poignant or hilarious scenes or lines of dialogue. Well, if this is who she is, or might be in the not-too-distant future, does she need to apologize for herself? And what if it truly isn't possible to be, simultaneously, both a full-fledged mensch and a bona fide writer, what then? She is miserable contemplating all of this, and apparently it shows on her face, because Riley is asking her now if she's all right.

She puts her hand on Desirée's. "So what's with you and Nick? He's cute, even if his clothes look like they've been slept in a couple of nights in a row."

"Well, there's a little something called love that was missing from his half of the equation," Desirée explains.

"Time to move on, then. Obviously."

"What about *you*?"

"What *about* me?"

"Come on, Riley, you can't be serious."

"Wes and me are a couple, okay? He's got this thing for my sister, we don't deny that. But am I going to be any better off if I throw him out? I'll be alone with two little kids and not enough money. So what's the sense in that? Where's it going to get me? No place better than where I am now, that's for sure."

"You don't still love him?" Desirée says, appalled. "You couldn't."

Smiling at her pityingly, Riley says, "You've made the really stupid mistake of assuming that because you happen to be from some big-deal place and go to some big-deal school, you know every damn thing there is to know about everything. So when I tell you Wes and I are a permanent couple, you need to listen up. This is someone I've loved since we were twelve, okay? The both of us knew it was our fate—maybe God's will or something—to be together and we just had to go with it. No matter what."

God's will, huh, that she stay married to an abusive, unfaithful low-life? What, exactly, are the chances that God has anything at all to do with it?

"And your sister's fate?" Desirée says, so disgusted she can hardly speak.

"Well, Allison's just one of those crazy fuckups who's got no sense whatsoever. The other day, believe it or not, I saw her slap Charles—that's her butt-ugly bulldog—across the face because he grabbed her ham and cheese sub from the kitchen table and made off with it. See, that's the kind of thing that keeps me from killing her with my bare hands," Riley says. "Because if I thought for one second that she was a regular, normal person, I *would* kill her."

"Kill who?" Nick says, arriving with two professional-looking plates of French toast, slices of orange artfully arranged around the edges.

"Very nice," Riley says. "But where's the syrup? And the silverware. If you're gonna do it, do it right."

"Coming right up."

"Wes never once fixed me breakfast in all the years we've been together," Riley says. "Wonder if he's made my sister breakfast in bed. If I ever found out something like that, I'd never forgive him."

"Wait wait wait—you forgive a black eye and a swollen lip but not breakfast in bed for your sister?" Desirée says.

"I've already *told* you," Riley says impatiently, "he only hit me because I nearly knocked his tooth out."

"I give up." Desirée is too outraged to speak; her fists are clenched and she doesn't know what to do with them.

"Don't bother trying to understand someone else's life," Riley advises. "It's one of those things that can't be done."

"I'm a writer," Desirée says, though even to her own ears this sounds laughably presumptuous. "It's my *job* to understand."

"Yeah, sure, good luck with that."

Their silverware scrapes against the thick ceramic breakfast plates, and the small sounds of chewing and swallowing seem magnified in the otherwise silent room. Desirée's elbow keeps brushing Nick's as they eat. They're far too close for comfort and all she wants from him is to finish up his breakfast and clear out of her life. Permanently. But why is this too much to hope for?

The door swings open and Bobby appears, followed by two gray-haired guys in overalls. Desirée's face flushes; every inch of her feels blisteringly hot and trembly. She waves to Bobby, but his response is curt, merely a nod.

"Hey Riley, how about some coffee over here?" one of the men yells.

"Have to get it yourself, Arthur," Riley calls back.

"Huh?"

"I'll have the usual," the other guy says.

"You want eggs over easy, *you* make them," Riley says.

"Huh?"

"Sorry, Tate, I'm only serving gals from now on. The rest of you are on your own."

Tate and his buddy are standing over Riley now, eyeing her French toast longingly.

"That sure does smell good," Tate says. He has a weather-beaten face and squinty blue eyes, just like Arthur; Desirée imagines him reaching down into her plate and helping himself to some of her breakfast.

"Sure do wish I could get me a taste of that," Arthur says, with a theatrical sigh.

"You're acting plain old crazy today, Riley. And who gave you that fat lip?" Tate says.

"I was sleepwalking last night. Right smack into the bath-room door."

"Dresser drawer," Desirée murmurs, as if the specifics of Ri-ley's lies are of any consequence.

"That's a dangerous business, sleepwalking into doors and such," Tate says. "My poor wife, AnnMarie, once . . . well, never mind about that, but if she were alive today, she'd be cooking those eggs over easy for me right now and I wouldn't be standing here begging you to take pity on a hungry old man who misses his wife so terribly he can't think of nothing else."

Running a finger thoughtfully over her bruised mouth, Riley says, "That's a load of crap, you big faker. You think I don't know about you and Margaret Keating? You think all of Honey Creek doesn't know?"

"But hey, that doesn't mean I'm not hungry," Tate says.

"*I'll* make you breakfast," Nick volunteers. "You guys come over to the counter with me."

They scoot after him, and Bobby, who has been keeping his distance, standing alone at the counter, makes his way at last to Desirée. He's in jeans and cowboy boots, a plain, perfectly white T-shirt, and, weirdly, suspenders, which remind Desirée of her grandfather, of the struggle it always is for her and her mother to get him properly into his clothes on Porsha's days off. She won-ders if her mother has succeeded in luring Porsha back, or if, at this very moment, Nina is breaking in someone new, someone who regards Marvin merely as a vacant shell, a man without a past or a future, just one more old geezer biding his time until he's ready to be fitted for a coffin. Guiltily, she considers walking over to the pay phone outside the Sweet Tooth's restroom and calling home, but the sight of Bobby McVicar with his braid undone, his beautiful pale hair lying loose just beneath his shoulders, roots her to her seat. She motions to him to come and sit with her; as he lowers himself into the booth, his hair drapes itself along her bare arm and she nearly falls into one of those classic Victorian swoons.

Bobby stares at Riley in silence. "Any broken teeth in that mouth of yours?" he asks finally.

"Nope, I'm okay."

"Look, want me to have Starshine give you a call?"

"About what?"

"About what I'm guessing is behind those sunglasses," Bobby says, his voice gentle. "You know."

"I'm grateful for your concern," Riley says, leaning across the table and snapping a suspender. "But the best thing you can do for me is to stay out of my business and concentrate on your own, which is making sure that your parents tie the knot nice and tight and live happily ever after like the rest of us."

This sounds more or less like a curse, Desirée observes, but if *she* were in Riley's Nikes, wouldn't she be unlikely to smile upon the McVicars' impending marriage, as well?

A newcomer, a short, bull-necked guy in a Kansas City Royals baseball cap, is addressing Nick crossly. "What the hell are you doing back there behind my counter?"

"Helping out?" Nick says.

"Are you on salary here?" the little guy asks. "Do I pay your workmen's comp? Have I ever seen your face before?"

"Not exactly," Nick admits.

"Well, then, get out from behind the counter. And take off that goddamn apron!"

It pains Desirée to see the way Nick shrinks ever so slightly from the overbearing little guy, the way he whips off the starched white apron and folds it meticulously before handing it over.

"Hey, you can't do that, Cliff, he's in the middle of making us breakfast," Tate says. "And we're starving."

"If anyone's making breakfast, it's Riley. And what's she doing in those sunglasses?"

"Resting my eyes," Riley calls out.

"Well, break time's over. These guys are hungry over here."

"That's *their* tough luck," Riley mutters as Cliff approaches and takes in the sight of her swollen lip.

Desirée, who's always been suspicious of men who sport jewelry more lavish than a plain wedding ring, notices the thick gold ID bracelet around his wrist and the gold-and-onyx ring on his pinky.

"You didn't get that lip on the job, did you?" Cliff is asking Riley.

"I've been sleepwalking, is all."

"Well, you're awake now, in which case I recommend you get back to work."

"I will," Riley says. "Just as soon as some gals walk through the door."

"You've got some perfectly good customers right here."

"They're men," Riley points out. "And I won't be serving men anymore."

Cliff gives the onyx ring a couple of violent spins around his pinky. "Is this one of those feminist things?"

"No, I don't think so."

"Well, what am I supposed to tell people? That the best employee I ever had just up and turned racist overnight?"

"Sexist," Desirée calls out.

Observing her for the first time, Cliff says, "So who are *you*?"

"Oh, no one at all, really," Desirée says as Bobby places his hand over hers in her lap.

"Hey, are we getting our breakfast or what?" Tate says.

One-handed, Riley yanks the sunglasses from her face, then hooks them around the salt and pepper shakers at the center of the table. "I just can't."

"Jesus Christ Almighty!" Cliff says, getting a good look at her spoiled face. "If I find out Wes did this to you, I'll break his legs."

"I'm a sleepwalker," Riley insists. "Been doing it all my life."

"I'm still gonna break his legs," Cliff says. "And you can wait on the customers of your choice, Riley. At least for a while, okay?" Having dispensed with her, he heads straight for Nick. "Where're you from, stranger?" he asks, as if they were actors in some old TV western, *Bonanza* or, perhaps, *Gunsmoke*.

"Wisconsin," Nick says coolly.

"Okay, look, sorry I yelled at you, buddy. You wouldn't happen to be in the market for a temporary job, would you, you know, maybe for a week or so?"

"Maybe." Clearly trying not to look too interested, Nick concentrates on his knuckles, cracking them one by one.

"You could do worse than working for me."

"Excuse me, but don't you have an application you want him

to fill out?" Desirée says. "And aren't there blood and urine samples you need for drug testing or something?"

"This is the Sweet Tooth, not Wal-Mart," Cliff says. "And this is the personnel dee-partment right here. If this guy from Wisconsin can cook and clean up and be friendly to everyone who comes in here, including the guys, he's hired."

"All right, sure," Nick says. "But I need a place to stay."

"Get your apron back on and I'll find a real cheap room for you at the Bambi. They got a special weekly rate that'll knock your socks off."

"I'm in!" Nick says.

"Hold it, don't you have to think this over?" Desirée says desperately. Because isn't it clear that he's invading her territory, and doesn't she have every right to feel choked with resentment? She'd like to insist that this is *her* little town, *her* Honey Creek—after all, she'd discovered it on her own, become entangled with its people, fallen in love with at least one of them. And here's her ex following directly behind her, settling in with a job and a place to stay, for a special weekly rate Desirée thought had been formulated just for *her*.

So look, I'm pretty sure we're happy to have you in Honey Creek, and even if we're not, at least you're not a homosexual or a woman lesbian. And so I've decided to offer you an extra-special weekly rate.

Sure sure sure.

Nick has slipped into his apron again and rolled back his sleeves before answering Desirée. "It's a free country, honey," he says, a conversation stopper par excellence. And then, turning away from her, he resumes his place behind the Sweet Tooth's grill.

SHE AND BOBBY RETREAT to her room at the Bambi, where, postbreakfast and prelunch, he undresses her tenderly and lifts her spirits considerably. She hears Bobby murmuring *I love you* and she answers, truthfully, *Me too me too me too.*

Her wrists are pinned under his, their ankles entwined, their hips locked together sweetly. "I don't want you to go back to New York," Bobby says. "Or to Yale, either."

"Oh, it's just the heat of the moment," she says, feigning nonchalance.

"We're sizzling!" Bobby agrees. "But there's more there than just the sizzle, Desirée." He nips at her neck, licks the curve of her ear. "When the heat of the moment's gone, we've still got plenty." She smiles at him lazily, contentedly. "Talk to me," he says. "You're not saying anything, Desi."

"That's because *you're* saying all the right stuff."

"Which is why you're going to forget Yale and come to KU with me?"

What? She tells him that though she hadn't planned on leaving until she absolutely has to—until the new semester starts—now that he's raised the subject, even at Margaret Keating's supersaver rate, she's racking up a big bill at the Bambi. "I'll have to pray that one or both of my parents will take pity on me when it's time to pay up," she says.

"Move in with me until we have to go back to school," Bobby says. "And then we'll figure something out after that. Like how you can take courses at KU and transfer all your Yale credits there. Since I can tell you right now that Yale's never going to be impressed with me and my less than stellar GPA."

Trade Yale for the state university in Lawrence, *Kansas*? (Probably a perfectly good school, the town itself former home to no less a literary luminary/drug addict/accidental killer than William Burroughs, a cosmopolitan guy who'd lived in London, Paris, Tangiers, and New York, yet chose to spend the last years of his life in Kansas.) But really, who would make such a counterintuitive move? What kind of wack job would even *contemplate* it? Only someone truly, madly, head over heels. And it occurs to Desirée now that, surprising—even shocking—though it may be, this wack job might very well be her.

"How about one step at a time," she tells Bobby. "So you mean move in with you and the soon-to-be newlyweds?" she says.

Bobby laughs.

"Well, technically speaking, anyway, they're about to be newlyweds."

"Technically speaking," Bobby says, "you and I have known each

other for what, almost six weeks, but that only makes what there is between us more like a great romance, don't you think?"

Romance. A word that never held even a tentative place in the vocabulary of anyone she's ever dated. Coming from Bobby McVicar, the word itself is thoroughly heartfelt and warmly intimate, and she can do nothing but embrace it, embrace *him*, wrapping her arms around the damp base of his spine and holding on for dear life.

"So am I still saying all the right things?" he asks her.

"Oh, you have a real gift for it." Unlike someone else she happens to know, someone in a grease-spattered apron and holding a spatula in his hand, someone who doesn't know the first thing about love.

CHAPTER 31

IT'S AS IF SHE AND KINGSLEY have had a whirlwind affair and then abruptly, awkwardly, ended it, Nina thinks. Serves her right for getting involved with a student after hours, sticking her nose where it never did belong. Kingsley barely looks at her these days when Nina addresses the class, and when Kingsley herself speaks up, as she does so often and so incisively, she looks everywhere but in Nina's direction. Whatever intimacy there'd been between them has vanished; that Nina had taken her student into her home, given her Desirée's bed, prepared meals for her, even thrown Kingsley's laundry in with her own, well, all of that seems like something she might have imagined in a particularly vivid dream. Kingsley has disappointed her, grievously, and Nina herself has failed her, but there's one thing, at least, that they can both count as a success: somehow, Kingsley has managed to stay awake through every one of Nina's classes. And whether it's sheer force of will, crystal meth, or megadoses of caffeine that have kept her alert and on her toes, this, too, is none of Nina's business.

Lesson learned: those who meddle will only come to grief.

"Students who would like to speak to me about the final drafts of their portfolio can see me after class or make an appointment during office hours," Nina says now, sounding, to her own ears, unusually businesslike.

Hands go up, misunderstandings are clarified, class dismissed. Davis approaches her to report, with unconcealed haughtiness, that he's transferring to Wesleyan this coming semester; turning her gaze slightly as he talks, Nina sees Kingsley and Elaina Whitacre laughing it up together, elated about something, and she is stung by the sudden coziness between those two. Her hunger to be included is, she's well aware, needy and inappropriate. Her students are not her friends; why would she want them to be? She doesn't—it's just a momentary bit of lunacy, she decides.

"Congratulations, Davis," she says. "Best of luck to you."

• • •

CONFIDING IN DR. PEPPERKORN later in the afternoon, Nina asks, "Do you think all this anxiety is just a reflection of how desperately I want my daughter back from Kansas?"

Pepperkorn strokes the top of his shaved head. "What do *you* think?"

Oh, come on, buddy, don't play that stupid game. "I asked you first," Nina says, smiling faintly.

He is not amused. "Therapy is hard work," he tells her. "I thought we'd established months ago that you were prepared to engage in that hard work, but perhaps you're no longer willing to do so . . ."

"Today on the subway I saw some teenaged kids dressed as zombies," Nina says, changing the subject just because she feels like annoying him. "They were all in whiteface, and carrying buckets of eyeballs in plastic pails."

Chewing his thumbnail aggressively, Pepperkorn says, "Uh-huh."

"There was one with a bloody, severed finger protruding from his mouth. It actually looked very lifelike."

"And how did it make you feel, looking at something like that?"

"No way at all. I'm just sharing with you one of the many outrageous things to be enjoyed on the New York City transit system."

"I think you're avoiding the subject of your daughter," Dr. Pepperkorn says. "The helplessness you feel when she doesn't heed your pleas to come home."

"Maybe."

"Good. What else?"

"My biggest fear," Nina confesses, "is that she'll trade Yale for the University of Kansas so she can be with this kid she's convinced she's in love with. And that, I can tell you right now, will kill me. Because Yale just isn't a school one drops out of. No way."

"Your daughter isn't allowed, at the age of twenty, to make her own decisions?"

"Not about THIS!" Nina says, and here come those tears, a steamy rush of them, and even as she's fishing in her handbag, she knows there are no tissues to be found there, only a bulging, forest-green suede wallet, Tic Tacs in a plastic dispenser, pens in green, red, and lavender ink, two flavors of sugarless gum, her cell phone, keys, and a twenty-seven-dollar tube of Chanel Aqua-lumière Lip Shine. None of which can be used to wipe her leaking eyes. Or—and this is mortifying—her nose.

Without a word, Dr. Pepperkorn hands her the box of cheap, no-name tissues on his desk, and she plucks one and then two more, quickly mopping up her face and remembering Desirée asking, in her preschool days, *What do I need a tissue for when I can just use my sleeve?*

Dr. Pepperkorn puts his feet up on his desk, hooks his hands behind his neck. Nina is startled to see that he's wearing slippers—backless, round-toed ones constructed of some kind of microfiber, and which render him schlumpy and unprofessional. Ordinary. Someone unfit to analyze her subconscious or any other part of her, for that matter.

"Feeling better?" he asks.

"Not really."

"Would it make you feel any better if I told you I'm confident that, ultimately, you'll do the right thing when it comes to your daughter?"

"I will?"

"You're an intelligent woman, smart enough to know that interfering with Desirée's life is, at this point, inappropriate. She's old enough to vote, old enough to join the army, old enough to choose where she goes to school. She is, if I may quote Bob Dylan, 'beyond your command.'"

This is the worst advice she's received from him today or any other day; the only consolation is that her health insurance is picking up the tab for it. *"Blood on the Tracks* is my favorite album," she offers, and clumps the bargain-brand tissues into a single soft ball. "You know, 'Idiot Wind'?"

"It appears you are, yet again, avoiding the subject at hand," Dr. Pepperkorn says, unable to conceal—as he is supposed to—the disapproval in his voice.

Id-i-ot wind, blow-ing ev-ery time you move your mouth.

. . .

"YOU WANT ME to do WHAT?" Patrick says.

"First of all, calm down," Nina says into the phone. "Take it easy. All you have to do is fly to Kansas City, rent a car at the airport, drive out to Honey Creek, and make sure you get Desirée on that plane with you. Twenty-four hours and you'll be back on Riverside Drive with Jordan. I'd do it myself, but I still have a few classes left to teach. And obviously I can't leave my father. But you've had the whole summer off from school, Patrick, give me a break."

Sushi the cat flies neatly onto Daniel Rose's dining room table, then brazenly dips a paw into Nina's glass of club soda. "Bad boy!" she scolds, and is surprised at how awkward the moment feels, as if she's admonished someone else's disobedient child in the presence of his father. But Daniel merely laughs, and sweeps Sushi off the table and into his lap.

"What do you mean you can't leave your father? Can't Porsha take care of him?" Patrick says.

Oh Porsha, whom she still hasn't heard from since the day she visited her in Brooklyn. Perhaps she's deceiving herself, but Nina's still harboring hopes for Porsha's return. "We had a falling-out," she tells Patrick. "Don't ask."

"Sorry to hear it. But honestly, I just can't imagine myself in Smallville, USA," Patrick says. "Not even for twenty-four hours. There's something unnatural about the picture, if you know what I mean."

"No worries—you're the straightest gay guy in the world," Nina says. "I mean, if that's what you're concerned about."

"No, no, it's not that. I don't know, it's just the *idea* of Smallville that makes me uncomfortable. But look, if I go—and I'm not saying that I will—I'm bringing Jordan with me. For moral support, et cetera."

"I can't tell you how much I appreciate this, sweetie." *Sweetie.* Her face colors; the familiar word they traded so easily between them is now off-limits, no longer appropriate. She looks to see if Daniel has been listening, but he's busy massaging the underside of Sushi's chin.

And Patrick doesn't seem to have taken note of it, either. "Desirée will never forgive me," he says. "And it *is* sort of unforgivable,
you know."

"Leaving Yale for the University of Kansas solely for the
purpose of being with your boyfriend is what's unforgivable."

"Who says she's going to drop out of Yale? You really think
she would do something so . . . patently idiotic?"

"She's been hinting around recently, an e-mail here, a quickie
phone call there," Nina says. "Love makes people stupid, don't
you know that?"

"You're quite the romantic, kiddo."

"Well . . ."

"Well, what?"

"Listen, can I count on you or not?" Nina says. "Come on, you
know you owe me. And more important, you owe Desirée. Just
put in a personal appearance out there in Kansas and get her to
see the light."

"And what light is that?"

"Oh, just the clear bright light of reason. You've heard of it,
haven't you?"

"Sounds familiar."

"Be the good father you've always been," she instructs him.
Well, not always. She remembers a disastrous dinner, years ago, at
the home of friends; Desirée, four or five at the time, had been an
infuriatingly fussy eater, a child who would only eat grilled cheese
cut on the diagonal, pasta adorned with nothing but salt, chicken
tenders that resembled, as closely as possible, those offered at
Burger King. Her refusal to venture beyond the margins of her
severely limited menu drove Patrick crazy. He worried that her
growth would be stunted, and maybe even her character, as well,
and had taken to standing over her, insisting that she finish every
morsel on her plate, including the broccoli, baby carrots, and
sliced bamboo that he stir-fried for her every few nights, hoping
that, at the very least, she'd try a mouthful from time to time. The
evening that they'd had dinner at their friends' apartment, Laura,
Nina's college roommate, had bought a box of beautifully decorated cupcakes, each studded with inch-high, wafer-thin, pastel-
colored sugar stars, and further tricked out with silver glitter. What

Nina remembers, so miserably, these fifteen years later, began with the sight of Laura's two little boys tucking into cupcakes of their choice while Desirée struggled to polish off the chicken and smooth hill of mashed potatoes on her plate; unless she finished up, Patrick warned, there would be no cupcake for her. The potatoes, which she detested, were her downfall. Teary-eyed at her failure, Desirée sat quietly, disgraced, as Patrick handed her a dinner roll from the basket still on the table. This *is your dessert*, he announced, Laura's sons staring, bewildered, their faces smeared with glittery frosting. That Nina herself hadn't defied him at that moment still mystifies her, as does Patrick's bullying cruelty to the child she knows he loved (and loves) deeply. Oh, the foolish, foolish mistakes well-meaning parents make, always in the name of love! (And what must her friend Laura have thought then of Patrick, and of Nina herself, married to a pitiless guy who would deny his own child such an alluring dessert.)

"You *owe* her," Nina says now, "you owe her *everything*," she insists, sounding just like Porsha claiming the Weight Watchers sundae as her own. And Nina's voice so fierce that Daniel raises his eyes to look at her, a frown of surprise marking his face.

"You're right," Patrick says quietly.

"Okay then. You'll do this for Desirée?"

"I will. And listen, there's something I've been meaning to mention, which is that Jordan and I are having a commitment ceremony next weekend. Nothing too elaborate, just some of our close friends and family . . . Desirée, of course, if I can convince her to come back with me. And you, if you're willing. I'd love to have you there, to know that you're able to feel some . . . some measure of happiness for me, as I know I'd feel for you if you were—"

It's too soon, she wants to tell him. *Too soon not for them, but for her.*

"Oh, and we need to get this divorce going, too. It's time, Nina," he says gently.

This searing pain she's feeling, this rage and disappointment she thought she'd put aside, what's this all about?

"So we're good?" Patrick is asking her.

"We're good," she lies through gritted teeth. "In fact, we're great." Because he's going all the way to the ends of the earth, to godforsaken Honey Creek, Kansas, to bring back their daughter, and what does it cost Nina to say the things he wants to hear?

"Everything okay?" Daniel asks as she hangs up the cordless phone and returns to the table.

She tells him that it is, then sighs.

"You don't *look* like everything's okay," Daniel observes.

Absently she pets Sushi, allowing him to gnaw on her index finger. "Patrick and his honey decided they're having a commitment ceremony. And we're getting this divorce business started."

"Ah." Caressing the back of her neck now, he reminds her of the advice he offered on their first date. "Repeat after me: I. Don't. Give. A. Flying. Fuck."

Nina laughs.

"Say it," Daniel urges.

"I don't give a flying fuck," she says, mumbling.

"Once more, with feeling."

"Do I have to?"

"Doctor's orders."

"But you're not my doctor. Thusly, I'm free to ignore you."

"*Never* screw with the doctor's orders," Daniel says. "It's just too dangerous."

"But I don't *give* a flying fuck," Nina tells him, smiling.

"Funny."

"*I* thought so."

"One more time, and give it all you've got."

Nina tells herself the truth, that it was *her* lucky day when Desirée sat down in her assigned seat in coach next to Daniel on the flight to Kansas City; her lucky day when he memorized her phone number before washing his hands in his room at the Kansas City Sheraton; her lucky day when Daniel's wife ran off with the Hell's Angel lab tech.

"I DON'T GIVE A FLYING FUCK!" she announces loudly and enthusiastically, her fervor terrifying Sushi, who makes a run for it, and disappears behind the living room couch.

"Excellent!" Daniel says.

CHAPTER 32

DESIRÉE CHECKS OUT OF THE Bambi Motel just before 2 P.M., right under the wire. Margaret Keating, who, these past few weeks, might have given her a hard time about her stolen and canceled credit card, is, instead, surprisingly generous, saying she trusts Desirée to put things right as soon as she's able.

"I treat everyone fairly, Christian and New Yorker alike," Margaret says. "So where're you headed?"

"Oh, just going to stay with friends," Desirée says vaguely. Goliath, Margaret's two-pound teacup Yorkie, is asleep in a furry blue slipper on the counter and both of them smile at him.

"You know, my son, Big Curtis, was a great dog lover," Margaret says. "He had a pair of chocolate Labs and a scrawny mutt that were the love of his life after his wife left him. I kept nagging him and saying, 'Big Curtis, if you didn't spend so much time with those dogs of yours, maybe you'd have a social life to speak of.' And now he's gone and I can't nag him anymore. But if only I had the opportunity, I'd tell him, 'If you're even *thinking* of killing yourself, no matter what, no matter how much cash you may have stolen from me, just stop right there and turn your thoughts to something else. Because God gives us one life and one life only on this earth and it's a sin to throw it away like it was garbage.'"

"Uh-huh."

"So Jews believe it, too?"

"In the sanctity of life?" *For crying out loud!* "Of course."

"I figured, but I wasn't sure."

"Jews are ordinary people," Desirée says, amazed that she even finds it necessary to say these words. She strokes Goliath's silky ear.

"Of course they're not, silly. What kind of people don't believe in Jesus, for God's sake?"

Why bother? Desirée thinks wearily, but gives it a shot nevertheless. "Muslims, Buddhists, and Hindus," she says, "to name a few."

Margaret laughs. "Those aren't regular people! Don't be ridiculous! Now, take my grandson, Curtis Junior, for example. He calls himself a Buddhist, but he was baptized a Lutheran and there's nothing that can change that, I don't care how many times a day he's chanting away at that altar of his. He's just a crazy kid and I bet if I prayed hard enough, one of these days he'll come to his senses."

"I know it's tough for you," Desirée says. "But try not to be too disappointed in him."

"I'm a disappointed woman," Margaret confides, "and that's a fact."

Gazing beyond the glass door of the lobby, Desirée sees a teenaged couple embracing in the parking lot, the guy's back pressed against his pickup, his girlfriend's silver necklace glinting in the afternoon sunlight. "Looks like you've got customers," Desirée says, and makes her exit, wondering how many hours the couple will need one of Margaret's rooms, and whether she'll give them a lecture at checkout time. She herself doesn't know the half of what it takes to confess deep disillusionment to a near stranger—as Margaret has—but she leaves the Bambi with an unlikely sympathy for her and her sorrows.

"She's a miserable old woman," Bobby says after Desirée climbs into his car with her duffel bag. "It's kind of tragic that she lost her son, but that's still no excuse."

"Well, it's a little bit of an excuse," Desirée says. "At least by my lights." She smiles. "Hey, don't argue with me when I'm trying to do the Christian thing and forgive someone who's insulted me left and right."

"You should have done the New York thing and given her the finger."

"*You're* awfully cranky."

"Must be the wedding," Bobby says. "It's starting to seem momentous all of a sudden. And when I left the house today, my mother and father were fighting over the tie he was planning to wear with his wedding outfit."

"The print's too loud?"

"You could say that. It's got a foot-long image of *The Scream* on it."

"Awesome! So what's the problem?"

"My mother thinks it'll send the wrong message. You know, on their wedding day and all."

Desirée reconsiders. "Actually . . . I can see where your mother might be sort of offended."

"*Sort of?* She told him if he wears the tie, the wedding's off."

"And?"

"When I left, they were deadlocked."

"Weddings bring out the worst in people," Desirée says, though, in fact, she's been to only a few, and isn't particularly qualified to weigh in on the subject. The wedding she remembers most vividly, she tells Bobby, is that of a distant cousin, a guy not much older than she and related, in some labyrinthine way, to her grandfather. Because it had been held in an Orthodox synagogue, Desirée had been required to sit with all the other female guests, separated from the men by a gauzy curtain during the ceremony. She'd watched, mystified, as the teenaged bride solemnly circled the groom seven times. Unable to learn from her mother the meaning of what she'd just witnessed, Desirée asked a guest sitting next to her to explain the bride's slow circles around the groom. She was told that the groom was like a king (arrgh!), and just as a king had soldiers to circle and protect him, so did the groom. But what about the bride, Desirée wanted to know. Who was going to protect *her*? The guest, who might have been even younger than Desirée and held a toddler on her lap, didn't have an answer and seemed irked by the question; all Desirée could think was that the small, pale bride was on her own. Later, during the reception, where she was relegated, once again, to the all-girl side of the banquet hall while her father and grandfather seemed a world away on the other, she asked the same question. This time she chose a grandmotherly type who, Desirée sensed, was bound to know the right answers. The woman explained that the bride had circled the groom to protect him from the demons who'd been assigned to harm him. *Who knew demons could be assigned to you?* And who was going to keep the demons away from the poor, defenseless, eighteen-year-old bride? Apparently she'd have to keep an eye on them herself. Well, that didn't seem very fair, Desirée complained to the old woman, who responded with only a halfhearted shrug of her sequined shoulder.

"Demons, huh?" Bobby muses, slowing to a stop at the one and only traffic light in Honey Creek.

"Hey, look, a pedestrian," Desirée says, as a white cat with a dirty face scoots across the empty street.

The light changes, at last, and they're cruising at a cool twenty-five miles per hour. And there, in front of the bank, is Sarah Lee, standing with her arm slung over the shoulder of a spindly, bearded guy in sunglasses. Desirée leans across Bobby and honks the horn, but Sarah Lee pays no attention to them, and, inexplicably, turns away in the instant after she sees the car.

"What's up with that?" Desirée says as they take off.

"That was her brother. Wes the wife-beater."

"Her arm was around his shoulder!" Desirée says. "Riley's her best friend. What could Sarah Lee be thinking?"

"Um, let's see, that blood's thicker than water?"

Remembering the display of posters in Starshine's office offering salvation to just about every sort of hard-luck story you could imagine, Desirée asks, "Can't your mother help?"

"She's in need of a little help herself," Bobby says. "I've never seen her like this before."

"You've never seen her on the brink of marriage before," Desirée reminds him.

They are beyond Minnehaha now, driving on disconcertingly silent cobblestone streets, turning down Comanche Drive, Chippewa Lane, Chickasaw Road, all lined with maples, the houses on well-kempt lawns. There's a child or two running through a sprinkler, another peddling furiously on a Big Wheel, a couple of older kids shooting some hoops in a driveway. Desirée tries to imagine herself being raised in this landscape, imagines lonely Sunday mornings when the whole world is in church, her young self yearning to tag along, desperate to be part of some greater whole. And always, *always*, because of her Jewish mother, regarded with a measure of suspicion, maybe even by the friends who know her best. Probably she would take off at the first opportunity, persuading her parents to send her to college in some faraway city, someplace with a pulse, where skyscrapers rose from the pavement as naturally as weeds on an untended lawn, where the streets were choked with traffic, and strangers hurried past without noticing you. Even

222

now, as they pull up in front of Bobby's house, Desirée wouldn't mind being a passenger on the Lexington Avenue Express, in earshot of someone complaining, *Hey! Step on my foot one more time, asshole, and I'll break your fuckin' head!* This is the particular strain of homesickness she's suffering, and it has nothing to do with familiar faces and beloved voices, the affectionate touch of someone's kiss against her cheek—things her eight-year-old self dreamed of night after night at summer camp and couldn't let go of until visiting day, when she'd thrown herself at her mother and father as if years had come and gone since they'd last been together instead of a measly week. This homesickness she's feeling now is of another sort entirely—an adult pining for the very texture, the music, really, of the place that is undeniably home.

"Take a deep breath," Bobby orders. "We're going in, and it ain't gonna be pretty."

"Sure your parents don't mind having another houseguest? And a penniless, unemployed one, at that."

"Well, maybe Starshine can hire you as a receptionist or something—she's always saying she could use an extra pair of hands. And besides, she really gets a kick out of you."

The idea of temping for Starshine is an appealing one, actually, and Desirée can see herself sitting at the desk in her outer office, dispensing tissues to the bleary-eyed, maybe even taking down case histories, secretly accumulating details she might use later in her stories, her *real* work.

In the living room, installed in one of the wicker thrones, is Rusty Wallis, his hair slicked back with product, and his hands folded on his lap. He looks as if he'd been deposited there a while ago and had been instructed to sit quietly and behave himself while those in charge attended to important business.

"Hey there, Rusty," Bobby says. "Feeling any better?"

"In prison I'll be getting three square meals a day," Rusty informs them. "I don't like to cook, but when my wife took sick, I had to do it all, dontcha know. After a while, when Helen could hardly swallow anymore and I had to give her pudding and hot cereal and not much else, she tried to steal the food from my plate, which was an awful lot better than that mush I had to feed her. And I said, 'Helen, if you steal from me and choke on a hunk of meat, we'll be real sorry.' And she said, 'I hope and pray I choke to death on a juicy piece of steak someday real soon.' So pretty soon we started to pray for her to die, but the good Lord wasn't paying attention like He should have because every morning I woke up and Helen was still breathing, but it wasn't much of a life and what there was of it Helen didn't want anyway. So even if what I done was a bad thing, it was a good thing."

Bending on one knee, Desirée strokes Rusty's hand. The gesture seems familiar; it might have been her grandfather's wheelchair she is kneeling before, Marvin's hand she is patting. "Everyone knows you loved her," she assures Rusty.

"You want to watch some more TV?" Bobby says.

"Don't know *what* I want," Rusty says.

Just then Dr. McVicar appears, dragging a vacuum cleaner behind him. "Hey, amigos!" he says. He's wearing an animalrescuesite.com T-shirt; around his neck hangs the *Scream* tie, sloppily knotted. There is an iPod at his waist and earbuds in his big pink ears. "Guess you heard the wedding's off," he says, and plugs in the vacuum. Diligently, he vacuums the fuzz from the Berber rug underfoot, tilting his head from side to side, presumably in time to the music.

The vaccum's growl peters out as Bobby pulls the plug with a determined yank. "You're not getting married?" he says.

Ignoring him, Dr. McVicar sings, "'Lay down all thought/ Sur-ren-der to the void . . .'"

"Earbuds," Desirée says helpfully.

Bobby sneaks around behind his father, and disconnects him from the music.

"Hey!" Dr. McVicar says.

"What do you mean, the wedding's off?"

"Ask your mother."

"I'm asking *you*."

"Life is full of surprises," Dr. McVicar reports. "One moment you're sure the woman of your dreams wants to make it official, the next moment it turns out a goddamn necktie—which, I'd like to point out, the aforementioned woman gave you for Christmas— has come between you."

"Uh-huh. Don't you think you're being a little selfish, not to mention ridiculous?"

"Not at all. Ever hear the expression, 'Love me, love my tie'?"

"Does this mean I'm going to prison?" Rusty inquires.

"A prison of your own making, perhaps," Dr. McVicar murmurs.

"Dad!"

"What?"

"Rusty's in a very fragile state right now," Bobby says in a stage whisper.

"Well, so am I."

"You've got to man up. Take off the stupid tie and get on with it," Bobby orders.

"This tie, I'll have you know, is art, sir. Get a load of the colors, the richness of the blues, the violets, the—"

"Hold on. Have you been smoking something that doesn't belong to you?"

"I cannot tell a lie," Dr. McVicar confesses. "Nor an untruth. After it became clear to me that this wedding was not to be, I went straight to your undershirt and sock drawer—you know, the one where you hide all your good stuff—whereupon I stole a joint. But don't worry, I'll make it up to you."

Desirée laughs; she can't help but be amused by the very notion of a pot-smoking dad, and one ten years older than her own father at that.

"From now on, stay out of my dresser," Bobby scolds.

"I can't help it. I'm a child of the sixties—I see some weed in a drawer, I gotta smoke it."

"Grow up! Get married! It's time already."

"I was married," Rusty says. "And I do recommend it."

"Really?" Dr. McVicar says.

"A man's got no business being alone. And when the wife's yakkity-yakking gets to be too much, you just go outside and have a look at all the stars up there. And take a bottle of whiskey with you, of course. By the time you go back inside, the wife's probably asleep and won't bother you none."

"Imagine that," Dr. McVicar says. "Brilliant!"

"You can't see the stars in prison, though."

"No? Well, there's a compelling reason right there to stay on your best behavior."

Rusty nods. And just when Desirée is convinced that she can't feel anything but compassion for the poor old geezer, he stares coldly at Dr. McVicar and says, "You know, I keep having to remind myself that you're the fornicating dentist, the one what's been living a life of sin."

"Is that who I am?" Dr. McVicar says, smiling companionably. "I don't think so, sir."

"That's some other dentist you're confusing him with," Desirée says, and when Rusty complains that he's thirsty, she goes straight to the kitchen, where the breakfast things are still littering the table, and the clean dishes haven't yet been emptied from the dishwasher, further evidence that all is not well with the McVicars.

"Come on in!" she yells to whoever it is knocking so determinedly at the back door. In her hand is a glass of juice for Rusty.

The Reverend Billy Lee Ribbs, his clerical collar looking a bit dingy, steps into the kitchen uncertainly. "Desirée Christian-Cohen?" he says. "Is that you?"

"It is," she says coolly.

"And how are you? No hard feelings, I hope," he says.

All she has for him is one of those noncommittal shrugs.

"I'd love to hang out and chat with you, Desirée, but I'm looking for Starshine or whoever else here might have called for a spiritual advisor."

"In *this* house? Are you sure?"

"Sure as I am that Jesus loves you."

"Well," Desirée says doubtfully, "if she called you . . ."

"She did, indeed. Some kind of spiritual emergency, I gather. So where's the bride and groom?"

They discover Bobby and his parents playing Scrabble on the living room floor. Rusty Wallis is nowhere in sight.

"Hello, McVicars," Billy Lee says. "Anyone call for a spiritual advisor or am I in the wrong house?"

"Wrong house!" Bobby and his father sing out.

Starshine waves her hand. "Right over here, Reverend."

"I love Scrabble. Finest board game in all of creation. Mind if I join you?" Billy Lee says.

"Tell me you didn't call him," Dr. McVicar says. "Tell me it's just this drug-induced haze I'm in."

"When in the course of human events desperation strikes," Starshine begins, and leans over the board. *"Z-E-R-O-X."*

"Actually . . . there's no *Z* in 'Xerox,'" Desirée says. "And anyway—"

"And anyway," Bobby finishes, "it's a proper noun."

"Listen, if you young people are going to play by the rules, I'm quitting," Dr. McVicar says.

"In Scrabble, as in life, without rules we have chaos," says Billy Lee. "Take, for example, the venerable institution of marriage."

"Can't live with it, can't live without it," Dr. McVicar says. "Unlike the art of Edvard Munch, which speaks volumes about the postmodern world and cannot, under any circumstance, be ignored."

"Monk," Starshine corrects him. "'Munch' is pronounced like *M-O-N-K*. It's Swedish or something."

"Norwegian," Desirée says.

"Desirée knows everything," Dr. McVicar says. "It seems to me that the Jews—and sometimes even half Jews—are frequently the sharpest knives in the drawer."

"Well, I certainly don't know *every*thing," Desirée says, lowering her eyes modestly. "I'm no Einstein, of that I can assure you."

"My point precisely!"

"Well," Billy Lee says, "I must confess I find all this truly fascinating. And yet—"

"Not now, Reverend. My wedding day is fast approaching, you know."

"I do. And I also happen to know that a little premarital counseling seems to be in order."

"If you're going to counsel me to lose the *Scream* tie, you can forget it. If the tie's out, I'm out."

Starshine removes the *X* from "ZEROX." "Zero," she says. "A compromise we can all live with. Though of course I've lost quite a few points on the board there."

"Now there's a word rich in meaning," Billy Lee says.

"Zero?"

"I'm talking about 'compromise,' Starshine."

"No offense, padre," says Dr. McVicar, "but why don't you do us all a big favor and butt out."

"Hey!" Starshine objects. "He's an invited guest."

"He's not on *my* guest list."

Gazing up toward the ceiling, Billy Lee Ribbs shuts his eyes. "Oh Lord," he prays, "grant us now the wisdom to put aside all pettiness and stubborn stupidity and get on with the matter at hand, namely to convince these two to join in holy matrimony after years and years of living in what can only be called sin. An abomination, frankly. Amen."

"And you call yourself a Christian?" Starshine shouts. "Escort him to the door, Wayne! And hurry!"

"Front or back?"

"I don't care, just get him out of here."

"What did I say?" Billy Lee asks in bewilderment as Dr. McVicar shows him the front door. "I prayed for a setting aside of all stupidity and this is how you thank me?"

"No one insults my life partner and me in the sanctity of our living room," Dr. McVicar explains. He holds the door wide open. "Get going, padre."

"It'll be a frigid day in hell before I come to you for a simple cleaning and a checkup, Doctor. Even so, may the good Lord forgive you your sins."

"Likewise, I'm sure."

"I wash my hands of all of you," the Reverend Ribbs announces.

"Well, bye now."

"If you were the last dentist on earth and I had a rotting tooth in my mouth, I'd sooner pull it out with my own hand than come knocking at your door."

"You betcha!" Dr. McVicar says breezily, and shuts the door. And then, whipping the tie from his neck, he tosses it across the living room, where it comes to rest on the Scrabble board. "Casting aside all pettiness and stubborn stupidity probably isn't the worst idea in the world," he admits.

Though he's done nothing more than come to his senses, it seems a cause for celebration nonetheless, Desirée thinks.

CHAPTER 33

"CAN'T HELP FEELING A little guilty that I sent Patrick to do my dirty work for me," Nina confides to her father as she raises a can of Nutrament to his mouth, gently inserting the tip of a bendable plastic straw between his lips. "But we can't let Desirée screw her life up for this boy we know virtually nothing about, right?"

Her father attempts a small sip, swallows with difficulty, says something unintelligible.

"I'll take that as an unqualified 'yes,'" Nina says, smiling. "Because I know how proud you were when she got her acceptance to Yale."

"Yah," he says. Or maybe "Yale."

"It was over the Internet," Nina reminds him. "Do you remember I told you about the fireworks on the screen? One of the happiest days of *my* life," she says, recalling how she'd pulled Desirée joyfully from her seat at the computer desk in the den, she and Patrick enfolding her in their embrace, the three of them euphoric at the news that Desirée's years of fiercely hard—and stellar—work had been rewarded with the prize they'd all been hoping for. Their shared elation that night, their pride in Desirée as they toasted her with champagne before she ran out to join some high school friends blessed with equally good news from Princeton and Brown—well, in a way, it's agonizing to conjure up the wildly happy family they'd been that lucky night two years ago. Of course it's true that everyone's luck runs out eventually, but why so soon for *her*? Nina wonders. Why not years from now, instead?

As if there might actually be a particularly good time for your luck to run out.

"More?" she asks her father, easing the straw back into his mouth. "Good boy," she says absently, because this is what it comes to when you're a middle-aged woman in charge of your father, a man who's all used up, powerless in every conceivable way. Impotent.

When the phone rings, as it begins to now, it's Patrick's Lover-boy, calling from a stretch of highway somewhere between Kansas City and Honey Creek, his voice amiable as can be, letting her know they're on their way to rescue Desirée.

Whether she's in need of deliverance or not.

"I'm so grateful to you, Jordan," Nina is saying, and surely she means it, because isn't it true, she sees now, that they're all in this together? All of them wanting what is best for Desirée, which is, indisputably, that she get her act together posthaste and return home and then to school. And by school she means Yale, not the University of Kansas. KU, as the natives persist in calling it.

Who would condemn a mother for wanting what is best for her beloved daughter?

I am the way the truth the light, she hears Jordan say, but he must be kidding, right?

"You're breaking up," she tells him. "Call me when you get to Honey Creek!" she yells.

CHAPTER 34

AT TWILIGHT, HUMPY WILSON—Honey Creek's mayor and justice of the peace—performs the wedding ceremony in Bobby's backyard, where the crab apple trees are strung with Japanese lanterns and a pair of disguised bridge tables are loaded down with salads in cut-glass bowls and neat stacks of glossy paper plates, plastic cutlery fanned out gracefully beside them. Starshine holds a single white rose matching her cocktail-length white satin dress, and sniffles quietly and continuously during the exchange of vows and rings. Beside her, Dr. McVicar stands straight-backed in a navy blue blazer and a tie patterned with teensy, umbrella-toting frogs; Bobby's blazer is identical, his tie ornamented by minuscule chartreuse octopuses, each reading the newspaper as it soaks in its own bathtub. Desirée is the only bridesmaid, a sorry sight dressed in ill-fitting borrowed clothes—a low-cut sleeveless pink chiffon dress that Sarah Lee has given a temporary hem with special sticky tape (so that she herself can wear it again after tonight), and a matching jacket with enormous shoulder pads suitable for a football player in the pros. Swimming on Desirée's feet are high-heeled pink pumps still a size and a half too large despite the tissue paper stuffed in the toes. But what does it matter, really? After all, she's a minor player in the proceedings, and none of the thirty or so invited guests are looking in her direction anyway. Except when she comes forward with a wine glass wrapped in a dish towel—her contribution to the six-minute ceremony.

"Listen up, everyone," Bobby orders as Desirée positions the glass next to Dr. McVicar's left foot.

"I'm a far cry from what anyone would call a gifted public speaker," Desirée says, "but I'd like to explain why, in a moment, Dr. McVicar will be stepping on this wine glass and smashing it to smithereens."

"What the hell is he doing that for?" the mayor asks.

"Because," Desirée begins, "he's one-eighth Jewish and would like to acknowledge that part of his heritage today. So . . . once upon a time in the Jewish tradition, there were those who believed in the existence of demons wanting to destroy the happiness of each and every bride and groom. Theoretically, the noise of the glass breaking was just the thing to scare off the evil spirits. Actually, this is the very same reason church bells are rung and why a ship is christened by a champagne bottle smashing against it." She'd obtained all this information off the Internet less than an hour ago at Dr. McVicar's request, and hopes she sounds as if she knows what she's talking about.

She signals to him now, and a moment later he gives it his best shot. "Mazel tov," she murmurs, and claps her hands.

A puzzled silence follows.

"Now what?" Starshine says.

"Hold up the applause sign," Desirée instructs Bobby.

"Okay, everyone, let's put our hands together for the happy couple!" Bobby shouts; the sound of polite applause follows, precisely the sort you might hear watching a televised golf tournament.

"Did I forget something?" says the mayor, a chunky guy in his forties whose waxed handlebar mustache looks like a genuine fake. "Seems to me I did."

" 'You may now kiss the bride'?" Bobby suggests, but Starshine and Dr. McVicar are already at it, smooching ardently, oblivious of their audience.

"I am just so thrilled for the both of them," says Sarah Lee, who appears now at Desirée's side. "After all those years, you just know they've got something real good going there."

"If only every married couple in this town were so lucky," Desirée says.

Sarah Lee winces. "This is a happy occasion. Let's not spoil it by talking about certain members of a certain family, all right?"

"Okay," Desirée says, but can't ignore the temptation to add, "You understand why I wish Riley would throw your brother out on his ass, don't you?"

"I *do* understand, but don't make me talk about it," Sarah Lee repeats. Appraising Desirée in the clothes she's lent her, she says, apologetically, "You probably ought to put the jacket back on—at the very least, we should have gotten you a strapless bra, don't you think?"

"At the very least," Desirée agrees, laughing.

"Well, next time," Sarah Lee says.

As she approaches the bride and groom now, Desirée smiles. "You're sparkling," she tells Starshine, wanting her to know that in the light of the Japanese lanterns her small, pretty face is luminous. "So how does it feel?"

"Uh, unbelievably great?" Dr. McVicar says buoyantly.

"It feels . . . as if we've lost something," Starshine says. "Now we're just like everyone else in Honey Creek."

"Absolutely untrue! We're *us*, babe, and an official piece of paper with Humpy Wilson's signature on it ain't gonna change that."

"Who knows?" Starshine says. "Maybe it will and maybe it won't. We'll find out soon enough."

"Look at it this way, we can always get a divorce and go back to the way we were," Dr. McVicar says.

Ah, romance, Desirée thinks, and finds herself wondering when her parents will decide to officially get moving on their divorce. She herself is an adult, and hardly needs her parents' marriage to be intact for *her* sake. So why is it that she feels so bruised by the thought of its dissolution?

Starshine seems to have perked up at the mention of the word "divorce." "Honestly, the truth is I just find it impossible not to love you," she tells her brand-new husband.

Embarrassed to witness another of their lingering kisses, Desirée excuses herself and scrambles unceremoniously in her big pointy-toed shoes to the bridge tables/salad bars.

"There you go!" Bobby says. "Ready for your very first Private Lee show? The opening song's for you," he tells her, and then, because she's never had a song—or anything else, for that matter—dedicated to her before, she throws herself at Bobby, almost knocking him over. He puts down his plate of salad; shamelessly, he slides his hand down the front of her dress. "And here come the Beaudine sisters, goddamn it," he says, slipping his hand out of her bra and tucking it behind his back.

"I see someone's been enjoying my famous five-layer salad,

which, I have to admit, is the best thing here," Olive says. "Starting from the bottom up, you've got your chopped hard-boiled egg, you've got your bacon bits, you've got your—"

"Sorry," Bobby interrupts, "but I need to do a sound check before we start. Desirée and I have got to make sure the amps are in order."

"First I have to say how exciting it was to read all about you in this week's *Honey Creek Herald*, Desirée," Frances crows. "And the sweetest part, I thought, was where you said your only disappointment was that you hadn't had a chance to milk one of our shorthorns."

"I did?" Desirée says, wondering what other fictional disappointments have been attributed to her by that untrustworthy Jane Cowley. In fact, she'd allowed herself to forget all about that regrettable interview weeks ago, and is startled to hear that it's actually been published. "So a shorthorn is some special kind of cow, I take it?" she says. Of all the regrets she may have had in her life, not having milked a shorthorn—or any other stupid cow, for that matter—isn't likely to make the top of her list.

"Oh, very special—they're docile yet hardy, and . . . well, never mind, there you were on the front page of the paper, and really, Desirée, it was a kick to read about you."

Desirée can't wait to get her hands on that newspaper and then on Jane Cowley herself, she whispers to Bobby.

"Forget it," he says. "You know, I'd heard that Don DeHaven, the *Herald*'s editor, had killed the piece after Jane handed it in a while back, but I guess she managed to convince him to run it after all."

"I need a drink," Desirée says.

Filling up a plastic champagne flute for her with winey-scented punch, Bobby says, soothingly, "The *New York Times* is your paper, Desirée. The *Herald* is for Honey Creekers only and shouldn't mean a thing to you, okay?"

"Has this got liquor in it?" Miss Lavender, surprisingly grand and imposing in a billowy caftan, points toward the punch bowl with a shapely, polished fingernail. She smiles at Desirée vaguely; one look from her, no matter how innocuous, and Desirée is already a little weak in the knees.

"Only some rosé," Bobby says. "Nothing to be afraid of."

"Thank you kindly, sir. And congratulations to one and all," Miss Lavender offers. "I must say I especially enjoyed the destruction of the wine glass."

"Where I come from, there are a lot of people who can't have a wedding without it," Desirée says.

"Where *you* come from," Miss Lavender sighs, and her voice quickly runs out of steam.

"That's a very suspicious-sounding sigh," Desirée says.

"Please," says Miss Lavender; as she grabs Desirée by the wrist, her collection of silver bracelets clinks pleasingly. "Don't imagine that things could have been different."

"*What* things? Can't you give me a hint?"

"Certain things are classified information. Just be patient."

"Do you work for the CIA?" Bobby asks.

"My advice is that you two enjoy the time you have left."

"On this earth?" Desirée's pulse has instantly flipped into overdrive; though she has no particular plans for an imminent return to New York, visions of a 737 jet losing altitude en route to LaGuardia, rows of passengers mouthing the Lord's Prayer, play in her imagination.

"Now you're talking like a crazy person," she hears Miss Lavender say. The old woman saunters off, with her armfuls of bracelets, her ginger-colored dyed hair, and her future as uncertain as anyone else's. There's no denying that some small part of Desirée has yet again fallen under her spell—yet again reluctantly suspended disbelief and embraced her clairvoyance.

"Hey, come on, you're way too smart to swallow that stuff. Come on," Bobby says, squeezing her arm.

"I have to see the *Herald,* Bobby."

"You *don't,* actually. What I mean is, I wouldn't recommend it," he warns.

"Oh my God!" Desirée moans. "Oh. My. God." She hasn't seen a word of the article yet, but is already deeply humiliated.

"I'll hunt down Jane Cowley like a dog and strangle her if you want," Bobby offers sweetly.

"Where's the newspaper? You hid it from me, didn't you?"

"It's in my room, under the bed," Bobby confesses. "But I really wish you wouldn't go there."

Abandoning Sarah Lee's shoes in the grass, Desirée hustles herself barefoot through the kitchen door and into the house. There, leaning against the turquoise refrigerator, pinned against Nick, is Riley Maxwell, her head tipped back so he can tuck a few kisses under her lovely long neck.

"Pay no attention to me, guys," Desirée says. "I'm just on my way to the bedroom."

Nick pulls himself away from Riley so fast, it's as if he'd been blown back by an explosion.

"Just curious," Desirée asks, "but who invited *you*?"

"I did," Riley says, and wipes her neck daintily with two fingertips. "Starshine said I could bring a date."

"She means an escort," Nick explains. "Her, um, husband, is home with the, um—"

"Kids," Riley says. "They're the reason we got here so late."

Desirée snickers, having discovered that the recognition you're finally over someone is almost as exhilarating as the moment you realized you'd fallen for him. Not the most brilliant of epiphanies, but a surprisingly gratifying one nonetheless.

"Sorry to have interrupted," she says. "Please feel free to resume whatever it was you were doing."

"Actually," Riley says, "we just came in for some ice."

"For the punch bowl," Nick says.

Desirée recommends they try the freezer.

"Good thinking," says Nick, and these will turn out to be the last two words he will ever offer her.

ON HER KNEES, stretching her arm under Bobby's bed—the bed she's been sleeping in so blissfully ever since leaving the Bambi— she extracts his copy of the *Herald*. And, in truth, can't help smiling at the headline.

HONEY CREEK WELCOMES
ITS FIRST NEW YORK VISITOR

BY JANE COWLEY *Staff writer*

Desirée Christian-Cohen, a most interesting young tourist from New York City's Upper East Side, chose Honey Creek for her first visit ever to the Midwest because, she said, "It just sounded like the sweetest place on earth." Ms. Christian-Cohen, a redheaded visitor to our town, knew no one at all upon her arrival here, but has met quite a few people in Honey Creek since then, most of whom impressed her favorably with their warmth and generosity. Unfortunately, she was robbed at gunpoint, along with several Honey Creek citizens, after this interview took place (note: the robbery is still under investigation as of this writing). In this interview, however, she focused on the kindness with which she has been treated by, among others, the McVicar family, who offered her both friendship and free dental care. She has also developed a close personal relationship with their son, Mr. Bobby McVicar, noted Honey Creek musician, during her stay here.

We have learned that there is a dark side to our visitor as well: when invited by Levi Wheelwright to a Youth for Christ meeting, Ms. Christian-Cohen declined, despite Mr. Wheelwright's assurance that "even though she was a half Jew, she could still be saved." The Reverend Billy Lee Ribbs, in a separate interview, also confirmed Ms. Christian-Cohen's reluctance to accept the Lord Jesus Christ. Reverend Ribbs quoted her as saying, " 'Us heathens are happy just the way we are.' " The Reverend then added, "I must say I was real disappointed in her stiff-necked pride, her stubborn unwillingness to give the Lord Jesus just a little bit of her time. You win some, you lose some, I guess."

That aside, we are pleased to have Ms. Christian-Cohen here with us in Honey Creek, and hope to see more of this New Yorker whose one regret is that she hasn't yet had the time to get out to one of our numerous farms and milk one of those famous short-horns. To which we respond, Well, then, why not make *the time, Ms. Christian-Cohen!*

Desirée is seething! She rereads the article half a dozen times, as if there might be some hidden subtext she will stumble upon if only she keeps at it long enough. But really its message is unmistakable, and she heard it loud and clear the first time around. How foolish would you have to be to shed even a single tear over something so utterly, outrageously absurd? she asks herself. And yet the tears that spring now from being publicly ridiculed in a cheesy small-town paper mix with the bitter tears of humiliation over what has to be acknowledged as her own part in allowing this to happen. In willingly consenting to an interview that she'd secretly hoped would land her on the front page. All because the prospect of being transformed into even a D-list celebrity had simply been too exciting to pass up. How could she have known that she'd been suffering from a case of inflated vanity, known that backstabbing Jane Cowley had been on to her?

Shoving the newspaper back under the bed, she longs to hear her mother's voice saying, *What's wrong, pussycat, what is it?* And how vividly she can see her mother gently nudging her toward the shelf of her shoulder, how vividly she can hear her urging, *Park it right here, sweetie pie, and tell me all about it.* But wouldn't it be an act of selfishness, calling her mother only to fret, long-distance, about her lacerated ego, childishly seeking consolation and, in the process, causing her mother even more worry and anxiety?

And she doesn't need to hear her mother say, once again, *Why can't you just come home, pussycat?*

AFTER SHE'S THROWN handfuls of cold water on her face, and touched up her makeup, Desirée rejoins the party, surely, she thinks, the most bedraggled bridesmaid a wedding has ever seen. She can't remember where her borrowed shoes are; without them, the taped hem of her dress trails across the freshly manicured lawn. Blushing miserably, she wonders how many of the guests have read the *Honey Creek Herald* today.

Under the darkening sky, Private Lee is posed on a rented wooden riser that sets them above the crowd. Desirée hears Bobby's electronically amplified voice announcing, a trifle self-consciously, "We're going to start with 'Romantic Engineering,' which I'd like to dedicate to a certain someone—and I'm pretty sure she knows who she is." First there are a few tentative chords from his Stratocaster, then Sandy Swindell on the drums, his broken nose imperfectly healed. Now Luke Sadler, the bass player, comes in, a bit harsh. And Bobby again, sounding more confident this time.

The night is still summer-warm, the air sweet with the fragrance of scented candles arranged in a row on one of the bridge tables, and into this perfumed air, Bobby's baritone floats, his eyes shut as he sings to Desirée.

> *All our future's right in front of us*
> *Dead clouds are overhead*
> *Things may not go as planned*
> *I haven't stopped to wonder why*

Though she isn't quite sold on the lyrics, which could probably use a little tweaking, the melody is mournful and lovely, and every time Bobby and Luke harmonize into a single mike, Desirée feels a thrill of the purest pleasure. A cluster of people, including Sarah Lee and the newlyweds, stand close to the riser and seem to be listening appreciatively, though most of the guests continue eating and drinking and make no effort to lower the volume on their chitchat. Desirée thinks of the hail of lemon rinds and chicken bones that flew in the band's face in Greenville, and she has the urge, even now, to knock a few of those heads together. Wanting to exact revenge on the losers who'd insulted Bobby and his band—if this isn't evidence of the depth of her love, then she doesn't know what is.

"Private Lee rules!" she shouts, as "Romantic Engineering" comes to an end.

Dr. McVicar is calling her name now, threading his way excitedly through the crowd, followed by two people who appear to be—though reason tells her otherwise—her father and Loverboy/Jordan! She blinks at them. And immediately understands that something must be terribly wrong back home, that her father is here to personally deliver the sort of appalling news that can't be uttered over the phone long-distance.

"Hey, look who *I* found sneaking around!" Dr. McVicar says.

"I was just telling your father and his partner what a treat it is to have them here as our guests, uninvited though they may be."

"Hey kiddo," her father says. "Hug?" he asks, and spreads his arms expectantly.

"What's wrong?" Desirée squeaks, having finally found her voice. "What's happened?" Taking a step back from Patrick, her heart jackhammering furiously, she collides with Rusty Wallis, who gripes, "Nobody here wants to sit down to dinner with me because I killed my wife."

"He killed his wife?" Jordan says, then waves a friendly hello to Desirée.

"I don't think that's it at all," Dr. McVicar says. "I'm guessing they don't want to sit with you because, well, you're you, Rusty."

"I'm *me*? What's that got to do with it? And who are those two?" Rusty says, pointing a plastic fork at Patrick and Jordan. "They look like strangers," he says accusingly.

"Nothing's wrong," Desirée's father tells her. "Or, to put it more accurately, nothing's unfixable."

"It's like someone slipped me a hit of LSD," she murmurs, and grants her father his hug. "I mean, are you actually *here*? And if so, why?"

"Oh, just thought I'd check up on you, and check out the landscape, as well," her father explains. "And Jordan's along for the ride."

"It's delightful to see you again, Desirée!" Jordan says. "Sorry for showing up unannounced," he adds. In his black leather blazer and jeans, gold hoop pierced through the tip of his ear, he's looking, Desirée decides, pretty cool. Even his diminutive ponytail—that same inch-long ponytail that, weeks ago, she had only contempt for—doesn't, here in Kansas, strike her as objectionable. And she's grateful for his apology, which is more than her father has offered.

"What do you mean, you're checking up on me?"

"Just popping in to see what's kept you here so long," Patrick says.

"Who *are* these people?" Rusty Wallis asks.

"Well, this is Patrick, Desirée's dad, and Jordan, his partner," Dr. McVicar explains. "It's not that complicated, really."

"Partners in what? Crime?"

"They're college professors," Desirée says.

"College professors and business partners?"

"They're *life* partners," Dr. McVicar says helpfully. "You know, just like Starshine and me. Though without the marriage license, I gather."

"This sounds unnatural, just like homos and gays," Rusty says.

"Hate to break it to you, amigo, but gays, and homos—as you so quaintly put it—are one and the same," Dr. McVicar says.

"*Wrong.* The homos are what do the giving, and the gays are what do the receiving. Or maybe it's the other way around, I'm not sure," Rusty admits.

Reading the faces of her father and Jordan, Desirée is relieved to see not the horror and contempt she expected, but merely astonishment followed by amusement.

"How did you find me?" she says. "How did you find your way to the wedding?"

"Did you really think that in a town of 1,623 people, we wouldn't be able to track you down?" her father says. "But, if you must know, we're staying at the Bambi Motel, where we got the scoop from Margaret Keating, who knew just where you were. And of course there's a GPS in our rental car."

"I'm about tuckered out trying to figure how a homo can be a homo and a father at the same time," Rusty says. "Seems to me it's just plain impossible. But I do know what the Bible tells us, which is that God will judge homos unfit to enter the kingdom of heaven."

"You're a very rude old man," Patrick says, and leaves it at that.

"Well, I think we can all agree it's past the rude old man's bedtime," Dr. McVicar says. Taking Rusty by the arm, he leads him toward the house. "And if I may borrow from the late, highly decorated general Douglas MacArthur, 'I shall return!'" he calls over his shoulder.

"Friendly dude," Jordan observes. "I meant the groom, of course, not that fucking ignorant homophobe."

"Uh-huh. So . . . what's this unspeakable rumor I heard from your mother about you and the University of Kansas, kiddo?" Desirée's father says.

"First explain to me why you're *really* here."

"No way, you first."

"I think I'll go sample some of the wedding buffet," Jordan says diplomatically.

"Knock yourself out," Patrick says, and waves him away. "But forget the carrot and raisin salad, I hear it's got too much sugar in it."

"He's a sweet guy," Desirée says. "I'm glad he makes you so happy."

"He does, indeed. And so do you, Desirée, especially when you're generous like that."

She looks down at her bare feet, where cool slivers of grass nestle between her toes. "It's clearly taken me a while to get there, and I probably need to be forgiven for that."

"Whatever. But on the subject of Jordan and me," her father begins. She listens to those formal words "commitment ceremony" and learns that it's been scheduled for next Sunday afternoon in New York, just before she has to leave for Yale. "And of course we absolutely have to have you there, kiddo," Patrick says. "It wouldn't be nearly as meaningful without you. Really, I'd be crushed if you weren't there."

"You couldn't have told me this over the phone?"

"I could have, but sometimes it's much more effective to do things in person." Patrick falls silent for a beat. "Well, to be perfectly, completely honest, I'm here at the behest of your mother, to bring you home with us tomorrow night. I've already got a plane ticket for you. I'm sure you know your mother will shoot herself if you don't go back to Yale. And my orders, in fact, are to kidnap you if you refuse to go willingly."

Her father is smiling at all this hyperbole, but Desirée knows it's no joke. And she is outraged.

"Did you come with a chloroform-soaked handkerchief and lots of rope?" she asks.

"And a dark day for Honey Creek it is!" Dr. McVicar shouts from the buffet tables, raising a bottle of Heineken above his head.

"I'll be at the ceremony," Desirée says, "but you can tell *my mother* I'm not going back to Yale and leaving Bobby behind."

"Your boyfriend plays a pretty good lead guitar, by the way, and his voice isn't half bad. But this is Yale we're talking about, kiddo, not Podunk U."

Desirée kneads her toes into the grass. "You think it's necessary to tell me that? But no worries, I'll take courses at the University of Kansas until I can officially transfer," she's both startled and relieved to hear herself say. Because isn't it always a relief to have put aside fears and doubts and arrived at a decision, even an impulsive one? "Look, it's not like I'm turning my back on academia. I'll still be in school, right?"

"Albeit a school ranked eighty-ninth in that *U.S. News and World Report* thing that I happened to have looked into," her father says. "Just think what you'll be trading away. And you know, just because my job at Columbia entitles you to free tuition at Yale, that doesn't mean they have a reciprocal agreement with Kansas. In all likelihood, I'd have to pay your tuition out of my own pocket."

But doesn't love trump all? And if it doesn't, shouldn't it?

"I want to be with him," Desirée says. "Why can't it be as simple as that?"

"You *know* why not. You've already figured that out on your own."

But doesn't love trump all?

"Figured *what* out?" Starshine says. There are four kinds of salad overflowing on her plate, and a Heineken Light in her hand. Her unsteady gait announces the obvious, that surely this isn't her first sip of alcohol tonight. "And this, I presume, is your lovely father?" Introducing herself, Starshine says, "I hear Rusty Wallis was quoting from First Corinthians, and that later several other equally upstanding Honey Creekers joined the bandwagon. Please accept my profound apologies, Mr. Jewish-Christian, for the unfortunate narrow-mindedness of some of our guests."

"That's just plain 'Christian,'" Patrick corrects her. "My partner and I are atheists, or lapsed Catholics, or whatever you want to call us, *and* you can rest assured, not terribly offended. What I mean is, we know we're in Kansas."

"Well," Starshine says, "I'm in Kansas, too, or at least I think I am, and I swear to you that most of the people here are the proverbial, whatchamacallit, salt of the earth."

Really? Desirée would like to say. *And would that include Margaret Keating, Laurene at the chamber of commerce/dry cleaners, and Levi, the pizza guy/president of the Fellowship of Christian Athletes? And what about that double-crossing Judas, Jane Cowley?*

"Bet you didn't know you're referencing the gospel of St. Matthew."

"Not me. I don't know a *thing* about the Bible," Starshine boasts.

"Me, either," Desirée says.

"'Salt of the earth,' straight from the gospel," Patrick insists, smiling.

Olive, the tattletale twin who was only too eager to turn in Rusty to the sheriff's office the night of the armed robbery, swings by for a gander at Patrick. "I met your partner," she says, "and he's a very nice man. Even so, I feel obligated to warn you, sir, that 'if a man lies with mankind, as he lies with a woman, both of them have committed an abomination. And will surely be put to death.' And that's Leviticus, not some silly comic book."

Angrier, she believes, than she has ever been in all her life, *enraged,* really, by the calm, almost courteous manner in which Olive has delivered her hateful message, Desirée imagines with ease the satisfying smack of her own fist making contact with Olive's pale-lipped mouth, or maybe with that potbellied mound protruding from under her singularly ugly mauve polyester dress that shows off the puff of flesh above each middle-aged knee. She's floored by both Olive's cruelty and her father's equanimity; clearly Olive is beneath his scorn and he makes no attempt to respond to her except in the narrowing of his eyes.

And with his thumb and index finger, he gives Desirée's forearm a painful little pinch.

Why, she wonders, doesn't he pinch Olive instead?

"Jesus, enough with the damn Bible!" Starshine says. "This is my wedding day, wedding night, whatever, and we're supposed to be celebrating, not attending Sunday school."

"I'm just recommending that Desirée's father and his partner reconsider the path they're on. I'm trying to save them from eternal damnation," Olive says. "Just trying to help."

No one thanks her.

Shoving her plate at Desirée, Starshine announces that she's going to be sick. And staggers away.

"Poor thing," Olive murmurs, but it's Desirée who runs after Starshine, regretfully leaving her father in the company of his ignorant, well-intentioned, would-be savior.

"Are you going to throw up?" she says when she catches up to Starshine, who has seated herself on the stoop outside the kitchen door, her wedding dress flush with a black rubber welcome mat.

"I'm feeling simultaneously nauseated and pessimistic, not a good combination," Starshine reports.

"Plus, you're getting your wedding dress dirty."

"Really? Well, that's the least of it."

"Maybe you should stand up so you don't ruin your dress. Here, let me help you," Desirée says, extending one hand.

"Can't get up. And can't get comfortable with this whole marriage thing."

"You've got to give it a chance!" Desirée says, and has to shout, because the band has suddenly grown loud, even a little strident.

Gravity's the enemy
Anything that holds us down
The road ahead is motioning
We're on the road again.

"Oh, I'll give it a chance," Starshine says. "Forty-eight hours, maybe forty-nine."

This doesn't sound auspicious. "You can do better than that," Desirée says. "You *have* to do better than that."

"I've lived fifty-five years without a wedding ring," Starshine says, thrusting out her left hand to display the gold-rimmed jade band on her finger. "You're familiar with the expression, 'You can't teach a middle-aged dog new tricks'?"

"Is that from First Corinthians?" Desirée jokes, hoping to cheer her.

"No, but wanna hear about the greatest disappointment of my life? I had a chance to see the Beatles at Shea Stadium in New York in the summer of 1966," Starshine says plaintively.

"Awesome!"

"You'd think so, but my parents thought otherwise. I was fourteen and they forbid me to go, even though I had a free plane ticket to New York, thanks to my best friend, Rebecca Hostin, who, miraculously, got Beatles tickets for her birthday and only wanted to share them with me."

"Bummer," Desirée says.

"Precisely. And my point, in case you missed it, is that parents often pose obstacles to their children's happiness. And to *what* end, you may ask. So that forty-one years down the line, their children are still pissed off at them, still wondering if things might have turned out differently?"

"Your parents are dead," Desirée points out. "How can you still be pissed off at them?"

Starshine smiles drunkenly, but there's also a whiff of sympathetic sorrow playing across her face as she shakes her head at Desirée. "Don't be offended, okay, but actually, you're nowhere *near* the astute observer of life you think you are."

Ouch. Surely this can't be the most scathing charge ever leveled against her, but why does it feel that way?

Hand in hand, her father and Jordan stroll toward her now, a copy of the *Honey Creek Herald* tucked under Patrick's arm. "Can't believe you didn't tell us you were front-page news, kiddo," he says.

"Did you read the article?"

"Merely skimmed it," her father admits. "But did you really say, '*Us* heathens are happy just the way we are'? For Christ's sake, how could you have made a mistake like that?"

"Arrgh!" Desirée says, insulted. "My exact words were—and I swear this is the truth—'*We* heathens are happy just the way we are.' Don't you know me well enough to know that I would never say '*Us* heathens'?"

"In that case, I recommend you sue the bastards for misquoting you," her father says. "And if you're as upset by the article as you should be—as *I* am—well, it's one more reason for you to come home. And to reconsider your plans to ever come back."

"I *said* I'd come home with you for the commitment ceremony," Desirée reminds him. "But please don't ask anything more of me." Reluctantly, she makes her way toward the band, to give

Bobby the news that she's leaving tomorrow. When she reaches the riser, Private Lee is taking a break, setting their instruments carefully aside, wiping the sweat from their faces with paper towels torn from a jumbo-sized roll, and helping themselves to bottles of beer.

"Your father's here?" Bobby says, as he steps down from the riser. Perspiration still glistens at his temples, and he is looking at her worriedly. "I don't understand." When he does, and hears her plans, he seems only slightly less distressed. "Here's what I'm afraid of," he says. "You'll go back to New York, your parents will do everything they can to convince you that Yale is where you belong, and, in the end, you'll find yourself nodding your head in agreement. Because, Desi, it's not like they don't have a good, solid case. And you, I hate to tell you, don't really have much of a leg to stand on." Turning his palms upward, he lifts one higher than the other. "This," he says, "is Yale, and everything it has to offer. And this," he says, slowly lowering his palm while raising the other, "is me."

"Don't," she says.

It isn't that she doesn't understand his fears.

It isn't that they aren't hers, as well.

If only she were someone who could accurately describe herself as capricious and unpredictable, like that girl back in her bedroom on the Upper East Side, the one who closed her eyes, drew her arm across the map, and then touched down so decisively in Honey Creek. She marvels now at the impulsiveness of that moment, the sheer cheekiness of it, that instant in which she threw off her old cautious, watchful (and maybe even uninspired) self, and discovered someone capable of recklessness. But admirably so, she thinks.

Not to worry, she tells Bobby; grasping both his hands, she matches them together. She seeks out the two callused fingers he uses to play his beloved Strat, and tenderly raises them to her lips.

247

CHAPTER 35

MUCH TO NINA'S SURPRISE, her students have chipped in for an elegant coconut cake with meringue frosting to commemorate their last class of the summer. Even more surprising are the words "Thank you, Prof. Cohen" ornamenting the cake in magenta script. Really, she had no idea that a single one of her students felt even a soupçon of gratitude for anything she might have done for them this summer. Except, of course, for Kingsley, though she's continued to do her best to avoid Nina ever since leaving the apartment several weeks ago.

"I'm truly touched," Nina confides from her seat at the head of the seminar table, embarrassed as her eyes briefly fill. There are, she sees, floral-patterned paper plates, matching dessert-sized napkins, and even a stainless steel cake knife. An assortment of two-liter bottles of soda is arranged in a couple of neat rows at the center of the table. "And so flattered," she adds.

"Yeah, you can thank Kingsley for organizing everything," Elaina Whitacre calls out. Nina notes that she is, yet again, sporting her favorite DYNAMIC DYKE T-shirt, and there's also something new: a small, brilliant-cut diamond engagement ring on her left hand. *Well, good for her*—a long and happy partnership for her and her fiancée, Nina hopes.

Kingsley nods, curtly or shyly, hard to discern which—as Nina offers an effusive thank-you—and begins slicing up the cake, the first piece going straight to Nina, as if she were a guest of honor. Then Kingsley's cell phone rings; checking the number, she purses her mouth, excuses herself, saying, "Sorry, I've really got to take this."

Oh no you don't, Nina thinks of saying, but, ever reluctant to provoke any sort of confrontation either inside her classroom or out, she utters not a word as Kingsley rushes from the room, holding the cell to her ear.

As if Nina—and everyone else in the room—can't guess that

this must be a business call. But what's so urgent that it can't wait until class is over? Perhaps some high-profile customer, some titan of industry, has asked to book a whole night with Kingsley in the Champagne Room. Along with his wife, who gets the ultimate turn-on at the sight of her fully dressed husband dancing so intimately with Kingsley and her G-string. The forkful of delicate, subtly sweet cake turns sickening in Nina's mouth; if she were alone in her own kitchen, she would have already spit it out. Instead, she swallows it down with a chaser of Diet Pepsi.

Davis is staring at her disapprovingly, and it takes her a moment or two before she realizes that the source of his displeasure lies in her pathetic failure to stop Kingsley from leaving the classroom. But why does *he* care—isn't he transferring to Wesleyan in a couple of weeks? *Get a life, kid.*

"So," Nina says, and knits her hands together self-consciously, "any last questions about the literature we've been reading? No? The deadline for your portfolios?"

Joelle Friedlander, whose long struggle with bulimia remains yet to be clarified in the fourth and final draft of her first essay, raises her hand high. "Does anyone know where this yummy cake came from?"

"Magnolia Bakery on Bleecker Street," Kingsley reports, returning to her seat looking perfectly untroubled.

"Yummy!"

KINGSLEY STAYS BEHIND TO help clean up as the rest of the students drift out the door, a handful stopping first both to thank Nina and to warn her that they may need her help with a few "little things" before they hand in their final drafts.

"Feel free to shoot me an e-mail," she says encouragingly. She is always aware, at the tail end of every course she teaches, of a palpable sense of loss that lingers, ever so lightly, in the empty classroom itself. It's her own mild sorrow, of course, in the knowing that she will never see or hear from most of these students ever again, though some, usually the best ones, like Kingsley, will continue to send her their work—stories, poems, sketches, fragments of memoir—wanting Nina's generous assessment as they feed their hunger to write, sometimes awkwardly, but sometimes with the sort of grace, intelligence, and insight that startles her. And makes her thankful for her chosen, albeit ill-paid, profession.

"Please don't be angry at me," Kingsley is saying, maneuvering the leftover cake back into the box, sweeping crumbs into her cupped hand.

Angry? For what? For having the chutzpah to take a call on her cell phone in the middle of class? "I'm not angry with you," Nina says.

"Well, you're disappointed in me," Kingsley says. "Disappointed in the choices I've made. You think of me as a fuckup, but really what I am is a savvy businesswoman."

If you say so.

"In a couple of years, when I'm a senior and ask you to write me a letter of recommendation for grad school, will you do it for me?"

"Certainly," Nina says.

To the Admissions Committee:
It is a pleasure to write on behalf of Kingsley Harwood. Kingsley is a highly accomplished young woman, possessing many talents, among them a facility for lap dancing, pole dancing, and listening with feigned sympathy to a wide range of complaints from middle-aged men only too eager to admire her virtually naked bod. In addition, I found myself deeply impressed by her masterful critiques of her classmates' work, critiques that displayed an eye and ear for the sort of subtleties the rest of the students often missed. And so it is with great enthusiasm that I recommend her to your graduate department of English Language and Literature.

Sincerely,
NINA COHEN
(Ill-paid, overworked adjunct professor who, regrettably, failed to convince Kingsley that her sleazy, and possibly dangerous, career as a high-priced stripper was ill-conceived in the first place)

On the plus side, she muses, Desirée is, at long last, due home tonight! And perhaps Nina will, if she's lucky, have more success with her than she's had with Kingsley this summer.

"Oh, and what do you think about my idea to write an anonymous memoir about my life as an exotic dancer? Do you think I could get a publishing deal? Like for half a mil or so?" Kingsley asks.

How does a twenty-year-old come to *think* this way? Nina recalls herself at Wellesley all those years ago in the early eighties, never missing a single class, usually studying after dinner until the eleven o'clock news came on, always feeling that undercurrent of worry about her grades, always wanting to do better . . . and never once contemplating a lucrative part-time job as a stripper. Christ, what a dorky kid she was.

"Half a million dollars for your memoir? Sounds reasonable."

Kingsley smiles at her. "And maybe a movie deal?" she says, flashing the silver stud embedded in her tongue.

"Anything's possible," Nina tells her, because, well, generally that's the truth, isn't it?

"SATYRA!" SHE CALLS OUT when she arrives home after class, swinging the cardboard box containing the leftover cake that Kingsley insisted she take with her. "Satyra?" No response, and so she strides down the hallway to her father's bedroom, where, utterly astonished, she discovers Porsha in the midst of a diaper change. From the small, flat-screen TV perched on her father's dresser, a voice asks, "Where do *you* want your ashes scattered?"

"Oh my God, Porsha!" Exhilarated, she wants to fling her arms around her, but Porsha is busy painting Marvin's behind with Vaseline, and swivels her head only briefly to get a quick look at Nina.

"Grandpa's got a touch of diaper rash," Porsha says reproachfully. "*Someone's* been napping on the job."

"Oh Porsha!"

"Will you stop saying my name like I'm Jesus Christ himself?"

"I'm sorry, I'm just so . . ." Nina starts to say "relieved" but reconsiders and says, in all sincerity, "thrilled to see you here."

"If you want to know where that Satyra is—which you should—I sent her home and told her you would settle up with her money later. And I don't suppose she was very good, was she?"

"She was all right," Nina says, "but no better than that. Not like you."

"Well, I got to thinking that Grandpa deserved to have me back."

"But not me?"

"It's Grandpa and me got a little thing going on," Porsha explains, smiling; an instant later Marvin grunts in apparent agreement.

Porsha clicks onto a reality show now, where a woman contemplating breast enhancement surgery complains, "No wedding, no shower, no engagement party, and so I never got so much as a freakin' *can opener* from my family." And it occurs to Nina that she will have to buy a gift for Patrick and Jordan—whether or not she has the mettle to accept their invitation—when they tie ever tighter whatever knot it is that has bound them so comfortably together. She suspects they've registered somewhere, perhaps Bed Bath & Beyond, Tiffany, Williams-Sonoma . . . How about an automatic espresso maker with the automatic milk frother she admired recently in the window of Williams-Sonoma? At three hundred dollars, it's no bargain but certainly a generous gift. Never would she want Patrick, and especially Jordan, to think of her as stingy . . .

"You going to stand there staring at that spoiled girl on TV, or you going to help me get Grandpa back into his wheelchair?" Porsha is saying.

Gently bending her father into an upright position, then grasping his featherweight frame beneath the right knee and shoulder as Porsha does the same on the left, Nina wonders if Porsha would laugh, hearing that this is one of the most satisfying moments of her day, she and Porsha working together easily and so well, simply to do this small thing that needs doing, day after day after day. Taking her chances, she tells Porsha just that, then says, "Laugh all you want, I won't be insulted."

"Do you see me laughing?" Porsha says. Hairbrush in hand, she works out a tangle or two in the loose silver curls that extend

252

to the back of Marvin's shirt collar. "Baby, we *all* of us got this thing going on."

Yesss! "We do," Nina says.

"Give me some sugar, then," Porsha orders her, pointing to her own cheek. "Some sugar right here, baby."

CHAPTER 36

THE SAAB'S AIR-CONDITIONING is busted, and a hot wind blows through its open windows as Desirée and Bobby tool down Minnehaha, past the rickety WELCOME TO HONEY CREEK sign set on stilts across from the Bambi. She remembers how, weeks ago, as the bus that dropped her here had pulled away, she could hear in the sound of its leave-taking something sorrowful; now she hears something poignant in the dull murmur of the Saab's motor as, on their way to the airport in Kansas City, they drive along a road lit solely by the stars. Behind them, in a rented Mustang convertible, her father and Jordan follow closely.

The vast Kansas sky, speckled with those stars that hang miles above the never-ending cornfields, is a dazzling, unforgettable sight beyond their insect-spattered windshield. Desirée keeps one hand on Bobby's thigh; occasionally his right hand rises to spin a hank of her hair around his finger. Passing through Greenville, she gets another look at the billboard shrieking SIN IS A CANCER TO ALL PEOPLE! Illuminated at night, it seems even more threatening than in daylight, and she clutches Bobby's arm until the sign is visible in their rearview, along with the one that marks the exit for the Land of Make Believe. Which, Bobby informs her, is merely an old, run-down theme park whose owners are in Chapter 11.

THEY SLOUCH UNEASILY IN fake leather-and-chrome chairs attached all in a row in the departures area (where Bobby has been granted special permission to wait with her), uncomfortably aware of her father and Jordan, who are seated in their own row directly in front of them, engaged in the ritual of intently examining their BlackBerrys. Funny, she muses, that when hers had been stolen a couple of weeks ago, she'd worried that she couldn't live without it, when, in fact, she's come to enjoy the luxury of being incommunicado, especially with her mother always, irritatingly, wanting to be in touch.

It is nearly ten o'clock, and a uniformed airline employee behind the counter has already announced that passengers will begin boarding shortly.

"So tell me what I can do for you this minute," Bobby says.

This minute? "How about cutting off your braid so I can sleep with it under my pillow every night until I come back?" Desirée whispers. Without asking permission, she strips off the rubber band at its tip, gently takes apart the braid, and then shakes out Bobby's hair, just for the pleasure of getting her hands on it one last time before she leaves. When, soon afterward, the flight begins boarding, she hides her face beneath that lovely gold curtain of his hair, staying under until the final call.

"Let's go, kiddo," her father says. "You're out of time."

She and Bobby stand up together; reclaiming his hair, he offers her a kiss so long and leisurely, it's as if they still have all the time in the world.

"Let's *go,*" her father says sharply.

"See you in a few," Desirée tells Bobby, striking a note of insouciance that might set his mind at ease. "I promise."

"Counting on it," Bobby says, but, even so, he looks bereft.

THE LIGHTS OF KANSAS CITY quickly recede, and the plane itself seems to float aimlessly in a pitch-dark sea. Desirée takes out the information packet—containing everything she might want to know about Lawrence, Kansas, proud home of KU—that Bobby printed out for her before they left for the airport. She thinks of how Starshine and Dr. McVicar had positioned themselves side by side in the doorway of Bobby's bedroom while he yanked the sheets of paper from his printer, his mother and father looking on expectantly. As though the information contained in those three carefully paper-clipped pages might be enough to keep Desirée from her flight back home.

"You do what you have to do, Desirée, and then you come back to us," Starshine ordered.

"And in the meantime," Dr. McVicar added, "we'll bombard

255

the *Honey Creek Herald* with a shitload of irate letters to the editor decrying that retarded piece they ran on the front page."

"What's the matter with you, don't you know you can't say 're-tarded'?" Starshine said.

"I'll say anything I like, and that includes warning Desirée that if she doesn't come back, we'll be forced to take matters into our own very capable hands."

"Okay, enough, you guys," Bobby said, thrusting the pages at Desirée, who was fully convinced there was no cooler family to be found anywhere within the entire eighty-two thousand square miles that constituted the state of Kansas. And no warmer family, either.

She does her homework now on the plane, dutifully absorbing the information that Bobby's college town boasts two microbrew-eries, a half-dozen coffeehouses, a thriving music and art scene. Even the *New York Times* (her *New York Times*!) claims that the town has "the most vital music scene between Chicago and Den-ver." Sounds promising. And furthermore, several years ago no less an expert than *RollingStone* chose Lawrence as one of the "best l'il college towns in the US." (A citation no one has ever awarded to the city of New Haven, have they?) Sold! To the love-sick girl in row 15, seat F, one Desirée Christian-Cohen, the red-head accompanied by the two gay guys to her left, one of whom happens to be her father, a middle-aged man who's fallen asleep, his head resting on his lover, a man immersed in a journal article entitled "A Story of Love and Hate: Antidesign and Pictorials in Flaubert."

Desirée wonders if Jordan has even the vaguest notion of how much she envies him this instant. Not the particulars of his life, but merely the fact that he's sitting here on this Northwest Air-lines jet with his lover beside him, Patrick's bearded jaw angled cozily against Jordan's shoulder.

"Tired?" Jordan says, mistaking her sigh for weariness, and sympathetically offering her his other shoulder.

Thanks but no thanks.

CHAPTER 37

HAVING BEEN ENLISTED BY HER mother for a quick, early-morning run to the Bagelry, Desirée takes her time drifting along Third Avenue, past some Korean groceries, a couple of drugstores, a small bar/rock 'n' roll club, pizzerias (one strictly kosher), a health food store, two Starbucks, Japanese, Cambodian, Thai, and Indian restaurants, a seven-plex movie theater, three hair salons, four nail salons, a handful of newsstands/candy stores, a health club (where she catches a glimpse of a class full of crazed yuppies doing aerobics before work), a sporting goods store, and, of course, the ubiquitous Banana Republic and its more humble relation, the Gap, where employees are already at work in the window, replacing the posters on display. All this in less than half a dozen blocks, Desirée marvels—like some tourist from Honey Creek—and nearly has to restrain herself from crouching down to kiss the uneven patch of pavement beneath her feet.

If she kicked the bucket and took the express directly to heaven, she couldn't have been happier with the landscape.

The only thing missing from this paradise of brick, steel, and glass is, of course, Bobby McVicar.

AS SHE HEADS HOMEWARD WITH A small container of vegetable cream cheese and some warm sesame, pumpernickel, and onion bagels swinging from a flimsy plastic bag at her wrist, she sees a young mother sipping coffee at a bus stop and eyeing her little girl darkly. "You don't punch people in the stomach and then get a reward, Isabella. It doesn't work that way."

Isabella, who appears just old enough for nursery school, seems mystified. "It *doesn't*?"

"That's right. So no SpongeBob SquarePants gummy patties for you, not today, or tomorrow, either."

"Not even tomorrow?"

"Absolutely. This is what happens when you're ill behaved, baby girl."

"No it DOESN'T!"

"Oh yes it does!"

Desirée smiles at the ill-behaved Isabella. She smiles, too, at a trio of Tibetan monks who walk past her in their peach-colored robes, sandals, and vivid yellow socks. She saves her brightest smile for a big-headed bald baby in tiny, open-toed shoes, cruising by on his father's shoulders.

No one smiles back, not even the baby, who is disappointingly stolid.

Welcome to New York! Desirée whispers jauntily. But does not fail to remind herself that *GQ* magazine named the Replay Lounge in Lawrence, Kansas, one of the top ten bars and music venues in the country. It's imperative that she remember facts like this one, small points of information that will serve to comfort her when, late at night, lying in her childhood bed on the Upper East Side, she considers, and reconsiders, again and again and again, exactly how she plans to remake her life with love as its centerpiece.

She will miss her Yale friends but will make new ones. She will miss both her teachers and fellow students who illuminate the classroom with their fierce intelligence, their unrestrained ardor for literature, art history, psychology, anthropology, you name it.

Tough to give all this up, even for love. As she read in the *New York Times* today (a paper whose veracity she's never doubted), love is a dangerous disease.

CHAPTER 38

THIS ISN'T THE ENTRANCE TO hell she's approaching, Nina tells herself, it's merely the threshold of Patrick and Jordan's beautifully appointed apartment overlooking the Hudson. And yet "Abandon hope, all ye who enter here" are the words that come to mind as she and Desirée, accompanied by Daniel Rose, make their way into the living room. That measure of happiness that Patrick wants her to feel for him today—the afternoon of the commitment ceremony—well, she's just not feelin' it. Not yet, anyway. Mostly she's a little numb, her hands icy in this overly air-conditioned room filled with strangers, almost all of them men, though there are a few woman, too, a couple of slightly familiar faces, she realizes, from Patrick's department at Columbia.

Patrick and Jordan, dressed in matching white linen suits, come forward to greet them, dispensing kisses to Nina and Desirée. "It's so wonderful to have my girls here," Patrick says with obvious pleasure, and Nina recoils, offended. Can this really be the way he thinks of her? One thing's certain: she—a forty-something woman—hasn't been his "girl" for a couple of decades. Or, for many months now, his wife.

"Congratulations," Daniel says, shaking hands with Patrick, patting Jordan awkwardly on the shoulder.

"Congratulations," Desirée echoes, and smiles.

Nina can't discern what her daughter is thinking at this moment, but her smile surely looks genuine. After months of ill will toward Patrick, it seems that Desirée has finally come around, which Nina herself is grateful for, she realizes. She would never have wanted the estrangement between Desirée and her father to become something flint-hard, permanently etched into their family history. And, in fact, she is envious of the easing of all that simmering hostility, of the way her daughter has been able, at last, to let it go. If only Desirée would let go, as well, of her obsession with Bobby McVicar and this KU of his (why the

University of Kansas would call itself KU rather than UK is only further evidence of its inferiority, Nina can't help but think), and get herself back to New Haven where she so plainly belongs!

"This is our good friend Roger Bean," Patrick is saying, introducing them to a black guy in his thirties in a gray suit and an elegant bow tie, a tiny gold cross hitched to his lapel, his jacket cast across his right arm. His left arm is bare, save for the small tattoo of the Hebrew word *L'Chaim*. And Nina can't refrain from asking why.

"Your question has been put to me many times," Roger Bean says, "and I'm going to tell you what I tell everyone, which is that my ex was an Orthodox Jew, and the tattoo was just sort of a gift to him. Maybe it's time I had it removed, preferably with a laser or something else not too painful, what do you think?"

"Roger's the Universal Life minister who's going to officiate at the ceremony," Jordan explains. "Of course if we were hetero, he could marry us right here in the state of New York . . ."

"After my divorce was final, that is," murmurs Patrick.

"Not ashamed to say I got my ordination over the Internet," Roger Bean confides. "And as a legally ordained minister, I'm permitted to perform functions of the clergy, such as baptisms and weddings, and so on and so forth. I'm also qualified to be a ministerial counselor, having completed the Science of Understanding Life course in psychology—or SOUL, as we like to call it. So if any of you need counseling, I hope you'll think of me. May I offer you my business card?"

"Fabulous," Nina says, taking his card with one hand and gripping Daniel's hand with the other; inexplicably, she feels as if she's about to lose her balance in her high heels, and pitch headlong onto the pristine Persian rug underfoot.

"You all right with this?" Daniel whispers. "Because if you're not, we can get out of here. No one would blame you."

But she would blame *herself*, she thinks. For lacking the strength, the smarts, the graciousness to accept the unpredictability, the inconstancy of the human heart. And of life itself.

"I'm fine," she tells Daniel, and so what if it's one of those little white lies that serves her so conveniently from time to time. She takes a seat between Desirée and Daniel in the very last row of slatted black wooden folding chairs that have been set up facing the Hudson River. Two young Asian recruits from Columbia's music department are at the window playing their violins, those sprightly notes of the allegro movement of "La Primavera" from Vivaldi's *The Four Seasons*. Something of a wedding cliché, Nina observes, but can't deny its beauty.

Rudely cutting off the music mid-movement, Roger Bean announces, from his place between the violinists, "Subtlety not being my strong point, in essence we're here today to celebrate the love that these two dear men, Jordan and Patrick, feel so deeply for one another. And a big thank-you to the delightfully talented Xiao-ling and Tai-shu, who will, I've been assured, be playing more for us during the reception."

Xiao-ling and Tai-shu, dressed in black, floor-length gowns, smile modestly.

"And now we'll have the pleasure of hearing from the men of the hour, who've been waiting anxiously in the wings."

Patrick steps front and center, followed by Jordan; Roger Bean motions for them to face one another. "Our first selection is from the Song of Solomon," Patrick announces, his voice a little tremulous, perhaps not wholly reliable, reminding Nina of a performer in one of those overtly amateurish middle school productions, someone who only wishes he were in the audience with his friends, snickering delightedly, joining his pals in their mockery of the proceedings onstage.

Set me as a seal upon thine heart,
as a seal upon thine arm: for love is
Strong as death; jealousy is cruel as
the grave.
Many waters cannot quench love,
Neither can the floods drown it.

"Jordan?"

"This from Sir Walter Scott," Jordan says, and offers Patrick an encouraging smile before he begins.

Love rules the court, the camp, the grove,
And men below, and saints above;
For love is heaven, and heaven is love.

"And this from the immortal Shakespeare," Patrick says.

Haply I think on thee, and then my state,
Like to the lark at break of day arising
From sullen earth, sings hymns at heaven's gate;
For thy sweet love remember'd such wealth brings
That then I scorn to change my state with kings.

"Shakespeare was such a rock star, man!" someone calls out. Now Desirée is rising to join her father and his partner, a surprise to Nina, though of course isn't that her daughter's way, to reveal as little as possible, whenever possible?

"Emily Dickinson," Desirée says. Her posture could be better, Nina thinks, but her delivery is nicely paced, breezy and confident.

That love is all there is,
Is all we know of love;
It is enough, the freight should be
Proportioned to the groove.

"Way to go, Emily!"

Blushing, Desirée returns to her seat. "They asked me to choose something myself," she whispers to Nina, "and of course you can't go wrong with Dickinson, right?"

"Perfectly chosen," Nina says. But how long is this love fest going to continue? Isn't enough enough?

"We're going to conclude," Jordan reports, "with something else from Sir Walter Scott, who, though he died in 1832, even today seems like one smart cookie."

True love's the gift which God has given
To man alone beneath the heaven:

"Patrick, you'll finish up here?"

. . . It is the secret sympathy,
The silver link, the silken tie,
Which heart to heart and mind to mind
In body and in soul can bind.

Yadda yadda yadda, Nina hears some cynic behind her sigh at the same moment that Daniel's arm casually finds its way around her shoulders. Hard to know, or even to guess, whether the easy affection she and Daniel feel for one another will ripen into something deeper, or whether it will, in time, wither into indifference. She relishes his slightly rumpled appearance (even today, in his sport coat and tie, his wild hair fleetingly tamed by a spritz of water from her kitchen sink, he looks like someone who doesn't much care about the image he reflects), his innate modesty, his sweet nonchalance that makes her feel, in his company, like flushing her Lexapro down the toilet and giving Dr. Pepperkorn the ax. And yet if she allowed herself, she could worry about the two of them, examining their relationship from every possible angle, turning it this way and that, looking for the smallest things that disappoint her, ways in which Daniel doesn't quite meet her expectations. But what *are* her expectations? All she knows is that she wants that secret sympathy, that silver link—if not with Daniel, as she hopes, then perhaps with someone else. She and Patrick had it once, but it's perfectly transparent not only to Nina, but to everyone in the room, that it cannot ever be reclaimed. *Cannot.*

"Patrick Christian and Jordan Sinclair," Roger Bean begins, "it is now my distinct pleasure to present you with the Affirmation of Love certificate, which, by the way, is suitable for framing, should you so desire."

Affirmation of Love certificate—they've got to be freakin' kidding! A bit of a smile plays uncertainly at Nina's lips; as her daughter only recently pointed out to her, it's the twenty-first century and she needs to lighten up. Surprisingly wise counsel from Desirée, of all people, Nina thinks, and feels her smile growing more expansive, taking in the bounty of things she predicts are yet to come—some of it maddening, no doubt, some of it heartrending, but some of it damn near as good as it gets.

"Pussycat?" she says, wanting to thank her. "Pussycat?" she repeats, already knowing, as a mother would, that Desirée is somewhere else, out of earshot; ninety miles northwest of Kansas City, in the passenger seat of an aging, immaculately kept Saab cruising down Minnehaha Avenue, not yet page one news in the *Honey Creek Herald* but about to be noticed any minute now, her head tilted contentedly against Bobby McVicar, his thick gold braid shimmering endlessly in her imagination.

ACKNOWLEDGMENTS

WITH THANKS TO G.B. Ashland for driving me to Kansas; to Burt Schall for his sense of humor; to Dr. Barbi Kantor for easing the pain of Desirée's toothache; to Theo Fitzfebruary and Seymour Woodbury for their inspiring music; to Michelle Richter for never, ever dropping a stitch; and to Maria Massie and Elizabeth Beier for so warmly and generously embracing the very notion of "Lucy Jackson."